She Used to Be Nice

She Used to Be Nice

A NOVEL

ALEXIA LAFATA

alcove
press

Books should be disposed of and recycled according to local requirements. All paper materials used are FSC compliant.

This is a work of fiction. All of the names, characters, organizations, places, and events portrayed in this novel are either products of the author's imagination or are used fictitiously. Any resemblance to real or actual events, locales, or persons, living or dead, is entirely coincidental.

Copyright © 2025 by Alexia LaFata

All rights reserved.

Published in the United States by Alcove Press, an imprint of The Quick Brown Fox & Company LLC.

Alcove Press and its logo are trademarks of The Quick Brown Fox & Company LLC.

Library of Congress Catalog-in-Publication data available upon request.

ISBN (hardcover): 979-8-89242-274-1
ISBN (paperback): 979-8-89242-171-3
ISBN (ebook): 979-8-89242-172-0

Cover design by Meghan Deist

Printed in the United States.

www.alcovepress.com

Alcove Press
34 West 27th St., 10th Floor
New York, NY 10001

First Edition: August 2025

The authorized representative in the EU for product safety and compliance is eucomply OÜ Pärnu mnt 139b-14, 11317 Tallinn, Estonia, hello@eucompliancepartner.com, +33757690241

10 9 8 7 6 5 4 3 2 1

To every woman I've ever met

1

AVERY WAS FLAT ON her back. Her gaze drifted across the wrinkled brown curtains, drawn together in front of a half-open window. A bottle of contact solution sat on his bedside table, next to a pair of glasses he'd probably had since tenth grade. Every time Ethan (or was it Evan?) thrust into her, the corner of a *Pulp Fiction* poster taped to the wall flapped from the gust of his movements.

"You like that, baby? You like that?"

Avery scrunched her face and glanced up at him, trying to get him to register with his own eyes that she definitely did not like that, not even a little. But he wasn't looking at her. She sighed. You'd think she'd be used to this by now.

"Oooh, yes," Avery breathed as Evan (wait, *was* it Ethan?) continued pumping without regard for the human being underneath him. She willed herself to feel something, anything, besides the metal coil in his mattress digging into her spine. But there was nothing. There was always nothing.

"Are you—" *Pump pump pump pump pump.* "Are you close?"

Avery raised an eyebrow. This guy had clearly never heard of the clitoris. She decided to spare him the snarky comment and say nothing, her desire for this to be over surpassing her desire for an orgasm. Seconds later, he let out a loud, satisfied groan and collapsed on top of her, crushing her with his weight. She patted his back, which was slick and gummy with sweat. Then she peeked at the digital clock flashing on his nightstand. They'd started two minutes ago. She couldn't believe she'd waxed for this.

Ethan/Evan hoisted himself up, pulled on his boxers, and promptly unlocked his phone. The light from the screen illuminated his face, reminding Avery of why she'd swiped right on him a few hours ago. His angular jawline and icy blue eyes coupled with his CrossFit abs easily ranked him among the hottest guys Avery had ever hooked up with. But he had the sexual prowess of a seventh grader.

"So, I'll text you?" He was still looking at his phone, engrossed in what appeared to be a Reddit page with gifs of people screaming, though Avery couldn't get a close enough look to be sure.

She pressed her mouth into a line. "Sure," she muttered, but they both knew he wouldn't. Not that it mattered. She retrieved her jeans and silky black tank top from the end of the bed and dressed like she was being timed, then scanned the apartment for any remaining belongings. She didn't need this guy thinking she'd accidentally-on-purpose left her hoop earrings on his nightstand because she wanted an excuse to see him again.

As she slung her purse over her shoulder, ready to leave, she heard the tinny sound of someone yelling. Her eyes flicked to her hookup. He was biting his knuckles, enraptured by whatever weird shit he was watching.

She blinked at him. "Well, bye."

Avery stopped to use his bathroom, then slipped out of his apartment and onto the sidewalk, where she was greeted by the perfect cacophony of Manhattan: police sirens blaring down the block, bars pulsating with music so loud it thumped in her chest, a jackhammer drilling into a mess of broken concrete. She checked her phone for the time—11:30 PM shone in promising bright white letters on her home screen. The weekend, her salvation, had barely begun.

She hit her vape, feeling the tingles of restlessness that had become familiar to her since her breakup with Ryan a year ago, and began walking, following the nicotine buzz and city sounds wherever they led, which she hoped was somewhere good. She

SHE USED TO BE NICE

instinctively opened Instagram, her thumb stopping on a picture of her best friend Morgan and Morgan's boyfriend Charlie, posted ten minutes ago from Morgan's account. Charlie's arm was wrapped protectively around Morgan, and Morgan was gazing up at him, her entire face crinkled from grinning. The caption read *Love of my life*.

Avery's lip twitched as she double-tapped the picture to give it a like. Morgan and Charlie's love for each other seemed to increase in tandem with Avery's number of sexual partners. She'd gotten used to their PDA, though, for the most part. They'd been like this since they met at a pregame freshman year, when Morgan had summoned Charlie to be her partner in a round of beer pong, and he lifted her into a hug every time she landed a throw. Tonight, however, Avery wished Instagram had a *We Get It* button. Of course, she was thrilled Morgan had found the kind of love most people spent their whole lives searching for and especially rarely found in college, or at least in the frat-star factory that was Woodford College, their alma mater. But still. We Get It.

She sent Morgan a text. *still w Charlie? wanna get a drink?*

She stopped to lean against the brick wall of a bodega, vaping some more and waiting for her best friend's reply. With each silent minute that passed, she grew increasingly jittery, alternating between digging dirt out from under her fingernails and kicking pieces of mulch spilling out from a sidewalk tree pit garden. Morgan and Charlie *lived* together; they hung out every single damn day, from the moment they each got home from work until they went to bed, rinse and repeat. Surely Morgan could stop giving him attention for ten seconds to respond to Avery's text.

Avery's phone finally buzzed. *Sure!! Just finishing up*

Doc Holliday's? Avery texted back. Doc Holliday's was a solid dive bar nearby. It was loud enough to be lively, but quiet enough that you could hear yourself talk, unlike so many East Village bars at this time of night. It was nothing like that sweaty, crowded basement from that party senior year, with that lukewarm keg and sticky floor and—

4 ALEXIA LAFATA

Avery's phone buzzed again, interrupting her thoughts before the panic set in.

Cool, Morgan replied. *Give me 20*

Avery heaved a sigh and shoved her phone in her pocket. How was she going to kill twenty minutes? The bar was right around the corner. It would take her no time to walk there, and then she'd have to wait for Morgan alone, as usual. She put her lips to her vape, then tossed it back into her purse. She wanted a real cigarette, to feel actual smoke burn her lungs. She rummaged through her purse and found one, crushed beneath empty bags of chips and crusty tubes of mascara. *Gross,* she thought. She needed to clean this thing out.

She lit her cigarette. The tip illuminated bright orange, and off-white smoke billowed into the sky. As she inhaled, she made eyes at every guy that walked by, enticing them to ask her for a light. Entertaining herself with cheap male validation was better than feeling sorry for herself for how single she was. Annoyingly, though, most guys passed by without a glance. Some ogled her cleavage, on full display thanks to her push-up bra, so that was something. A homeless man wearing black slides approached her asking for a dollar, and she told him no. She never carried cash anyway—her favorite nail technicians had started accepting Venmo for tips—but after she'd paid her rent this week, she barely had enough money for her sad desk salads.

She spent a few more minutes smoking and trying to entice guys, to no avail. Nothing titillating was going to happen on this corner, and she was starting to feel pathetic. It was time to go. She stubbed out her cigarette butt and tossed it in the trash before making her way to Doc Holliday's, where a group of high schoolers stood at the front door trying to convince the bouncer to let them in. She frowned. Did these kids have nothing better to do tonight? They had their whole lives to get wasted at bars and do something they'd regret. She wanted to scream at them to go play on a swing set, to preserve their innocence before it was too late. Because once you lost it, she knew, it was never coming back. If only someone had

SHE USED TO BE NICE

told her that her senior year of college, before she put her trust in the wrong man's hands and watched it break apart.

She shoved the thought out of her mind as quickly as she shoved through the crowd and into the bar.

"Hi there," she cooed to the bartender as she sat down on a stool, batting her eyelashes like windshield wipers to fade away the memories. She tossed a curtain of her thick dark brown hair behind her shoulder and inhaled the sweet smell of booze. "Can I please get your finest cheap beer?"

The bartender regarded her with a smile. Behind him, a hodgepodge of outdated holiday decorations and handwritten signs threatening to ask for ID hung above the bar. He grabbed a bottle of Rolling Rock from a mini fridge and popped it open with a *tsst*, winking at her as he handed it over.

"Sure thing . . ." he began, offering an open-ended pause for her to fill in her name.

Avery met his eye, let her gaze linger. "Avery."

He nodded. "I'm Jim." He tapped the bar twice with the palm of his hand. "Let me know if you need anything else."

Avery took a hearty sip of her beer just as Morgan called out her name from the front door. She waved as she strutted through the bar in a little black dress that clung to her five-ten frame. Morgan was stunning, with waifish, model-length limbs and high cheekbones that contrasted with Avery's curves and round face. Someone definitely would have approached her outside on that corner.

"You're early!" Morgan said, hoisting herself onto the stool next to Avery.

Avery suddenly felt self-conscious about the way her thighs spilled over her seat. They looked like two loaves of banana bread bursting over their pans. "Shocking, right?" She tossed Morgan a coy grin, pretending she didn't hate herself.

Morgan flagged Jim down for a beer. "Extremely. Did your date end early? How was it?"

Avery shrugged. She'd hardly call what had happened tonight a "date." The cocktails they'd gotten at Lovers of Today earlier in the night were simply the accepted prerequisite for meaningless sex. But Morgan wanted Avery to fall in love-of-her-life love, like she had with Charlie. Avery never knew how to tell Morgan that it wasn't as easy for some women to get that. That some women, in fact, might never get that. But Morgan meant well. Avery would allow Morgan to be optimistic, even if it bordered on pathological. One of them had to see the good in Avery, after everything.

"It was fine," Avery said.

"What happened?"

"Nothing. He was hot, but kind of dull. He also lurks on bizarre subreddits."

Morgan raised a suspicious brow. "Well, did you have anything in common?"

"Not really." Avery paused and pointed at Morgan with her beer bottle. "Sorry, I lied. We both grew up in the tri-state area. Does that count?"

"Hardly," Morgan said with a laugh. "Did you sleep with him?"

Avery hesitated. "Yes."

Morgan's forehead creased in worry, like it had so often since Avery and Ryan broke up. But Avery ignored it. She didn't want Morgan worrying about her. She didn't want *anyone* worrying about her, not that any of their friends besides Morgan cared about her anymore anyway. She was perfectly fine with having surface-level hookups and forgetting guys' names by the next day. It was easier this way, keeping her distance so she couldn't get hurt again.

"I just came from his place, actually," Avery added. "The sex wasn't good though. He basically used me as a human Fleshlight."

Morgan sighed. "I totally get it. When Charlie and I first started dating, it took several training sessions for him to learn that there's a person attached to a vagina."

Jim slid Morgan a beer. She used a cocktail napkin to wipe the condensation off the bottle, her shiny, loose waves rippling like a current across her shoulders as she moved. Her hair was light brunette with streaks of blonde that, thanks to her half-Irish genes,

SHE USED TO BE NICE

looked red at certain angles. It reminded Avery of the way the ocean surface looked when it was dappled by sunlight.

"At least you had someone to teach," she said.

Avery regretted saying that as soon as she saw the beginnings of a crease on Morgan's forehead again.

"I'm sorry, Avery. Next time. Your guy's out there."

Avery waved Morgan off. She didn't need pity from beautiful people in happy relationships. Morgan didn't understand what loneliness felt like, the cavernous empty space Avery tried to fill in an attempt to feel whole again after she essentially ruined her own life. She was fine. Fine, fine, fine.

"It's fine, I'm fine." Avery took another sip of her beer. "How was your night?"

A coquettish smile crept onto Morgan's lips. She thrust her dainty left hand in front of Avery, and suddenly her smile exploded across her face. A massive emerald cut diamond sat on Morgan's ring finger, glinting beams of bright oranges and yellows. Avery gasped. She'd known a proposal was inevitable but not that it would happen only five months after graduation. Then again, she supposed they were in that delicate place between youth and adulthood now, where some people were settling down and other people were . . . well, other people were flashing their cleavage at creeps outside bodegas.

Avery shook off the feelings of self-loathing bubbling up inside her and clutched Morgan's hand, a grin taped to her face. "Charlie *proposed?!*" Avery marveled at the ring. Charlie had even remembered what Avery told him junior year, about Morgan wanting a solitaire diamond with a gold band.

"Yes!" Morgan cried, resting her hand on her heart. "And I said yes!"

Avery flung her arms around Morgan's waist, her happy tears seeping into Morgan's dress. "You're engaged!" She felt the wind knocked out of her from both breathless joy and a sucker punch to the chest. Her best friend was getting married, and thanks to her new compulsion to bolt from a guy's place immediately after sex, she was well on her way to dying alone. She never thought she'd be that kind of girl, but alas, this was who she was now. Avery released herself from Morgan's grip but kept her hands on Morgan's shoulders, digging her fingers into her skin. *Keep smiling,* she thought. *Don't be a bitch.* "How'd he do it? Tell me everything. I need every detail."

Morgan's caramel brown eyes misted, twinkling beneath the overhead lights of the bar. "We were getting dinner at Manhatta, that restaurant with the sky-high views sixty stories up. Our table was right by the window, overlooking all of downtown. We'd just finished eating, and then . . ." She pulled in a deep breath, holding it for a second before releasing. "And then he started talking about how much I mean to him, and how much he loves me, and finally he got down on one knee. It took me a second to realize what was happening. But when I did, I started sobbing, Avery. Sobbing! I'm surprised my makeup isn't all over my face right now. And then, a band just started playing *music.* And a bottle of champagne just *appeared.*" Morgan sighed dreamily. "It was perfect."

Avery hugged Morgan again with as much excitement as she could muster. All the while, she couldn't help but think that everyone was growing up, moving on, making something of their lives after graduation. Everyone but her. She was still stuck on that party senior year, on the moment Noah got her alone in that bedroom, and she was too drunk to give him a convincing no. It was her fault for being so friendly with him, for making him think she wanted to sleep with him when that couldn't have been further from the truth. She knew she wasn't supposed to think in such a victim-blamey way. Feminism and #MeToo and all that. But she couldn't help it. She felt like the exception, like those movements were talking about other women and not her.

"Now, I have something to ask you," Morgan began. She fanned tears from her face and took Avery's hands. "Will you be my maid of honor?"

Avery's jaw dropped slightly. Part of her had thought she'd be excused from this massive responsibility when it came time for

SHE USED TO BE NICE 9

Morgan's wedding, because Morgan's childhood friend Kim was an event planner and loved doing this kind of thing. Avery also hoped that Morgan wouldn't put her in the line of fire so soon, in front of all the people who thought she'd cheated on Ryan. What happened senior year didn't happen that long ago, and their group of friends still wanted nothing to do with her, while of course Noah hadn't suffered at all from the fallout. He was lucky his head was down when they were in that bedroom at the party, that Avery's face was the only one visible through that crack in the door. Everyone thought she'd hooked up with Ronald Archibald, the rando nobody was friends with who only lived in that room because he needed housing. Nobody knew it had been Noah sucking the life out of her.

Avery tensed. "Are you sure? I—I've never even been to a wedding before. I don't know the first thing about being a maid of honor."

"Of *course* I'm sure!" Morgan's face was wide-open, earnest. "And you'll learn. It's not like you're doing everything by yourself. I'll be with you."

"But what if I mess everything up? What if I forget to pick up your garter or something? Do brides even wear garters anymore?"

Morgan laughed. "You won't mess anything up. You're super responsible." She paused, then backtracked. "Well, you're capable of being responsible. I've seen it. You just gotta . . . I don't know. Tap into that again."

Avery bit her cheek, piercing the tender flesh with her teeth. Maybe there once existed a version of Avery who was responsible, a girl who used to read novels and spend her weekends going to brunch and was generally just normal. But now Morgan was making a huge mistake. Avery was the girl whose credit card got declined for a four-dollar coffee at Starbucks, who let her houseplants wither and die from lack of watering, who got both a pregnancy scare *and* a gonorrhea diagnosis from the same one-night stand. She was different now. Someone she hardly recognized.

Morgan folded her hands in front of her chest, pouting. "Please?"

Avery studied Morgan, her last remaining friend in the world. After Ryan broke up with her, Avery made it clear to Morgan that she didn't want her to pick sides, and Morgan did her best to stay friends with everyone. She forgave Avery for sleeping with Ronald while understanding why everyone else wouldn't. And it wasn't like Avery corrected anyone's version of events of what happened that night. She could never say out loud the terrifying things that Noah did to her. That would just make them real.

"Morgan . . ." Avery tasted blood inside her mouth. "I don't have a natural eye for wedding stuff. I can't help you, like, choose flowers. I don't know a rose from a chrysanthemum." *And all of our friends still hate me for what they think happened at that party and I'm too scared to tell anyone the truth. And I'm gonna be single forever while you and Charlie die together* The Notebook-*style because I won't be vulnerable with a man ever again.*

"We'll figure it out together!" Morgan held Avery's gaze, a tenderness settling onto her face. "I really want it to be you, Avery. You're the only person who can keep me in check. When I start obsessing over which cheese knife to put in my registry, you need to sedate me."

Avery fidgeted with the zipper on her leather jacket. She had no idea how she could be a strong, stable anchor for her best friend when she felt so lost in her own life. She'd need to pore over every *Brides* magazine she could find, study weddings like she'd studied for the SAT. She'd need to be calm and levelheaded and a source of sanity for Morgan, despite feeling like she had none of those comforts available for herself. It wasn't even that her well had run dry, but that at this point she couldn't remember the last time it was full. But she would have to move on from what Noah did to her at some point, wouldn't she? Surely she could keep convincing herself that what happened was just a stupid drunken hookup, which would help her get over it eventually. Right?

She wasn't sure of the answer to these questions. But she could pretend for Morgan's sake.

SHE USED TO BE NICE

"Plus," Morgan said, her eyes round and hopeful. "You're my best friend. That means way more to me than the stupid chrysanthemums."

The corners of Avery's lips pulled into a smile. "All right." Her voice was thin. She hesitated and then said it again like an incantation, as though repeating it might summon her long-lost confidence. "Yes, all right, I'll do it! I'll be your maid of honor!"

Morgan clapped and kissed Avery on the cheek. Avery beamed, feeling her shaky confidence strengthen and solidify. How could she have thought that she wouldn't be her best friend's maid of honor? Avery was always going to be part of Morgan's wedding. Whenever she heard Morgan fantasize about it in college, it went unsaid that Avery would be involved, and nothing about that was going to change now. Even though everything else—and everyone else—would be different.

Jim appeared on the other side of the bar, grinning apologetically. "Can I get you girls anything else?"

Avery slid her empty beer bottle toward Jim and leaned forward to show off her cleavage. "I'd love another one of these," she said.

Jim's eyes flicked to her chest before he walked away.

Morgan stared at him, cringing. "Avery, that guy has the most jacked up teeth," she whispered. "And he has *visible* dandruff."

Avery shrugged. "So what? My hair gets greasy. Nobody's perfect."

Jim grabbed Avery another beer and poured two Fireball shots, filling the glasses so high that liquid spilled over the sides and onto the bar. He pushed the glasses toward them.

"On me," he said with a wink. His teeth *were* a little yellowed, now that Avery got a closer look. Whatever. He was the only guy giving her attention tonight, and she needed the self-esteem boost, proof that someone, somewhere, could still find this broken version of her desirable. He'd have to do.

"Please tell me you're not going to sleep with him," Morgan begged as Jim brought a toothpick to his scalp and scratched his hairline. Dandruff fell like snow onto his black T-shirt. "He looks like an incubator for STDs."

Avery rolled her eyes. Again with the worrying. But Morgan wouldn't understand. While she racked up blissful nights with her fiancé, all Avery did was rack up her body count. Last weekend, there was Dylan, the guy Avery blew to completion who then ignored her to tinker with his fantasy draft after he came. The guy before that was Victor, or maybe his name was just Vic. Avery shook her head, reminding herself she didn't keep track for a reason: because it hurt too much when she forgot. Forgetting was a reminder that there had been way too many, that her pain dictated more of her behavior than she was willing to admit. Her logic went that the more men she slept with, the more that night with Noah would fade into irrelevance. It made perfect sense.

Avery nudged Morgan with her shot glass. "Forget about Jim. Tonight's about you. You're getting married!"

Jim brought over two glasses of water, stealing another glance at Avery's chest.

"Hopefully you'll even have time for me this year," Morgan said as she eyed Jim suspiciously. "Jim might want you all to himself."

Avery flashed a mischievous smile. "I'll allocate my time between both of you, don't worry. How's that sound, *Mrs. Durham*? If you plan to no longer be a Feeley, that is."

"I'm definitely changing my last name." Morgan's cheeks flushed. "Wow. Mrs. Durham. Can you say that again?"

Avery laughed. "Say what again? Mrs. Durham?"

"Yes. With my first name."

Avery spread her arms out wide as she shouted in her best emcee voice, "Ladies and gentlemen, Mrs. Morgan Durham!"

Morgan's eyes turned into hearts, like the emoji. "God, I love that. I love that so much."

"Now imagine it embossed on one hundred off-white thank-you notes."

They giggled and clinked their shots together, then flung the Fireball to the backs of their throats. Avery shivered once her

SHE USED TO BE NICE

stomach settled. Fireball had been her and Morgan's drink of choice in school, mainly because it was the cheapest of all the booze at the corner store near Woodford. It didn't taste that bad, either. But it had been a while, and that cinnamon burned horribly now. Forget college graduation, moving out of your parents' house, and getting a job: Outgrowing Fireball was the real transition into adulthood.

The bar started clearing out, save for a few tables covered in empty beer pitchers and a couple playing darts in the back corner. Avery was surprised that people were leaving already. It was only 1 AM—the night was young and teeming with potential! She was about to ask Morgan what bar they should go to next, until Morgan yawned and scooted off her stool.

"Okay, it's getting late. I'm gonna head home. Wanna split a cab uptown?"

Avery knew Morgan had the right idea. The night was not young at all. Nothing good came from being out alone downtown at one in the morning, scraping the bottom of the nightlife barrel to find something to do. Nights that seemed sparkly and infinite were just black holes that sucked Avery in, disintegrating her into dust. But going back home to an empty apartment sounded even worse.

"Nah," Avery said. "I think I'll stay out a little longer."

Morgan shook her head in disapproval, but it was lighthearted, like she knew she wouldn't be able to stop Avery so why even try. This was part of their dynamic now: Avery would be Avery in ways Morgan didn't understand, and Morgan would just let it happen, almost as a joke, unknowingly giving Avery the go-ahead to self-destruct. Avery would've felt guilty about it if she could feel anything besides panic at the threat of being alone with her thoughts again.

"If you say so." Morgan draped her crossbody bag over her shoulder. "Just promise me you won't black out and sleep with the bartender."

Jim grinned at Avery from behind the bar. A piece of spinach was stuck in his gums, right above his front tooth.

"He's *so* hot though," Avery cooed sarcastically, giving Jim a seductive wave. "It'll be tough to resist."

Morgan scrunched her face. "You're gross."

"But you love me."

Morgan sighed, her lips curving into a smile. "Unfortunately."

Avery hugged Morgan goodbye, then watched her walk out of the bar and disappear into the night. She could've sworn Morgan was moving slower and steadier than she normally did, like she was practicing walking down an aisle of a church. Avery put her hand on her chest, her heart warming at the idea of Morgan in a gorgeous white gown, a lace trail gliding on the floor behind her. She imagined Charlie, his usually disheveled curly hair neatly combed, waiting for Morgan at the altar. She imagined the mist in both of their eyes, their romantic exchange of vows, the roar of applause as they kissed for the first time as husband and wife. And she imagined herself running around the venue with bobby pins, holding Morgan's dress up as she peed, giving a heartfelt speech in front of the crowd—being the perfect maid of honor that her best friend deserved, proving to their friends that she wasn't the cheating monster they thought she was.

Avery pushed away her beer. There was half a bottle left, but she wasn't going to drink the rest. No, she was going to go home, back uptown to her apartment. She was going to put on her matching pajamas, make some peppermint tea, and read a book, the way the old Avery would have behaved, content and serene with peace and quiet. She wasn't going to let what Noah did to her affect her anymore. She might have lost her boyfriend, her friends, and her dignity all in the same night, but she needed to get her shit together for the sake of this wedding. And, she supposed, for herself.

2

AVERY SWIVELED ON HER stool to face Jim. "Can I get the check, please?" she asked.

Look at her, being responsible! Morgan would be so proud.

Jim was behind the bar punching numbers into a touch screen computer when he met her eye. Avery winced when she saw the dandruff still visible on his shoulders. Morgan didn't have to worry. There was no way Avery was sleeping with this man. Her first task in getting her shit together would be to raise her standards so they were at least higher than the floor.

"Sure thing, little lady," he said.

A whiff of Jim's powerful cologne startled Avery's senses, sending them into overdrive. She relished the smell, surprised by how much the pungent scent turned her on. And "little lady" was far from the worst name she'd ever been called. Ryan had called her way more awful things when he broke up with her.

She drummed her fingers on the bar. Maybe she could stay out a little bit longer. Or maybe just until two. New rule: Nothing good came from being out alone at *two* in the morning.

Avery waved a dismissive hand. "Actually, never mind the check." Morgan would never have to find out about this. Not that she'd judge Avery, exactly, but Avery wasn't dumb. She knew Morgan didn't approve of her behavior lately, could see it in Morgan's eyes every time they parted ways on a night out or recounted their weekends spent separately. And frankly, Avery didn't blame her. But this didn't need to be Morgan's problem, nor could Avery handle seeing the person she'd become through her best friend's worried gaze. Morgan was probably halfway home by now anyway, fantasizing about her wedding and her future with her fiancé, like she should be doing. Avery could handle herself fine. Being forced to learn how to be alone had made her very self-sufficient.

"You sure?" Jim asked.

"Absolutely. I'm enjoying your company too much." Avery leaned forward, effectively serving up her cleavage on a silver platter. She knew this was all you had to do to get a guy to sleep with you: boost his ego, show some tit. It was too easy. She almost wished it weren't. Maybe then she'd stop doing it. But it was too tempting of a power trip, seeing the way a guy's face lit up at the mere suggestion of her cleavage. She couldn't resist dangling herself in front of them, controlling them with the tease of her body, she the magician and them awaiting her next trick. That night with Noah was the last time a man would control her first, or ever again.

Jim chuckled. "Well, thank you. Seems like your friend got bored of me, though."

"Nah, she's just got a fiancé waiting at home." Avery's mouth twisted at the word *fiancé*, but then she snapped herself out of her ridiculous jealousy. She refused to be one of those single women who resented happy couples. She was once just as happy, just as in love, with a man she thought was her forever. Until he wasn't.

"Can I get another shot?" she asked. "The Fireball's fine. Pour one for yourself, too." She batted her eyelashes. "On me."

"Ah, I can't," Jim said. "I'm on the clock." He pointed at an analog clock mounted to the wall above the bathroom. "I get off at three."

"Awww, really? Nobody's even here. Who'll know?" She gave Jim a playful, inviting smile, turning on the charm as high as she could. "Do it for me?"

SHE USED TO BE NICE

Jim poured her the shot and slid it over without a word. "I can't. Sorry."

Avery scowled. Some girls were worth marrying but she wasn't worth *one* drink? Even one she was going to *pay for*? "In that case . . ." She tossed back the Fireball, her adrenaline racing so much that she didn't even feel the cinnamon prick her body with chills. She dug through her purse for her credit card and slammed it onto the bar. "I'll take the check."

A flicker of fear flashed across Jim's face as he gave her the bill. She scrawled something illegible on the dotted line and thrust the paper back to him.

"Thanks," she said, her voice tight. "And fuck you."

She darted out the door and took a lap around the block, the sting of rejection burning a hole in her insides. When Ryan dumped her, she'd fully abandoned the idea that anyone would love her ever again, but they were still supposed to want her body. Her boobs were supposed to be foolproof.

She peered into the windows of the bars she passed in search of somewhere crowded. She wanted to get lost in a sea of people and forget her own name, if she was lucky. She stumbled into the first Irish pub she saw and shoved her way through the two feet of walking space toward the bartender, then asked for a double shot of tequila and a beer. After taking the shot, she glanced around, trying to make eye contact with a cute guy. But there were none.

"Where *is* everyone tonight?" she said out loud to nobody. She supposed it was time for the apps, ignoring the voice in her head scolding her for seeking out a second hookup in the same night when she hadn't yet showered after the first. She opened Tinder and started swiping, her thumb aching from how fast she was moving it across the screen. She matched with a couple of guys and beamed at the boost of confidence. Both of them were hot, too, and probably looked even better in person. Ever since she started using dating apps, she found that guys were more attractive in real life than in photos, because they had no clue how to choose flattering pictures of themselves for their profiles. Unlike women, who were far too in tune with their appearance from every possible angle, cognizant of their good and bad sides and when a picture displayed each. Avery knew her left side was her good side, how to twist her body in full-length mirror pictures so that she looked slimmer, and that she would immediately untag any Instagram photo that prominently featured her side profile.

She often wondered how much easier her life would be if she were a man. What it'd be like for her body to be hers, not something that existed for others to ogle at and consume. Surely nobody had ever made Noah feel as powerless as he made Avery feel at that party senior year. Avery never should've danced with him in the basement, even in a silly way in a circle of people on the crowded dance floor. All it did was provide him with an opportunity to sweep his eyes across her chest, then lead her up the stairs under the guise of getting some fresh air. God. She shouldn't have even *glanced* at him, let alone been so naive as to giggle and dance in his vicinity. She should've looked for Ryan first to see if he wanted to join them upstairs. But she wasn't thinking. She was fully drunk by the time she and Noah reached Ronald's bedroom, incapable of being anything but a body for Noah to bleed dry.

If she was going to be just a body, she would wield it like a weapon. Demanding back her power.

"Can I get a beer and a water?"

Avery startled at the sound of a man's voice, her ears perking at his pronunciation of "water," like *wudder*. Sometimes her own accent slipped out when she was pissed off, though it was pretty much gone otherwise.

"Hey," she called out to him, sitting up straight to maximize his view of her chest. "I like your accent."

The guy turned to look at Avery. He flicked a lock of dark brown hair out of his arresting blue eyes, which were made even brighter by the glow from the neon Guinness sign on the wall above him. "My accent?"

She gave him a drunken smile. The double tequila shot had hit her; she felt warm and buoyant, like a hot air balloon rising higher

SHE USED TO BE NICE   19

and higher, suspending her above reality. She was free now, detached from it all. "Don't act like you don't know you have one. I'd recognize that *wudder* anywhere. Where are you from?"

"New York, born and raised." He rested his arm on the back of his stool, his button-down shirt lifting slightly to reveal the waistline of navy chinos. And, she noted with interest, some abs. "The accent definitely slips out sometimes. If I'm drunk enough, I start going full Tony Soprano."

Avery laughed. "I can relate. I'm an Italian-American girl from New Jersey. I'm basically a real-life Meadow."

The guy took a sip of his beer without taking his eyes off her, drinking her in. Avery knew that look. It meant he wanted to have sex with her. The rush of validation coursed thick and hot through her veins. Maybe she wouldn't have to go home alone after all.

"Well, I'm assuming Meadow isn't your real name," he said.

"Your assumption is correct. I'm Avery. What's yours?"

"Nice to meet you, Avery. I'm Pete."

Pete grinned, and Avery admired how straight and white his teeth were. Fuck Jim and his rotted smile.

"Do you wanna do a tequila shot, Pete?"

Pete gave her an enthusiastic nod. "Hell. Yes."

Avery waved over the bartender and ordered the shots, and he brought them over complete with salt and limes. "We need to toast to something first." Avery grabbed her glass. "You can't take a tequila shot without celebrating."

"All right," Pete said with a chuckle. "What are we toasting to?"

Avery raised her brows suggestively. "To the night *just* getting started."

"Cheers to that," Pete said before taking his shot. Avery took hers, too, then set her empty glass down on the bar. She made pointed eye contact with Pete as she sucked on her lime wedge, letting her tongue dance along the fleshy green surface. Pete's eyes lingered on her mouth, just as she intended. Then he quickly met her eye, seemingly catching himself staring for too long, and cleared his throat.

Avery took a satisfied sip of her beer. She was ready to ride this wave until she crashed. "So, *Pete*." She liked Pete's name. One syllable, short and sweet and easy to moan in throes of passion. "How's your night going?"

"Not too bad." Pete pointed at a man and woman in business casual arguing in the corner by the pool table. Patrons were maneuvering around them to access the cue balls. "I've spent the whole night third wheeling my friends over there. They're fighting now, though."

Avery squinted at the couple. Through her tipsy blurred vision, they looked almost like a watercolor painting.

"We work together, too," Pete added. "So it's gonna be awkward on Monday."

"What do you do?" Avery asked.

"I work in finance."

Of course Pete was a finance bro. Avery should've known that the second she met him. The guy was wearing a fleece vest. No judgment, though; Avery loved finance bros. They never wanted relationships, since they were usually too busy working late during the week and spending their weekends in the Hamptons. But they were always down for a one-night stand, especially one with a girl who wasn't interested in turning it into something more. Avery never had to worry about anyone catching feelings or having expectations; she could stop the inevitable disappointment and heartbreak that would follow if they got to know her, her shameful past remaining a door she could keep bolted shut.

Avery gave an amused grin. "A finance bro, huh? Classic."

"Hey, I resent the *bro* accusation," Pete teased. Then he grinned back. "But yeah, I know it's not original for Manhattan. At least I don't live in Murray Hill. That has to count for something, right?"

"It does, for sure." Avery wobbled a little in her seat. Was this stool as wonky before? She felt like she was on a boat. "I'll give you more points if you haven't been to The Gem Saloon in the last month."

SHE USED TO BE NICE

"Dammit." Pete mock-slapped his forehead. "I lose. Although I actually spend a lot more time in SoHo. I like Kenn's Broome Street bar, if you've ever been."

"I haven't. But SoHo's near my office. We're near Union Square. I do audience development at *Metropolitan*." Distantly, Avery could hear her voice slurring, could feel her jaw muscles working overtime to help her articulate words. She hadn't planned on getting so drunk, but she supposed there was no turning back now. She really *was* as irresponsible as her college friends thought, wasn't she? She was still the girl who could put herself in the most compromising positions imaginable. She shouldn't have drunk this much tonight, or that night senior year. Look where that got her. Just look.

"*Metropolitan* is an incredible magazine." Pete sounded genuinely impressed. "I read it all the time. Very cool that you work there."

Avery squinted as she tried to focus on him. "You think so?"

"Definitely!" He was smiling big now, his perfect teeth like spotlights shining from his face. "I follow you guys on Instagram, too. The captions crack me up. I especially love the posts about Taylor Swift and Travis Kelce. I'm not a big football guy but I will happily root for the Chiefs for Taylor's sake."

Avery tried to laugh without falling over. "Are you telling me you're a Swiftie?"

"Of course I am! Who isn't these days? She's a powerhouse. Her lyrics, the melodies, the production." Pete pressed his fingertips into a bud and then to his lips in a chef's kiss. "It's perfect."

Avery leaned forward, resting her elbow on the bar and her chin in her hand. She knew her body was her one redeeming quality that made up for everything else. It was all she was good for; she'd received that message loud and clear. But her eyes, hazel with specks of gold, were among the features she liked the most about herself. She widened her eyes, hoping Pete would notice the flecks more than her chest.

"Now it's *my* turn to be impressed," Avery said. "I mean, I also love Taylor Swift, but the fact that you admitted you do too is pretty great."

Pete shrugged, unbothered by her implication. "Well, it's true. And I like her in a genuine way, not in a guilty pleasure way either."

The corners of Avery's lips turned into a loose smile. "That's even *more* impressive."

"I actually don't believe in guilty pleasures, as a concept. Who you are and what you like aren't things to feel guilty about."

Pete seemed so self-assured, even about something that other guys might find embarrassing. Avery admired it, found it incredibly charming. What was that like, to be so confident in who you were that you didn't care what other people thought? She longed to know.

"You make a good point," she said. "I pretty much feel guilty about everything all the time. Probably the Catholic in me."

Pete laughed, nodding in agreement. "I can relate to that. I'm not saying this mindset is easy, but it's worth it. Much less stress."

Avery couldn't remember the last time she'd possessed the carefree freedom of confidence. It felt like the person she was now, after Noah, was the person she'd always been. He had embedded himself in her DNA and changed her on a nuclear level, so that even her children's children's children would be subjected to his cataclysmic influence.

"I could use that," she said.

He gave her a playful nudge. "Stick with me, Avery. I'll bestow all my life wisdom upon you."

Avery's skin buzzed where he'd touched her. Her ears savored the sound of her name in his mouth. "I'll take whatever you've got, Pete."

She chugged the rest of her beer, the last gulp tasting like water as it slid down her throat. Maybe she and Pete could get out of there. They could go back to his place and listen to some Taylor Swift, and she could learn more about him, more from him. She didn't even need to have sex with him. Just his company would be nice.

When she finished her drink, she slammed her arm on the table with a *thump* and flagged the bartender down for the check, listing dangerously far left.

SHE USED TO BE NICE
23

"Whoa there!" Pete was suddenly by her side, holding her up. "Maybe we should get you some water?"

The lights above the bar blurred in Avery's eyes, making her head hurt. "I don't *want* water."

Pete rubbed her arm. "Water is good for you, Avery. I'd like to get you some."

Rage thrummed like an engine under Avery's skin. Who did this guy think he was, telling her what *he'd* like her to do? Men were so selfish, concerned with only *their* needs, and it looked like their selfishness continued beyond college as well. She thought of Noah letting Viraj Gupta say he saw Avery Russo fucking his roommate Ronald the rando the night of his party senior year. *Fucking* him! Like they'd had *sex*! Did Noah forget that Avery had tried resisting him, that it was not *fucking* so much as it was *committing a fucking crime?* She might have been too drunk to communicate her desire clearly, but her attempt alone, however sloppy, should've been enough for him to stop. But he didn't, and she couldn't make him, so she was forced to resign lest he do something worse, though she could not fathom what could possibly be worse.

Avery hadn't even known it was Ronald's room that Noah had taken her to that night. Nobody ever paid attention to Ronald's comings and goings. Months later she heard that Ronald moved back home with his parents after graduating early, but who knew why his room was empty that weekend? All she knew was that he wasn't around to confirm or deny what happened, so she just let the rest of their friends believe what Viraj said. Even though Viraj was an idiot for thinking Noah was Ronald. Sure, they had the same dirty blond hair, and yes, it was Ronald's bedroom, but come *on*. Viraj probably only looked through that door crack for a millisecond before coming to a conclusion about what was going on. That meant Noah got away with it completely unscathed. Triumphant. The prick.

"You don't *know* me," Avery snapped now to Pete. "You don't know shit about what's *good* for me."

Pete put his hands up in surrender, but it was too late. Avery was officially furious. Would men always get exactly what they wanted the precise moment they wanted it, no matter the cost? She wished they didn't live in such a world. Maybe then she would still be someone she recognized instead of this sloppy, insecure coward who couldn't tell anyone the truth about what happened at that party.

She threw a wad of cash on the bar and rose from her stool, feeling Pete's eyes follow her as she wobbled away.

"Hold on!" he called out. "Where are you going?"

"I am *not* listening to a fuc—" *Hiccup.* "A fucking *man.*"

Avery's vision blurred in and out as she teetered out of the bar and whirled her head around, scanning the area for a landmark or a subway line or anything she recognized. But the outlines of the buildings were too fuzzy and the lights were too bright and everything was spinning . . .

"Let me at least help you get a cab," Pete said, holding Avery's arm to stabilize her. She jerked away from his touch.

"I can do it *myself,*" she said, or maybe she only thought she said it, because soon her eyes were rolling to the back of her head and her knees were wobbling and everything was fading to black.

3

Beepbeep. Beepbeep. Beepbeep. The high-pitched sounds pierced Avery's throbbing skull. A light shone in her face, the heat scorching her eyelids. It felt like she was propped up on a bed with her back against a pillow.

Her eyes fluttered open.

"She's awake."

Three people in white scrubs hovered over her and scratched notes on clipboards. An IV drip was attached to her arm, limiting her mobility. Everything around her was bright yellow, sterile.

"Where am—" Her voice came out hoarse. The inside of her mouth tasted like burnt gasoline. "Where am I?"

"The hospital," one of the people in scrubs said.

She looked around wildly. "I'm *where*?" The scent of rubbing alcohol tickled her nostrils, making her cough. She blinked rapidly. Mascara flaked off her eyelashes and fell onto her cheeks. She felt simultaneously panicked and like her brain had turned to oatmeal.

"NewYork-Presbyterian. You were experiencing the effects of alcohol poisoning," Scrubs continued, all business. "And you took a fall, but you're all right now. This young man called an ambulance and brought you here."

He pointed in the direction of a guy slumped in a blue plastic chair in the corner. Avery remembered him from last night. Or tonight? What time was it?

She wiped the smudged mascara off her face, pulling at her eyes. She felt the ridges of a wound scabbing over on her temple. Bruises blossomed on her left arm, purpling her skin and leaving her sore. The beeps from the various monitors connected to her body did not let up.

"I'm so sorry about this, uh . . ." She hesitated. She knew she'd met him at some point after she left Morgan at Doc Holliday's. It was at another bar. Somewhere Irish. O'Something. McSomething.

Oh no, she thought. She'd drunk too much. She'd been with a guy. Her cleavage was out. There were some holes in her memory. *Please not again.*

"W—what happened?" she asked, her heart racing.

"You passed out," the guy said. "Outside the bar. And I couldn't wake you up so I called an ambulance. Here." He handed Avery her wallet, meeting her eye. "They needed your ID and insurance card."

Avery blew her stringy hair out of her face as she took her things, relieved. "Thanks."

"Don't sweat it." He glanced away, seemingly to hide a blush spreading across his cheeks. Had she been *flirting* with this guy last night? The beer goggles must have been strong, because that fleece vest was hideous. It was an ugly slate gray, and the name of some financial firm was embroidered on the chest. But the man wearing it was handsome, with wavy brown hair, light blue eyes, and lean arms poking out of the rolled-up sleeves of his button-down. And at least he'd been nice enough to take her here. If he'd been someone else, someone like Noah, this night could've ended way differently, terrifyingly so. The thought made her shiver.

The door suddenly swung open, hitting the cinder block wall with a deafening *bang.* Morgan burst into the room and threw her purse on an empty chair.

"What happened to you?" she shouted, the messy topknot on her head swinging loose.

Shit.

SHE USED TO BE NICE · 27

"Hey!" Avery said uneasily. Her heart hammered in her chest. Avery didn't want Morgan to see her esteemed maid of honor like this. She tried to sit up straighter in the bed and greet Morgan like nothing was wrong, but the IV drip stopped her from moving much more. She plastered on her cheeriest smile, as if that would distract Morgan from the chaos. "What's up? What are you doing here?"

Morgan's chest rose and fell in rapid bursts, and for a second she said nothing. Avery held her breath, bracing herself. This was it—Morgan was going to fire Avery from being maid of honor. She was going to realize that Avery could barely take care of herself, let alone shoulder the responsibility of a wedding. She was going to finally see that their friends had been right to ditch Avery senior year and maybe Morgan should have, too.

"I got a call from someone saying you were here!" Morgan cried. "What's going on? Are you okay?"

"Oh, sorry," the guy—dammit, what was his name?—called out from his seat. "I scanned your phone open with your Face ID and called the last person you texted. Sorry if that's invasive. I wanted someone to know where you were. Hope that's cool."

Avery glared at him. The thought of this stranger touching her while she was unconscious made her feel all sorts of ill. But he could have left her for dead instead, so she supposed she had to be grateful.

"Yeah, that's . . . um, thanks," she said.

Morgan whirled her head around to face him, then did a double take. "Wait. I know you. Your name is Pete, right?"

Pete's face scrunched in confusion. Then his eyes flew open. "Oh shit, you're Charlie Durham's girlfriend."

Avery leaned backward into her crunchy hospital pillow, watching carefully as this interaction unfolded.

"Fiancée, actually," Morgan said with a smile. She held up her left hand, her ring glittering with rainbow beams of light. "I'm Morgan."

Pete pointed at her. "Yes, Morgan! I knew that. And congratulations."

Avery had no idea how to feel about this. "How . . . do you two know each other?"

"I know her fiancé," Pete said. "We met when I was a senior at UGrant and he was a senior at Woodford. We both worked at this record store in Boston and hung out sometimes. But we've kinda lost touch now."

"Charlie invited you to some parties on campus, too, right?" Morgan asked. "I remember you were at a couple."

"Yeah, UGrant had a shit nightlife. Charlie took me to a few Woodford parties, actually. I remember a Dino-Whores theme party specifically." Pete chuckled at himself. "Kind of offensive. But also hilarious."

Morgan sighed like she couldn't believe she was associated with such people. "Yeah, that one was something." She looked at Avery. "I don't remember you being at that one. Maybe you had to study or something."

Nervous sweat pricked Avery's armpits. "Hold on." She stared Pete down. "You went to school in Boston? And you've been to Woodford?"

"Yeah." Pete cocked his head. "Why?"

Now Avery knew exactly how to feel about this, and what she felt was not good. "*I* went to Woodford."

Pete laughed in disbelief. "No way!"

Avery groaned and rubbed her temples. As if getting so drunk that she needed to be taken to the hospital wasn't embarrassing enough. Now she risked Pete knowing how much of a mess she *really* was. The city of Boston was essentially populated solely by college students, so it wasn't unlikely that she would meet someone who had also gone to school there. But the fact that Pete also knew Charlie and Morgan put him way too close to their friend group. Who had Charlie introduced Pete to senior year? What if Pete met Ryan somehow and heard that Avery had cheated on him? It was certainly possible Pete had learned about her from someone at one of the parties Charlie took him to. What a terrible first impression.

SHE USED TO BE NICE 29

"I was—am—friends with Charlie and Morgan, but I don't remember meeting you at school," Avery said. "Don't take that the wrong way."

"I don't, don't worry," Pete replied, and seemed to mean it because he laughed a little as he spoke. "I didn't get out that much. Still don't, really."

Avery waited for him to tell her that he didn't remember her either, but he didn't offer up the information on his own, and she wasn't sure if she should ask for it or not. Last night, though—at least from what was crystallizing in her memory—he hadn't shown any signs of knowing her previously or treated her like anyone other than a girl he was bonding with over Taylor Swift. Avery remembered admiring how self-assured he was, too, in admitting he was a Swiftie. Yes, it was coming back to her now. Pete was so easygoing, so self-assured. She coveted those qualities.

"I can tell," she teased. "Look at your vest. Your investment firm is monogrammed on it."

Pete laughed, the sound like a song. "Harsh! But you're right. I need to stop wearing this to the bar. It's not doing me any favors."

A doctor put two fingers on Avery's neck and studied the monitor by her bed, where a thin, squiggly line moved up and down to the rhythm of her heartbeat. Avery felt strangely comforted by the visual proof that she still had a beating, functioning heart. Her chest had felt emptier than ever lately, and her attempts to fill it always seemed to go awry. Although Pete kept his gaze soft on her and there was a whisper of a smile on his lips, like maybe he didn't mind that she'd derailed his night. She smiled back, something warm and hopeful blooming in her chest.

Then her eye snagged on Morgan, who had busied herself with gathering Avery's medical files. Avery frowned. Responsible Avery, the Avery everyone once knew, would've been fast asleep right now, dreaming about floral arrangements and save-the-date cards, not having her bride-to-be best friend pick her up from a bender the morning after her engagement. Avery imagined

Morgan snuggled up with Charlie in their warm king-sized bed while she lay passed out in the middle of a filthy Manhattan street surrounded by judgmental onlookers.

She jumped out of bed and slipped on her black booties in her effort to hurry of there. The less time they spent in this hospital room, with reminders of Avery's behavior ticking across monitors and scribbled on paperwork, the better.

Pete cleared his throat awkwardly, like he didn't know what to do next. Avery didn't know either, at least as it pertained to Pete. She just knew she needed to go.

"Well, hey, thanks for giving me an excuse to leave my annoying friends." He spoke in a tongue-in-cheek kind of way, like Avery was supposed to know what he was talking about. But she didn't. She must have been tanked last night if she'd met his friends or otherwise involved herself in a guy's life in a semi-meaningful way. There was no way she'd have done that sober.

"Oh, sure," she muttered. "Happy to help."

"Maybe you could let me know how you're doing in a few days." Pete took out his phone and offered it to Avery. "Can I get your number?"

He sounded so sincere that Avery thought it was a prank. Her lips were horribly chapped, and alcohol seeped through her pores like she was a dirty sponge festering on a kitchen sink. The fact that any of this appealed to Pete—who, for what it was worth, looked somehow cute, clean, and sprightly after a night spent in the hospital with a stranger—was mind-boggling.

"Oh, I, uh . . ." Avery scrambled for an answer, though as soon as she started speaking she had no idea where her sentence was going. There was clearly something about him that she liked, and her distrust of men made that hard to come by lately. She should just give Pete her number. Was it so shocking that someone would care about her well-being after a trip to the hospital? It wasn't like he was trying to date her. But he was looking at her so intensely and curiously, like he was interested in more than just

SHE USED TO BE NICE

checking up on her, like he was trying to *figure her out*. No way was that happening. What man would honestly want to deal with this? To deal with *her*? And then there was the fact that she had no idea what impression Pete had of her from school, what he may or may not have heard about her from his proximity to her friend group. She'd rather not start off with a guy on that foot. The prospect of spending so much time with her college friends during Morgan and Charlie's wedding events this year already filled her with dread. She didn't need to add another person from Boston to that mix.

She shook her head. "I'm sorry."

Pete cast his eyes down, dissolved his face into a nod. He looked embarrassed now. "Don't worry about it," he said quickly. "Hope you feel better. Nice meeting you."

He made an about-face and bolted toward the door, practically leaving behind a cartoon cloud of dust. For a moment, Avery felt bad and considered calling after him, but then she tasted leftover booze on her tongue and her head throbbed, and she immediately dismissed the idea.

"What time is it?" Avery asked as Morgan handed her a manila folder of discharge papers.

Morgan yawned as she checked her phone. "Four in the morning."

"Ugh, it's so late. I'm sorry." Avery wrapped her arms around Morgan's waist and gazed up at her, pouting. "Thanks, Mom."

Morgan met Avery's eye and tightened her lips into a smile. Despite probably being exhausted, Morgan was trying to be a good friend, and for that Avery was grateful, even though she knew she didn't deserve it. But that was Morgan. The most compassionate, sympathetic person Avery knew, the kind who'd put a bowl of water outside her apartment to feed stray animals and who cried when she saw old people eating alone at restaurants.

"Listen, don't worry about it," Morgan said, rubbing the back of Avery's head. "I'm just glad you're okay."

Avery nuzzled her face into Morgan's soft and worn-in buttery denim jacket. This was her going-out jacket from college, and its familiarity both filled Avery with warmth and made her pulse quicken. This jacket had been around for everything. Avery remembered Morgan was wearing it when she hugged Morgan and Charlie goodbye the night of that party at Viraj's house senior year. If only Avery had left with Morgan when Morgan wanted to leave. She could have ended her night in the dining hall eating mozzarella sticks with her best friend, not with Noah holding her wrists down behind her back as he fucked her frozen, unprotesting body from behind.

Avery and Morgan exited the hospital, where outside it was dark except for a row of street lights flickering down on them from overhead. The only sounds were the fizzle of a fly bumping into a light bulb and a homeless man snoring on a bench next to his overfilled cart of belongings. Avery's limbs felt heavy with exhaustion; it took quite an effort to stay upright, let alone walk. She fantasized about how late she was going to sleep in tomorrow. Or, rather, later today.

"Well, I was gonna text you about this tomorrow, but I guess that's technically now," Morgan said. Thankfully she didn't sound pissed about this fact. She was merely stating it. "Are you free to get dinner tomorrow with me and Charlie and his best man? We want to celebrate the engagement."

"I'm down. Who's the best man?" Avery tried to act casual, but the concern in her voice was obvious. She just hoped she had some time before she'd have to see her old friends again, before she'd be subjected to their sneers and hatred for what they thought she did to Ryan.

"One of Charlie's friends from the lacrosse team. He wasn't in our friend group. I hardly know the guy, actually, but he and Charlie have gotten really close."

Excellent start. "Sounds good," Avery said, at ease now. "I'll be there."

Morgan leaned forward and smelled Avery's shoulder. "But make sure you shower first. You smell like onions."

Avery sniffed her armpit and recoiled. "Ewww. You're right."

SHE USED TO BE NICE

Morgan laughed. "I'm, like, half joking. But also half not."

"No, you're right. It's not good."

Morgan laughed again and looped her arm around Avery's shoulder, and they held each other tightly as they crossed the street. Tomorrow night's dinner, Avery vowed with a yawn, would mark a brand new, freshly showered beginning.

4

THE NEXT MORNING (READ: a few hours later), sunlight burned behind the closed off-white curtains in Avery's bedroom, bathing the room in a dull glow. Her brain pounded in her skull like a pressure cooker about to burst. Her contacts, which she'd forgotten to take out last night, were glued to her eyeballs. Groaning, she ripped them out and flung them onto the hardwood floor, where they curled and hardened with her other forgotten lenses. She felt around on her bedside table for the bottle of Gatorade she'd left there and chugged half of it. She, genuinely, wanted to die. Weren't hangovers not supposed to feel this bad until your midtwenties? Avery was only twenty-three. She thought she still had time to be this level of self-destructive without consequence, at least to her physical health.

She pulled her pillow over her face and tried to fall back asleep, but it was fruitless, because now her stomach was growling. She couldn't tell if it was from impending beer shits or if it was time for a bagel. She waited for more clues. She was nauseous, yes, but also hungry. Starving, in fact. The hunger wrestled and then overpowered the queasiness, and would probably even cure it. Confirmed: She needed carbs.

She threw on a pair of leggings and her oversized Woodford crew neck sweatshirt and trudged outside. The fall air was cool but the sun nearly blinded her, its harsh rays shooting straight down

SHE USED TO BE NICE

through a cloudless sky. She placed a curved hand on her forehead like a visor to shield her eyes, then crossed the street to Tal Bagels for a bacon, egg, and cheese on an everything bagel. She desperately hoped her credit card would go through. A couple months ago, she maxed out her credit after spending too much at a Madewell sale, and the guy at Tal let her have her bagel for free because he knew she'd be back, dragging her hungover ass to his counter the following Saturday morning and every Saturday after that like clockwork.

After successfully securing her bagel, she crossed over the shops and skyrises of York Avenue back to her building. The gray, stark lobby wasn't very inviting, resembling a jail cell more than a cozy room welcoming tenants, but still she found comfort in the fact that she was almost back in her bed, where she could rot for the rest of the morning. She dragged her feet up the five flights of stairs to her apartment, unlocked the front door, and tiptoed to her bedroom, doing her best not to jostle the creaky floorboards in the hallway too much as she passed her roommate Celeste's room. Avery's overprotective parents had panicked when she told them she'd be moving in with an executive assistant she'd never met who she found on Craigslist. They had probably envisioned Avery and Ryan living together after graduation, then pulling a Morgan and Charlie and getting married not even a year later. They would've seen no reason to wait. They got married young, at twenty-one, and had somehow managed thirty-five years of a perfect marriage. They were always in sync and hardly fought—a rarity for an Italian-American couple from New Jersey, for whom it was essential to navigate the difference between yelling as speaking, which happened often, and yelling as anger. If they ever *did* get angry at each other, they seemed to make up swiftly and easily, remembering above all else that they were on the same team.

Growing up, Avery couldn't help but admire her parents and wanted to manifest the same love and commitment for herself. She thought she'd found it in Ryan, the handsome, charming lacrosse player she met through Morgan and Charlie in the dining hall during their freshman year. They were together after that for almost three years, and had even begun thinking about their future after college: where they'd live (in a suburb outside New York City), when they'd get engaged (around their fifth anniversary), how many kids they wanted to have (two, maybe three). Until Avery ruined everything, thinking she could safely dance and drink and get some fresh air with a guy who seemed nice and everything would be fine. But now she knew.

Avery's phone buzzed with a Snapchat from Morgan as she crawled back under the covers. It was a picture of a tres leches latte from 787, Morgan's favorite coffee shop, with a caption that said *When your amazing future husband buys you a coffee that supports your fellow Boricuas* ♥

Avery stared at her bagel, haphazardly gnawed on like it had been attacked by pigeons. She held it up next to her face and took a selfie, then with greasy fingers typed *Same!! Love a breakfast surprise from my thoughtful fiancé!!* and hit send.

Then she paused, wondering if that joke was too bitter. Avery was ecstatic for Morgan, she really was. She was thrilled to support her best friend's happily ever after, even while hers was put on hold indefinitely. For now she could live vicariously through Morgan's romantic success, getting the fun and satisfaction of a wedding out of her system by being with Morgan as she went through hers. Plus Morgan had been dreaming about marrying Charlie practically since they met, when she told Avery in their dorm room freshman year that she knew he was "the one" after only a month of dating. By junior year, Morgan had their kids' names picked out: Riley for a girl, Brooks for a boy. And when their girlfriends started applying to corporate jobs and dreaming about breaking glass ceilings, Morgan pranced around monologuing about marriage and women's rights. "The point is that women don't *have* to get married and do the whole white picket fence thing if we don't want to," she'd say. "But if I *want* to get married and do the whole white picket fence thing, then that's my choice."

Avery's phone buzzed with a reply from Morgan. *LOL what a nice guy.*

SHE USED TO BE NICE

Avery breathed a sigh of relief that her message wasn't interpreted as bitchy. Morgan always saw the best in people, Avery included, which was probably why she trusted Avery to be her maid of honor in the first place. It was also probably why she didn't turn her back on Avery senior year like all their other friends did, instead attributing Avery's perceived infidelity to a moment of bad judgment. Avery would have understood if she'd felt differently, considering the story everyone believed that Avery would never correct. But Avery was more scared of confronting the reality of what Noah did to her than she was of losing her boyfriend and her friends. And so here she was, facing the consequences of her own actions. Single and alone.

Morgan texted again. *Let's meet at 7 tn at The Spaniard? I booked a res*

sounds good! Avery replied.

The Spaniard was a gastropub in the West Village and a schlep from Avery's apartment, which was tucked away in the easternmost corner of the Upper East Side on Eighty-Eighth Street. But she figured she could use the long subway ride to prepare herself for the evening. She absolutely needed to be on her best behavior tonight, because the last thing she wanted was to disappoint Morgan. At least she wouldn't have to be around any of her old friends yet. That she wouldn't have to white-knuckle through an evening of painful conversation with her most judgmental critics already made for a good time by default.

Still, she laid down some ground rules for herself: no bitchy jokes, no self-pitying about being single, no excessive drinking, and definitely no hospitals. The thought of alcohol made Avery nauseous right now anyway. She couldn't imagine being ready to drink again in a few hours, though she could use some weed to help this hangover. She smoked some from her purple glass pipe and let her eyelids flutter closed, just for a second. She awoke several hours later and stretched, drawing the last of her hangover out of her limbs, and checked the time.

It was 6:30. She needed to leave ten minutes ago.

She leapt out of bed and jumped into her small, cramped shower, then threw on last night's jeans and a fresh tank top, grabbed her leather jacket and crossbody bag, and sprinted to the subway. Once she arrived at The Spaniard, sweat beading on her temple, she pushed open the heavy glass front door and locked eyes with Morgan waving from the back. Her pulse returned to normal when she realized Morgan's booth was empty.

She navigated through the restaurant, passing the other emerald green half-moon-shaped booths until she approached Morgan's.

"You made it!" Morgan said as Avery slid in beside her. She gave Avery a hard stare and sniffed her. "And you showered."

Avery winked. "Only for you."

"The cut on your forehead looks better, too."

Avery touched her injury, which she'd hastily covered with foundation. "Yeah, I'll be fine."

The Spaniard was just beginning to fill up, with people surrounding occupied stools near the bar in the hopes that one would soon be free. Waiters holding trays of food weaved through the crowd as the smell of whiskey and kitchen grease swirled in the air. A few minutes later, Charlie appeared at their table, looking handsome in a chambray button-down and beige chinos. He kissed Morgan on the cheek with a wet *pop* and she giggled in response. It reminded Avery of the adorable candid she'd snuck of the two of them junior year, when they were giggling by themselves in the corner at a tailgate.

"Hey, beautiful," Charlie said, nuzzling into Morgan's face.

When was the last time anyone called Avery beautiful?

"Babe! You scared me," Morgan said breathlessly. "And your stubble itches. You gotta shave."

"I know, I know." Charlie rubbed his chin, then turned to Avery to offer her a fist bump, which she accepted. "What's up, Avery?"

Avery and Charlie were close the way you were close with your best friend's boyfriend, in that the friendship went deeper than surface level small talk but rarely developed further outside of

SHE USED TO BE NICE

a group setting. Plus he hadn't turned his back on Avery senior year. Probably because of Morgan.

"Not much," Avery said, smiling. "Congrats again on the engagement! Super exciting. And great job on the ring."

Charlie beamed. Avery knew how much he adored Morgan, purely and uncomplicatedly. He probably loved her slightly more than she loved him, but in the way those old wives' tales say it's supposed to be, in that women always give more in a relationship and need to be with men who appreciate it. If given the choice, Morgan would quit her job tomorrow to stay home and take care of Charlie, dedicating her whole life to nurturing their future family. Not all men were deserving of that.

"Thanks, yeah, I'm really happy," he said. Then he moved to the side, revealing a man drenched in shadow, the warm glow from the round lamps perched above the tables just out of reach of his face. "Avery, you remember Noah, right?"

Avery stiffened. Noah?

Her heart stopped when he came into the light.

It was, unmistakably, him. The man who'd led her upstairs to Ronald's bedroom. The reason her relationship with Ryan came to a screeching halt.

The reason everything in her life had changed.

Noah sat down in the only available spot in the booth, which happened to be right next to Avery. She froze as he reached over her to grab the bottle of wine, then watched as he poured himself a glass. *Glug, glug, glug.* She listened to the wine splash around. Yes, her ears were working. That was wine being poured, liquid sloshing into the bowl toward the rim.

But her eyes had to be tricking her.

"Nice to see you again, Noah," Morgan said with a smile.

Avery blinked a few times. Was she dreaming? Maybe she was still at home in bed and sleeping off her hangover. She had to be. After all, she'd never been capable of both showering and arriving somewhere early. Nothing about this current reality made sense.

40 ALEXIA LAFATA

Noah returned Morgan's smile with a grin of his own. "You too, Morgan."

Avery's breath caught at the sound of his voice. A few hours ago, she wasn't so sure that she'd be drinking tonight, but now she reached for the bottle of wine and poured herself a glass, filling it to the top. Because this wasn't a dream. He was here.

Noah was Charlie's best man.

"And this is Avery," Charlie said as he draped his arm behind Morgan. "Morgan's maid of honor. She went to school with us. Not sure if you guys hung out a ton."

Noah gave Avery an almost imperceptible head nod. "Yeah, I think we met at a party once. What's up?"

Avery narrowed her eyes. That was all the recognition she'd get from him? That they'd *met*? Fine, she could play that game.

"Hey, yeah. Great to see you again," she said, clasping her glass with trembling fingers.

Noah took a sip of his wine, and a drop of purple pooled on the corner of his lip. Avery's stomach lurched as she watched him lick it away.

The waitress brought over the steak tartare and kale and artichoke dip that Morgan had ordered for the table, but neither of them were appetizing to Avery right now. All she wanted was a long, comforting sleeve of Oreos and infinitely more bottles of wine all to herself. She brought her glass to her lips, wondering how Noah and Charlie became this close. Avery had seen Noah before Viraj's party senior year, at one of Ryan and Charlie's lacrosse games. At that point Noah and Charlie were only teammates and acquaintances at best, and nowhere near best friends.

"I'm so glad you could be part of this, Noah," Morgan said, helping herself to a piece of steak tartare. "You've been such a good friend to Charlie since the divorce."

Noah unrolled his silverware. "I get it. Having divorced parents is tough. I handled mine all right, but my little brother was really upset."

Avery took a swig of her drink. So Noah helped Charlie through his parents' divorce, and that was why they were close

SHE USED TO BE NICE

41

now. Avery supposed Charlie did take that divorce hard. Morgan had gone with him to Massachusetts so they could move his mom out and get her settled in a new place, and he was distraught the whole weekend. But had Noah really helped Charlie this much, to the point where Charlie made him the best man in his *wedding?* Avery thought men bonded by playing Fortnite and grunting at each other during football games, not by talking about their fucking feelings.

"I remember your brother visited you a lot senior year," Charlie recalled. He sounded very sympathetic, more than Noah deserved. "You missed so many pregame pasta dinners to hang with him."

Noah nodded, making Avery hold her breath. With every flick of Noah's head, his cologne diffused into the air and tightened its grip around her throat. She knew that scent. It was one of her clearest memories of that night senior year, which otherwise mostly came to her in blurred, intoxicated flashes. She remembered the sour and spicy musk wafting off of him as they talked and laughed in the basement. She remembered smelling it in his wake as she followed him up the stairs for fresh air, then later when it hit her in the face as he decimated her from behind. His scent had engulfed her, locked them together in a cage from which she could not escape, despite her desperate attempts and drunken *nos.*

She buried her nose into her wine glass, its sweet fumes like a tonic.

"I know, dude," Noah said. He bit into a piece of bread and chewed with his mouth open, munching violently, like a serial killer. "That sucked. But I wanted to comfort him whenever I could, you know?"

Avery was still inhaling her wine when Morgan glanced at her with a raised eyebrow. This was not Avery's best behavior. She was being too quiet, acting too strange, which was probably confusing to Morgan because Morgan had no idea who Noah was to Avery, the horrifying things he'd done to her. Nobody knew. And Avery planned on keeping it that way.

Avery lifted her head but kept her wine glass underneath her nose for comfort. "That's *so* nice of you," she said to Noah, her voice as sturdy as a tree. "So, what do you do for work?"

Noah took a sip of his wine and looked at Avery over the rim of the glass, his green eyes flashing. Those eyes. Another detail from that night she would never forget. Her palms went slick with sweat.

"I actually founded a start-up," he said. "Meow Monthly. Ever hear of it?"

"I haven't." Avery rubbed her palms on her jeans. His eyes were sickeningly green, like puke. "What is it?"

Noah set his glass down pointedly, as though he was preparing to give a speech. "It's a monthly subscription box for pet owners, specifically cats. Every month, we send a package of treats, litter, toys, and other stuff to take care of your cat, so that you can just focus on your bond. We're about to expand to dogs and other pets, but I've always been a cat guy. Had to start with them."

He grinned to himself like he'd nailed his pitch. What a loser. And *cats?* Really? Cats were creepy and mean. Which, actually, made complete sense for Noah.

"I was so impressed when Charlie told me about this!" Morgan said, annoyingly charmed. "It sounds like a cool company."

"Thanks! I'm very proud of it. I started working on it our junior year. I got the idea during my Intro to Entrepreneurship class and just kept at it. We got a nice round of funding recently. And I'd love to get on *Shark Tank* at some point."

"I'm sure you will, bro," Charlie said. "You went to the *esteemed* Randall School of Management." He mocked what was surely proudly printed on Woodford College brochures for prospective students. Woodford's lacrosse team was D2, but their undergraduate business school was ranked #2 in the country. "If anyone knows anything about business, it's you."

"We'll see," Noah said bashfully. But there was a current of self-importance under the surface, like he was relishing Charlie's

SHE USED TO BE NICE

compliment because he knew it was right. Because he couldn't imagine a situation where he didn't win.

He flashed his eyes at Avery again. She really should've gouged them out of his face that night.

"Your company sounds cool," she murmured, trying to sound normal as bile rose in her throat. The image of his eyes, the last thing she saw before he flipped her over on her stomach and pinned her wrists behind her back so hard he left bruises, refused to leave her head. "I mean, not for me. I don't like animals." Avery never usually admitted that—she could feel people judging her for it, thinking she was even more of a bitch than she already was—but her visions were grabbing hold of her attention and refusing to let go.

"No?" Noah asked.

"Avery isn't an animal person," Charlie explained.

"Yeah, I keep sending her dog memes to change her mind, but it's not working," Morgan added. "I really want a golden retriever one day. They're so cute."

Avery willed herself to focus. "I got bit by a German shepherd when I was younger, and now all dogs freak me out. So, whatever."

"And now she's the kind of coldhearted asshole who didn't shed a single tear during *Marley and Me*." Morgan grinned lovingly at Avery. "But she's *my* coldhearted asshole, so it's okay."

Morgan suddenly gasped, like she remembered something, and told everyone about her and Charlie's tour of the Brooklyn Botanic Garden last week. Morgan had always dreamed of getting married there, and it was Charlie's idea to take her on a tour of the venue during their trip last weekend, probably because he knew he would pop the question soon. ("Right, babe?" she asked, beaming, to which Charlie shrugged with mock innocence.) Morgan described the beautiful outdoor area for the ceremony and the huge glass dome in which they could have their reception, where you could see all the flowers blooming from inside the hall. Avery smiled and nodded and squealed at each moment that called for a reaction, all while Noah sat mere inches away. Someone get her a medal.

"But we don't know if we can afford it," Morgan said with a frown. "So we'll have to see."

Charlie put a reassuring hand on his fiancée's arm. "We'll do our best, babe. We have awhile to save."

"Do you have an idea of a date yet?" Avery asked, and suddenly Noah reached over her to grab a forkful of steak tartare. She stiffened at his closeness. She could see every hair on his forearm, every freckle on his skin, the bulging veins revealing the strength he used to pin her down . . .

"We're hoping to book about a year from now," Morgan said. "Maybe less, if it's available and we can swing it."

A year. Avery had to be around Noah for a whole year.

She squeezed her eyes shut and opened them again, forcing herself to stay present as the conversation morphed to rising rent prices. She didn't know how they'd transitioned to that; in between her blinks she mentally left the table and also Earth.

"One of my coworkers at the ad agency used to live in Bushwick," Charlie said. "He said it wasn't too bad of a commute."

Avery took slow, deep breaths. One year. It sounded long now, but the older you got, the less time it was. Today it was one twenty-fourth of her life, for example, but when she was twenty-nine it would only be one thirtieth. Etcetera. She commanded herself to internalize this or else she'd lose her mind.

"Even that deep in Brooklyn has become pricey, though," she said. "I considered it before I moved here but I couldn't afford it."

"Brooklyn Heights is the same," Noah agreed. "That's where I live. Brooklyn is just expensive in general."

Avery was so glad she lived in Manhattan, where people from Brooklyn rarely made the trek and vice versa. It wasn't unheard of for New Yorkers to remain firmly, stubbornly in their borough. Avery hoped Noah was one of those. Manhattan was *hers*, after all. In fact, the entire city of New York was hers. He wasn't allowed any piece of it. She didn't know or care where he was from originally, but he needed to go back there—now.

SHE USED TO BE NICE

"Hold on, Charlie," Morgan said, her nose scrunched in disgust. "Are you talking about that gross video editor you work with?"

Charlie nodded sheepishly. "The one who got suspended for sending offensive messages about a female producer, yeah . . ."

"Ooof," Noah said. "What were the messages?"

He locked eyes with Avery for a beat before they both looked away, Avery's heart slamming against her ribcage. Then he took a sip of his drink, all casual and unbothered as if they had not been exchanging knowing eye contact all night. The normality of his behavior sickened her. This must've been how he acted at school when he heard the story of her infidelity spreading like wildfire through her friend group and the wider lacrosse team. Just took a proverbial sip of his drink and said nothing.

"He wrote, 'Rachel has the most fuckable ass' in our corporate-wide group chat," Charlie said.

"Well, does she?" Noah asked, laughing briefly before adding, "I'm kidding. That's bad."

Charlie grimaced. "Yeah. It was clearly meant to be private. I felt kinda bad for him."

Morgan held her hand up. "I don't feel bad for him. He shouldn't be saying that about a female coworker at work. And she *saw* his message? Traumatizing."

Charlie and Morgan spent the next few minutes bickering about the severity of what happened. *Practicing for marriage*, Avery thought rudely as she drained the rest of her wine. At least they had someone to bicker with. They had someone to *be* with, for richer or for poorer and in sickness and in health and all the romance that goes along with that. They had a *plan*.

Avery had a plan once, too. She was going to graduate from Woodford College at the top of her class and live in a one-bedroom apartment downtown with Ryan, maybe in the West Village. She would pursue her lifelong dream of being a writer by working and networking in the city, and then eventually she and Ryan would get married, have kids, and move to the suburbs like her parents did, where she could write essays and books in peace. A simple, happy life. But now she spent her postgrad days floating around like an astronaut lost in space, hovering deeper into the open-ended nothingness that was her future. And she was too chicken-shit to talk about what Noah did to her, choosing instead to let everyone believe the lie that she'd cheated on the man she once thought was the love of her life.

Noah reached over her for another bite of steak tartare. As he pulled backward with the tartare in his hand, his arm lightly grazed Avery's skin. She jumped at the contact, the silverware on the table rattling from her sudden movement.

Everyone whirled to face her. Blood rushed in her ears.

How dare he touch her.

"Sorry," she muttered. "I'll be right back."

Avery hurried to the bathroom and slammed the door closed as Noah's touch burned her skin. She hovered over the marble sink to examine her reflection in the mirror. Her makeup was smeared around her sunken, red-rimmed eyes. Her lips were dry and pale, vanishing into her washed-out face. She leaned forward, searching for a spark of recognition in the person staring back at her, but there was none. All she saw was a ghost, the faded remains of a woman she once knew, of a woman who'd disappeared at the hands of the man sitting outside at that table. And now he was back in her life, the best man to her maid of honor in Morgan and Charlie's wedding. And there was nothing she could do to make him go away.

5

AVERY WOKE UP FROM her tired, zombie-like state on Monday morning by Snapping Morgan a picture of her eyes fluttering closed. Morgan replied seconds later with a close-up of her mouth, spit bubbling between her teeth and the metal wire of her retainer. Avery laughed out loud. Sending Morgan ugly Snapchats before work made her feel like they were still living together in college, hanging around the dorm in their sweatpants and slept-in buns. Avery knew they would've been roommates in the city if Morgan and Charlie weren't so serious, though it made sense that Morgan had decided to live with Charlie instead. Avery wasn't offended by it as much as she couldn't believe the finality of it, what it represented. It was like the door to that carefree part of their lives, where their biggest problems were writing tedious term papers and deciding which top to wear to the bar, was officially closed. Everything really was different now.

And worse, these last several months since graduation had felt like the purgatory of adulthood. Nobody warned Avery about this uncertain, confusing period where she would feel both too young and too old for everything. She was too young to pay her own phone bill, but too old to live back home with her parents; too young to wear heels and pencil skirts to an office, but too old for the leggings and crewneck sweatshirts she wore across campus. The in-betweenness of her identity was disorienting. It made her miss the comfort of college even more, when she had a firm grasp on who she was. At Woodford College, she'd been a student who got straight As in her journalism classes and wrote for the school paper, and her only concerns were to study and to squeeze as many fun memories into four years as was possible. She'd loved college.

She interrupted her thoughts with a sigh. She was doing so well before Noah showed up last night. She was ready to prove to her friends and to herself that she was still capable of achieving something good after everything. But now, with Noah around, she had no idea how she was going to manage that. His presence was going to send her a million steps backward when all she'd wanted to do was forget him and move on. Already her memories from that night senior year were like quick flashes of video from an old VHS tape, Noah's firm grip and searing gaze interspersed with static darkness.

It was easy for her to tell herself she'd just cheated, too, because the bare bones of the truth of what happened—sexual intercourse with a man who wasn't her boyfriend—perfectly mirrored cheating. It's like how police can interrogate suspects into admitting to crimes they didn't commit, only Avery basically interrogated herself as a form of self-protection. If her flashes of memory fit into an existing version of events, why add complexity about consent that would've only caused her more anguish? And now that some time had passed, if she'd decided to come clean, people would think she was just covering up a mistake that she'd already essentially admitted she'd made. It was much easier to continue lying to herself than to tell any semblance of the truth. Lying was as essential to her survival as water.

She glanced at her phone. It was 8 AM, and she was officially running late for work. She shuffled to the bathroom to brush her teeth, then headed to the kitchen for a breakfast bar. As she ate, her hips leaning flush against the countertop, her phone buzzed with a text from Morgan.

Noah seems cool, right? I wish we hung out with him more at Woodford but I think he was mainly friends with Randall kids

SHE USED TO BE NICE 49

Avery's chest tightened. Noah's name was the only word she saw in that text, and now it was branded onto her retinas. She supposed she'd need to get used to these startling reminders of him, after having spent the last several months pretending he didn't exist. How infuriating that he seemed so normal last night. So *cool,* according to Morgan. She could never know the truth about him now. Not that Avery planned to tell her or anyone else anyway, but this solidified it. Morgan had enough to worry about with the wedding, and the knowledge that Charlie's *cool* best man could be capable of such a heinous act would ruin everything about the year that was supposed to be the best of her life. No, the truth would remain locked inside the filing cabinet of Avery's brain, collecting dust and yellowing away, curling at the edges, until it disintegrated into nothing.

yeah, sounds like it, Avery texted back.

Maybe you guys can become friends now. We could go out like last night more often!

Avery choked out a laugh. Her and Noah. Friends. That was fucking hilarious.

for sure! she replied.

As she made her way west across the avenues toward the Q, passing a yoga studio, a specialty grocery store, and a couple of boarded-up restaurant fronts, her anxiety morphed to irritability. She projected her anger onto everyone in the subway car, like this elderly woman who kept knocking into her because she wasn't grabbing onto the metal pole. And this disgusting mouth breather who kept huffing his lox and onion breath directly into her eyeballs. And these idiots trying to squeeze into this clearly overcrowded car, holy shit, couldn't they wait for the next one? What was the rush? Where were they so eager to get to? *Work?* Fuck these people. Fuck her life.

Once the train rolled into her stop, Avery stormed up the steps and into her office building. She headed to the communal kitchen to brew a cup of weak coffee, cursing herself for being so distracted and forgetting to stop at La Colombe for their stronger brew. At her desk, she powered on her laptop and shared the morning stories onto *Metropolitan*'s social channels. One story, about a woman who was groped on the sidewalk near Times Square, gave her pause. She thought briefly about what she would've done in that situation and decided the last thing would have been to tell a newspaper, because she would have murdered him instead. Like she should have done to Noah.

She checked her email. There was a monthly "Editor's Note" from Patricia Gruyere, *Metropolitan*'s editor in chief, and a few pitches from PR people who always made the mistake of thinking Avery was a staff writer. Which was truly the cherry on top of this morning's shit sundae.

"Good morning!" Larry, a staff reporter in his sixties, said cheerfully, leaning against Avery's desk. "How many pageviews did my article about the homeless population in the subway get?"

Larry used his hands to make air quotes when he said "pageviews," as if he were saying it hypothetically.

Avery took a long sip of her coffee, which had already become tepid. She was just about ready to kill herself. "Morning, Larry." Larry covered the public transportation beat at *Metropolitan*. These stories got low traffic and were always at risk of being cut, but they were Larry's pride and joy. Sometimes Avery thought he insisted on the importance of the section just so he had an excuse to complain publicly to the mayor about how inconsistent his morning F train was. "Let me see."

Avery perused the stories she'd shared across *Metropolitan*'s social media channels on Friday: an explainer on bipolar disorder pegged to an actor's recent diagnosis, a feature about what a rare bird spotted in Central Park meant about climate change, a story about a white pop star apologizing for using the n-word, a list of horror movie remakes worth watching. Eventually she found Larry's feature, about the increase of homeless people living in the subway over the last twenty years. Avery had read the story last week. It was sad but incredibly well-reported and beautifully written. Larry was a talented writer, despite being a chipper pain in her

SHE USED TO BE NICE 51

ass right now. Avery was talented too, once. Maybe she should email those PR people back. She wouldn't use any of their pitches for story ideas. She would just act like she was considering them, maybe give them her work address to send over a sample of their supposedly "revolutionary" psoriasis cream or ask some follow-up questions about their ex-Mormon client's "mesmerizing" self-help memoir. That's what real writers did anyway. Who would know she wasn't serious?

She would know. She would know she was pathetic.

"That one did pretty well for your section, Larry," Avery said. "Four thousand pageviews so far."

"Nice! Quadruple digits!" Larry gave Avery a high five and practically skipped away, the scent of mothballs and artificial hazelnut lingering in his wake.

Kevin, the only other person under thirty in the office, messaged Avery on Slack. *How does that man's wife have sex with him?*

Avery laughed. *Awwww, be nice*

Do you know how long it took me to delete all the drafts he made in the CMS yesterday? He must have started the same article 15 times in 15 different pages

As senior product manager, Kevin was tasked with teaching all the writers and editors about *Metropolitan's* in-house technology. Some of them had a hard time understanding the basic inner workings of a content management system.

He'll learn! Avery replied.

I've showed him how to do this so many times!! Can we have our 1:1 earlier? I need a bitch sesh NOW

Avery headed to the conference room with her laptop to meet Kevin, feeling extra thankful for him today. If it weren't for her work husband, she would be even more miserable at *Metropolitan*. Being around so many writers and never writing herself only exacerbated her confusing postgrad identity feelings. As a kid, writing had been her escape from her cushioned suburban life. She kept the same Five Star journal throughout her adolescence, documenting her angst in painstaking, dramatic detail. She loved journaling, the way the act of putting her thoughts and feelings on the page helped her make sense of things. Sometimes she'd even write stories—narratives of real-life moments she didn't want to forget or scenes she completely made up. She never felt more invigorated, more alive, than when she was immersed in a world of her own creation, the master of her own universe.

Then in college she wrote essays and op-eds for Woodford's student newspaper, *The Golden*. She was ecstatic when her columnist application was accepted and saw the gig as her first step toward a real writing career. But senior year, when it was time to put the clips she'd generated to use in job applications, she didn't apply to any staff writer openings anywhere. She'd been so depressed over everything that happened that she could barely muster the energy to walk across campus to class, let alone fix up her résumé. Now any writing she did for *Metropolitan* needed to be quippy and condensed into 280-character social copy. If she never wrote another pun again, it would be too soon.

Kevin appeared in the conference room and flung himself into a leather chair. He fumbled with a charger cable emerging like a snake from a hole in the table and plugged it into his laptop.

"Patricia's driving me nuts about the site redesign," he said, clicking a pen over and over again. "She's asked me to QA it a hundred times."

"I thought it all looked fine," Avery whispered as she closed the door. She may hate her job but she didn't want to get fired for talking about hating it. She needed the money, especially for all the wedding expenses this year.

"It does! I feel like she thinks I'm missing something. But she doesn't even know how to add page numbers to a damn Word Document." Kevin pounded his fingers against his keyboard, not looking up. "I'm so over this place. I applied to ten different jobs last week. Really hope one of them gets back to me."

Avery frowned. "Kevin, you can't leave. I can't be the only person around here who can embed a video into a draft. I will lose my shit."

SHE USED TO BE NICE

"You can leave, too. Nobody's stopping you."

The sound of chairs shuffling around echoed from the conference room across the hall, where the writers were preparing for their weekly pitch meeting. Avery peered longingly at them through the transparent glass wall of their meeting room, wishing she could join. Kevin followed her gaze.

"Or you could move departments," he added.

Avery glared at him. "I can't."

"Come on, sure you can! Just go pitch something. Patricia's always complaining that the writers don't come up with good ideas anymore."

Avery opened her laptop to pull up *Metropolitan*'s RSS feed, which she used to track the stories being published throughout the day so she could share them on their social media channels. Watching the feed deflated her. It made her feel benched from the big game, like she was watching the editorial action happen from the sidelines without ever getting called in. The worst part was, she wasn't even a player. She was the waterboy.

"I don't know, Kevin. I haven't written anything since college."

She brought up *The Golden*'s website and searched for her name to see if her essays were still there. She clicked on her favorite essay, a piece she'd written junior year about how watching trashy reality television was beneficial for your mind. Avery was a sociology major and used to love finding the meaning and significance of seemingly insignificant facets of popular culture. In her essay, she argued that reality television allowed your imagination to wander into the extremes of experiences and return safely without any consequences. A communications professor she talked to called it "vacationing." Her editors at *The Golden* had loved it. They thought it was pegged perfectly to the season finale of *The Bachelor* and ran it a week before, and it got the most reads and shares out of any *Golden* essays published that year. Avery had been so proud of it.

Rereading it now, though, she thought it was juvenile and pointless. And her writing had surely gotten worse now that she hadn't practiced in so long. She hadn't written a single word since before her breakup. Since before that night.

Kevin leaned over the table to look at Avery's screen. She slammed her laptop closed.

"What?" he asked with a dramatic gasp.

"You can't read it."

"Girl, I have Google. I'll find it myself." A second later, Kevin smiled. "Found it!" He squinted at his screen to read the article while Avery wished she could jump out the window and fall to her death. She'd forgotten what it was like for people to read her writing, the bravery and confidence it took to share your thoughts and feelings so openly with the world. The version of herself who could do that was such a stranger to her now.

"Avery, this is so smart and well-articulated," Kevin said. He sounded shocked. And Avery would be, too, if she had to reconcile the girl she was now with the girl who'd written that article. "You *have* to write something for us."

Avery mumbled a vague response. Something resembling "no."

"Why not?"

"*The Golden* was a silly student paper," Avery said. "*Metropolitan* is a legit magazine. Nobody cares what I have to say."

Kevin sighed impatiently. "The media craves voices like yours and mine. Everyone's gotten sick of cis-het white men projectile vomiting their opinions all over the place without any of us getting a say. You should capitalize on this moment."

Kevin's computer dinged with a message from Patricia. He stood up from his seat and left the room, leaving Avery alone with her essay up on her laptop screen, a relic from before Noah stole all her life force. She closed the browser. She was much better off continuing to be quiet.

• • •

Avery didn't hear Noah's name again for the next couple of weeks and went back to pretending that he didn't exist. Her irritability

SHE USED TO BE NICE

toward her job, too, had calmed down. As the weeks passed by, she reverted to her normal feelings of apathy, which she tempered after work with her usual glass of wine (or three), reality television marathon, and 2 AM doomscrolling. She didn't once ask Morgan about who else would be in the wedding party, preferring to live in ignorance for a bit longer despite knowing it was only a matter of time before she would be faced with her old friends-turned-enemies. By the time the following Saturday afternoon rolled around, when she met Morgan in SoHo to go shopping, she felt like herself again, or at least the version of herself she'd gotten used to since graduation.

"I asked for a sample of this brightening eye cream from Sephora," Morgan said. She took a sip of her caramel macchiato. "I hope it works. My dark circles are extra dark lately. It's not fair that guys get to walk around with circles and nobody says anything, but if I do, I look *tired*."

Avery paused in front of a window to admire a pair of sneakers, then kept walking to match Morgan's long-legged strides along the sidewalk. Avery broke a sweat to keep up with Morgan sometimes. At five-seven, she wasn't short, but next to Morgan she felt like a troll.

"I don't think it'll work," Avery said. "*Metropolitan* did a whole story on those eye creams last week. They just moisturize."

"Really? Damn, this one's supposed to be good. I won't buy the regular size one then."

Morgan scooted out of the way of an interracial couple holding hands and a family of tourists fighting in another language. She and Avery were walking away from the overpriced boutiques and heading to Broadway, where the options mirrored more of what you'd find in a suburban mall. Last week, Avery found a gorgeous gray wool sweater around here for only sixty bucks. Which, in hindsight, maybe wasn't that cheap. Avery sighed. She needed to be more thoughtful with her money instead of following every impulse she had, as though her net worth were bottomless. She'd never think to sample something before committing to a purchase like Morgan did. She wasn't one of those college grads whose parents helped with rent or a gym membership or even a roll of toilet paper; her dad told her she was moving back home to New Jersey before *that* ever happened. With the wedding and all its related maid-of-honor expenses, some budgeting would be necessary. She'd have to pay for not just gifts, but her bridesmaid dress and shoes, her part of the bachelorette party and bridal shower, travel expenses . . . the list went on and on.

Avery walked over a street vent at the exact moment a gust of wind from a subway rushing by underground made her skirt fly up. She tried to cover herself, but it was too late: She'd flashed a group of construction workers leaning against the side of a building, and now they were heckling her. She made a sharp right into whatever the next store was—they hadn't quite cleared the side streets yet, so it was another expensive boutique—and furiously combed through a rack of clothes, with Morgan beside her.

"Creeps," Morgan muttered.

Avery held up a white crop top that would've been cute if it wasn't a hundred dollars and didn't have the words "Allergic 2 Mornings" written on the front. It would also, maybe, be a bit tight. She put it back, hating those construction workers for making her question her outfit choices. It wasn't fair that what she wore dictated whether men respected her, that basic parts of her anatomy were seen as an invitation. Sometimes now she purposely used revealing outfits to attract guys before they had a chance to weaponize how she dressed against her. But men were often swift to remind her who really had the power. As if she could ever forget.

"Hey, I was thinking," Morgan said as she moved on to a table of folded jeans. "Did anything happen with Pete?"

Avery glanced at her, looking away quickly. "No. I didn't give him my number."

Morgan made a disappointed face. "Aw, why not? He's cute! And really sweet."

"He was fine, I guess. It was nice that he took me to the hospital, and I know he knows Charlie, but to me he's a stranger. He

SHE USED TO BE NICE   57

could've taken advantage of me when I was passed out. I was dumb to get drunk with him."

Morgan cocked her head, confused. "But he didn't take advantage of you. He got you help."

"And I'm supposed to reward him with my number because he's a decent person? That's a bare minimum requirement."

Morgan sighed. "Okay, I see your point. However, it's not the bare minimum for him to stay in the hospital with you until 4 AM, so, let's give him some points for that."

Avery considered this. "Fine. Sure. You're right." She hesitated. She didn't want to talk about this, had hoped Pete would become a distant memory like everything from senior year. "But I'd be nervous to go out with someone with such a close connection to our friend group. Who knows what he and Charlie have talked about, or what he's already heard about me?"

"Charlie doesn't gossip. Men don't talk like that with friends. I have to literally pry details out of him after guys' nights."

"Well, he could've heard about me from another one of our friends at the Dino-Whores party or wherever else. And maybe Charlie doesn't gossip but you *know* everyone else does, especially when they're drinking." Avery shook her head, like this was final. "Pete might already know about everything that happened with Ryan. I cannot imagine a worse first impression."

Morgan fingered a scarf hanging off a hook on a wall nearby. Then she met Avery's eye, her face soft. "Even if Pete *did* hear something about you—and we don't know if he has—I would hate to see that holding you back. You and Ronald hooked up, yes, but it was a mistake. What's done is done. All of that is in the past now. At some point, you have to forgive yourself and move on."

Avery looked down at the ground. She'd definitely made some mistakes that night. Just not the mistake everyone thought she'd made. But no matter how that night ended, she'd started it, asked for it. She'd giggled too much and drunk too much and shown too much cleavage, and then later she failed to get Noah to stop. The end result was still her fault.

"It's just hard, Morgan."

Morgan didn't say anything for a few moments, letting the silence fill the empty space between them. She knew this was difficult territory. "Can you at least tell me how many days it's been since you've stalked Ryan's Instagram?"

Avery bristled. "It's been a whole month! But even when I *was* looking, it wasn't for any real reason. My finger just magnetized to the search bar and some greater force dragged my fingers to spell out his username."

"Riiiiiight." Morgan wasn't buying it. "And then you'd duck down, hiding from the phone screen like he'd catch you peeking."

Avery gave a casual shrug. "I did what I needed to do." Then she chuckled to herself. "Remember when you caught me ducking three times a day, and you tried to go all Pavlovian on me with your pillow?"

Morgan laughed. "That thing could really scratch you if the sequins hit at the right angle."

"That's why it was so effective. You got me down to once a day." Avery's laughter trailed off into a frown, her face becoming hard and serious. "Look, I'm trying not to think about him anymore. But I obviously still have some feelings for him." Her eyes burned with tears. She blinked them away before they fell. "I thought I was going to be with him forever. And now we're over and he can't stand me."

Morgan stopped walking, settling in beside a mannequin modeling a lavender athleisure outfit. Avery watched her as she took a nervous breath.

"Okay, I have something I need to tell you," Morgan said. "And you're not going to like it. And I want you to know that I fought extremely hard for it to not happen."

"What?"

Morgan tucked her hair tight behind her ears. "We're inviting Ryan to the wedding."

Avery's heart thudded. Pressure built behind her eyes, like she might faint into this massive rack of sports bras. "Are you kidding?"

SHE USED TO BE NICE

"I'm sorry! I'm sorry. He might say no, he really might." Morgan's words blended frantically, the syllables coming out faster than her lips could enunciate them. "He lives in Seattle, so that's a trek and probably an expensive plane ticket, and none of us have enough money for that right now. And Charlie told him you're the maid of honor, and, well, you know . . ."

Avery held up a hand. "You don't need to say it. I know he hates me."

Morgan regarded Avery's comment with a frown. "Charlie only liked a few guys from the lacrosse team, and Ryan was one of them. They're still pretty close. And I just . . . we can't not invite him." Morgan suddenly looked very, very pale. "I'm in a tough spot, Avery. You have to know that."

Avery did know that. And she'd never forced Morgan to be loyal only to her. It wasn't normal to expect that kind of one-sidedness from your friend in the real world; this wasn't a dictatorship or the *Vanderpump Rules* universe. She knew Morgan was in an impossible situation. Especially now, during the most important year of her life, when Morgan would no doubt want to invite everyone she and Charlie had stayed close with to the wedding. And that would be fine. It was what Avery had wanted. She didn't want to be responsible for splintering the friend group any more than she already had, even if that meant seeing Ryan again.

"I get it," Avery sighed, resigned. "Let's just hope he doesn't come, I guess."

Morgan's face brightened in what seemed like relief. "Exactly. Yes. Let's hope." She absentmindedly picked up a pair of loafers and inspected them for scuffs. "But maybe soon you won't even care about him . . ." A delighted, mischievous smile spread across her face. "Because maybe you'll see Pete again. And then you'll go out with him. And then you'll bring him as your date to the wedding. And whether or not Ryan is there won't bother you at all!"

Avery held back a grin, feeling endeared to her best friend, someone who truly only wanted the best for her. Love was so easy for Morgan. Her thinking went that if you liked someone, you should act on it. Period. Her straightforward confidence was how she and Charlie first got together. But it was easy to open up to a guy when you had nothing to hide, when you hadn't done anything you were ashamed of and were afraid of being judged for. It wasn't so simple for Avery.

"That's a lot of hypotheticals, Morgan."

"But they're all possible!" Morgan said, deep in her fantasy. Her voice swung up an octave at the end, the way it sometimes did when she looked desperately on the bright side. "I could totally see you with a date at the wedding, and for that date to be Pete. I saw you guys being flirty at the hospital."

Avery rolled her eyes. "You know, if you want Pete at the wedding so badly, you could just invite him yourself. You don't need to involve me in that."

"No, that would be weird. He and Charlie were never that close, and now they don't talk. We're not even inviting all our family members, never mind a distant college acquaintance. No offense to Pete."

Avery shrugged. "Just saying."

"No. Pete is only invited as your plus-one." Morgan's eyes twinkled. "Just think about it. Pete could be *exactly* what you need to be happy and move on."

Morgan hadn't always had this uncomplicated, optimistic view of romance. Around all the career-oriented go-getters at Woodford, she'd felt a little insecure that her main aspiration was to have a family, and that aspiration only intensified when she met and fell in love with Charlie. She worked in marketing now but wasn't passionate about it, even when she'd majored in it, and she often joked to Charlie that he'd better start editing those big-budget action films that people overseas love so she could become a stay-at-home wife. Avery always listened to Morgan vent about her complicated life and career feelings without judgment. It was almost impressive that Morgan had no interest in girlbossing, that she could stay so true to herself in a world that didn't always take caregiver dreams seriously. But the way Avery saw it, if the worst

SHE USED TO BE NICE

61

of Morgan's insecurities revolved around whether it was socially acceptable for her to put her romantic relationship above everything else, she was lucky. There were some women who'd never know what that kind of love felt like in the first place, let alone wonder whether it was okay to have. Some women were too broken for someone to see them as beautiful. Some women were just . . . unlovable.

On their final lap around the store, Morgan picked up a black puffy quilted purse with a thick gold chain strap. It looked like a Chanel bag, the classic style that Morgan had loved since she was a teenager and first saw her Irish Grandma Peggy wear to her dad's fiftieth birthday party at the country club in Rhode Island, where she was from. She was about to hand the cashier her credit card when Avery flung out her arm.

"I'm buying it for you."

Morgan shot Avery a confused look. "What? No, you don't have to do that."

"I want to! I didn't get you an engagement present." Avery handed the cashier ten twenty-dollar bills. After she'd gotten paid last week, she'd taken out some cash; it made her wallet feel thick, giving her the illusion that she wasn't living paycheck to paycheck. But eternal love was worth celebrating. For Avery's parents' thirtieth wedding anniversary, she and her brother, Hunter, had given them a set of Tiffany silverware, which they now used during every holiday and family dinner when Avery went home for a visit. Avery was excited to watch Morgan and Charlie's love blossom over the years in the same way that her parents' had. It even made her feel a flicker of optimism about her own love life. Maybe love could find her through osmosis, if she stayed close enough to it and didn't forget what it felt like when you got it. That it was still worth something.

"Are you sure?" Morgan asked. "I know you struggle to pay rent sometimes . . ." Her forehead creased in worry as she watched the cashier separate the bills, place them in the drawer, and hand Avery her change.

Avery gently lowered Morgan's credit card back into her purse and handed her the shopping bag with a smile. "Happy engagement, bitch."

Morgan let herself smile back. "Thank you so much. You didn't have to, but thank you." Her phone buzzed with a text, and a gray iMessage bubble reflected in her eyes as she scanned her screen. She giggled to herself as she typed a reply. "Sorry, it's Charlie. He just got off the phone with the Brooklyn Botanic Garden. We're going to sign our contract with them later to officially book! Save the date, August twenty-second next year!"

Avery snapped her wallet shut, now that she officially had no cash left. And she desperately needed to pay off more of her credit card bill this month. She hadn't even spent her whole paycheck yet and already it was gone. "You guys figured out how to afford that place?"

"Well, yes and no." Morgan slipped her phone into her bag. "Noah hooked us up!"

Avery's breath caught in her throat. Panicked heat erupted inside her body. She'd somehow convinced herself she'd never hear his name again.

She swallowed. "How?"

"Turns out one of his Meow Monthly investors' wives is a senior-level botanist at the garden! She did Noah a favor and got us in at a *super* discounted rate. Like literally half off."

Avery's head spun at the thought of everything she'd have to fork over for the wedding this year, and it wouldn't come *close* to matching the level of financial support that Noah had already given to Morgan and Charlie. It was probably so easy for him to use his Meow Monthly connection, too, because when you've already convinced everyone to give you exactly what you wanted, what was trying for one more thing? And to ask it from a woman, no less. His smile, so arrogant and disingenuous, could fool even the smartest of them.

Avery took a breath. Only she knew that Noah's generosity was a facade to hide the piece of shit he really was. But she couldn't let that derail her. She just needed to focus on herself, on figuring out how she would contribute financially to the wedding, too. She just needed to save some money. To stop getting expensive takeout from Seamless and start doing her laundry at a self-service laundromat instead of dropping it off at that place with the good softener down the block. Just because Noah was fooling everyone didn't mean he was fooling Avery. And Avery would need to stay strong in the face of that until the wedding. She had no other choice.

6

A VERY DECIDED TO WALK home from SoHo, through the cobblestone side streets lined with townhouses in neutral colors and luxury designer stores she'd never be able to afford. It would be a long walk uptown, but a refreshing late November breeze swirled in the air, and she needed to clear her head.

The sound of Ryan's laughter was echoing in her mind, making her heart ache. There was so much she'd loved about him—his boyish charm, his athletic prowess, how dedicated he was to his friendships—but his sense of humor was her favorite. When you heard that infectious laugh booming across campus, you *knew* it was Ryan Donohue, and you wanted to know what the joke was so you could laugh, too. All their friends loved him for how much of a goofball he was. He was the kind of gregarious guy who rounded everyone up at a party to do haircuts, pouring peppermint schnapps and chocolate sauce into people's mouths and encouraging them to swish it around so it tasted like a York Peppermint Pattie when they swallowed. He would always let Avery cut the line of people waiting for one, and if anyone tried to argue with him, he'd yell "But you're not my girlfriend!" at them. He mostly did it to be funny, but it still made Avery feel special when he ushered her to the chair and winked at her while proceeding to use her mouth as a cocktail shaker. Everyone wanted a sliver of his attention, and all he wanted was to put his attention on her. Being

SHE USED TO BE NICE

in Ryan's corner was a good place to be. And for a while, for Avery, that corner was home.

And then she burned it all down, leaving nothing but ashes.

She still couldn't believe their friends thought she would sleep with another man. How could they think she was capable of betraying Ryan in such an unforgivable way? She'd only slept with one guy before meeting Ryan at eighteen, and it was her high school boyfriend, Thomas, who'd been equally as nervous about losing his virginity as she was of losing hers. She even remembered not taking her shirt off. When they finally had "sex," it ultimately amounted to just sixty seconds of trying to knead a large piece of Play-Doh back into its canister, because Thomas was too limp to make anything meaningful happen. After it was over, Avery was like, "That's it?"

In other words, she had not exactly been a femme fatale.

But now she'd spend the rest of her life climbing this mountain of regret over how she somehow led Noah on. And with the wedding in August, it would be an even *more* treacherous ascent, since she'd also have to navigate the rocky terrain of his presence for the next nine months, particularly the way he'd started tricking Morgan and Charlie into thinking he was a decent guy. What else besides that generous gift did he have up his sleeve this year? What other behaviors of his would Avery have to grit her teeth through? She felt like she was looking down the barrel of a gun, like she could not possibly survive this without bleeding nearly to death.

She approached a crosswalk and shoved everything out of her mind, trying to calm herself down as she waited for the light to change. While peering around at fire escapes climbing up fronts of buildings and orange cones from construction sites blocking off parts of the street, the foggy window of Kenn's Broome Street Bar caught her eye. The name of that bar sounded familiar. She thought about where she'd heard it before—

Of course. She'd heard it the night she met Pete, when he told her it was his favorite bar in SoHo. Out of idle curiosity, she squinted across the street through the murky glass window at the front of the bar. A guy who looked like Pete was sitting right up against the glass, rolling the neck of a beer bottle between two fingers. Avery blinked a few times to adjust her vision and get a better look. Then, to her surprise, Pete came clearly into view.

And seconds later, he met her eye.

Fuck, she thought. She considered rounding the corner, disappearing from his line of vision, but instead she quickly studied him through the window. He wasn't wearing the dorky monogrammed fleece vest this time. He was in a maroon flannel with the sleeves rolled, and he looked *good*, especially under the glow of the warm light of the bar. He'd grown some stubble, too, and it was working.

He tore away his gaze, leaving her be. She pursed her lips in thought. She truly never thought she'd see him again. She knew if she'd given him her number at the hospital, she would have felt like he risked getting too close to her. Acting with some intention of seeing him again on purpose would have been too vulnerable, would have invited him in too much to get to know her and her past. But here he was, right in front of her, having spotted her in plain sight, and something about that made her stay put. Because now she could chalk seeing him again up to a chance run-in, making it easier to justify giving him another shot, which she never would have done on her own volition. She still wasn't sure if he'd heard the story of her infidelity in Boston, but right now her mind was drifting off to the connection they'd made at the pub a few weekends ago and Morgan's fantasy for her at the wedding. She couldn't deny that she'd feel better about seeing Ryan in August if she was already together and happy with someone else.

There was something different about Pete, too. Whereas Ryan was always trying to be the popular life of the party, Pete seemed to unapologetically do his own thing. Avery was intrigued by it, by this unique sort of confidence. Maybe Pete really could be what she needed to move on, from everything.

She opened the door to the bar. A bell jingled above her, echoing in the near-empty room. Sunlight sparkled through the

SHE USED TO BE NICE

stained-glass windows on the wall, and a list of specials written in colorful markers hung over the bar. Pete's eyes flicked up and he froze, staring at Avery. His expression was unreadable.

Avery lifted her hand in an awkward wave. "Hey, Pete."

Pete leaned backward on his stool, then searched her face and said nothing. Maybe this was a bad idea.

"Look who it is. Morgan and Charlie's friend," he said. His lips twitched into a strained smile that didn't reach his eyes. "Avery, right?"

Avery couldn't tell if he was *acting* like he'd almost forgotten her name or genuinely had. She decided to respond in earnest. "Yeah, that's right. It's nice to see you again. Sorry, I was just—I saw you at the window and thought I'd, um . . ." She hesitated, one eye on the front door in case he told her to get lost, then gestured to the empty seat beside him. "Can I sit?"

He put out his hand. "Please."

She sat down. Nervous sweat bubbled on her back, making her already-tight sweater cling even harder to her skin. She felt almost as humiliated now as she had when she woke up at the hospital. But she'd already decided to walk into the bar and give him a chance. She owed it to herself to keep going.

"Thank you again for getting me to the hospital the other night," she said. "And I'm sorry I got kind of . . . weird and distant at the end. Blame the alcohol poisoning, I guess." She smiled uncomfortably but hopefully, like this excuse for rejecting him would suffice.

He shrugged. "Don't worry about it." He sipped his beer and swirled the liquid around in the bottle, the fruity hops wafting into the air. Avery would love to order one for herself—the bartender was wide open, just scrolling on her phone—but stopping this conversation for a drink after Pete called an ambulance on her for alcohol poisoning would not be a good look. "The same thing happened to me during SantaCon in Boston. I was rushed to the hospital while wearing a Santa crop top."

Avery chuckled at the image forming in her mind. "Why were you in a crop top?"

"Why not? A red fur suit would've been so lame. I wanted to stand out."

"Weren't you freezing?"

Pete shot her a knowing glance. "Let's just say I gave new meaning to blue balls."

Avery's chuckle turned to a full-blown laugh. Pete was exactly how she remembered—cute and funny and the perfect amount of self-deprecating. And it seemed like he was letting his guard down. She kept talking.

"I'm surprised I never saw you there," she said. "My friends and I loved SantaCon. All the bars in Boston just played dumb, knowing we were all underage and letting us in anyway."

"I know, it was a riot. The chances we would've run into each other were slim, though. That event was always packed. And I only went that one year." Pete met her eye, tossed her a grin. "You know, I wish Charlie had introduced us in school. I would've definitely remembered you."

Avery's heart skipped. So she was a stranger to Pete, too. "Is that right?"

"You're not easy to forget, Avery."

Avery leaned in closer, encouraged by this. She was glad she'd taken the risk to talk to him again.

"Well, I'm glad we met now," she said. "So we can have a fresh start."

Pete held her gaze. Avery's cheeks flushed warm and pink. His eyes really were so blue.

"A fresh start." He mulled this over. "I like the sound of that."

Avery smiled. She couldn't believe how fast her heart was beating. How badly she wanted this conversation to keep going.

Pete took a sip of his beer, then set it back down on the bar. "I was actually so excited to graduate for that exact reason. I wanted to finally start my real life, as a real adult. We can all be whoever we want now."

Avery loved the way Pete's mind worked. She felt like she'd never be able to break free from the death grip that night senior

SHE USED TO BE NICE 69

year had on her identity, but she longed to remember who she once was. Maybe with Pete, she could.

"For sure," she said. "I'm also thrilled to no longer have to do homework."

Pete nodded vigorously. "The fact that we no longer have homework is insane! I had homework for eighteen years of my life. And now I get to spend my free time doing anything I want?" He pressed his fingers to his temples and made a *mind blown* gesture, which made Avery laugh.

"I know, right? And now we have some money, too. Which is also insane."

"Don't even get me started on that. Sometimes when I put on my tie every day, I feel like a kid playing dress-up in his dad's closet. And then I get a paycheck, and I'm like: okay, never mind, I *am* a legit adult."

Avery laughed again. Pete returned the grin, and their eyes stayed locked on each other for a few beats, until he broke away to take another sip of his beer. She was feeling some déjà vu from the night they met, except now she was sober and had her wits fully intact. Maybe now she could close the deal with him, the way she'd failed to the other week.

She rested her hand on his thigh. "Well, again, I really appreciate you being there for me after the pub. You saved my life."

Pete's eyes followed Avery's thumb as she rubbed it back and forth on top of his jeans. He seemed a little unsure, though not enough to pull away.

"Nah, that's not true," he said, his voice low and somewhat bashful. "I mean, someone else would've found you."

He glanced at her mouth. She could feel him coming around to her flirtatiousness, slowly wrapping around her finger.

"But I'm glad it was you," Avery said, and when Pete glanced at her mouth again, she knew that was her moment to lean in. When their lips touched, she was surprised by how different it felt right away. Even with her eyes closed, unable to see him, she was excited that it was Pete she was kissing, and for some reason this was the detail she focused on the most: not just on the feel of a pair of lips pressing against her own, but on the fact that it was *Pete's* lips. It was an awareness she hadn't felt during a hookup in a long time.

She dug her hand into Pete's hair and sighed into his touch, prying open his lips with her tongue and exploring his mouth. When he pulled away a few moments later, his cheeks were red. Her face slowly zipped open into a smile.

"Well—uh. . . ." Pete coughed to clear his throat, then exhaled a quick laugh. Yes, those teeth. Avery remembered now how flawless they were, like a row of white Tic-Tacs. "Sorry. That was just, um, unexpected."

Avery hovered her lips close to his. "Good or bad?"

"Good!" he said quickly, reassuringly. "Definitely good. Sorry. Just surprising. Since you didn't give me your number and all."

Pete ran his hands through his thick shiny hair and fluffed out the strands, his movements emitting delicious whiffs of pomade, at the same time that Avery realized she needed to sleep with him. More specifically, she needed to fuck him. She needed to fuck away his memories of their night at the hospital, of the girl who drank so much that she passed out and woke up attached to an IV drip. Because when Pete thought of her, he was *not* going to think of someone like that, someone so weak and helpless. She wasn't either of those things. She wasn't like that when Noah pinned her wrists down senior year, and she certainly wasn't like that now. She was strong. Powerful. In control. She just needed to prove it.

"I'm telling you, it was the alcohol poisoning." She didn't want to talk about it. She just wanted to get this done, show him who she really was, excavate his existing memories of her like old bones from an archaeological site. "How would you feel about going somewhere else?"

"Yes. Let's do it." Pete took out his credit card to pay for his drink. "Do you live close? I can grab a cab."

Avery shook her head. "I can't do my place. My roommate's hosting a potluck dinner for her club soccer team." That was a lie.

SHE USED TO BE NICE 71

Celeste didn't play sports. But inviting a man over to her apartment was too intimate. She much preferred their place. It was easier to escape afterward, leaving no trace of herself except the version they'd gotten in their bed. That's what they always wanted anyway: something that existed for their pleasure and nothing else. Except now she'd lead with it on her terms, not theirs. Never again theirs.

"I was thinking maybe yours?" she asked.

Pete slipped his signed bill to the bartender. "Well, we could, but . . ." His voice trailed off.

"But?"

He met her eye. Like she should brace herself. "But I live on Staten Island."

Avery stared dumbly at him. Pete might as well have suggested they board a spaceship. Staten Island was part of New York City, but it was another planet entirely. No subways went there. It was quite literally an island. If you didn't have a car, you could only get there by taking a bright orange ferry on which the words "Staten Island" were written in a Windows 95-era script font. Lots of newspapers advertised the ferry to tourists as the place to go to see the Statue of Liberty, but nobody ever suggested that you get *off* the boat when it docked.

"Staten Island," Avery repeated slowly. "Like Pete Davidson. Wow."

Pete rolled his eyes. "Yeah, yeah. You think that's the first time I've heard that?"

Avery chuckled. "Definitely not but I still had to say it."

"Of course you did." His playful annoyance turned devilish as a smirk spread across his lips. "You up for an adventure?"

Avery had been to Staten Island a couple times as a kid to visit family, but she didn't remember anything about it, except that some of the buildings looked like barracks.

"How many women have you presented a trip to Staten Island as 'an adventure'?" she asked.

"Oh, come on! You know you want to . . ." Pete let his words linger, attempting to dangle them like a carrot on a string in front of her, but Avery wasn't going all the way to Staten Island just for sex. She wasn't that desperate.

"Not happening," she said.

But she did want to kiss him again. And so she did. She kissed him hard, tugging his bottom lip with her teeth and lacing her hands through his hair, trying to summon her power. But it wasn't enough. She needed him closer than clothes allowed. She needed sex. She whipped her head around, searching, thinking. They needed to go somewhere, somewhere that wasn't right in the middle of a bar with floor-to-ceiling windows. Somewhere with privacy.

Somewhere like that bathroom a few feet away.

Avery scanned the bar. Besides an elderly man drinking a scotch and two middle-aged women gossiping over cosmos, there were no other patrons. The bartender was standing behind the well drinks, engrossed in her task of inspecting highball glasses. Nobody would care if two people scurried to the bathroom at the same time.

Avery stood up. She wasn't desperate enough to go to Staten Island, but she was desperate enough to go into a public bathroom. This was a truth about herself she now needed to live with.

She pointed to the black nondescript door down a narrow hallway toward the back. "Let's go in there."

Pete choked out a laugh. "You're joking."

"Nope." She grabbed his hand. "Come on."

The bathroom was small, with rainbow graffiti and wads of gum decorating the walls, and reeked of garbage masked by nondescript berry air freshener. Avery ignored it all and took Pete's face between her hands, then pressed her lips to his more urgently than before. Their kiss deepened and intensified, their mouths slipping and sliding in a frenzy of breaths and groans. She pinned him against the green tile wall with her knee and peeled his clothes off like they were on fire. Then he wiggled his way out of her grip and kneeled in front of her onto the sticky floor, pulling her skirt and underwear with him. When he was eye level with her hips, he moved his face between her bare thighs and began to flick his tongue.

SHE USED TO BE NICE 73

Avery's breath hitched. Warmth pooled between her legs as he kept his rhythm steady. She gripped the wall with one hand and grabbed a lock of Pete's hair with the other, paying no attention to the open garbage pail beside her. She ground her hips against his mouth and the pressure mounted, building and building and—

He stopped. Avery flung her eyes down, panting, the lower half of her body burning hot. For a second their eyes met, and he moved his lips away to toss her a smile. Her heart leapt. She had forgotten that sex was supposed to feel good, that sex *could* feel good, and was even better with someone you actually liked.

Although nobody, not even Ryan, had ever gone down on her like this.

"Don't sto—" she began, but before she could finish her sentence Pete was between her legs again, flicking his tongue and holding her steady. She writhed and implored him to keep going. Once again, though, he stopped short. And then he did it again. And again.

Suddenly, there was a knock.

"Hello?" said a slurred female voice behind the door. "Is someone in there?"

Avery stiffened against the wall. She couldn't speak, could barely breathe. All she could focus on was the feel of Pete's hands gripping her thighs and the dizzying heat rising in her body as he edged her.

"Hold on!" Pete called out, still crouched on the ground. The woman tapped her foot a few times and stomped away. Avery tugged at Pete's hair, a silent, desperate plea for him to finish her off. She felt woozy from the pressure coiling between her legs, begging to be released.

Knock.

"Whoever's in there, open up." That was another voice, a man's this time.

Pete cleared his throat. "We—uh, I'll be out in a minute!" He sprang up from the ground and hoisted Avery into his arms, then pressed her back against the wall, slipped on a condom, and swiftly entered her, filling her completely. He kept his gaze locked on her as each of his thrusts pushed her closer to bursting open. When she finally cried out, the release nearly ripped her body in half, aftershocks pulsing through her limbs until she settled into quiet whimpers. Pete didn't take his eyes off her the whole time she came, like he wanted to see all of her, defenses down. And to her surprise, she didn't want him to look away.

The bathroom door flew open, and a bald man with a ring of keys stood at the doorway. Avery sprung off the wall and crouched down to shield her naked body from this stranger's view. Pete tried to shield her, too, as best as he could, a gesture that was almost heartwarming enough to make Avery forget what was happening.

"Seriously, guys?" the man who was probably the manager said. He sounded more impatient than pissed off, like he'd seen this happen a hundred times before. He took out his phone menacingly. "It's 7 PM and I only have one working stall. Get out or I'm calling the cops."

Avery's fuzzy postorgasmic bliss completely disappeared, replaced now with the sharp sting of real life. The man folded his arms across his chest and rested them on his beer belly as he watched Avery throw on her clothes, flatten her tousled hair, and wipe the lipstick smudges from the corners of her mouth. She stopped abruptly and stared at him, wide-eyed and wild.

"Please don't do that," she begged. She would not be able to live with herself if she went to the hospital and got arrested in the same month.

"If you get out right this second," the manager hissed, "I won't."

Avery hobbled out of the bathroom, disheveled and panting, her right shoe halfway on her foot, and bolted out of the bar. She didn't even care if Pete was behind her. She needed to get out of there. Once outside, she sat on the curb a few feet from the entrance and smoked a cigarette, taking huge pulls and trapping the smoke in her lungs for as long as she could.

"Whew!" Pete suddenly appeared next to her, sitting down. Without the lights shining onto the awning of the bar, his face

SHE USED TO BE NICE 75

would have been hidden in the near-blackness of night. "That was fun. Definitely a close one though."

Avery took another long pull of her cigarette. She wished she could disintegrate into a pile of ashes. "What are you saying? We got caught."

"Well, yes." Pete stretched out his legs and propped himself up on the concrete, getting comfortable. "But we're not going to jail. That's good, right?"

"Oh, *sure*. That's fan*tastic*. Everything's fine because we're not going to jail. Glad that's the standard we're working with."

Pete narrowed his eyes, watched her for a few seconds. Then he lifted himself up off the ground, brushed the dirt off his pants, and made an about-face, like he was going to leave Avery to wallow in her bitchiness. But she couldn't help herself. On top of all the terrible, impulsive decisions she'd made lately, on top of the awful choices she made senior year, she'd just made another one.

But she didn't need to take her anger at herself out on Pete.

"Hold on," she said with a sigh.

Pete turned around and stared at her, looking like he'd had about enough of her bullshit. She didn't blame him. She'd had enough of it, too.

"I'm sorry. I'm just mad at myself." She hesitated. "I get myself into bad situations all the time. It—it just sucks."

Pete sat down beside her again, softening. "Avery, it takes two people to have sex. We were both in the same situation."

"But it was my idea."

"So? I agreed to it. And guess what? I had a pretty great time. I might even go out on a limb and say you did, too." His eyebrows bounced up and down on his forehead suggestively.

Avery nudged him. "Fuck you."

He grinned. "Already did that."

The corners of Avery's mouth pulled into a smile. Maybe she could trust that Pete was right. That maybe everything *was* okay. No, that maybe everything was more than okay. Because despite the near-arrest, she was here. With him. And against all odds, enjoying it.

She wondered what would happen if they stayed on this street corner for the rest of the night. Maybe they'd make their way to another bar, one of those dark cozy pubs illuminated year-round by Christmas lights. Maybe they'd talk and laugh until two in the morning, their surroundings slipping away as conversation took them under, and she'd ride home in a cab with a cheesy grin on her face as she replayed the night in her head, wondering when she'd see him again. Wondering if this was the beginning of something. Just like Morgan had hoped.

"What were you doing in that bar by yourself, by the way?" Avery asked.

"Woooow," Pete teased. "*Someone's* judging."

Avery giggled, unable to resist making the girlish sound. "Not at all! People our age just don't normally do that. Feels like a divorced dad kind of thing."

"Well, how do you know I'm *not* a divorced dad?"

"I guess I wouldn't."

Pete smiled with his perfect white teeth. Avery's stomach did a cartwheel.

"No, I'm kidding," he said. "I was just hanging out. My buddy left to go deal with his drunk girlfriend, and I was finishing my beer."

Avery cocked her head. "Was it the same friend from the other night?"

Pete's eyes widened. "You remember that?"

"Vaguely. They were in a fight? Something like that."

"I'm impressed! Yeah, same guy. Maybe you didn't need to go to the hospital after all."

Avery choked out a laugh. "Tell that to the concrete I planted into face-first."

She smoked the last bit of her cigarette as they sat in comfortable silence. There weren't many people around either, just a group of women carrying shopping bags and a man in a suit rushing by while talking into his AirPods. It was often more desolate at night

SHE USED TO BE NICE 77

in this part of the city, especially on the weekends; most people were heading farther downtown or farther uptown. Avery didn't mind. She liked being alone with Pete.

He fixed his eyes on the flicker of orange light at the tip of Avery's cigarette, then cleared his throat and rubbed the back of his neck.

"So, what are your plans tonight?" he asked. "Do you wanna hang out? Maybe get a real drink?"

He stared carefully, hopefully, at Avery, his blue eyes round and sparkling. She locked eyes with him, feeling her heart swell.

Was this the beginning of something?

"Sorry, I can't," Avery replied quickly. "I've got plans with some friends. I should head home to get ready, actually."

She stood up and threw her cigarette butt in the trash. She had no plans. She had no friends anymore either, besides Morgan. She just knew where a drink with Pete could go and was putting a stop to it now. She didn't deserve any happiness he could give her. She didn't deserve any happiness at all. She deserved the pain of making all the wrong choices with Noah, deserved the wrath of all her friends thinking she'd cheated on Ryan. She deserved to suffer, to be lonely and alone.

"Oh." Pete stood up, too. His eyebrows were furrowed in confusion. "Okay. No worries. Maybe we could do a rain check?" He handed Avery his phone, which was open to a new contact page. "Here."

Avery clutched Pete's phone and stared at the screen, feeling his eyes on her as she contemplated what to do. Pete wasn't the only guy she'd met who didn't have her number. No guys ever got it. The dating apps had their own messaging systems, so there was no need to move platforms just for sex. And if she met a guy at a bar, they didn't need a permanent way to contact each other, because she was going home with him that night and he'd be irrelevant by morning.

She didn't know what it was about Pete, though. Perhaps it was the earnestness of his continued pursuit of her, the way he didn't seem to balk even when she gave him every reason to. Perhaps she simply liked him. Something about him sparked the tiniest flicker of hope, the first since her breakup, and she found herself wanting to let it guide her through the darkness instead of blowing it out before it could combust.

When she finished typing her number, she handed back his phone before she could change her mind. In the middle of the exchange, her fingers brushed softly against his, sending a jolt through her arm and up to her heart. It was the most innocent touch they'd shared all night. And yet, somehow, it was the most invigorating.

7

THE SUBWAY CAR ON Monday morning was suspiciously empty. Avery didn't realize why until the car was already zipping underground, rumbling through the dimly lit transitions between stops. From her seat, she spotted a man in ripped black sweatpants and a black sweatshirt slowly walking around in circles and weaving through the empty spaces between passengers. The few people who'd either been brave enough to ride in this car or who, like Avery, hadn't realized he was in here ignored him.

Avery held her breath and remained seated, praying he'd walk past her and move along. After a few stops, he sat down next to her and eyed her cleavage, and then, to her horror, began stroking himself underneath his boxers. Her heart pounded. She kept her nose buried in her phone and managed to not make eye contact with him even as his gaze bore into her. With a lurch of nausea, she realized that looking down provided him with a perfect view of her cleavage, more explicit imagery with which to get off. But she was frozen. Too frozen to move. It was a feeling she knew well, the quiet resignation after putting up a fight with a man who wouldn't leave her alone.

When the train finally approached her stop, she sprinted out of the station and to her office, where Patricia was waiting by her desk.

"There you are!" Patricia said, twirling a pen between two fingers. "How are you this morning?"

Avery was so shaken up she couldn't form words. "I'm . . . fine," she said softly, shuffling some papers to give herself a minute. "You?" She'd never felt more exposed, like she could button her shirt up to her chin and still be someone's nonconsensual sex object. Why did being a woman mean paying a toll on your ability to move about the world freely and with dignity? If the pink tax didn't already include "being eye-fucked by sickos," someone should add it. Or was there something specific about Avery that attracted the most disgusting men that walked the earth? Maybe that night with Noah set something cosmic in motion. She wished she hadn't worn this button-down shirt today. She wished she hadn't done a lot of things. Maybe, if she'd done everything differently, Noah would've stopped.

"I'm wonderful, thanks for asking." Patricia tapped her pen against the wall of Avery's cubicle. The sound made Avery's teeth hurt. "Listen, I wanted to talk to you about something. We need to find some fresh younger audiences on new social media platforms. Start meeting the kids where they're at online. Our readership has grown stagnant."

Patricia spoke to Avery like she was bestowing some newfound knowledge about the capital-I Industry, but *Metropolitan*'s existing audience was dwindling faster than any of their competitors, and Avery could have told Patricia they needed to diversify their traffic sources the day she started working here a few months ago. Unfortunately, the responsibility of creating kitschy videos over viral sounds or doing whatever else she needed to do to maximize reach was going to fall squarely on Avery. She needed a coffee the size of her head.

"Start on it today," Patricia said. "And when you create the new accounts, ask Kevin to build a feature that pushes all our published content onto each platform at the same time. With one button. So that we don't even have to think about it."

Avery peered longingly at the coffee machine over Patricia's shoulder. "I . . . don't know about that."

"Why not?"

SHE USED TO BE NICE

"That would probably be a big challenge from a technical perspective. Also, isn't that why you hired me? To keep tabs on these different platforms and share our content in ways that make sense for different audiences?"

"Hmm. I suppose it is."

Avery stared at her.

"Look, I don't care how we do it," Patricia said, rubbing her temples. "Our numbers are down and we need them up." Her pep from earlier completely dissolved. She started walking away, back in the direction of her office. "You guys are smart," she called over her shoulder. "Figure it out."

Avery made herself some coffee, then messaged Kevin. *I assume you heard all that*

Kevin responded immediately. *That woman needs a lobotomy*

Back at her desk, Avery researched the different social media accounts of other publications, including *New York* Magazine, *Cosmopolitan*, and other places she'd once dreamed of writing for. As she worked, the thunderous sound of applause came from the writers' meeting across the hall. She watched the writers through the glass wall of their conference room, willing herself to get up. Her project could wait another hour. She should go over there and pitch something. Take a seat at the table, as they say. Or, better yet, just approach the damn door.

But she couldn't do it. She'd lost her voice and, in truth, she'd probably never find it again.

• • •

Later that week, Avery headed to Morgan and Charlie's apartment after work to flip through bridal magazines with Morgan while Charlie was out with his coworkers. Morgan had already researched so many dresses online, but for more inspiration, she enlisted Avery's help to make mood board collages using cut-outs from paper magazines. Avery was excited and ready, bottle of red wine in hand. She might be the fuckup who ruined her relationship with Ryan, but one thing you couldn't say about her was that she was a bad friend.

The lobby of Morgan and Charlie's apartment building in Lenox Hill was decorated with bouquets of flowers set atop an assortment of oak side tables. Across a brown leather couch set, a massive red brick fireplace carved into the wall roared with flames. Under Avery's feet was a large ornate Turkish rug, and beyond the lobby, black-and-white tile flooring stretched down the hall toward a gold-rimmed elevator. When Avery first visited during the summer after graduation, right off the heels of senior year, she had joked to Morgan that she understood why Morgan didn't want to room together, because Avery was way too poor and unremarkable to live in a place like this. With a frown, Morgan had replied that wasn't the reason they weren't roommates in the city and Avery knew that, but by that point Avery's need to disparage herself had become like a tic.

As Avery approached the doorman, her phone buzzed with a text from an unknown number. *Pretty sure there was a piece of toilet paper stuck to my shoe this whole week and I only noticed it now . . .*

Avery's lips played into a smile as she typed a reply. *toilet paper is this season's hottest accessory. i would know, i work for Metropolitan*

Pete's reply came soon after. *Yeah, you definitely know what's fashionable way more than I do. Some of my clothes have been around since high school. I gotta do a closet audit.*

Avery laughed. *"audit"? you really do work in finance, huh?*

Unfortunately. It's my biggest flaw. Unless you count my fear of air plants.

Avery laughed again. Pete was so comfortably, hilariously himself. It was inspiring. *wait, what's wrong with air plants??*

They're WEIRD, Avery. Where are their roots? How do they stay alive? They just FLOAT?! I do not get it.

hahaha wow i never thought of that but you're so right. just give me any air plants you're afraid of and i'll kill them instantly. i have the worst black thumb

I'd love to be your accomplice in those murders.

"Hello?" the doorman said from behind his desk, irritated. "*Hello?*"

Avery jerked her head up from her phone. When she gave Pete her number, she simultaneously hoped he would never speak to

SHE USED TO BE NICE 83

her again and would also text her right away. Even just smiling at a text made Avery feel tense with vulnerability, made her worry about the ending before their relationship began. She tried not to think about it only being a matter of time before he realized she wasn't good enough for him. He needed someone more on his level, someone as cool and confident and funny.

Avery told the doorman that Morgan was expecting her. She rode the elevator to the fourth floor and knocked on Morgan's door, still grinning like an idiot at Pete's texts.

"Are you smiling at a text?" Morgan asked in a singsong voice when she answered the door, nodding toward Avery's phone. "Is that *a guy*?!"

Avery tossed her phone in her tote bag. "No, just a work thing." No way could she tell Morgan about the latest development with Pete. Avery had no idea what to make of him yet, but Morgan would be so thrilled Avery had his number that she'd start making room for him as Avery's plus-one to the wedding. And they were a long, long way from that.

Avery removed her ankle boots and dug her toes into Morgan's off-white rug. A navy-blue couch was pushed up against the wall, which was covered in abstract art, framed photos of Morgan and Charlie, and gold antique mirrors in different shapes and sizes. On the round marble coffee table, the licking flames of a candle burned the warm, cozy scent of vanilla and cedar. Morgan had such a knack for creating a homey space. In college, she used to spruce up her and Avery's hundred-year-old dorm room for all the holidays: pumpkin string lights above the windows for Halloween, a plastic turkey centerpiece on the table for Thanksgiving, red paper hearts taped to the front door for Valentine's Day. Avery thought briefly about her apartment now: the bare walls crusted with spackle from the last tenant, the stiff couch covered in lint from her scarves and sweaters, the empty kitchen table with its peeling composite wood. She sighed.

Avery set her wine bottle down on the coffee table and dug into an opened box of Oreos. Next to the box, a bridal magazine

84 ALEXIA LAFATA

was flipped open to a page showcasing a gorgeous gown with a plunging neckline. Avery pointed at the dress.

"Morgan, you need that."

"I know," Morgan said longingly. "I've been staring at it all day. I love column silhouettes."

Avery cocked her head. "Column?"

"It's a type of wedding dress, yeah. A little form fitting. Follows the natural shape of your body."

The doorbell rang. As Morgan padded to the foyer, Avery wiped the Oreo crumbs from her mouth and buried her face in a bridal magazine, preparing to hear the familiar grating Southern twang of her ex-best friend. Morgan had told Avery that Blair was going to be a bridesmaid only a few days after she told Avery about the engagement. Avery could tell Morgan had been nervous to talk about it, the way she kept tucking her hair behind her ears and talking at rapid-fire speed. But the three of them had been best friends once—Morgan and Avery had been assigned as random roommates freshman year and met Blair down the hall, and they'd been inseparable all throughout college—so the news wasn't exactly a *surprise*. Still, Avery tried not to show too much of her actual reaction, which was one of dread; she just told Morgan that it was her special day and she could do whatever she wanted. She didn't see Morgan's continued friendship with Blair as a betrayal of some sort anyway. The friendships were kept separate and it was whatever. It was easy to do when Blair was up in Boston and Morgan and Avery were in Manhattan. The way it worked was that Morgan would never mention Blair to Avery, and if Blair visited, Avery would occupy herself for the weekend with guys from dating apps and dissociative rewatches of *Bake Off*.

"Aver-*ay*!" Blair squawked. Her drawl seemed extra obnoxious today. "How are you, girl?"

Blair hung her beige peacoat on Morgan's coat rack, which made Avery's leather jacket fall to the floor. Morgan hurried over to pick it up after Blair ignored it.

SHE USED TO BE NICE 85

"I'm great!" Avery replied. She used the quintessential high-pitched, fake-nice voice every girl has down pat, the kind that could crack glass thousands of miles away. "How are you?"

"I'm great!" Blair's voice rose even higher than Avery's, some-how. "It's so good to see you!"

Morgan darted her eyes back and forth between Avery and Blair. Avery could see the wheels turning in Morgan's head as she tried to figure out how to diffuse the tension, which could be sliced with the mini foil cutter knife sticking out of the wine bottle opener on the coffee table. Avery busied herself by grabbing three glasses from the kitchen and opening the wine. Blair was the one who gossiped the most about how Avery had cheated on Ryan, not only within their friend group after Blair heard about it from Viraj but with the whole lacrosse team as well. Avery wasn't naive enough to think Viraj wouldn't have told anyone if it weren't for Blair, but maybe he wouldn't have made it this huge dramatic thing. Blair, meanwhile, loved to talk shit. Things weren't the same between Blair and Avery after that.

Morgan flashed a pained grin. "We're just browsing through some bridal magazines and looking at dresses. Sit, Blair!"

Blair sat on the couch, on the opposite end of Avery. With her off-white manicured nails, she grabbed a magazine and a pair of scissors from the coffee table. Avery sat a glass of wine down on the table in front of Blair, as an attempt at normalcy.

"Have you decided on a veil yet?" Blair asked Morgan, point-edly not acknowledging the wine with a thank you. "That'll inform so much of your look."

"I'm not sure if I'm doing a veil, actually," Morgan said. She reached for the glass of wine Avery offered her. "Oh, thanks, Avery."

"You're very welcome," Avery said.

She glared at Blair. *Bitch.*

Blair sat up straight and tall, like she was about to conduct a business meeting. Avery scanned Blair's outfit: a puff-sleeve blouse, cropped black jeans, and gold kitten heels. There was once a time when Avery admired how elegant and put-together Blair was, when she found Blair's South Carolinian formalities charming instead of the result of a stick up her ass. She'd even sought Blair's help for her first date with Ryan, and Blair spent hours doing Avery's hair and makeup and sifting through Avery's closet to give her advice on what to wear. Their friendship was special to Avery in college. Sometimes she still couldn't believe they'd fallen so far, that Blair had so viciously and vocally turned against her and encouraged all their friends to do the same.

"Well, there are lots of options," Blair said. "There's the cathedral or chapel veil. Those are pretty formal. Or short veils, which I don't love, but they're a bride favorite. There are mantillas, but they kind of look like tablecloths. My favorite is the fingertip."

Avery flipped a page of her magazine so forcefully it almost ripped. "Morgan *just* said she doesn't know if she wants a veil, Blair."

Blair lifted her chin slightly, staring Avery down. Avery stared right back.

"I'm only trying to help," Blair said with a shrug. The innocent tone of her voice was a skewer through Avery's eardrums. Blair took a compact mirror out of her polka dot makeup bag and touched up her lipstick. "I was the maid of honor in my cousin's wedding. I did *so* much research, so I have a lot of context." She snapped her mirror shut and met Avery's eye again, like a dare. "Have you ever been a maid of honor before, Avery?"

"Nope. First time." Then Avery kicked herself for allowing Blair the moment of superiority. She and Blair weren't best friends anymore. There was no place for honesty in their relationship.

"It can be *super* overwhelming. Did you know some brides have their maids of honor sign their marriage certificate as a witness? What a responsibility!" Blair popped her lipstick cap back on, then gave Avery a sickly sweet smile. "Seriously, let me know if you need help with anything. Being a first time maid of honor is *tough*."

Avery cleared her throat, the only appropriate response to Blair's passive aggression. Then she summoned the fake-nice voice again.

SHE USED TO BE NICE

"So how long are you in town for?" It was exhausting, being this phony, obliterating people with kindness. Avery didn't know how Blair did it all the time.

"I'm actually staying until the middle of next week for a work conference!" Blair launched into a long-winded, self-indulgent monologue about all the "challenging but fulfilling" responsibilities she had at Deloitte, which Avery tuned out immediately. Blair always thought she was better than everyone in college because she worked the hardest, and clearly nothing had changed. Back then, Blair would even skip out on parties if she knew she'd be too hungover to do schoolwork the next morning. It gave her this false sense of morality, like *she* could stay in and be responsible while *everyone else* was easily swayed by childish vices. Avery used to laugh it off as Blair being Blair, and would sometimes even join Blair if she didn't feel like going out either. Now, knowing how far that superiority complex could go—knowing it made her think she knew *everything*—Avery wanted to smack her.

"That's amazing," Avery said when Blair's speech felt over.

Morgan taped on a smile, sensing it was time for a subject change. "My mom's making coquito for the engagement party. 'Tis the season. Get excited."

"Hell yes!" Avery cheered. Gabriela always used to send Morgan back to campus after Thanksgiving with two homemade bottles, and it got everyone through the final slog until the December holiday break. "Your mom's coquito is the best."

"I know, I miss it. I've started looking up decorations for the party, too. I'm thinking pink. To match the color scheme of Sel Rrose."

Sel Rrose was a rustic restaurant in the Lower East Side, with an entrance bordered by two pink doors and a bar with gold stools and exposed brick. It was beautiful, expensive-looking, and Instagrammable—the perfect spot for an engagement party. Avery had suggested the spot to Morgan after it was featured in a *Metropolitan* story, and Morgan loved the urban, industrial romantic vibe.

"But you don't want a hot pink," Blair said, like this was the most astute clarification. "You want something chic. Like a muted dusty pink."

Avery heaved a sigh. "Right. That's the shade of pink in the restaurant."

Blair blinked like a robot programmed to do human movements. "Great, just confirming. There are lots of shades of pink, you know."

Frustration bounced around in Avery's throat, like a cage fighter preparing for the ring. *Shut the fuck up!* she wanted to shout. *Just shut the fuck up!*

"This isn't a Sweet Sixteen, Blair," is what finally came foaming out of her mouth. "We wouldn't do hot pink either way."

Morgan's lip twitched.

"Right." Blair blinked again. "And maybe, *Morgan*, you could get some bubble letter balloons that spell out 'love.' I see them all over."

Avery had seen those balloons online too and was going to suggest them to Morgan days ago. She chugged her wine, annoyed that she didn't bring them up sooner.

"That's a cute idea!" Morgan said. "And I agree on the dusty pink. That'll match the flowers, too. We're getting bouquets of soft pink roses and ivory ranunculus, tied together with a gold band."

"Ranunculus," Avery repeated, holding back laughter. "That sounds like the name of a dinosaur. *The Ranunculus*," she began in a dramatic, vaguely British nature documentary voice, "*with its slender neck and tail hung low—*"

"Ranunculus is actually a very common bridal flower," Blair said, unamused.

Avery stifled an eye roll. She could've sworn Blair had a sense of humor once.

"You should mix in some anemones and hellebores, too," Blair continued. "They're in-season and very popular for the winter."

"Definitely," Morgan agreed. "They're kind of expensive, but maybe now I can consider them. Noah's connection to the venue alleviated so much financial stress."

SHE USED TO BE NICE

Avery's heart seized, startled by the sound of his name.

"Yes, I heard about the amazing discount!" Blair said, a smile curling on her lips. "He is *so* generous." She turned to Avery. "Last month, he got us a table at Sons of Essex and paid for *all* the alcohol."

Avery couldn't have given less of a shit. "Wow. Cool."

"He's also so hot." Blair folded her lips together and made a *mmmm* sound as she sank deeper into the couch. "He's a tall drink of iced tea, that boy."

Avery's eyes darted around the room in frantic search of the wine bottle. Noah was not hot. He was a predator. He reminded Avery of this guy she once saw on an episode of *Worst Roommate Ever* who was so smart and charming that he could trick people into living with him until they found out he was secretly a creepy serial squatter.

"You're such a sucker for tall guys, Blair," Morgan encouraged.

"He's six-four! Who *wouldn't* love that?" Blair was practically swooning. "And I love blonds. Specifically Noah's shade, where it's, like, a dirty light brown. And his *eyes*."

His eyes.

Following Avery everywhere she went.

She took out her phone to reread Pete's text message. She thought of that night at the bar: how he teased her so deliciously, how that final release made her see stars, how that glimmer of happiness thawed something deep and cold inside her. She'd give anything to do that again, anything to feel that again. Anything to get away from talk of Noah.

She sent him a text. *hey, are you busy tonight? what are you up to?*

Her phone buzzed almost immediately. Avery had to laugh at Pete's lack of chill. Usually, a two-second reply time would make Avery want to ghost; a guy that was too eager tended to be looking for more than she was willing to give emotionally. But right now, in her desperation, she was grateful for Pete's urgency, regardless of what it might mean. The faster she could have sex with him, the faster she could convince herself that Noah didn't have power over her anymore.

Not much, Pete replied. *Chillin at home on the island. Why?*

Avery scratched her head. Getting to Staten Island would require two subway transfers, a boat ride, and then who knew how much farther? Avery hadn't exactly spent her weekends exploring Staten Island like people explored Williamsburg. Was she about to do this?

She texted him back. *send me your address?*

"Sorry guys. I, um, just got an email from my boss." Avery kept her brows creased and her fingers moving across the keyboard, because this was a very, very, very important email. "I need to run home to finish up some work."

Blair flipped through a magazine without looking up. "Bummer!"

"You sure?" Morgan asked, frowning. "I was gonna order pizza . . ."

"Yes. I'm sorry." Avery threw on her leather jacket and hoisted her tote bag over her shoulder. "Next week we'll do Rubirosa's— on me. Promise."

She paused for a moment to stare into Morgan's sad, downturned eyes. She hated that she was disappointing her best friend, but she hurried out of the apartment before Morgan could say another word. She pressed hard on the elevator button, the skin under her nail turning white, until the elevator rumbled and ascended from the lobby. As she waited for it, she closed her eyes to block out the sounds of Blair and Morgan's conversation wafting into the hallway. Avery didn't want to chance hearing Noah's name again, even low and muffled through Morgan's front door. She couldn't bear the sound of it, the mere thought of it. It was just a reminder of how she'd have to spend the next eight months until the wedding lying through her teeth around him and everyone else. Pretending that she was okay.

8

A VERY TOOK THE MOST agonizing forty-five-minute subway ride filled with inexplicable slowdowns and unintelligible loudspeaker announcements to the Staten Island ferry terminal. She hustled under the blue sign at the entrance and up the stairs to the boat just as the gates were about to close. She grabbed a seat next to a window on the lower level, and a beat later the boat took off across the bay. Choppy sea water splashed against the glass, mirroring the seasickness churning in Avery's stomach. A group of tourists stood on the outside decks fighting the harsh December wind to take whatever blurry picture of the Statue of Liberty they could get. Avery related to their feelings of desperation as she willed the boat to go faster, to take her as far away from Noah as possible and closer to tonight's distraction.

Twenty minutes later, after the boat docked on Staten Island, she was in an Uber on her way to a gray townhouse nestled between other gray townhouses. An empty, run-down pizza shop stood lifeless on the corner of Pete's street, which stretched out underneath a row of telephone pole wires dangling dangerously low to the ground. Avery shook her head, wondering what the hell she was doing here. There was no reason she needed to go all the way to Staten Island for a booty call. It was even a trek to get to Brooklyn from her place on the Upper East Side, and subways *went* there. She should've just picked up a guy at a bar or swiped mindlessly on dating apps, like she usually did.

But as she stood at the base of Pete's driveway, feeling hopeful in a way she was too scared to acknowledge out loud for fear of the crushing disappointment later, she knew those guys wouldn't be good enough anymore anyway. Because none of them would be Pete.

Thunderous barking sounds suddenly roared from behind a barbed wire fence. Avery sprinted up the stoop that she hoped led to Pete's front door and rang the doorbell in distress. Seconds later, Pete opened the door wearing a blue waffle knit shirt that made his eyes sparkle in a way Avery had never seen. Her heart fluttered at the sight of them, how the reflection from his clothes made them look bigger and brighter than she remembered.

Then the Rottweiler barked again. She let out a shriek.

"I hope that isn't your dog," she breathed in a panic.

"Nah, that's Milo. He's my neighbors' dog. He can be scary." Pete opened his door a little more and put his hand out, gesturing inside his apartment. "Come on in. I'll keep you safe," he added with a wink.

Avery gave a playful eyeroll, blushing earnestly. "Such a gentleman."

"I try."

When Avery stepped inside, her eyes widened in awe. In the foyer, where she stood, a massive chandelier hung from the ceiling, and a glass coffee table topped with a photography book of famous bands took center stage in the living room a few feet away. Pressed against the back wall of the living room was a champagne couch covered in rust-colored throw pillows arranged artfully and purposefully.

"Wow," Avery marveled. "Your place is stunning."

Pete smiled. "Thank you. Can I get you a drink? I have soda, seltzer, beer, wine . . ."

Avery waved her hand and sat on the couch. "Whatever you're having," she said distractedly, unable to take her eyes off her surroundings: the high tin ceilings, the massive flat screen television

SHE USED TO BE NICE   93

mounted on the wall, the floor that was so shiny you could eat off it. Pete could probably get a lot more space for his money in Staten Island than he could anywhere else in the city, too, so it was smart to live here. In Avery's next life, she was working in finance.

Pete pulled two beer bottles from his fridge and set them on the coffee table. "Hope the trip here wasn't too bad."

Avery swallowed a mouthful of beer. "It was fine." She was uninterested in small talk. She scooted closer to Pete on the couch and kissed him, pressing her body urgently against his. But then he pulled away and smiled strangely, like he was holding something back that was making him laugh.

"What?" Avery asked.

Pete shrugged innocently. "I don't know. You just got here. Why don't we just chill for a second?"

Avery stared at him. She didn't transfer two subway lines, endure a bout of seasickness, and pay twenty bucks for an Uber to have a *conversation*. She tried to jog his memory. "But I haven't been able to stop thinking about the other day . . ." She pulled down the neckline of her V-neck sweater. "Don't you wanna do it again?"

"Of course I do." Pete didn't even glance at her newly exposed cleavage. "But I'd also like to get to know you. Is that wrong?"

Get to know her? What was there to know? That her friends thought she'd cheated on her college boyfriend and now she was a shell of a human being, everything good about her gutted out like a fish? The real her would only repel Pete like it had repelled everyone else. This, right here on the couch moments from hooking up, was much better, for everyone involved.

"I feel like we all do this stuff so backward," Pete added with a chuckle. "I know what your naked body looks like but I don't know your last name."

"Russo," Avery deadpanned.

Pete flashed her a boyish grin. "Well, now I know everything, don't I?"

Avery set her beer down on the coffee table. Pete was lucky he was so good at oral and looked so good in that blue shirt. And maybe a small part of Avery liked that he wanted to get to know her. Nobody had wanted to in a while, or at least she hadn't given anyone a chance to decide if they wanted to in a while. Her walls were industrial strength thick. But Pete always managed to crack her.

"Fine." She needed to tread carefully. "What do you wanna know?"

Pete thought it over for a moment. Then he said, "What's your favorite color?"

She raised an eyebrow. "Seriously? Why does that matter?"

"Oh, come on. I'm starting easy."

She sighed. "Purple."

"Very nice. I'm a blue guy myself. Favorite food?"

"Spaghetti and meatballs." The corners of her mouth raised slightly.

"Hold on." Pete squinted dramatically, focusing hard on her face. "Is that a smile I see?"

Avery covered her mouth with her hand. But she'd been caught. It was too easy to give in to Pete's effortless charm. She wondered how good it would feel to just relinquish herself to him. How freeing.

She put her hand back in her lap, the smile lingering. "Is that your next question?"

Pete draped his arm over the back of the couch. "Okay, here's a real question. What do you want to be when you grow up?"

"Really? Aren't we already grown up?"

"I mean, yes, technically. But I'm still trying to eat more vegetables and submit my tax forms on time. I'm a bad grown-up."

Avery nodded in agreement. She'd only recently learned what a 401(k) was. "True. I guess when I grow up I want to be a writer." She squirmed in her seat, regretting the words as soon as they came out of her mouth. Too much. She'd revealed too much. She worked with so many writers but was too nervous to enter a pitch meeting for reasons she was nowhere near ready to tell Pete. She never should've brought this up.

SHE USED TO BE NICE   95

"A writer, huh?" Pete eyed her curiously, intrigued. "What do you want to write about?"

"I don't know. Anything." Avery ran her palm over the silky couch, watching the fabric darken, before pivoting the attention away from her. "What about you?"

"I want to work in music. Maybe producing or marketing. But I feel the corporate world sinking its teeth into me, like it's done to my dad." Pete sighed wistfully. "He's never home and always complains that he wished he had more free time to spend with family or to golf. But he doesn't know how to get out. I'm not sure how I'll get out either. I'm only an analyst, so I'm pretty low on the ladder, but already I'm so overwhelmed all the time."

Pete gazed at Avery with his hands wrapped around his beer bottle. Avery could tell by the softness in his voice that that wasn't something he told a lot of people. The weight of that responsibility sat heavily on her shoulders. This was getting way too intimate.

"Yeah," was all she could say.

Pete fiddled with the sticker on his beer bottle. "My coworkers and I talk about quitting and, like, moving to Brazil or something all the time. You ever think that? Just leaving everything behind and starting over?"

More than anything, Avery thought, but she took a long sip of beer to put off saying that out loud. That conversation would be dangerous, would risk Pete learning more about her than she was comfortable with him knowing. She was already grateful he didn't remember her from college and they could start fresh. She didn't need to allude to that part of her life now, or ever.

Luckily she was saved from responding by the sound of a garage door rumbling in the distance. Avery heard a key jimmy into a lock, then a few doors slam shut. "Pete?" an older woman's voice called out. "You home?"

"Who's that?" Avery asked. Pete hadn't mentioned any visitors.

Pete whirled his head around, then took a deep breath. "One second." He set his drink down on the coffee table and sprinted away. The sound of muffled voices drifted into the living room, growing louder until a middle-aged man and woman stood in the door frame. Next to them, Pete's face was splotchy and red.

"So, Avery . . ." He scratched his head. "These are my parents."

Avery's lower jaw practically unhinged from its socket. She shot a glance at the front door, ready to make a run for it. "Oh," she said. She racked her brain for a more cohesive thought, but the next most intelligent thing she could think of was, "Hello."

Pete lived with his *parents*. How had she not noticed that? Did she honestly think a guy's apartment would be this clean and orderly? The apartments of most guys she'd met in the city were usually in disarray, with beige L-shaped couches covered in mysterious stains, video game consoles overflowing from beneath television stands, containers of Muscle Milk taking up all the counter space in the kitchen. She should've known.

"You guys want some cantaloupe?" Pete's mom asked in her thick Staten Island accent as Pete's dad gave Avery a quick hello before heading upstairs to do some work. Avery watched Pete watch his father disappear, a forlorn look on his face.

Then he shrugged in Avery's direction. "Well, do you?" he asked.

Avery studied Pete's mom as she shuffled around the kitchen, which was decorated in that Tuscan style of sand-colored furnishings and grapes everywhere—another clue that this apartment did not belong to a twenty-something man. With her long French-manicured nails and highlighted hair, Pete's mom looked exactly like the women back home in New Jersey, who'd wear heels and a full face of makeup just to go to the grocery store. Pete's mom caught Avery's eye as she set the container of cantaloupe on the wooden kitchen table. Avery found herself smiling, comforted by this woman's presence. Staten Island and New Jersey, certain parts at least, were similar in a lot of ways, most notably their strong populations of loud, fussy Italian-Americans. Pete's family seemed to be cut from the same cloth as Avery's, and right now his mother

SHE USED TO BE NICE

reminded her of home, of her life before college. A life she didn't need to spend forgetting. A life she was excited about, even, when she dreamed about finding someone with whom she could share the kind of special romantic bond her parents had. Whether it was fate or a coincidence that Pete's family culture mirrored hers, she wasn't sure, but she allowed herself to feel a small thrill about the similarities.

Avery joined Pete and his mother at the table. The bowl of bright orange cantaloupe sat in the middle beside a stack of plates and a row of forks.

Avery gestured toward the utensils. "Can you please pass me a plate, Mrs. . . . uh . . ."

"DeFranco," Pete said with a pointed grin.

"Yes, of course," Pete's mom said. "And you can call me Gina, honey."

Avery helped herself to some cantaloupe and took a bite. It was delicious. "Gina. Got it."

"So, where you coming from, Avery? You live in Manhattan?"

Avery nodded.

"Your parents from New York, too?" Gina asked. "Any siblings?"

"I have a younger brother, Hunter," Avery said. "And I grew up in New Jersey. But my parents did the whole Brooklyn to Staten Island to New Jersey trek, so we still have family here."

"Ah, the classic northeast Italian-American voyage," Pete declared, like he was a cartographer mapping a new world. "Hopefully we're not secretly cousins or something."

Avery nudged him with a laugh. "Ewww, don't be weird."

"Hey, I wouldn't like it any more than you would."

Gina rolled her eyes. "You're sick, Pete."

Avery's heart warmed at Gina's familiar pronunciation of "you're." *Yaw-uh.* "My parents hate that I moved out. They wish I still loved home. They're a little overprotective. One time, in college, when my mom couldn't get a hold of me because my phone died, she sent the campus police on a search for me."

Gina and Pete burst out laughing. "That's hilarious," Pete said.

"It was. I mean, *now* it's funny. But at the time I was mortified." Talking about her parents made Avery realize she hadn't talked *to* them in a while. The last time they spoke, though, they got into an argument about why abortion should be allowed for any reason a woman decided upon with her doctor, not just the extreme exceptions touted by Republicans, and it turned into a massive fight about women needing to "take responsibility for their actions." Maybe she should wait a little longer.

"You gotta understand something, Avery," Gina began. "You guys are our babies. Doesn't matter if you're sixteen or sixty. When our babies are out of our sight, we are in a constant state of distress." Gina reached over the table to squeeze Pete's cheek. "All this is to say, I'm gonna cry the day Petey moves out."

"Ma!" Pete ducked away from her grip. "Goddammit."

Gina wagged a finger at Pete. "Don't use the Lord's name in vain in this house."

"Sorry about her," Pete muttered to Avery.

"Don't be," Avery said, charmed by how embarrassed Pete was. She could imagine her mom reprimanding her for the same thing.

Pete stabbed a piece of cantaloupe with a fork, the juice sliding down and pooling onto his place. "I'm definitely moving out soon." He seemed to direct that statement more to Avery than to his mother. "To Manhattan, most likely. I'm just trying to save up some more. I've almost got enough to rent a place and have some extra cushion in the bank."

"That's a good idea," Avery said. The familiarity of Pete's home made her feel so loose, so open. She kept going with it. "I lived with my parents for a month after college. It helped a little with savings. But I couldn't stand the commute."

"Where'd you go to school?" Gina asked.

"Woodford College. In Boston. Just like Pete."

"But we never knew each other," Pete added. "And I definitely would've remembered if I'd met her."

SHE USED TO BE NICE

He met her eye across the table and smiled. Avery resisted the urge to grab his hand, as a thank you for seeing something good in her. For giving her a chance that she wasn't sure she deserved.

"Get outta here!" Gina squealed. "So how'd you two meet then?"

"We met at a bar downtown," Avery explained. "And it turns out Pete knows my friends Charlie and Morgan."

"Yeah, Charlie worked at the record store with me, Ma, if you remember," Pete said. "He brought me to Woodford to hang a few times."

Gina gasped. "Now *that* is fate." Her eyes darted between Avery and Pete. "This is all God's work. You two were meant to be, I just know it."

The suggestive smile on Gina's face punctured Avery's chest with guilt. Avery knew that look. Gina thought she was meeting her son's new girlfriend.

Avery felt her walls shoot back up around her. She let this conversation go on too long, open up too many possible doors. She knew she needed to keep Pete at arm's length, but she also knew the more they hung out, the harder that would be. Because this was how it all began: First you told them your favorite color, and then they found out everything. Even the things you were the most ashamed of, all the things you wanted to hide. And she liked Pete so much already. She'd rather spare herself the pain of his inevitable rejection when he found out what a mess she was. What she was capable of.

"Well, it's getting late," Avery said, shoving a final chunk of cantaloupe into her mouth. "I think I should get going." She stood up. It was only 9 PM, which wasn't late, but she didn't have another excuse.

"Already?" Gina reached out to give Avery a hug. "Come back soon, will ya?"

Avery returned Gina's embrace. "For sure." Avery was grateful for the hug so that she wouldn't have to look Gina in the eye when she lied.

"Let me drive you to the ferry," Pete said. He was so earnest in his offer to help, not thinking anything of Avery needing to leave. His trust in her made her feel even worse.

"Oh, you don't have to," she said, feeling shy. "I'll just take an Uber."

"Let Pete take you!" Gina winked. "He should learn what it takes to care for a woman."

Avery's heart sank. She'd led them on enough; she didn't want to be even more of an asshole for putting up a fight. "Okay, sure. Thanks."

Pete drove Avery to the ferry. He tried to make conversation but she gave him clipped, one-word answers and claimed she was tired, then turned on the radio to let the chipper voice of a Z100 host fill the air. She leaned her elbow on the windowsill and stared out into the street, watching blurred images of buildings and cars zoom past in a blend of bright lights and colors. She caught her reflection in the side mirror and glanced away, disgusted with herself. She knew she shouldn't have come here. Pete didn't deserve to be with someone who could hurt him the way Avery hurt Ryan. She was helping Pete out by leaving. Eventually he'd find someone with less of a past. Someone better.

Pete pulled into the terminal and put the car in park, cutting the radio abruptly. The silence pierced through the still night air. Avery reached for the passenger car door and gripped the handle, half waiting for him to say something, half ready to bolt.

"So, I guess we skipped right to meeting the parents," he said with a playful lilt.

Avery returned a joyless grin. "I guess so."

"Seems like things are getting pretty serious between us now, huh?"

Avery closed her eyes. The more he tried to crack her with his jokes, the more she fortified her walls, which made her feel even guiltier for letting the night go this far in the first place. Without responding, she went to open the door, but then Pete put his hand on her shoulder.

SHE USED TO BE NICE 101

"Avery, wait."

Avery glanced at his hand, felt the heat of it through her sweater and jacket. She inhaled through her nose, savoring his touch one last time before disappearing from his life forever.

"I'm sorry I didn't say anything about my parents," he said with a sigh. "I thought they'd be out all night."

Pete took his hand off her shoulder. The loss of physical contact made Avery ache with longing. She was still inside his car and already she missed him. How much pining would she do when she left? She couldn't handle any more emptiness, when she already felt like such a husk of her former self. That night with Noah had taken everything from her, and the only way she could stop it from taking more was to keep everyone at a distance. Because if she didn't gain anything else, she had nothing else that she could lose. Because if you never knew what happiness was, you couldn't know what you were missing without it. She never wanted to see Pete ever again.

"I was also embarrassed about it, to be honest," Pete continued, so soft it was almost a whisper. "I mean, I'm twenty-three, and I still sleep in my childhood bedroom. It's not exactly very attractive."

Avery didn't care that Pete lived with his parents. It was pretty responsible, actually, considering the astronomical cost of living in New York City. Pete was responsible. He was funny. Charming. The best sex she'd ever had. And way too good for her. This was for the best.

"It's fine," Avery said. "Really."

She got out of the car and closed the door before Pete could say anything else, before she could trick herself into thinking she was enough for him, that what Noah did to her didn't break her beyond recognition. On the ferry back to Manhattan, she swiped through her dating apps and fired off messages until someone invited her over. She dragged whoever he was to his bedroom and didn't let him ask her a single question, just let him use her for her body like all the others, her flesh like armor keeping her battered heart safe.

9

AVERY SPENT THE NEXT month distracting herself from reaching out to Pete—and from the fact that he hadn't exactly reached out to her either—by throwing herself into planning Morgan and Charlie's engagement party at Sel Rrose. She helped Morgan curate a guest list and menu, and arrived early to the restaurant on the day of the party to help set up the decorations and trays of Puerto Rican food that her mom and aunts made. Now, dusty pink candles were scattered on all the tables along the walls, a gold "Charlie & Morgan" banner hung from the bar, and a white gift box was placed next to the front door. This, Avery thought as she arranged a bouquet of white roses in a vase near the buffet, was where she needed to direct her attention. On her best friend's wedding. Not on a guy whose life would be better without her. And luckily he'd become irrelevant before either of their feelings deepened or before she could even consider bringing him as a plus-one to Morgan and Charlie's wedding. Maybe Ryan wouldn't come to the wedding either, so then it wouldn't matter if Avery had a date anyway. This was all working out perfectly. Good riddance, Pete.

Morgan flitted by in her white lace knee-length dress and nude heels, and Avery flashed her most genuine attempt at a smile. Tonight was important. It was Morgan and Charlie's first official wedding event with their most beloved friends and family, which

SHE USED TO BE NICE 103

included all the people from Woodford that Avery hadn't seen or heard from since graduation. Her plan was to keep a low profile and not be too visible, maybe give a brief hello but spend most of the night hanging out with Morgan's family.

This plan would also, ideally, help her hide from Noah.

Who would be coming tonight as well.

"You look stunning," Avery said to Morgan in her attempt to take her mind off him, though her body remained on edge. The moment she arrived at Sel Rrose, she buzzed with fight-or-flight adrenaline, her heart jolting and throat tightening at the sight of any broad-shouldered blond man or whiff of cologne reminiscent of Noah's. She felt like an exposed nerve, sensitive to the tiniest of stimuli. This engagement party felt like a test, one she should've studied for but didn't, leaving her hovering panic-stricken over a blank sheet of paper. It was one thing to be ambushed by Noah's presence at that first dinner a few months ago—she could forgive herself for acting strange under that circumstance—but theoretically she'd had time to prepare for tonight. From this point forward, it was crucial that she keep it together, despite having no idea how.

"Doesn't she?" Charlie said, adjusting the sleeves of his white button-down shirt. He wrapped his arm around Morgan's waist and kissed the side of her head. "She's way out of my league."

Morgan smacked Charlie playfully across the chest. "I am not!"

Avery touched her own hair. She'd tried to straighten it, but it frizzed up on the way over to the party and looked like shit now. But she kept her mood light. "I don't know, Morgan. He might be right." She swept her eyes over the room. There was, thankfully, no sign of Noah yet. "Look at your hair. It's so shimmery. And Charlie, your hair is, well . . ."

Charlie dangled a piece of sliced prosciutto into his mouth. "Covered in prosciutto grease."

Avery laughed. "Precisely."

"You're both ridiculous," Morgan said with an eye roll.

Morgan spotted her parents across the restaurant by the windows looking out at the street and waved them over to say hello. Avery loved Joe and Gabriela Feeley. Morgan was an only child, so they often referred to Avery as their "other daughter" and invited her to spend the summer at their house in Rhode Island whenever she wanted. Avery always had a great time with the Feeleys up in Westerly. The house was Morgan's dad's childhood home near the beach and had been in the family for almost two centuries. While there, Avery and Morgan would spend the whole day out by the ocean, and at night they'd stay up late talking on the wraparound porch, bundled up in gray sweatshirts while the salty breeze tickled their faces. She hugged Morgan's parents, grateful for the distraction from searching for Noah again.

Moments later, someone shrieked at the front door. Avery recognized the screeching sound. It belonged to Emma Smith, a bridesmaid and one of Avery's ex-best friends, who was now running toward Morgan in a fit of giggles and flinging her arms around Morgan's neck. The two of them jumped up and down in a tight hug, Emma's California-boho jewelry clanking as it smacked against her body.

Avery headed to the buffet and shoved a croquette in her mouth, keeping her distance.

"Great setup, girl!" Blair called out to Avery, hovering next to the gift box.

Emma peeled herself off of Morgan, her eyes skimming past Avery's without a word.

"Thanks," Avery replied with her mouth full. More people crowded into the restaurant, joining other guests sitting at the small tables along the perimeter or congregating by the bar for a drink, which prompted Avery to crane her neck in search of Noah again.

"Did you get those 'love' balloons, by chance?" Blair asked.

Avery ignored her and continued scanning the crowd, only to see more of her ex-best friends arriving. Viraj came through first and gave Charlie one of those dude-hugs with an aggressive slap

SHE USED TO BE NICE 105

on the back. He was on the lacrosse team with Charlie and Ryan, and now he was a groomsman and wouldn't even glance at Avery, considering what he thought he saw her doing in Ronald's bedroom. Behind Viraj was Parker Stein, Viraj's bio lab partner from sophomore year. Everyone had become close to Parker through Viraj, and now he, too, was a groomsman, exchanging more dude-hugs with Viraj and Charlie. Emma and Morgan joined in the circle next, and soon it was a full-blown Woodford reunion, complete with shrieks and cries and *oh my Gods* and *it's been so long*s.

Avery snorted. Her friend group was always loud and commanding in college, bulldozing like a bunch of Kool-Aid men through parties and tailgates, but today they seemed more obnoxious than ever. Or maybe it was just that Avery was watching them from the outside, excluded.

Blair repeated her question, now tinged with impatience.

Avery heaved a frustrated sigh. "Yes, I got the balloons."

"Where are they?" Blair asked.

Viraj's eyes flicked to Avery as he made his way to the buffet. A lump formed in Avery's throat.

"There were problems with the delivery." Avery did her best to keep her voice even. "They're coming."

Blair frowned sympathetically, but her eyes were empty, like she didn't mean it, because she didn't. "Bummer! You should've said something. I would've picked them up on the way here."

Avery's nostrils flared. The balloons were such a fucking ordeal. Avery had arrived at Sel Rrose as they were getting delivered, and it turned out some idiot at the balloon place brought "Happy Birthday!" balloons instead, so Avery had to send them back. Not that Blair would care about this. She would only use it as proof of Avery's incompetence.

"I'm sure we'll survive without the balloons," Avery said flatly.

Blair gave Avery a look like she was the stupidest person alive, like how could Avery possibly think Morgan could have a good engagement party without the balloons. Sometimes Avery wasn't sure how much of Blair's attitude toward her was actually the result of Blair's mom's affair. The fact that Mrs. Montgomery cheated on Mr. Montgomery with a twenty-five-year-old she met at work certainly did not help Blair's feelings about Avery's alleged infidelity.

"Fine," Blair nearly spat.

Avery suddenly realized she had no drink in her hand and went to order a whiskey. Neat.

She leaned against the bar and sipped her drink, the smooth brown liquid warming up her insides. She knew she needed to keep it together tonight, but after graduation she'd genuinely thought she would never see these people again. But it was inevitable now with this wedding. For any other normal friend group, this would be a happy occasion, a chance to laugh and reminisce about the fun times they had in college and make new memories as adults. That wouldn't happen here. Everything was tainted by Avery's actions senior year, a dense awkwardness looming over everyone like haze. But Avery would just have to deal with everyone's version of events of that night. It was the dominant narrative she had no interest in rectifying. Let Blair be sickly sweet to Avery's face but call her a ho behind her back, tell everyone that Avery was a horrible person who wasn't to be trusted. Let it all happen again and again, a million times over. All of it was better than admitting what Noah did to her was real.

Morgan flitted by again, the loose waves in her hair perfectly intact, and stopped when she spotted Avery. Avery smoothed down her flyaways.

"You should go grab some pasteles before they're all gone," Morgan said. "Titi Julia sort of only made enough for family since it's a big undertaking, but I told her you count." Then she eyed Avery's drink. "Since when do you like whiskey?"

"Since now." Avery took another swig and winced. She hated whiskey.

Suddenly her pulse flared at the sight of Noah. There he was, tall and broad-shouldered with a head of blond hai—

Nope, that wasn't him. That was Morgan's cousin.

SHE USED TO BE NICE   107

"Come with me." Avery needed a distraction. "I wanna show you something."

She led Morgan to a long table by the front door, where she'd hidden her gift inside a white and pink striped bag. She dug into the bag and took out a collage of photos of Morgan and Charlie pinned to a corkboard inside a glass box. They were Morgan's favorite pictures from their relationship: Charlie giving Morgan a piggyback ride by the reservoir near Woodford, Charlie and Morgan holding hands on a beach in Turks and Caicos, a selfie of Charlie kissing Morgan's cheek. Avery had sprinkled gold sparkles on top and written "Future Mr. and Mrs. Durham" in swirly pink script.

Morgan gasped. "Did you make this?"

Avery smiled. She was proud of the gift. It was necessarily cheap but also thoughtful, the latter of which, Avery hoped, counted more. It was fun to bring out her creative side again, too. Since she wasn't writing anything meaningful at the moment, she figured she would try scrapbooking as an alternative. It scratched the itch sufficiently enough for now.

"You bet," Avery said. "I was gonna include that picture I have of you guys making out at that bar junior year, but I didn't want Joe to flip."

"You know he would have. The WASPiness is strong on my dad's side." Morgan ran her fingers over the embossed text, admiring it. "I love this. But you already got me an engagement gift!"

"I couldn't show up empty-handed today." Tears burned Avery's eyes. "I'm so happy for you and Charlie." The homemade gift was a little cheesy, but if there was ever a time for cheesiness, it was today. Her best friend was getting *married*. No matter the stress it brought into Avery's life, this wedding was a big deal, and she was honored to be Morgan's right-hand woman, that Morgan still saw the good in her when nobody else did.

Morgan gave Avery a hug, holding her in a long embrace. Avery felt immensely satisfied with herself, with the gift, with how well she was keeping it together around these ghosts of her past life. All she needed to do was maintain her composure until the end of the night and then in each wedding event after this one, and in seven months it would be August and this all would be over. She could do this.

A burst of laughter came from the corner of the restaurant, where a group of Woodford people had gathered near the buffet. Avery tightened her grip on her whiskey.

"Come on," Morgan said, nodding toward the group. "Let's at least try to mingle."

Avery pressed her mouth into a straight line. "I'm good here."

"Please? I know it's uncomfortable, but just for a sec. Then you can go. I promise."

Avery sighed, acquiesced with a brisk nod. She held onto her whiskey like a life raft and shuffled slowly behind Morgan, trying not to draw attention to herself as they approached their friends and stood side by side in an opening next to Charlie.

Viraj shifted his eyes toward Avery, then looked away immediately.

"Charlie, you hitting the gym, kid?" Parker asked as he squeezed Charlie's bicep.

"If by 'hitting the gym' you mean 'eating pizza,' then yes," Charlie said. He gave Avery a small smile. "'Sup, Avery?"

Viraj continued looking away. Emma crossed her legs and stared down at the ground while Parker coughed into his arm. This was brutal. Avery thought she could spend the rest of her life hating herself enough for all of them, but evidently that wouldn't come close to how much they hated her on their own.

"Hey, Charlie," Avery muttered. At least she had him.

Morgan rubbed Charlie's stomach affectionately and took the wheel on the halted conversation. "We're trying to cut back on pizza when we go out, but the late-night slices here are too enticing."

"They're on every corner and they cost a dollar!" Charlie exclaimed. "It's like they strategically placed these pizza shops by the best bars."

SHE USED TO BE NICE

Morgan put her arm around Avery, encouraging her. "Avery, remember when you were so drunk you asked that pizza guy in the Lower East Side if he had pizza with sushi on top?"

Avery offered a tiny shrug. "I remember."

Morgan laughed a bit too loudly. "I wish I'd recorded that conversation. You literally fought him when he said it wasn't a thing."

Avery wasn't sure where to focus her attention. Her old friends had no interest in acknowledging that she was in the circle, let alone that she was now the subject of a story being *told* in the circle, especially a story that made a joke out of how much she drank. Avery's drinking wasn't amusing to people who thought it made her cheat on one of their best friends.

"Yeah, that was funny," Avery muttered.

"It wasn't just funny! It was hysterical!" Morgan laughed again, in a deranged way. This poor girl was trying so hard to make Avery comfortable. Avery didn't know whether to hug her or relieve her by running away.

Parker responded by coughing again. Then Viraj walked away and left a giant, obvious gaping hole. The tension in the group was heavy, pressing down onto Avery's chest and making it hard to breathe. Morgan's arm was still around Avery, too, which only suffocated her more.

"Well, now *I'm* craving pizza," someone said.

Avery's body stiffened. Noah.

He had materialized from thin air like a fucking hologram. Avery was never letting her guard down again, not for a second. She gulped down her whiskey until her glass was nearly empty, and soon everyone started debating whether late night pizza at school was as good as New York pizza. But Avery couldn't focus. All she could do was hold her breath. Noah's musky cologne was way too strong tonight, stronger than it was when they had dinner with Morgan and Charlie at The Spaniard, stronger than it was that night senior year. Her stomach twisted, tight like a wet towel wrung bone dry.

"Speaking of late night, did you guys hear about that sophomore who stole ten buckets of cheese fries and got caught by a cop?" Emma said, her voice hushed with juicy gossip. "He told her he wouldn't get her in trouble if she blew him."

Charlie cringed. "Yikes."

"I *know*," Emma replied.

"That's awful," Morgan said. She turned to Avery. "Isn't that awful?"

Avery held her breath again. "Awful," she managed to squeak through her closed airways. This whole night. This whole wedding. Awful. She exhaled quickly, then held her breath once more so the foul musk of Noah's cologne wouldn't attack her senses. She would do this all night if she had to, if it would stop the memories from coming up like vomit.

Emma winced. "And apparently she did it."

"No!" Morgan cried.

"I mean . . ." Viraj looked around. "It worked, right? She didn't get in trouble, so . . ."

Morgan scoffed. "Because the officer abused his power, Viraj. That doesn't mean it *worked*."

"Are you talking about the campus police officers who rode around on those gay ass segways?" Noah held back a spurt of laughter. "And honked those little horns when students were in their way?"

"Yes, exactly," Emma said. "Although I wouldn't have used *gay* as a slur—"

"Those officers were a joke," Noah interrupted. "Not exactly guys I'd call powerful. I think I only ever saw one who was above a hundred and fifty pounds soaking wet. She should've just told him to get lost."

Because men always listen when you say no, Avery thought sarcastically. *You're proof they don't.*

"Well, if he was enough of a creep to offer that kind of deal, who knew what would've happened if she'd denied him?" Morgan said. "She was probably scared."

SHE USED TO BE NICE 111

At this, Noah made a dismissive sound. "Did she get to keep the cheese fries, at least?"

"I have no idea." Emma shrugged. "I guess so."

Noah sniggered. "Then the blowjob was worth it. Those fries are amazing."

He high-fived Viraj, who'd joined in with laughter, while Charlie shook his head and Morgan and Emma exchanged a disturbed look. Then Noah took a sip of his drink, the movement of his arm sending a rush of his cologne straight into Avery's nostrils. Avery held back a dry heave as he remained unbothered and indifferent to her presence, not once looking her in the eye during the entire conversation. It wasn't that she wanted him to talk to her, especially not when his contributions were unsurprisingly offensive garbage. There was just something about the fact that *he* was ignoring *her* that pissed her off. It wasn't fair of him to pretend she didn't exist; he'd made it clear enough that he thought she was invisible the night of the party senior year. He didn't get to keep doing that now and getting away with it. Why was he allowed to keep belittling her like this, after everything he'd already done to make her feel so small?

Everyone moved on to talking about the dining hall food at Woodford again, about whether the Philly cheese steaks were better than the chicken fingers were better than the onion rings. Avery could not have cared less. She desperately wanted to escape this conversation, this party, this life.

"What late night meal do you miss most, Avery?" Morgan asked.

Avery shot Morgan a confused scowl. She knew Morgan was only trying to involve her in the conversation, but Morgan knew it was the buffalo chicken sandwiches.

Everyone stared Avery down, daring her to speak.

"None of it. The food sucked." Avery drained the rest of her whiskey and shook her empty glass. "Be right back."

Avery hustled to the bar and inhaled a deep, cleansing breath once she was far enough away from Noah. She needed to take some control here, needed something to make her feel like a regular functioning person, even though she wasn't exactly behaving like one. She stared at the bartender, with his deep tan and muscular arms, then leaned over the bar and asked him for another drink. Soon the two of them fell into easy conversation about where he learned to bartend, like any two people meeting on a night out, his eyes lingering on hers just long enough for her to know he was flirting with her. Finally, something normal was happening. Everything was okay now.

As the conversation continued, Avery almost forgot where she was, until she glanced over her shoulder and spotted Noah gesticulating around the room while telling some elaborate story that had everyone double over laughing. At one point, midsentence, he locked eyes with Avery. And before she could look away, her vision began to tunnel. She tried blinking to clear it, but the pull was too strong and she zeroed in on his eyes. His olive green eyes, with that hint of sage and the navy dot by his pupil, the last thing she saw before he flipped her around and pressed her face into the mattress . . .

She tore away from him and asked the bartender for another whiskey, a double this time. She drank it all in two gulps. The booze rushed to her head and emptied her thoughts so that she was filled only with nothingness, with air, like she was inflatable. *Much better.*

Charlie stood in front of the room and used a knife to tap his beer bottle. Or maybe it was a wine glass. Avery's vision was too fuzzy to see what he was drinking. She could barely make out his movements, let alone his beverage, as he gave a speech thanking their friends and family for coming out to celebrate and sharing a few words about how excited he was to marry Morgan. Avery did her best to channel her drunken energy into cheerful whoops and claps, imagining subtitles translating her inebriated babbles.

When he finished his speech to a round of applause, a blurred figure gestured for Charlie's wireless microphone, making Avery's breath catch again. She knew it was Noah, despite her poor

SHE USED TO BE NICE

113

intoxicated vision. If Noah ever murdered someone, she'd be able to help the FBI pick him out of a lineup of one trillion blond, green-eyed men.

"I'll be quick." Noah eagerly tapped the microphone. Then he clasped an open palm on Charlie's shoulder. "First, I wanted to say thank you to Charlie for letting me stand by him as his best man. We've only recently gotten closer, but now I don't know what I'd do without this kid."

"Same here," Charlie murmured into the mic.

Avery held back a gag.

"As some of you know, I founded a start-up called Meow Monthly," Noah continued. "You might've seen us on Instagram. Our account is at 400,000 followers now and this is only the beginning, because we plan to post a *lot* more cute animal videos."

He paused for reactions and laughter from the audience, eagerly looking around in a self-satisfied way.

Avery did not chime in.

"Every Saturday, my company and I volunteer with the Humane Society to help abused and neglected animals," he continued. "Sometimes, we'll even take one home with us."

Noah grabbed a cardboard box from behind him. He removed the lid and held up a golden retriever puppy like fucking baby Simba in *The Lion King*. There was a chorus of gasps and squeals from the crowd.

"I was gonna wait until the end of the night," he went on, "but my friend at the shelter dropped this guy off early, and I didn't want to keep him in the box for too long. Happy engagement, guys!"

Avery's mouth dropped open. Who gives a *live animal* as a surprise gift? Wasn't this how animals ended up abandoned—because of "gifts" that recipients didn't necessarily sign up for? Even Avery knew that a puppy was a major life decision and she didn't fucking like animals. Noah *the animal lover* should absolutely know this. But he didn't care, of course he didn't, because he only cared about how these grand generous gestures would make him look, with no regard for the people whose lives would change because of them.

Avery studied Morgan, who had tears pouring down her cheeks and was clamoring about how she'd always wanted a golden retriever. Emma and Blair rushed to the microphone stand, begging to hold the puppy, while Charlie nuzzled his face into its soft yellow fur. Avery stared at her pitiful collage sitting upright on the gift table, which now looked like it was made by a blind toddler. Then she glared at the puppy, at Morgan and Charlie practically throwing themselves into Noah's arms and howling with gratitude. Avery clenched her fingers into a fist. Every note of praise Noah received for this gift sent her deeper into a spiraling rage. The commotion crescendoed around her until the room spun, too, prompting her to stumble to the bar and grip the wood to stabilize herself.

She tossed back a shot of whiskey. As the warm, spicy liquid hit her stomach, she felt a tap on her shoulder.

"Hey, girl!" Blair said with her hands on her hips, her fake-nice voice extra high-pitched.

Avery plastered on a smile and said nothing. She could not deal with one more thing right now.

Blair eyed Avery's shot glass. "Whiskey can really screw you up. You're much better off sticking to something lighter like champagne." Blair tapped her flute, the bubbles trickling to the rim.

Avery once again said nothing, because fuck that. Blair took a dainty sip of her champagne.

"You know, Avery, this is your best friend's engagement party." Blair's voice was serious now, almost threatening. "You should probably have your wits about you."

"Thanks for—" Avery hiccupped. "The tip." She waved her empty shot glass at the bartender. "Can I—" *Hiccup.* "Another one? Thanks."

Blair sighed audibly, drawing out the sound for an unnecessarily long time. "I'm just looking out for you, girl. I would hate to

SHE USED TO BE NICE

see you get too drunk and hurt someone you love." Blair took a step closer to Avery. "Again."

Avery clutched her chest. She stole another glance at Noah, at the man who was frighteningly good at making everyone believe he wasn't a bloodsucking parasite, and felt lightheaded, like she was standing on the roof of a skyscraper and peering over the edge to her death. She threw back the other shot of whiskey and sprinted through the front doors, out under the street lights.

• • •

Avery awoke groggy and hungover the next morning with a stabbing pain in her head, like pieces of shrapnel were lodged in her brain. How had she gotten back to her apartment? She closed her eyes and waited as bits and pieces of last night crystallized in her mind. She saw herself running out of Sel Rrose, hailing a cab in the freezing cold, swiping mercilessly on Tinder, matching with a guy—named Donovan?—and inviting him over. He was cute, but she remembered him sending her a gross politically charged pickup line that, in her desperate, drunken state, somehow did not turn her off. She opened her phone and peeked at her Tinder messages from him, one of which said: *I may be a liberal, but I don't believe in giving your pussy a safe space.*

Jesus.

Avery closed the conversation and navigated to her home screen. Her eyes bulged when she saw she had fifteen unanswered texts, all from Morgan.

Hey where are you? We wanna take a group wedding party photo!
We're gonna wait for you. You ok?
Avery where'd you go? We're doing the cake
Did you leave???
???????

Avery slammed her phone on the mattress. What was she *thinking* last night? She wasn't thinking at all, that's what. She was too busy being drunk and selfish, just like she'd been senior year. But Blair should've kept her mouth shut, because as usual she was clueless and didn't know what she was talking about. The thought of having to deal with her snide, arrogant comments about that night all the way up until the wedding day made Avery want to scream. There was no need for Blair to keep bringing it up, but of course she would. She didn't stop in college, continued to rub salt in the wound even when it was obvious that Avery was maxed out on suffering. Blair said horrible things about her mother all the time, and that was her *mother,* so what made Avery think Blair would show Avery any mercy? Avery didn't need more reminders that she'd made a mistake, that the chain of events of that night senior year all started with her, even if they ended with Noah.

With shaky fingers, Avery typed a response back to Morgan. *hey omg i am SO sorry. i got too drunk and couldn't be there anymore. i'm so sorry.* Then she hit send. She waited for a response, but each second passed by with excruciating slowness and no reply. It was only the first wedding event of the year and already Avery had fucked up because of Noah, which was the exact thing she'd been hoping to avoid by keeping quiet about him. Gutted by the silence, she picked up the phone and called Morgan three times. Each call went unanswered, ringing into infinity and then to voicemail. Tears stung Avery's eyes. She couldn't lose Morgan. Morgan was the only person who cared about her, the only person who hadn't turned their back on her, the only person who still loved her despite what she thought Avery had done.

Avery stared desperately at her phone, willing Morgan's reply to appear on the screen. She filled the silence with sobs.

10

A VERY SOMEHOW FELL BACK asleep and was jolted awake by the deafening sound of her phone ringing. Her pulse quickened as she grabbed her phone off her nightstand. *Please be Morgan,* she thought. *Please, please, please be Morgan.*

But it wasn't. It was her mother. Who seemed to have forgotten that she'd called her daughter a "baby murderer" for believing that forcing a woman into motherhood was dystopian. At least her dad wasn't emailing her articles from .info websites about Hillary Clinton's child pornography ring anymore.

Avery stabbed the green phone symbol with her finger, too exhausted to deal with her mom's inevitable second, third, and fourth subsequent calls if she couldn't reach Avery the first time. Mom was always a worrier, but her propensity for panic increased tenfold after Avery's breakup.

"Hello?" Avery's voice was thick with sleep.

"Hi, Avery." Mom sounded completely normal, like they were just going to brush their fight about abortion under the rug. Fine. It didn't matter. Wouldn't be the last argument about politics she'd have with her conservative parents. "How are you? You don't sound good."

Avery rubbed her eyes and flicked away a yellow piece of crust. "I was sleeping."

"It's a little late to be sleeping, Avery."

118   ALEXIA LAFATA

Avery checked the time. It was only noon. She could've slept for another twelve years. "I had a late night."

"Why?" Suspicion crept into Mom's voice. "What were you doing?"

Avery put her mom on speaker and rested her aching head on her pillow with her phone face up beside her. She closed her eyes. "I was at Morgan's engagement party. It ran late."

Mom acknowledged this with a *hmph* sound. After a few beats of silence, she said, "Can I ask, were you drinking?"

Something was up. Avery could feel it, the way her mother's questions were more like interrogations than attempts at making conversation. It was classic Jackie Russo.

"Yes?" Avery wasn't sure what was happening. "It's a wedding event. There was obviously alcohol."

Mom cleared her throat. "Your blasé tone worries me, Avery Marie. This morning we got a five-hundred dollar medical bill for a hospital visit. Daddy nearly had a stroke. Care to explain yourself, or do you want me to tell you everything I already know?"

Avery sat up abruptly and covered her face with her hands. Fucking fuck. Had she seriously forgotten that she was still under her parents' health insurance when Pete took her to the hospital?

"I'm *so* sorry," Avery said stupidly, anxiously. "I forgot you'd be getting a bill. I should've warned you."

"You're damn right you should've. What the hell happened?"

Avery chewed on her lip. She lay back down and pulled the covers snug over her body. "Nothing. I fell and needed to get stitches."

"Really? Stitches?" The sarcasm bit hard. Mom did not believe Avery for one second. "So the stomach pump and IV drip we were billed for was because of a *fall*?"

Avery massaged her temples as she gathered her thoughts, trying to come up with a way to talk about what happened without sending her mother to an early grave. Once, after Avery shattered her iPhone screen, her mom freaked out because she thought a glass shard was going to come loose and slice Avery's finger off.

SHE USED TO BE NICE 119

The fact that Avery drank so much during a night out that she wound up in the hospital would launch Jackie into another dimension of panic.

Avery drew in a lungful of air and prepared for the worst. "Okay, yeah, that's not what happened. I . . . drank too much."

Mom gasped. "Tell me what that means, Avery. Now. What were you *doing*?"

Avery buried her face in her pillow, wishing she could suffocate herself with it. Her parents had no idea she'd started drinking this much. They weren't naive enough to think she wouldn't drink in college, but they certainly had never thought she'd be the type to pass out from drinking. To be fair, Avery hadn't thought she would be either.

Their ignorance wasn't exactly their fault, though. After graduation, Avery didn't tell them anything about her breakup beyond the cursory update that she was single now but it was fine. They hadn't asked any more questions, and she had not provided any more answers.

"I was out with Morgan and I just drank too much!" Avery shouted. "That's it! It was no big deal."

But it was a big deal and she knew it. Avery had always imagined herself responsibly enjoying a drink with her future husband the way her parents did their happy hours on Fridays after work, as a relaxing end-of-the-week ritual complete with a charcuterie board. Not in the desperate way she drank now. To forget.

"No big deal?" Mom was shrieking now. "Avery, you went to the hospital! For alcohol poisoning! Is everything okay with you? Do we need to come to Manhattan?"

"No!" Avery sputtered and shook her head, as though erasing the word from the air. "I—I mean, yes, everything's okay! That was my first and only hospital visit."

"Something awful could've happened to you! How did you even get to the hospital? Was Morgan with you?"

Avery hesitated. Her mom would not like this answer. "No. A guy took me."

"A guy? Who?"

"You don't know him."

"Do *you*?"

"Kind of . . ."

Mom groaned. "That's great. That's *really* great." Her scorn was palpable, vibrating like a tuning fork through the phone speaker. "How do you know he didn't take advantage of you when you were drunk? You need to be careful out there."

Avery stared at her wrist, watching her blood pump thick and spider-like through her veins. Pete would never do that to her. She didn't know how she knew that, exactly, after everything she'd been through. But she was certain. He made her feel safe. Cared for.

Mom's reply was also the exact kind of well-intentioned yet misguided thinking that made Avery never want to speak about what happened to anyone, and especially not her conservative parents. Her mom thought she was being protective. She had no idea she was part of the problem.

"He didn't, Mom," Avery said. "Everything's fine."

"Well, I'm glad you're all right, but you're still paying for this. If you think we have an extra five hundred dollars just waiting around, you are very mistaken."

Avery grabbed hold of her phone, held it flush against her ear. Five hundred dollars was more than what she had in her checking account. "Mom, I can't afford that. I've been trying to set aside money for all the maid of honor stuff I need to do for Morgan."

"I don't care. You need to take responsibility for your actions." Mom sighed. "You're worrying me. I think I need you under my roof a little bit. Daddy had to go to the city for work this morning. Maybe he can pick you up and bring you home for the rest of the weekend."

Avery whined. "But *Mom*, I—"

"Nope, it's settled. You're coming home."

Avery used to love being at her parents' house, but now she hated it. She hadn't been able to get out of there fast enough after

SHE USED TO BE NICE

graduation. She felt so resentful of their lives, of the fact that all they seemed to do was mosey around Costco and buy new mums for the yard and watch HGTV and still, somehow, be happy. Call it jealousy if you want. Plus they treated her like she was a rebellious sixteen-year-old if she dared to leave the house, prying for unnecessary details about her whereabouts. Where did they think she was going to go? It was the suburbs. The worst she could do was get high with some teens at the mall. And she hadn't even done that when she was younger and the opportunity was presented to her.

Though she had to admit that she could use a break from her life in the city. Being in Morgan and Charlie's wedding was eroding her already weakened self-esteem, and she didn't mind the opportunity to smell some trees and enter the portal of her childhood, a time before everything in her life went to shit. A time when she thought she could have all the trappings of simple and normal joys.

"Fine," Avery muttered. "Whatever."

Mom sighed, the kind of sigh that precedes a change in tone. "I knew you shouldn't have moved to the city so early." Her voice was soft and distant, like she was talking more to herself than to Avery. "You should've lived at home for longer. You weren't yourself after your breakup. And those grades . . ."

"Mom, they were Cs. It's not like I failed." Avery had felt awful about those Cs. Though she wished getting a C was the worst thing that happened senior year.

"That's failing to me. You had straight As nearly all of college. And then, well . . ."

Avery could feel the sadness in her mother's voice. But Mom didn't say more. She knew better.

"Anyway," Mom continued. "Daddy will text you on his way over."

The line went dead.

Avery pulled herself out of bed and threw a random assortment of clothes into a backpack before her dad arrived to pick her up. She climbed into his car and gave him a terse, guilty hello, and then he drove away from her apartment in silence. She wondered if he was being quiet because Mom had told him not to say anything. Dad wasn't usually the type to spark emotional heart-to-hearts anyway, but Avery would've figured he'd have *some* opinion over the hospital bill. Though perhaps Mom thought Avery was too pitiful to get yelled at twice in one day, over the same thing. Avery almost would rather have gotten yelled at again. It was better than being treated like she was too weak to handle a simple conversation.

They headed up the ramp out of Manhattan, where the skyline passed by one final time. Avery tried to admire the twinkling buildings across the river, the warm yellow sparkles from the windows of high-rises brimming with life, but right now, though she knew it was irrational, she was angry with this city, with its seemingly limitless opportunities for her to get herself in trouble. Would she behave this irresponsibly if she lived somewhere less stimulating? That was a stupid thought. Yes she would. Because no matter where she went, there she was—the same girl who'd put herself in the same situation in college and tried to act like she didn't. And her coping mechanisms were all short-lived balms that seemed to only make her feel worse.

Her phone buzzed with a text from Morgan. *I'm glad you're alive. What happened?*

Avery put her phone in her lap, thankful that Morgan wasn't icing her out like everyone else.

Her phone buzzed again. *Did Blair say something to you??*

Avery knew telling Morgan about her conversation with Blair would only exacerbate Morgan's existing stress about having them both in the wedding party. At the time, in her drunk one-track mind, running from Blair's comment had been the only thing Avery could think to do to get away from it all—literally. But Avery didn't want to give Morgan more reasons to worry. She would just need to forget about what happened with Blair and move forward, to suck it up until the wedding. Then she could go back to her regular life.

SHE USED TO BE NICE

no, she was fine, Avery said. *my mom's making me come home this weekend tho. hang when i get back?*

Avery spent the next thirty minutes peeking at her phone for Morgan's response, refreshing their text message window over and over. Until, finally: *Sure.*

That period was like a stab in the gut.

• • •

The public housing and warehouse buildings of upper Manhattan slowly morphed into the corn fields and rolling plains of grass of suburban New Jersey. Avery's heart swelled at the sight of her hometown. New Jersey was so much more than the stretch of highway that smelled like farts you had to drive through to get to New York City. Avery had a magical childhood here, filled with summers at the beach and late nights at the diner and long drives to nowhere. Maybe she should've stayed here after high school instead of going away to Massachusetts for college. She could've gone to Rutgers, worked for the *Asbury Park Press*, and dated a local guy, maybe a teacher. They could've spent their days going to restaurants by the ocean, listening to live music at The Stone Pony, and saving up for a modest home with a yard. She could've run in a different social circle, been someone different, gone to another party senior year. She could've had the life she'd always envisioned for herself as a kid. She should've taken a cue from her parents who rarely left the state. There was nothing for her beyond the confines of their town in New Jersey. Everything she needed to have a happy life was right here, along Route 22. Mike and Jackie Russo knew it best.

Avery's dad pulled into the driveway, and the car wobbled over the bumps in the familiar way it always did as her white-paneled childhood home with navy shutters came closer into view. She headed through the front door and snuck up the stairs to put her bag away in her old bedroom, where everything looked the same as it had when she first moved out, fossilized like artifacts in a history museum. Her comforter had the same yellow swirls, the colors faded from the sun streaming in through the window above her bed. Her bookshelf still overflowed with books, including a short story she wrote in elementary school called *The Brownie Sale on Our Block*, but there was a tiny layer of dust on all the spines. Her walls were covered in academic awards, drama club awards, a first-place spelling bee ribbon. She couldn't believe this person had once existed, and that that person was somehow her.

Mom suddenly appeared in the doorframe. Without a word, she reached over to give Avery a hug. Avery, also wordlessly, returned the embrace, breathing in the familiar scent of Mom's rosewater perfume and expensive hairspray.

"I'm glad you're home," Mom said softly.

She pulled away and tenderly stroked Avery's cheek, making Avery feel like a kid again. Avery wished her mom could hold her in her arms and make everything go away like when she used to scare the monsters out from under Avery's bed. The fight with Morgan, that night with Noah, the constant debilitating fear that Avery wouldn't make it to August—all these new monsters, bigger and scarier than anything Avery had feared before.

Avery's eyes became wet, burned with tears. "Me too."

Avery followed her mom downstairs to the kitchen, where a pot of hot water was boiling on the stove and a "Bless This House" plaque was nailed to the wall above a set of French doors leading into the yard. Dad was sitting at the table reading the paper, and Mom went over to rub his shoulders and give him a kiss, as though he'd had to journey through a treacherous jungle to pick her up and he'd made it out unharmed. Avery rolled her eyes. It was just Manhattan, for Christ's sake, despite their favorite Fox News pundits convincing them the city was twenty-four/seven mayhem. Though if Avery were in a better mood, she would find their protectiveness of each other sweet.

Hunter was kicking the soccer ball around outside when he spotted Avery through the window and sprinted inside to greet her. Avery hadn't spoken to her little brother in a while, but he was

SHE USED TO BE NICE

only seventeen—young and naive enough to think she was busy being an adult, not that her life was falling apart.

"Hunter, no more soccer until your science project is done," Dad reprimanded. "You need to get working on it."

Hunter exhaled loudly. "I *know*." He turned to Avery and told her about his indoor soccer game last weekend, when he outran the other team's fastest defender. "The goalie had no chance. He was cursing like crazy. I won't repeat what he said because Mom will kill me, but it rhymes with puck and sit."

"Hunter!" Mom barked.

"I didn't say the words! Just what they rhymed with!"

Mom poured Avery a cup of tea in her Woodford College mug. Avery dunked the tea bag up and down and watched the brown liquid swirl around inside the hot water. Avery had gotten this mug during freshman orientation week. She remembered feeling a sense of belonging those first few weeks on campus as she walked among Woodford's majestic gothic buildings and classic manicured lawns. Cheering on Woodford's top-tier football team, thumbing through pamphlets of extracurricular activities, and enrolling in enriching academic courses, Avery had felt part of something bigger than herself, something that would help her make her lasting mark on the world.

"Hunter's trying to get into a summer program for science and engineering," Mom said. "Soccer's been taking up too much studying time."

Hunter scoffed. "I'm gonna get in, Mom. I got into their space camp two years ago. That'll give me a leg up."

"I'm sure it will, honey." Mom ruffled Hunter's hair, beaming proudly at him. "You just wait, Avery. Hunter's gonna give you a run for your money with his grades. He'll graduate high school with an even higher rank than you."

"He probably will." Avery was less enthusiastic than she should've been, but Mom was right. Hunter easily had a shot at being valedictorian when he graduated high school next year. Avery, meanwhile, didn't even walk in her commencement ceremony at Woodford, still reeling and alone from her breakup and the aftermath. She'd spent all of graduation day in her dorm room drinking Rubinoff by herself, telling everyone she had the stomach flu.

Dad put down his newspaper and fixed his attention on Avery. "How's work going? I've been meaning to tell you, my coworker's daughter was a copy editor at a travel magazine, and she became a staff writer after working there only a year."

"Oh wow, Mike, that's great!" Mom said. "Did you hear that, Avery? You can leverage your social media job in the same way. You gotta show them your essays!"

Avery offered a tiny shrug. Her parents had always been supportive of her writing, which Avery used to share on all her social media pages. Her mom was especially supportive on Facebook, where, in addition to writing unnecessarily long posts about relatively minor life events and commenting on everything in all caps, like "YOU LOOK GORGEOUS" or "WHO'S HE? CUTE," she used to like every single *Golden* article Avery posted. But Avery never posted anything now.

"I haven't been able to write at all lately," Avery said matter-of-factly. "Been going through way too much this past year."

Avery's parents exchanged a sad look.

"What do you mean?" Mom asked.

Avery froze. She'd slipped too easily into the cozy cocoon of her parents' love and support. But she forgot that they didn't know any details about the breakup. Nor did she want them finding anything out.

"I just—I just mean that, uh . . . work's been busy," she said. "I don't have time to pitch anything if I wanted to."

Mom was still frowning. Dad's lips were a straight, concerned line. Avery tossed them another shrug and an unbothered smile, like *oh well, what can you do?* But she could tell what her parents were thinking, which was that they'd raised her in a nurturing, loving environment and even that wasn't enough to prevent her from failing miserably in her adulthood. At this point they should

SHE USED TO BE NICE 127

just focus their energy on Hunter. She wondered what they told their neighborhood friends during run-ins at Wegmans. *Oh, yeah, Avery's still making tweets,* she imagined them saying. *Hunter, on the other hand, is gonna be the next Bill Gates!*

"Well, maybe you should reach out to those other magazines you applied to, then," Dad suggested. He sounded cautious, like he didn't want to startle a skittish animal. "They could have a staff writer opening now."

Avery scrunched her face as she recalled the magazines she'd told her parents she applied to after Ryan dumped her but did not.

"Maybe." She gulped down the rest of her tea, preparing to leave. She had no interest in hearing about her lost potential or being the subject of her parents' pity once again. "I'm gonna go for a drive."

Avery headed outside and climbed into the white Honda Civic she'd had since high school and couldn't afford to park in the city now. She pulled out of the street and cracked open the window, letting the cool, piney air refresh her skin. She passed the bagel shop, where she used to get bagels because she wanted to and not because they soaked up the booze in her gut; the strip mall parking lot, where teenagers more sexually deviant than she'd been with Thomas in high school used to hook up. She passed the road that led to her high school, too, which reminded her of a fight she got into at lunch once with her childhood friend Joan. She couldn't remember what caused the fight, but she remembered that after the argument, Joan shouted across the table, "Well, Jacob imprints on Bella and Edward's baby!" Avery was in the middle of reading *Breaking Dawn.* Joan might as well have told her to go fuck herself.

Avery missed fighting with Morgan about stupid things like that. Like the time Morgan put up an Instagram post and Avery didn't like it right away. *Why haven't you liked my post yet?* Morgan had DMed her. *My likes-to-minutes ratio is terrible.* Or the time Avery got annoyed when Morgan bombarded her with dog memes that did not spark the warm and fuzzy reaction Morgan had wanted

128   ALEXIA LAFATA

them to. *this isn't making me like dogs,* Avery had texted. *it's making me feel like a bitch.*

Avery wasn't even sure if they were fighting now as much as Morgan was disappointed in her, which was undoubtedly worse. But Avery could never tell Morgan why Blair's comment rattled her enough to make her run out of the engagement party. Because for all her friends knew and for all they would continue to know, Avery *did* get too drunk and hurt someone she loved senior year, like Blair said. Avery had, indeed, had sex with someone else. It hadn't been her choice, but it was the only version of the truth that mattered.

Avery pulled into the park, then sat down on a bench in front of the frozen lake that disappeared into the horizon. She wrapped her arms around her upper body to warm herself up. A man in black workout gear jogged by before stopping to lean against a tree and catch his breath, white clouds of air billowing up into the sky as he exhaled. His brown wavy hair glistened appealingly with sweat and fell in thick ropes into his face, and he had some of the nicest arms Avery had ever seen.

A beat later, he caught her staring at him, and she glanced away. Then she looked back again. "Jonathan?"

He squinted at her before his face opened in recognition. "Avery?" Jonathan jogged over and went to give Avery a hug but quickly pulled back. "Actually, no, you don't want to touch me. I'm covered in sweat."

Avery let her eyes wander up and down Jonathan's firm, toned body. She and Jonathan had been friendly in high school drama club, but they lost touch after graduation and grew further apart for no reason except that they led different lives. There were rumors that he'd had a crush on her, too, but he never acted on it, and she never saw him that way. Now he was much cuter than she remembered.

"No worries! How are you?" she said.

"I'm great," Jonathan said with a very nice smile. "So funny I ran into you! Did you know the high school is doing *Fiddler on the*

SHE USED TO BE NICE 129

Roof this year? Are we that old that they're recycling the plays now?"

Avery laughed. "That's so funny. It's been, what . . . six years since we played husband and wife?"

"I know. Sometimes I'll wake up in the morning to that freaking 'Miracle of Miracles' song ringing inside my skull. It's the worst." Jonathan smiled again. The crow's feet that crinkled next to his eyes made him even cuter. She noticed, too, that his eyes were blue. Like Pete's.

She shook away the thought of him. He'd certainly forgotten all about her by now after the hasty way she left his parents' house. And if Ryan *did* come to Morgan and Charlie's wedding, surely it didn't matter who Avery's plus-one was as long as it was *someone*. Maybe that someone could be Jonathan. He could help her show everyone that she'd moved on just as well as Pete could, even if he wasn't her first choice.

"Anyway, how are you?" Jonathan asked. "I heard you moved to the city."

Avery tensed at the reminder of what was waiting for her back home, at the trail of destruction she'd left behind. She tried to focus on the park. The sky shone a beautiful, cloudless blue, and the winter air was energizing and crisp. She came here so often as a teenager. It made her so happy. She just wanted to be happy again.

"I did, but I'm home for a couple of days," she said. "You still live around here?"

"Yeah, can't seem to escape this town." Jonathan playfully rolled his eyes. "And the law firm I'm interning at is about ten miles away."

"Of course you're gonna be a lawyer. You were always so good at public speaking. What kind of law do you wanna do?"

"I'm thinking litigator, but who knows? I'm trying to go to law school next year." Jonathan kicked back his foot and grabbed his ankle to stretch out his leg. "Yes, I'm just as nerdy as you remember."

Avery watched his thigh muscle clench through his running tights. "Perhaps even nerdier."

Jonathan glanced at his watch and started jogging in place. "Hey, you around tomorrow? I'd love to catch up more when I'm not a sweaty mess."

Avery's eyes brightened. This could be her chance to try something new with a guy from home. She liked the responsible, well-rounded version of herself that she was when she was friends with Jonathan as a teen. Hanging out with him could help her tap into that side of herself again. In high school, she didn't yet have any regrets, wasn't yet tainted by the selfishness of a man who felt entitled to her body. She'd love to remember what that felt like.

"Absolutely," she said.

"How about lunch?" he asked. "1 PM?" Avery nodded, and Jonathan took out his phone. "I think I still have your number in my contacts from high school." He recited her number to confirm, and they exchanged a smile before agreeing to see each other tomorrow. Then she watched him disappear deeper into the park.

11

AVERY WAS TAPPING THROUGH Instagram Stories while waiting outside the salad place where she and Jonathan had agreed to meet when she came across Morgan's Story. Her heart stopped. Morgan appeared to be spending the entire day hanging out with Blair.

First, the two of them got brunch at Via Carota, the most difficult place to snag a reservation, and Avery knew they were there because Morgan had geotagged the restaurant in a video of her and Blair cheering across the table with matching mulled wines. Next, they wandered around the Whitney, which Morgan once again geotagged on pictures of a massive, sweeping gallery room and the view of buildings and spiky snow-covered trees from the rooftop. Following their museum trip, they went to some boutique with a French name on the Upper West Side that Avery had never heard of nor could afford, also geotagged across pictures of them trying on flowy midi dresses and making kissy faces into the camera. The geotags mocked Avery, making her loneliness not just apparent but also worldly and far-reaching, spanning neighborhoods and cultures and socioeconomic classes.

Avery clicked off her phone and chucked it into the backseat of her car. She was fuming now. She hadn't wanted Morgan to pick sides after senior year, but now she was reconsidering. And even if Avery hadn't asked her to, she should've just done it anyway! Morgan had so many friends, so many better and more worthy people to ask to be bridesmaids. She didn't need to pick the person who betrayed Avery the most. Avery hadn't been surprised by some of the people who took Ryan's side after the breakup, but she'd been surprised by Blair and her actions. Blair could have shown Avery some compassion for her mistake instead of spewing so much vitriol about it across campus. At least when Morgan heard that Avery had cheated, Morgan was sympathetic, knew how badly Avery was hurting and was kind enough not to make it worse. But Blair didn't offer Avery any sympathy at all. It wasn't so much that Avery blamed Blair for thinking she cheated as much as she hated that Blair was so cruel and unrelenting about it.

Avery spotted Jonathan walking across the parking lot looking sharp in a dark navy suit. She exited her car. Using Jonathan to tap into a past wholesome version of herself was going to be difficult now that her present-day trash self needed a confidence boost.

They greeted each other and entered the café together, then ordered their salads and drinks before grabbing a corner booth tucked in the back, away from the rest of the lunch crowd. Jonathan took off his suit jacket and rolled up the sleeves of his white button-down. Avery's gaze lingered approvingly on his muscular forearms. He'd come a long way from the nonsexual thespian he'd been in high school.

"I like your suit," she purred. Fuck it. She wasn't sure if sex was on the table this afternoon, but she was now officially trying to put it there. She was going to turn on the seduction and charm, to make herself seem as unaffected by Blair and Morgan as she could.

Jonathan's face flushed pink. Good start. "Why, thank you. I've gotta wear one every day."

"Sucks that they make you come in on the weekends."

"Yeah, but it's okay. Excited to continue the family legacy." Jonathan shoved a forkful of salad into his mouth. "My dad is thrilled that my brother and I are into law. Marissa couldn't give less of a shit about it."

"Is she still into the environment? I remember her activist group in high school. Everyone joked that you guys had the

SHE USED TO BE NICE 133

perfect combination of skills to end global warming." Avery wrapped her lips over her straw and sucked hard, on purpose. Jonathan's pupils dilated as he watched.

"I remember that," he said, meeting Avery's eye. "But my sister is actually brilliant. I was just good at pretending I was. You're smart, too, Miss Six-AP-Classes-Junior-Year."

Avery scoffed. "I *was* smart. Now I do audience development for *Metropolitan*. Not exactly on my way to becoming a CEO."

"That's cool, though! I love *Metropolitan*. I read it all the time. Love their Twitter presence. Or X now. Whatever it is."

Avery smiled, trying to keep their conversation playful. "That's all me." She was getting kind of bored. She didn't want to talk about work. She wanted to talk about fucking.

But Jonathan continued, as though they were just friends catching up. "You kill it. Twitter's the only social media I use, so I can't judge your ability on anything else, unfortunately." He took a long, unsexy sip of his soda. "Twitter's fun. I debate with people on a burner account. I love pissing people off. Whenever someone says something political, I say I feel the opposite."

Avery held back a groan. So he was one of those "devil's advocates." "Your stances on things change that much, huh?"

"Nah, I'm just a troll. In reality, I'm probably a centrist. There are two sides to everything, aren't there? And both parties have equally terrible people anyway."

Avery shoved her salad into her mouth. What she wanted to say was that sounded like a whole lot of both-sidesism bullshit, but she ignored the words coming out of Jonathan's mouth and stared at his face instead. Jonathan was hot. Jonathan was stupid. Hot. Stupid. Stupid hot.

Avery folded her arms under her chest to accentuate her boobs. She was glad this skin-tight baby tee was tucked in the back of her closet at her parents' house. Her tits looked incredible. She swallowed the last mouthful of her salad and put her fork down. Jonathan was never going to be her date to any weddings, ever, but she couldn't believe she was still trying to have sex with someone who for sure thought reverse racism was a thing. She was ready to get this over with.

"Well, I'm also a talented Instagrammer," she said. "You should check us out there, too."

Jonathan's lips curved into a smile. "I'd be happy to check you out anywhere, Avery."

His voice was husky and knowing. Avery narrowed her eyes, hoping he meant what she thought he did.

"Would you now?" she asked.

"If you'd let me, of course." Jonathan scrunched his face in what appeared to be a moment of self-consciousness. "Sorry, was that presumptuous?"

"No, no, not at all." Avery threw her crumpled napkin into her empty plastic bowl. Time to get out of there. "You mean, right now?"

Jonathan looked around. "I mean . . ." He shrugged. "Yeah. Sure. When else?"

Avery flicked her head in the direction of the parking lot, and Jonathan nodded in understanding. Then she got up to throw her trash in the garbage by the front door, with Jonathan following right behind. The silence between them was flammable as they walked side by side across the lot, Jonathan's hand brushing against Avery's hip and igniting the tension.

"This is me," Jonathan said, pointing at a black BMW a couple yards ahead.

"If I cared about cars, I'd say this is a cool one," Avery said.

Jonathan stopped walking, then pulled Avery in for a hug. She kept her face buried in his chest, enveloped herself in the linen fragrance embedded into his shirt, trying to find something to enjoy about this experience. When he released her, he kept his hands on her triceps, staring at her lips and licking his own with his tongue.

"Come here, you," he said. And then he leaned down to kiss her. His kisses started soft and without tongue before morphing into something too sloppy and wet. But Avery didn't care. He

SHE USED TO BE NICE

wanted her. They were going to have sex and she wasn't going to hate herself anymore.

A few moments later, he pulled away, a suggestive grin playing on his lips. "You know, there's a walking trail around the corner. The parking lot is almost always empty . . ."

"We could be the rebellious teens we never were," Avery joked.

Jonathan laughed. "Exactly what I was thinking."

They climbed inside his car, Jonathan in the driver's seat and Avery in the passenger side. A revoltingly masculine-scented Black Ice air freshener swung from the rear-view mirror. As Jonathan drove out of the parking lot, Avery leaned over the armrest from her seat to nibble on his ear, eager to get this done. He parked his car in the discreet lot next to the trail, unbuckled his seatbelt, and jumped into the back seat, pulling Avery with him. The back seat was tight, but Avery leaned into the closeness, letting Jonathan trail kisses down her neck, across her shoulders, and onto her upper back. He began to rotate her body so that he was behind her, but she tried to keep him in front of her by grabbing his head and kissing him.

"You taste amazing," he breathed. "God, I've wanted to do this since high school . . ."

He tried to turn her around again by putting his hand on her back and bending her forward. Then her knee slipped off the backseat.

"Ow," Avery whispered. She forced out a laugh. "Sorry, it's tight back here."

Jonathan put his hand on her back again. Avery's heart galloped as he pressed himself against her. She could feel him getting harder and her palms getting sweatier. Forgetting where she was, she shot upright and banged her head against the low ceiling.

"Shit!" she shouted, rubbing her head.

Jonathan winced. "You okay?"

Avery massaged her head. Pain exploded from the tender spot on her skull. "I'm fine. I just . . . I just think it's too tight back here for . . . for that . . ."

"I've done it before. Here." Jonathan scooted Avery's body backward and lifted her ass. She resisted.

"Stop, Jonathan. It's too tight."

He lifted her ass even higher. "Just hold on. I think we can do—"

She smacked him away, hard, and he drew back, a horrified expression flashing across his face at the red welt materializing on the side of his stomach.

"I said *stop*," Avery snapped.

She faced forward and inhaled a shaky deep breath, then released herself from his grip, felt around in the backseat for her lace underwear, and slipped it on as fast as she could. She rested her hand on her chest, which ached from how fast her heart was beating, and closed her eyes to block out the feel of Noah's large, imposing body pressing down on her back.

"Is everything okay?" Jonathan asked quietly. His dick was soft now, dangling between his legs like a tube sock with no foot. Avery busied herself by massaging her chest, begging her heart to slow down. If her body was the crime scene from that night senior year, where was she supposed to go when she still felt in danger?

"Yeah. I'm just not in the mood anymore." She zipped up her jeans and crawled to the front seat. "Sorry."

Jonathan cocked his head in confusion. Avery mumbled an apology again before flinging open the car door and slamming it shut.

• • •

By the time Avery got home, her heart rate had slowed to a normal pace. What she wouldn't give for a glass of wine to dull her senses and help her pretend this afternoon never happened. It was too early to start drinking, though, and she didn't want her parents thinking she was more of a degenerate than she already was, so she'd have to settle for carbs. She went into the kitchen, poured a bowl of Cap'n Crunch, and dove into Instagram, the dopamine from scrolling through her feed sufficiently distracting her from the fact that Jonathan had almost fucked her from behind. Her forbidden position, thanks to Noah. She clicked on a red notification

SHE USED TO BE NICE 137

in the top right corner of her screen as she went to take a bite of cereal. Then she dropped her spoon.

Pete had started following her.

Avery navigated to his account, which was public. Charlie was following him. She browsed through Pete's pictures. The first picture was cropped, and judging by the red Solo cup in his hand, appeared to be from a party. A Woodford party? She zoomed in; she didn't recognize the background, so maybe not. She scrolled to the next picture, where he was in a tuxedo with his hands folded in front of him. In the next picture, he was flipping burgers in front of a grill, the bright red and orange leaves on the trees behind him signaling the onset of fall. She scrolled down his page some more, scanning a picture of him playing Ultimate Frisbee, standing on top of a mountain, smiling with his arm looped around a girl in a pale blue dress. Avery scrolled through the likes and comments on that last one; there were tons. Definitely an ex. The thought made her jealous, irrationally.

She came across a video still of a prepubescent Pete playing guitar, with the caption *A legend in the making*. She let the video play. Preteen Pete hummed to himself to find his starting note, then strummed the guitar with his clammy fingers and began to sing in a sweet high-pitched voice. Avery had a feeling he'd posted this video to laugh at himself, but the earnestness of it all tugged on her heartstrings, made her want to reach through the screen and wrap her arms around him in a tight hug. She liked Pete's heart, his confidence, his sense of humor. She liked so many things about him.

The garage door rumbled open. Avery turned her phone face down on the table just as her mother came into the kitchen and dropped her purse on the countertop.

"Hi, hon," Mom said. "Saw the car parked in a different spot from where it was this morning. You went out today?"

Of course Jackie would notice that. Avery had never missed the subway more. "Yeah, I had lunch with Jonathan. Jonathan Williams, from drama club."

"Oh, sure! I remember him. What's he up to?"

"Nothing much. He wants to go to law school."

"Good for him." Mom grabbed an apple from the fruit basket on the counter by the sink and took a bite. "He was so handsome. I always thought you'd end up with him. I cried in the audience during that wedding scene in *Fiddler on the Roof.*" She tried to hide the smile prompted by her reminiscing. "I don't know. You two looked good together."

Avery did not want to continue talking about Jonathan. "Okay, Mom."

Mom sat down at the table and tapped the surface with her nails pensively, like she was debating whether to say the next thing she wanted to say. "You meet anyone special in the city yet?"

Avery rolled her eyes. Mom always tried to be casual about how painfully single Avery was, but she'd been so transparently upset after Avery and Ryan broke up. She would do anything to have grandchildren running around soon, continuing the traditional Italian-American family culture that she'd surely dreamed of before she had kids of her own. Avery had dreams of that, too, of Sunday dinners with fun-loving shouting and marinara sauce simmering on the stove, a mighty Feast of the Seven Fishes on each Christmas Eve, the velvety sounds of Frank Sinatra crooning through every speaker in the house. A month after Ryan dumped her, she looked up statistics around marriage to see how much time she had left before she was doomed to be alone forever. She learned that the average age women got married now was twenty-eight-and-a-half, and that number went up to almost thirty when you looked at just the New York area. She had plenty of time, but the clock was certainly ticking, and she wasn't exactly trying to find a boyfriend to settle down with. All she did with guys was fuck them. It was all she could do. Her secrets turned her body radioactive from the inside out, poisoning any man who got too close.

"Nope." Her voice was clipped. She took another bite of cereal.

SHE USED TO BE NICE 139

"Well, are you going out on dates?" Again Mom sounded breezy in that awfully manufactured way.

"Sure." Semantics.

"Maybe Morgan could hook you up with one of Charlie's friends?"

There was nothing more unappealing than a pity setup with one of Charlie's old lacrosse teammates, who were also Ryan's teammates. The ones she already knew and had been friends with hated her now. The other one was Noah.

"I'm not interested," she said.

Mom sighed and peered out the bay window overlooking the front lawn of their neighbor's house. Avery noticed that there was a little kid's swing set in the backyard and wondered if that meant that old man Heath finally moved out. She hoped so. In middle school, Heath used to stop her during her walks around the block to tell her he liked her outfit. It always started that way, at least, and then in high school his comments got even more predatory. One day, he'd tell her he liked her shirt. The next day, he'd say he liked her hair. The next, she had beautiful eyes, they reminded him of his dead wife's, and oh, by the way, did she have a boyfriend? Sometimes now, when she wore a low-cut top, she thought of suffocating Heath with her chest so he'd never objectify underage girls again. Although that was something that would probably happen over and over again in those girls' adulthoods, through the hungry eyes of men they didn't know as well as men they did. And when those women tried to take back their power, the memory of their degradation would put them right back in their place, making them leave in the middle of lunchtime car sex in distress.

"Well, whoever you meet," Mom said, "I hope you don't get too drunk with them. Like you did the night we got that hospital bill for."

Avery closed her eyes. She felt like a child putting their hands over their ears. "Mom, *please*."

"I just worry about you, Avery! You need to be careful. The world's a dangerous place. I want you to be smart."

It was painful to realize you couldn't seek comfort from the people whose job it was to comfort you, that her mother's perspective on this would never change. Avery buried her face in her phone, too frustrated to argue that as long as people focused on keeping women from becoming victims, the men who perpetrate would have free reign to terrorize. Where was the outrage with the men? Who blamed *them* for *their* actions? Avery was tired of shouldering the burden of her own self-protection. It was too heavy to carry all by herself. And yet she felt like it was her only option. Because it wasn't just her mother who made her feel like that night was her fault. It was the evidence itself. It was the fact that she'd participated in at least some way in the beginning, by peacocking her body and being friendly at the party, or else why would Noah have made a move? And then she had ultimately not tried hard enough to stop him. So she was a victim, but she also wasn't innocent. It was the most exhausting seesaw.

"Nothing *happened*, though," Avery insisted. "That guy I was with saved me."

Pete's Instagram page was still open on Avery's phone, the video of him singing paused on his openmouthed face. Avery ran a finger over the screen, careful not to like it by accident. She felt strange referring to Pete as "that guy," even casually to her mom. Because Pete wasn't just that guy. Avery had never met someone like him. And sometimes her feelings for him—the fact that she could feel anything at all—tricked her into thinking she could be worthy of someone like him. That maybe parts of her heart had remained open after everything, and Pete could see a version of her that was softer and more loving, more lovable. Most of the time, though, she knew the truth.

She didn't follow Pete back. She'd be doing them both a favor by staying away.

12

A VERY CAUGHT THE 6 AM bus from her parents' house to Port Authority on Monday morning, sleeping the whole hour-and-a-half-long ride into the city. Once there, she hustled through the maze of the terminal, first down a long escalator and back up two more, until she reached the subway, then went to check the time on her phone while waiting for a car. Her gaze lingered on her wallpaper. It was a picture of her and Morgan at Phebe's in the East Village a few months ago; they were facing each other and laughing, and Avery's lipstick had bled into the corners of her mouth from having accidentally made out with a forty-seven-year-old man.

"I can't believe he was a college professor!" Morgan had cried. They were outside Phebe's while Avery was taking a vape break. Richard—that was his name—had left to go somewhere else, probably some whiskey bar to smoke a cigar and discuss Foucault with his peers like the intellectual he thought he was.

"He looked so young in the dark! I thought he was thirty, max," Avery said.

Morgan shivered in disgust. "Well, the license in his wallet said otherwise. He probably thought you were a student. Which is even more gross."

"He totally did. He asked what I studied in school. I thought it was to be relatable, but it was, like, in a dad way." Avery chucked her vape into her purse and searched for a cigarette instead.

"Come on," Morgan insisted as Avery popped an unlit cigarette into her mouth. "You don't need one of those."

"Yes, I do," Avery mumbled.

"Why?"

"Because I'm an idiot."

Morgan took the cigarette out of Avery's mouth and flicked it into the garbage. Then she threaded her arm through Avery's and smiled. "But you're *my* idiot."

Tears burned Avery's eyes now. She sat down on an empty seat in a subway car that smelled of breakfast sandwiches and the tangy mix of strangers' freshly applied perfume. It had only been a couple of days since she and Morgan last spoke, but since they usually talked every day, two days felt like a lifetime. Avery wondered if she'd gotten too used to screwing up, knowing her best friend would be there for her unconditionally. Not only had Morgan forgiven Avery senior year after thinking Avery made one of the most unforgiveable mistakes you can make in a relationship, but she had stopped Avery from charring her lungs with cigarette smoke, had once sent her money for a train ticket home after a drunken bender ended in Philadelphia, and had accompanied her to CityMD for her various STD scares. She'd helped Avery out of the hospital, offered emotional support, sacrificed sleep. And she did it all without complaint. But she shouldn't have to deal with Avery's screwups now, during what was supposed to be *her* year.

Avery emerged from the subway and went to La Colombe near her office for a black coffee. She chugged nearly half of her drink in one gulp, letting the stifling liquid scald her throat as she lingered in front of her building and stared at her phone. If she didn't call Morgan right this second, she was going to chug more hot coffee and spend the rest of the day with a burning, aching mouth, and this would be a punishment she would deserve wholeheartedly.

She dialed Morgan's number with her shaky fingers.

"Hello?" Morgan answered.

"Hey!" Avery said, breathless and grateful. "Wow, I'm so glad to hear your voice."

SHE USED TO BE NICE   143

"What's up? How was your weekend?"

Avery blinked back tears, stared up at the sky. Morgan's voice was suspiciously normal, but Avery didn't want to sweep what happened at the engagement party under the rug. She knew, from that last *Sure.* text, that Morgan was upset.

"It was fine." Avery moved out of the way of a young-looking intern carrying a four-cup drink holder filled with beverages. "Look, I wanna say again how sorry I am for leaving you at the engagement party. I was hammered and I just couldn't be around everyone anymore. I hope . . . I hope you understand."

Morgan sighed. A fire engine wailed in the background on her end of the line. "I do understand. I just want everything to go as smoothly as possible this year. Minimal casualties."

Avery nodded desperately into the receiver. "I know. I want the same thing."

"And I know that's tough for you with our friends around, and I'm sympathetic to that, but . . ." Morgan trailed off. "But I need you to try. For me."

Avery tossed her coffee into a steel trash receptacle. She needed to pull it together. She'd known that their old friends would be in the wedding party, at all the wedding events. She may not have known Noah would be around, too, but she needed to get over that, lest he ruin her friendship with Morgan like he ruined everything else. She needed to be better at keeping his effect on her a secret. All she had to do was make it to the wedding in August, and then this whole thing would be over. And it was already nearly the end of January. She could do this.

"I swear I'll be okay, Morgan. I'm gonna be the most incredible maid of honor you've ever had. You'll see."

Morgan didn't respond right away. Avery approached the entrance to her office with her key in her hand, ready to go through the double doors and scan herself through the security turnstiles. But she did not want to stop this phone call. Not even the massive German shepherd police dog barking a few feet away prompted her to move inside for safety. She wasn't hanging up until they

144   ALEXIA LAFATA

were okay, until Morgan knew that Avery was going to support her like she'd supported Avery, through everything.

"Come with me to a bridal expo in Williamsburg later?" Morgan said when she finally spoke. "I'm warning you though, it's kind of deep in Williamsburg. Like, thirty-dollar-cab-ride-from-Union-Square deep."

Avery threw her fist in the air. "Count me *in*."

• • •

The bridal expo was actually a fifty-dollar cab ride into Williamsburg.

Avery probably could have taken the subway, but Morgan wanted to meet promptly at 6 PM, before all the good vendors left, and Avery didn't get out of work until 5:30. Her credit card wailed in agony as she sliced it through the machine in the cab. She made a mental note to pack lunch next week. Leftover takeout from the night before or peanut butter and jelly sandwiches—that was it.

She opened the cab door to the sight of Morgan waiting outside and scrolling idly through her phone.

"Hi," Morgan said when she looked up.

It was possible there was a hint of sadness in Morgan's voice, but perhaps Avery was imagining it. Avery walked slowly, cautiously, toward her best friend.

"Hi." She bit the inside of her cheek to stop herself from tearing up as they hugged hello. The embrace lasted longer than it normally would have, with Avery holding on tighter as a silent reaffirming of her apology, and Morgan letting her.

When they released, Morgan gave a small smile that put Avery at ease. Avery smiled back. Maybe they really were going to be okay.

"Ready?" Morgan asked.

She led them both toward the expo, held in a sprawling banquet hall inside a luxury hotel. Conversations among brides-to-be echoed throughout the space, where bakeries, limousine services, photography studios, and dozens more vendors were lined up in neat rows. Morgan and Avery made a beeline to sample red velvet

SHE USED TO BE NICE 145

cake at a bakery booth before continuing around the rest of the expo, stopping at a station selling cornhole boards that you could personalize with your and your fiancé's initials. Avery raised an eyebrow. She hadn't even known this kind of thing existed.

Morgan excitedly ran her fingers over the initials engraved on the display sample. She turned to a tired guy doing a crossword puzzle who appeared to be manning the booth.

"How much?" she asked.

He glanced up from behind his reading glasses. "Three thousand."

Morgan paused like she was considering it. Avery ushered her away.

"No way," Avery said. "You're not wasting your money on that."

They meandered through more rows of booths, eating more slices of cake and listening to more DJs' mixtapes and talking to more makeup artists. Morgan asked Avery for her opinions on everything—yes to the red velvet cake, no to this DJ's bizarre eighties synth playlist, absolutely not to this makeup artist's cat-eye pinup looks—and Avery swelled with pride every time she answered Morgan's questions, every time she felt herself getting Morgan's trust back. That Morgan was a compassionate person didn't mean Avery had free reign to screw up and be welcomed back into the friendship with open arms every single time. Love between best friends was not always unconditional. You had to be there for each other even when it was hard, otherwise trust could weaken and your relationship could demote to something more distant. As long as Avery acted exactly this supportive until the wedding, manifesting these same good feelings whenever she had to be around Noah, all would be well.

After another lap around the expo, Morgan and Avery took a break at a photographer's booth. Lots of couples had the same idea, packing themselves tightly into the small walled area to admire all the sample photos scattered around the space. A man scooted behind Avery, sliding his hand across her lower back and lingering at her hip bone. She jumped at the icky feeling crawling all over her skin. How had he managed to touch her there? Her black puffer coat completely concealed her hips. Sometimes it seemed to Avery like every man fell somewhere along the spectrum of entitlement. On one end were the men who stared openly at a woman's cleavage, as though they were permitted to be creeps simply because they had eyes. The disgusting man in this booth who'd copped a feel fell somewhere in the middle. And then, on the other end, was Noah.

Morgan slumped on top of a photo album on a high-top table. "I'm so tired. Taking care of Scout is exhausting. At night he barks every hour. I'm lucky if I fall asleep for forty-five minutes before I have to wake up again." She smiled sleepily to herself. "But I love him so much."

That stupid fucking dog. "Well, let me make your life easier." This could be Avery's chance for redemption. "Let me get started on planning your bridal shower. Actually, I'll do it all."

"Really? You don't have to do it by yourself."

"No, I want to! You can be involved with whatever you want, but let me do all the heavy lifting. I already know a spot."

Morgan brightened. "Where?"

Avery grinned to herself as she thought of Gallow Green, a rooftop bar in the Meatpacking District, where leaves and flowers burst from the ceiling in a style of décor that *Metropolitan* once called "garden-green chic." The theme matched perfectly with the Brooklyn Botanic Garden, completing Morgan's urban-nature wedding of her dreams. It wasn't a *puppy* like Noah had gotten her, but it was still meaningful in a different way, an opportunity for Avery to show Morgan that she could pull out the wedding stops, too. And the shower would be girls only, so Noah wouldn't be there to ruin it.

"You'll see," Avery said. She was genuinely excited about this.

Morgan beamed before absentmindedly flipping through a sample photo album, lingering on a formfitting dress—a column silhouette! Avery recognized it!—with an illusion neckline. Then she said, "I'm planning on going wedding dress shopping next

SHE USED TO BE NICE 147

month, by the way. That was the only time I could get an appointment at Kleinfeld. I want you to come, obviously."

"Duh, I'll be there."

Morgan sucked in a breath. "And Blair's coming, too."

Avery paused, probably for a beat too long. She threw Morgan a comically wide smile. "Awesome!"

Morgan frowned. "I know. I'm sorry. It's just, she offered, and I know you guys—"

Avery held up her hand. "It's okay." And it was. "No drama. I promise."

• • •

The following week, Avery's phone buzzed with a text from Morgan that included a link to two Groupon vouchers for a yoga class in the Lower East Side. *Come with? I know you hate working out, but yoga is an excellent stress reliever.*

Avery didn't answer right away. She'd never done yoga before, nor had she ever meditated or used aromatherapy or done any of that woo-woo shit to alleviate her anxiety. She didn't fit in with the chill, alternative culture of yogis and hippies; she was too brash and basic and thought those colorful elephant pants were ugly. She failed to see how she could relax enough for any of their relaxation methods to work. And she had horrible allergies. A drop of lavender oil on her temples or whatever would only make her sneeze.

Her phone buzzed again. *And if you don't wanna do it for yourself, do it for me. My dad is on my ass about me not inviting my creepy Uncle Ted to my wedding and I swear if I'm not face up in happy baby within the next hour I will kill myself.*

Avery sighed. She supposed she could try yoga. Morgan wasn't exactly relaxed at her natural state either; when the weather was warmer, the yoga classes she took on Saturday mornings in Central Park seemed to transform her into a different, more serene person. By agreeing to go to this class, Avery would not only be doing something healthy for herself, but she'd be doing something for

148   ALEXIA LAFATA

Morgan. And that was what great maids of honor did. And that was what she'd vowed to be.

She stopped by the sales rack at Lululemon on her way to the class to pick up some leggings and a sports bra. She only had one of each, and they were collecting dust in the back of a drawer somewhere in her parents' house. At the studio, she was greeted by a woman named Greer, who'd be leading the class. Greer had long gray hair and wore a baggy T-shirt covered in peace signs, and introduced herself to everyone with not only her name, but also how she thought she'd be reincarnated after she died.

"As a sunflower," she cooed.

Her voice was squeaky and drawn out, like a balloon releasing helium.

Avery went to exchange a judgmental glance with Morgan, but Morgan was enraptured by Greer's discussion of healing crystals.

Be open-minded, Avery thought. *You could use some centering.*

Inside the studio, a faded tapestry hung from the ceiling and covered the wall in the front of the room. A massive Buddha sculpture stood tall on the mantle behind Greer's yoga mat, and dozens of other multicolored mats were laid out on the rest of the floor in front of hers. The spicy incense burning from a stick perched on the small table next to Greer started giving Avery a headache.

"Welcome to our practice," Greer said. She stood on her mat and folded her hands together. "Please choose a mat, and let's start in Baddha Koṇāsana."

Morgan and Avery snagged two mats next to each other. Avery's eyes flicked to Morgan in her attempt to figure out what to do next, and she watched as Morgan sat down, pressed the soles of her feet together, and held them in place with her hands. Avery attempted the same, albeit much less gracefully.

Greer closed her eyes. "Let's bring our attention to this room. Feel the soles of your feet as they press against one another. Elongate your spine and feel it stretch toward the sky. What is your intention for today's practice?"

Avery's intention was to do yoga. Was that wrong?

SHE USED TO BE NICE   149

"Breathe in," Greer said.

Everyone in the room inhaled. Avery did the same.

"And out."

Someone made the most obnoxious flapping sound from their mouth, like their lips were the wings propelling them into outer space.

"Breathe in."

Avery breathed in again.

"And out."

Greer repeated these instructions five more times, and by the end Avery could barely keep up. She inhaled when she should've exhaled and exhaled when she should've inhaled, practically hyperventilating in her attempt to match Greer's pace. Christ. Yoga was stressful.

Soon the breathing instructions stopped, and the class was instructed to begin a flow that Greer called a "heart-opening sequence," which involved a bunch of movements Avery couldn't for the life of her keep up with. The flow ended in cobra pose, which felt . . . good. Avery stretched out her spine and opened her upper body, imagining the tightness in her chest bursting through her ribcage, her skin, her sports bra, and dissolving into thin air. Her breathing miraculously started matching Greer's, too, and then Greer concluded the class with ten minutes of corpse pose, which was essentially ten minutes of sleeping. *This* Avery could get behind.

"So, how do you feel?" Morgan asked afterward. They were outside the studio, on their way to grab some postexercise bubble tea. "Zen as hell?"

Avery smiled as she realized she'd gone the whole hour without thinking about Noah. She wasn't sure if it was because of the yoga class, her resolve to be there for Morgan no matter what, or both, but she felt as good as she'd felt in a while.

"Totally," she said.

She looped her arm through Morgan's and they headed into the tea shop.

13

"THE NAPKINS MY MOM wants me to use are the *ugliest* bubblegum pink. I get that they're cheaper, but my wedding is not going to be sponsored by Pepto-Bismol."

Morgan nervously bounced her leg up and down under the table as she shoved pad thai in her mouth with her chopsticks. It had been a few weeks since she successfully dragged Avery to yoga, and their friendship was back to normal. Blair had remained up in Boston, where she could easily be forgotten. Avery's old friends were scattered in their respective towns, no longer shooting her glowers about cheating on Ryan. Avery hadn't seen Noah since the engagement party, and thankfully nobody brought him up. Because of all this, her mind was freed in a way that allowed her to focus her energy on supporting Morgan with whatever she needed for the wedding. Today, that meant a reality check about napkins.

"Morgan." Avery put her hand on Morgan's knee under the table. They were at Up Thai, one of the best Thai places in the city. "Nobody's going to notice the napkins that much. They're going to be used and then tossed aside. If the bubblegum shade will help you cut costs, maybe you should consider it."

Morgan rubbed her temples with her fingers. "Ugh. You're right. This wedding is turning me into a crazy person. Who cares about napkins?"

SHE USED TO BE NICE

"Exactly. Plus, if you save money on the napkins, you can spend more on your dress when we go to Kleinfeld tomorrow. That's a pretty good trade." Avery pointed at Morgan with her chopsticks. "Also, people love Pepto-Bismol. It's the only thing that got me through my bouts of heartburn last summer. Gabriela could be onto something."

Avery wondered if she'd be this picky over something as silly as napkins when she planned her own wedding. Then again, she hadn't spoken to the guy she'd come the closest to wanting to be in a relationship with since she bolted from his parents' house. Pete had probably resigned himself to stop trying with her anyway after she didn't follow him back on Instagram. Lately she'd started staring at his little follower notification, willing herself to change her mind and follow him back. But then she would snap herself back to reality. If following her was going to be his only show of effort, that made it even clearer to her that he didn't want to be with her. Their communication would devolve into him emoji-reacting to her Stories once every few months and her either double tapping it because she felt weird or ignoring it. And that would be that.

Avery contemplated the colorful lamps hanging from the ceiling while Morgan angrily poked around in her dinner, trying to think of a way to shift this conversation to something happier. Her eyes landed on the empty plate of curry puffs on the table between them.

"Isn't it crazy how neither of us had Thai food until college?" Avery asked, gesturing with her chin to the plate. Her parents' idea of ethnic food was the Americanized Chinese restaurant two blocks away from their house in New Jersey. "We were pretty sheltered."

Morgan replied with an almost imperceptible laugh. "Speak for yourself. I grew up with sofrito seasoning everything and was basically born with a bottle of hot sauce in hand. Your parents think Tabasco is exotic."

"I know. They were so nervous about what I'd eat when we went to Mexico with everyone for spring break junior year. They were like, 'Watch out, the food's spicy!' And they were right, honestly."

"It really wasn't spicy, Miss I-Can't-Handle-Black-Pepper. I remember it being gross, though. I still have nightmares about cold slices of unmelted cheese laid on top of nachos. That hotel sucked."

"Remember when Viraj felt queasy after eating that taco and purposely drank the water in the shower so he'd throw up?" Avery mimicked the sounds of Viraj slurping water and dry heaving, and Morgan threw her head back laughing.

"What was the name of those ridiculously sweet cocktails we drank?"

Avery snapped her fingers, trying to remember. "Adios Motherfucker!" she said when it came to her.

Morgan squealed. "Yes! That's it!"

"And then there was Mountain Dew Me."

"I forgot about that one! Those were disgusting."

"Viraj had, like, ten of those. Which was probably what sent him over the edge."

Avery doubled over laughing, but inside a deep wave of sadness crashed over her. Ryan got sick that week, too. She remembered running around town in search of saltine crackers and bottled water, and spending their last night cuddled in bed together watching *The Parent Trap* with Spanish subtitles.

Avery took a sip of her Thai iced tea. "Have you heard anything else about Ryan coming to the wedding, by the way?" She tried to sound innocently curious, but even asking the question made her nervous.

"I haven't talked to Charlie about it again," Morgan said. "But I can inquire if you want."

"No, that's okay. Better to not bring it up. Maybe Charlie will forget."

Sometimes Avery wondered how Ryan would've reacted if she'd told him what happened the night of that party senior year. Not that that was on the table if he came to the wedding or was on the table back then. He'd been furious when he confronted her about cheating, so Avery had no doubt that he would've seen the

SHE USED TO BE NICE
153

truth as a convenient excuse to put the blame of her mistake on someone else. Plus he wasn't exactly the most progressive guy around. Even though Avery had adored him, at the end of the day he was a bit of a typical bro, always the first to laugh at the sexist memes that were sent around in the lacrosse guys' group chat, and she wasn't always sure that he was laughing ironically. He probably wouldn't have believed her anyway.

"I care more about whether Pete's coming, to be honest," Morgan said suggestively.

Avery wasn't sure when or if she was going to tell Morgan that she'd met Pete's parents and was currently sitting on his Instagram follow. She needed to figure out what to do about it herself first, and right now her plan was to let him fade into unimportance.

"I don't have his number, Morgan," she lied. "Remember?"

"Charlie has it if you want it. Just say the word. And just know there is a chair on the seating chart with Pete's name on it whenever you're ready."

Morgan smiled, her spirits officially lifted. Avery was glad she could boost Morgan's mood, even if it involved a brief interrogation about Pete.

"We'll see," Avery said.

They decided to go out after dinner to continue the evening's good vibes. They each went home to change and texted each other pictures of their outfits—a black crop top and loose jeans for Avery, a midi dress and white sneakers for Morgan—before agreeing to meet at Ace Bar, a dive bar in the East Village notorious for its throwback music and five-dollar Bud Lights. They elbowed their way through a group of underage guys wearing pastel button-downs to get to the sticky, wooden bar, then ordered two shots of tequila. After the booze settled in their stomachs, they jostled their way to the crowded dance floor, where they screamed "I LOVE THIS SONG!" after every song, laughing and grinding against each other as the DJ played a perfect mix of throwbacks and popular bangers. Chests and arms bumped into them from every angle, like a hurricane of limbs.

Suddenly, Avery's breathing became shallow. Her vision darkened. Everything around her began to tunnel.

She looked around wildly, put her hand on her heart to steady her erratic breathing. This sweaty, crowded room was shapeshifting. . . .

She was in a basement. The basement of that party senior year.

The walls were covered in discarded boxes of beer, the different labels distorting like in a fun house, closing around her menacingly. The floors were sticky with who knew what, so sticky she couldn't move, quicksand sucking her under. The music was so loud she couldn't hear herself think, the bass bumping inside her and hollowing her out. The—

She jerked her head to the left. Did someone just pull her arm? She blinked once, twice, three times, but her vision kept darkening, kept blurring. Sweat pricked her scalp and back. She couldn't breathe or speak, couldn't stop her arm from being pulled away, upstairs . . .

She grabbed Morgan's wrist with clammy hands. "I need to pee!"

"What?" Morgan shouted back.

Avery shoved Morgan through the oblivious crowd toward a two-stall bathroom. She sat on the graffiti-covered toilet and buried her face in her hands as she waited for the memories to go back into the little box inside her brain where she'd locked them away. The sweat on her body slowly evaporated, her skin becoming cool to the touch. She inhaled a shaky deep breath, trying to get her heart rate to slow, trying to remember she wasn't with Noah. That he wasn't here.

She was safe. She was safe. She was safe.

Her phone buzzed. With trembling hands she fished through her purse to find it.

The screen lit up with a text from Pete. *Hey you. What are you up to tonight?*

Relief rushed through Avery's body like a flood. What perfect timing. Sex was just what she needed, just the thing that would help her feel in control again.

SHE USED TO BE NICE

She checked the time. It was 11:00 PM. Was this a booty call? Generally, if a guy texted you after midnight, it was widely accepted to be a booty call, but between 10:30 and midnight was vague. Some people may not have left their apartments yet. To them, their night hadn't even started. But Avery was drunk and desperate to feel better and thrilled by the prospect of seeing Pete again, so she decided that yes, he was giving her a booty call. And she was proud of him. He finally understood that she was only capable of giving him sex, and now she'd be able to enjoy his company while keeping an emotional distance.

i'm at Ace Bar. let's hang later? she typed back. If she wanted to hook up somewhere that wasn't a disgusting bathroom, she had no choice but to invite him over. *my place,* she added with her address.

She put her phone back in her purse and exited the stall, calmer now. Morgan stood outside the bathroom near the increasingly crowded dance floor, where the artificial smell of makeup and cologne mixed with the earthy odor of perspiration and wood. Morgan's face lit up when she spotted Avery.

"I'm having so much fun!" she shouted over the music, her alcohol-tinged breath sharp in Avery's ear. "I looooove you!"

Morgan never got this drunk. It was cute.

"I love you, too!" Avery said. "How are you feeling?"

Morgan yawned. Her mascara was smeared around her eyelids. "Sleepy."

"Yeah? Wanna get out of here?"

Morgan nodded loosely, like a bobblehead. Avery led her outside, sidestepping an entire discarded takeout meal squished into the concrete, and hailed one of the yellow cabs zipping down Avenue B. Once Avery ushered Morgan into the backseat and the two of them were settled, Morgan zipped off her booties and flung them to the floor.

"Whoops!" she said with a giggle.

Avery laughed as she grabbed Morgan's shoes. "I got these for you, don't worry." Drunk, adorable Morgan rested her head on Avery's shoulder while Avery shot a quick text to Pete: *be home in 30 min*

156 ALEXIA LAFATA

"I'm *so* glad I'm getting married," Morgan slurred.

Avery patted Morgan's head like she was a sweet little toddler who'd done a good job. "I'm glad you are, too! You're gonna be such a beautiful bride."

Avery's phone buzzed with Pete's reply. *Sounds good*

Morgan's head lolled backward on Avery's shoulder as the cab made its bumpy way through the East Village. "Oh, *stop*. You're the bestest friend in the whole world. But really, I am, like, *so* happy I don't have to deal with men anymore. That bar was so . . . crowded! The guys were so . . . disgusting! Sweaty and loud and pounding their chests like gor—" Morgan hiccupped. "Sorry. Gorillas. How can you actually talk to anyone in there? It reminded me of parties at Woodford. Oh my God. Everyone just scream—" *Hiccup.* "Screaming and bumping into each other and who's going upstairs with who. So dumb! So . . . dumb . . ."

Avery focused on the blur of the storefronts and streetlights through the cab window, her stomach in her throat. "Yes," she said. "Very dumb."

Gentle snores purred from Morgan's mouth. The cab dropped her off first before heading farther uptown to Avery's apartment. Once Pete arrived a few minutes later, Avery buzzed him up and pressed her lips to his without a word, the kiss like a button that turned off her brain.

• • •

Avery and Pete woke up in her bedroom the next morning spooning, their legs entwined in layers of bed sheets. She couldn't believe she'd fallen asleep cuddling. She normally hated the way sweat collected under every fold of her skin, the way a guy's arms crushed her in an uncomfortable wrestling hold. She never got enough surface area on the pillow either, because guys' heads were always twice the size of hers. Relaxing enough to pass out was usually impossible.

Avery untangled herself from under Pete's grip and studied his face. He looked handsome and peaceful in her bed, his lips parted

SHE USED TO BE NICE 157

slightly and wavy hair tousled across her pillow. She padded barefoot to the bathroom to splash water on her face, feeling her hangover in the marrow of her bones. She needed to guzzle a whole bottle of Advil if she was going to make the Kleinfeld appointment with Morgan later this afternoon.

Pete stirred under the blankets, then rolled over and propped himself up with his elbows. A grin spread across his face. "Morning, sunshine."

Avery folded herself back under the covers. Her temples throbbed. She didn't have the energy to kick him out yet.

"Morning," she mumbled.

Pete yawned, the grin returning when he finished. "Last night was fun, huh?"

Avery nodded but said nothing else. Sex with Pete *was* fun. She was glad she could have that with him, at least.

"Sorry for texting you so late," he said. "I was pretty drunk."

Avery closed her eyes to block out the grating sounds of a garbage truck humming and a child screaming outside her window. "Same. I'm very hungover."

"Too hungover for Taylor Swift?" Pete navigated to Spotify and jerked his head toward the window. "She'll help with the noise."

"I can only handle *folklore*. Or *evermore*."

Pete hit play on "my tears ricochet." Taylor Swift's breathy vocals trickled into the air, a balm over the chaos happening outside. Avery rested her head on her pillow, feeling soothed.

"Nice choice," she said.

They listened in silence for a few minutes, exchanging the occasional peaceful glance and lazy, tired grin. A warm tranquility settled over Avery as she buried herself deeper into her bed, let her bare leg press against Pete's under the covers. She could stay just like this all day with no complaint. Maybe he didn't have to leave. Not yet.

When the song was over, Pete smoothed down his slept-in cowlick and turned to face her. Avery tensed. He looked like he was about to say something important.

"You know, I'm surprised you answered me last night," he said. "You didn't follow me back on Instagram."

Avery very much hoped they weren't going to have this conversation. "So what?"

Pete picked at a lint ball stuck to the sheets. "I kind of thought you hated me. After what happened with my parents when you came over."

Avery rubbed the sleep from her eyes. "I don't care about that. I don't hate you."

"Well, maybe hate is the wrong word . . ."

Avery narrowed her eyes. Pete clearly had something to say, and he should just say it before Avery's hangover worsened. Already she felt the beer shits gurgling in her stomach.

"I guess I thought you were done with me," he said simply. "That's why I haven't reached out in so long. If you were wondering."

Avery rubbed her hands up and down on her face. And here she was thinking this was just a booty call and not that deep. She should've known there was too much history between them to keep things casual, that he'd already shown her he was interested in more than she could give him.

"What do you mean, *done*?" she asked.

"Like . . . I don't know. We were starting a thing. A *fresh* start, I might add." His voice was soft, calling back to their conversation at Kenn's Broome Street bar. "And then we stopped."

Avery walked to her closet to grab a worn-in hoodie. Pete stared at her. She knew he was waiting for a response, but she needed to think carefully about how she was going to phrase this, how to tell him there was no beginning here because all it would lead to was an end.

"I mean, we haven't stopped anything," she said, slipping her head through the neck of her sweatshirt. "You can't stop something that never started."

"Of course it started. We're practically engaged. You've met my parents! My mom's already got her Italian-American grandbabies' names picked out."

SHE USED TO BE NICE

Pete tried to play off his reply with a smirk, but Avery didn't budge with even a chuckle. After a beat, she relaxed her face. His jokes weren't funny right now, but she didn't need to be such a bitch. Even though she *was* such a bitch.

"Sorry, it's early," she mumbled as an explanation. "And my head is pounding."

Pete gave a brisk, clipped nod. "Right."

Avery crossed her arms. She was disappointed. She thought Pete finally understood her and was giving her what she wanted. She thought they could hang out in a way that would allow her to remain surface-level. But she could no longer subtly dodge his attempts at emotional intimacy. She had to confront him directly, for his own sake. It was the only way. He would thank her in the long run when he found someone better.

"I hope you know nothing's going on here." She pointed back and forth between them. "You booty called me last night, and I responded to your booty call. That's all that happened."

Pete tipped his head to the side. "Booty call? What are you talking about?"

"You texted me at 11:00." Avery pulled her knotted hair into a loose bun on top of her head. She remained standing by the closet, away from Pete. "That, by definition, is a booty call."

"What is this, a nineties issue of *Cosmo*?" Pete asked through a burst of contemptuous laughter. "What makes 11:00, by definition, a booty call?"

Avery pressed two fingers onto the bridge of her nose. He wasn't getting it. "I don't want to date you, Pete."

Pete stared at the foot of the bed. Outside, the M-31 bus made a low buzzing sound and then drove away, belching an exhaust pipe into the street.

"Well, I mean, we don't need to be in a relationship or anything. Not right away." He hesitated. "But in the future, maybe. After we get to know each other."

After we get to know each other. The words rang loud between Avery's ears, over and over like a cast iron bell.

"I can't do that," she said.

"Why?"

Avery shook her head without responding. Pete could never get to know her. He would hate everything he found, everything that happened to turn her into this broken, unlovable person. She was so ashamed of what she'd done, of what Noah did to her. Of who she'd become as a result.

"Why?" he asked again, more urgently.

Avery stared out the window as tears welled on her lower lash line. She couldn't look at him. Her glassy eyes would betray her, would reveal the pain she kept buried deep inside, where nobody could find it. Where not even she could find it if she had it her way, if it didn't sneak up on her all the time without warning.

She swiped angrily at her eyes, removing the evidence. "I . . . I'm sorry," she whispered. "I just can't."

Pete removed himself from under the covers. He sat down on the edge of the bed and slipped on his shoes, and all Avery wanted to do was pull him toward her and plead with him to stay. Instead, she stared at a dust bunny gliding on top of her dresser, and watched him leave.

14

WHEN THE DOOR SLAMMED shut, all the tears Avery had been waiting to cry spilled out, like a thunderstorm breaking humidity. She spent the next hour curled up in a fetal position in her bed, alternating between shaking with sobs and staring numbly at her wall. All Pete had done was try to show her that he cared about her, and all she did was push him away. But she didn't know how to let him in the way he wanted to be let in. She would always keep a part of her past hidden, which would prevent him from truly knowing her. But if they started dating, eventually he'd find out about the infidelity. Eventually they'd talk about their exes, or one of her friends would slip something to him during a group hangout or—God forbid—at the wedding, or she'd just blurt it out herself out of guilt for lying to him. And what guy wouldn't immediately distrust someone with a history of cheating? What an awful start to a relationship. She wouldn't even be able to tell him what really happened either. He'd be judging her for something she didn't fully do.

She was about to drift off to sleep when her phone rang with a FaceTime from Morgan. She bolted upright and wiped the remaining tears from her eyes before answering the call. On her screen, Morgan's face was covered in the sticky remnants of different kinds of candy. A lollipop shaped like a strawberry was stuck to her cheek, the white dust of Sour Patch Kids made her lips sparkle, and melted streaks of what looked like red, blue, and green Skittles painted her forehead. Avery erupted in a fit of laughter.

"Morgan, *what* is going on?"

Morgan darted her eyes left and right, her mouth open in shock. "I literally woke up exactly like this."

Avery laughed so hard she couldn't catch her breath, thankful for Morgan's sweet tooth for making her feel better. During their junior year, after Morgan came home tipsy from the bar, she tried to bake an entire chocolate cake from scratch in the kitchen. Avery nearly peed herself watching Morgan spill milk everywhere.

Morgan pulled the lollipop off her cheek, wincing as it tugged at her skin. "I guess I decided I needed a snack last night and went to the bodega." Then she wiped the Skittle smears from her forehead.

"You are a disgusting person." Avery wiped tears of joy from her eyes. "Disgusting."

"I don't even remember eating them!" Morgan cried.

"Clearly you *didn't* eat any of them!"

A male voice mumbled something next to Morgan. Morgan turned the camera toward Charlie, whose face was swollen with sleep.

"Charlie, did you know your soon-to-be wife had a threesome with candy last night?" Avery asked.

"What?" Charlie sat up quickly, grabbing the blankets and clutching them dramatically. "You *cheated* on me?"

Morgan giggled. "I'm sorry, they were so juicy and delicious!"

"And I'm *not?*"

Charlie tackled Morgan in a hug, and Morgan tried to steady the camera on herself as Charlie tickled her. He kissed her over and over again, making her giggle so much that the phone fell out of her grip. Avery tried to admire their bond with a smile, but her expression didn't reach her eyes. She wondered if she'd ever have someone swollen-faced to wake up next to in the morning. Some-one who kissed her on the cheek and tickled her just to make her

SHE USED TO BE NICE

163

laugh. Someone who could see her for exactly who she was, and maybe love her regardless.

. . .

Racks upon racks of wedding dresses filled the massive showroom at Kleinfeld. The store was airy and bright, with white walls, cream carpeting, and elevated platforms where brides modeled dresses for groups of friends and family sitting on blue couches. Some brides looked upset, like none of their chosen dresses fit the way they'd imagined. Avery hoped that wouldn't happen with Morgan today. It would be disappointing if the dresses Morgan wanted to try on didn't live up to her expectations, but realistically, everything looked good on Morgan. She never needed Spanx and had a thigh gap a pickup truck could drive through. Avery once asked Morgan if she wanted to borrow some deodorant to rub between her thighs for chafing, and Morgan was like, "Huh?" Avery couldn't imagine what her body would look like in any of Morgan's picks. The cellulite lumps in her stomach and thighs would be on full display, pushing their way through the fabric to say hello. She'd have to suck herself into two layers of Spanx to shut them up.

"Good morning!" Morgan said brightly when Avery arrived at Kleinfeld holding an extra-large black coffee. "Afternoon, rather."

"Morni—I mean, afternoon." Avery squinted at her. "I have no idea how you're this not-hungover."

"I have no idea either. But who cares? It's wedding dress day!"

Avery couldn't help but laugh, even though she'd spent all morning sulking over Pete. On the subway ride to Kleinfeld, every time she'd seen a couple holding hands or leaning together against a pole, she would replay her and Pete's last conversation inside her head like a reflex. She couldn't stop hearing the desperation in his voice, couldn't stop summoning the image of him leaving her apartment. And she wasn't hopeful that being at Kleinfeld around all these happy brides would help her feel better. Avery wondered if any of these women had ever felt unlovable, and if so, how they overcame it enough to let someone promise to love them forever.

A woman in kitten heels approached Morgan, Avery, and Gabriela in the lobby that opened into the main showroom. A big glass case of tiaras sparkled across from the reception desk. The woman beamed. "Welcome to Kleinfeld, ladies! My name is Donna and I'll be helping you with your appointment today." Avery took a swig of coffee as Donna's chipper voice rattled her throbbing hungover skull. "Now, who's the bride?"

Morgan jutted her hand skyward. "Me!"

Donna smiled so wide her cheeks nearly popped off her face. "How wonderful! And this must be the beautiful mom?" Donna gestured to Gabriela, and Gabriela nodded, blushing.

"Wonderful!" Donna said.

Avery wondered how many times Donna had used the word "wonderful" with bridal parties today, or when she decided to replace it with "nice" or "sweet" or any other adjectives she had on rotation.

Donna looked expectantly at Avery, meaning it was Avery's turn in the roll call. Avery knew the drill. She'd seen *Say Yes to the Dress*.

She cleared her throat, preparing to amp up the enthusiasm and shove her thoughts of Pete out of her mind once and for all. Her fears around opening up to him were neither Donna's nor Morgan's fault.

"And I'm Avery, the maid of honor," she said.

Morgan squeezed Avery's hand. "We've been best friends since freshman year of college. I wouldn't want anyone by my side today but her."

"How *wonderful!*" Donna chirped.

Donna led the group through the showroom to a private dressing room, where three wrought iron white chairs were pushed up against the wall and a lilac silk robe hung from a hook behind the door. She took out some paperwork while Morgan explained the details about the styles she wanted—column silhouette, with a spaghetti strap or plunging neckline or both—while Donna wrote everything down and murmured her understanding. In the middle

SHE USED TO BE NICE 165

of the conversation, the door to the dressing room flung open, with Blair bursting through.

"Hey, y'all! I'm so sorry I'm late. My train from Boston was delayed and then I got lost on the subway and stuck in a cab in traffic. It's been awful." Blair turned to Donna and shook her hand. "Blair, bridesmaid." She turned to Avery next, a disturbingly wide grin plastered onto her perfectly made-up face. "Hi, Avery!"

Great, Avery thought. Just when she'd swallowed her sour mood. "Hey," she deadpanned.

She glanced at Morgan, who was thankfully too wrapped up in wedding dress bliss to notice the stilted greeting.

Donna ushered everyone out onto a couch in the showroom so Morgan could change into the first dress. As they sat down and shed their coats, Gabriela asked Blair how work was going, prompting Avery to roll her eyes and take out her phone to scroll through each of her social media apps in rapid brainless succession. Blair didn't stop bragging about her various roles at Deloitte until Morgan emerged in a spaghetti strap gown with a plunging neckline and a column silhouette, exactly as she'd requested. Avery's heart nearly burst through her chest as she took in the sight of her best friend, in a gorgeous wedding dress, as a *bride*. Avery didn't feel any bitterness about the lack of Spanx under that gown. Morgan looked perfect.

"You look stunning," Avery said, overflowing with joy and pride and delight and all the other overwhelmingly positive emotions you could only feel during the wedding season of the most important person in your life. She'd even momentarily forgotten about Blair.

"This one is amazing," Blair added.

Never mind.

Morgan's eyes misted as she spun around in front of the mirror on the platform. "I love it so much, but it's the first dress. This can't be it, can it?" She glanced nervously at Donna.

"Some brides fall in love at first sight!" Donna said. "But I always recommend trying on a few more, just in case."

Blair turned to Avery and gestured to the back of the store. "Wanna go look at bridesmaid dresses? Morgan asked me if we could figure out some styles we liked today."

Morgan shot Avery a concerned look, asking with her eyes if Avery would be okay. Avery met Morgan's gaze before confidently turning back to Blair.

"Sure," Avery said. "Let's do it."

Avery followed Blair to the back of the shop and started pulling some dresses from the racks to try on. Everything between them seemed strangely normal, given the circumstances of the last time they interacted at the engagement party. Any hope for reconciling their friendship was long gone, but maybe they could be civil with each other until the wedding. Then they never needed to speak to each other again. Avery could handle this, no problem.

"I love this one," Blair said, holding a green ruffle-trim faux-wrap dress in front of Avery's body. "This one would look beautiful on you. A-line dresses are great for curvy girls."

Avery opened her mouth to respond, but no words came out. Blair did not mean "curvy" in the nice way.

"That's, uh . . . pretty." Avery pulled out something pink and off-the-shoulder. "What about this?"

Blair pinched her eyebrows together and ran her fingers down the front of the dress. "I don't love the sash."

She pulled out a few more options, a yellow pleated tulle maxi dress and a light blue silk midi dress, and they headed to the dressing rooms at the back of the store before separating off to change. When they finished, they emerged in front of the huge wall-to-wall mirror to stare at their reflections. The silence between them expanded and filled the room, until Blair broke the dam.

"Can we talk for a minute?"

Avery remained stone-faced. She'd promised Morgan there would be no more drama, and she was sticking to her word, so she kept her eyes fixed on her dress. She'd tried on the pleated dress, and it was fine, nothing she couldn't find cheaper online.

SHE USED TO BE NICE 167

"I don't want to talk, to be honest," Avery said.

"I don't care." Blair tossed her hair over her shoulders aggressively. She was already seething. "I would do anything for that girl out there. She's my best friend. And you running out of her engagement party the way you did was *so* messed up. Morgan cried for half the night wondering where you went."

Avery kept her composure. "I get it. She and I talked about it. I apologized. Everything's fine."

"It's not fine to *me*. And it won't be to Morgan if you don't get your shit together." Blair's shallow Southern kindness was officially gone; Avery could practically see the shiny plastic melting off of her in hot fury. "This is an extremely special time in Morgan's life. I don't want you and your attention-seeking antics ruining it."

Avery was so naive, thinking she and Blair could get truly along. Avery wondered if the members of Blair's women's empowerment group at Deloitte knew she was actually a huge bitch.

"It's crazy how little you've changed, Blair. Still so judgmental."

"And you're still a skank ho, so we're even."

Avery was stunned into silence. At school, Blair had mostly called her names behind her back or in comments on Avery's Instagram posts left by burner accounts. Avery knew Blair was sensitive about infidelity after her mom cheated on her dad, but Avery hoped the passage of time would soften at least some of Blair's prickly frustration toward Avery. The fact that Blair could still muster up enough rage to spit such a name to Avery's face, however, seemingly proved the opposite. The state of their relationship was worse than Avery thought.

"I don't know where Morgan got off making *you* her maid of honor," Blair added, as though this fact inflamed her resentment. "How're you gonna juggle all these responsibilities when you've got your mouth around the groomsmen's dicks?"

Avery stood up as tall as she could, which was a solid three inches above Blair. From the outside, she looked strong and untouchable, but under her dress she was soaked in a cold, nervous sweat. She felt transported back to senior year, alone in her dorm room and stalking her friends on social media as they hung out without her, with Blair leading the charge on making plans that excluded Avery.

But she wasn't going to let Blair intimidate her now.

She took a breath. Only seven more months until the wedding, and then she'd never have to see Blair's smug, prissy face again. *Keep it together. You got this.*

"It sounds like you're jealous that you're not maid of honor," she said.

Blair huffed. "Please. I would never be jealous of someone like you. Women who betray kind, undeserving men should go to hell."

Okay. That's it. Avery jabbed a pointed finger in Blair's self-righteous face. She refused to be a punching bag for Blair's anger over family issues that had nothing to do with her. And she was done taking shit from someone who didn't know what the fuck they were talking about.

"You know what?" Avery said through gritted teeth. "I know we're in the same bridal party, and we have to put on a happy face for the sake of this wedding, but I'm not speaking to you anymore unless I have to. So you can fuck right off." Avery stole one last glance at herself in the three-way mirror. "And this dress is hideous. I'll find nicer ones online for half the price."

Avery stormed into her dressing room and peeled off her dress, which was sticky from her agitated sweat. She left the dress pooled on the floor before heading back into the showroom, where she slammed her body into the couch and tightly crossed her legs. Her insides buzzed with adrenaline; she felt legitimately high from telling Blair off. Avery tried to maintain a neutral expression so Morgan wouldn't suspect anything, especially since she already reacted too much to Blair at the engagement party. But she couldn't help it. She stuck up for herself more than she ever had before and she needed to relish it.

SHE USED TO BE NICE 169

Blair came in behind Avery a few minutes later and sat on the opposite end of the couch without making eye contact. Then Blair set her phone down next to her as she rummaged through her purse. The phone buzzed with a text, the name "Noah McCormick" flashing on the screen. Avery squinted at the screen to read his full message to Blair.

And then her breath caught.

Blair snatched the phone away before she could read it all. But not before Avery swore she saw the word "babe."

The walls around her caved in. Were Blair and Noah *dating*?

Avery massaged her temples in dismay. Her only consolation about this was the fact that nobody knew about Noah's involvement that night senior year, so of course Blair didn't know either. God, Avery hated Noah so much. He was like a scummy politician skating by on his lies, and Blair just *fell* for it.

"Random question," Avery asked Morgan as nonchalantly as she could on the subway after they left Kleinfeld. "Is Blair dating, um . . ." She mashed her lips together, unable to bring herself to say his name out loud. But she needed confirmation that this was real.

Morgan raised an eyebrow. "Noah?"

Avery swallowed. "Yes."

"You know, I saw him on her Story last night and had the same thought." Morgan took out her phone to play an Instagram video of Blair and Noah at a sushi restaurant. Rows of sashimi were splayed out on the table, and a bottle of white wine sat in a cooler. The next slide was a picture of Blair and Noah standing outside the restaurant. Blair was facing him with her hand flat on his chest and her leg flicked out behind her, and they were kissing.

"Looks like it," Morgan said. Horrifyingly, it sounded like she approved. "Good for her! Cute, smart, and rich. Very nice catch."

Avery rubbed her eyes so hard that she saw stars, trying to make the images go away. She couldn't believe she was the only person who knew the unspeakable things Noah was capable of and

170 ALEXIA LAFATA

had to continue keeping her mouth shut until the wedding. She was suddenly struck by a loneliness that penetrated bone deep.

"What, are you jealous?" Morgan asked.

Avery shot daggers from her eyes. "Absolutely not."

The subway pulled to a slow stop. Avery bolted out of the car, with Morgan trailing behind.

"If you were interested in him, you could've told me!" Morgan called out as they hustled down the street. "I would've given you dibs."

Avery kept making rapid, determined strides forward, almost knocking over an elderly woman carrying grocery bags in her effort to be out of earshot of Morgan's asinine comments. She only stopped when she approached the front door of Morgan's apartment building, at which point Morgan caught up and flicked her eyes to Avery, waiting for a response.

"Morgan, I am nowhere near interested in Noah," Avery snapped. "Things with Pete have picked up, actually."

Dammit, she thought. It just slipped out.

But if Noah and Blair could find love, two people who were nightmarish in their own unique ways, why couldn't Avery? Did Avery honestly think she was more unlovable than *those* two?

"Really?" Morgan asked.

Avery studied Morgan's sparkling eyes, the upturned corners of her lips, the rush of color on her cheeks. There was no turning back. Morgan was already writing Pete's name next to Avery's in black permanent marker on the Brooklyn Botanic Garden seating chart.

"Yeah!" Avery smiled warily at her lie. Well, half lie. Things had *sort of* started picking up with Pete, in that maybe they were going to be each other's booty calls. But then she'd kicked him out of her apartment. All because he liked her for more than her body. Because he wanted to get to know her as a person—the thing most sane women longed for after a few dates. What a crime, for him to be so normal.

"Wait, how did this happen?" Morgan asked. "I thought he didn't have your number."

SHE USED TO BE NICE

"Well, he didn't. Then I ran into him in SoHo and now he's . . . got my number, I guess." Avery flashed an uncertain smile.

"Wow, this city is so tiny." Morgan squeezed Avery's arm excitedly. "I'm so happy for you! We should double date! I bet Charlie would love to see him again. This is so promising for the wedding!"

Avery laughed. "Slow your roll on that one. I gotta see how things develop first."

"I get it, I get it. Like I said, Pete's invite is up to you." Morgan grinned with all her teeth. "But I'm remaining hopeful."

As they made their way through Morgan's foyer and stepped onto the elevator, Avery realized she could deny it no longer. She wanted to be with Pete. He'd gotten under her skin, like that dark dot of lead that buried underneath you after you accidentally stabbed yourself with a pencil in elementary school. It might've hurt going in, but now it was there forever as a part of you, like a new birthmark. A new beginning. A fresh start.

She took a deep breath and texted him.

15

TWO DAYS WENT BY without a reply from Pete. On the third day, after putting together some admittedly sloppy traffic reports for Patricia, Avery took a stroll outside and stopped at a small gated park by her office, where a teenager with a handlebar mustache passionately played the saxophone and pigeons congregated around an old woman feeding them breadcrumbs from a plastic baggie. Avery flinched as she walked past the pigeons vigorously ruffling their feathers to sit down on a bench far away. Then she stared at the text she'd sent to Pete: *hey i'm sorry for being weird this weekend. can i buy you a drink to make it up to you? totally understand if you hate me and never wanna see me again, but i figured i'd give it a shot*

She tightened her grip on her phone, like if she squeezed hard enough those three little dots would pop up. But the screen remained agonizingly blank. She was starting to lose hope. She wasn't clueless enough to think Pete lost his phone or was too busy with work or whatever people say to convince themselves they weren't getting rejected. She knew he was ignoring her. She almost didn't want her phone to buzz again because she knew it wouldn't be Pete. It would just be someone else, or worse, one of those phantom vibrations that only come when you're waiting for a text, and she'd have to relive the disappointment all over again.

SHE USED TO BE NICE 173

Defeated, she spent the next few minutes listening numbly to the saxophone player before dragging herself back to her office building. The doorman didn't say hello to her, nor had he acknowledged her at all over the past few days. He was always nicer to her when she looked pretty. Lately, though, the dark circles under her eyes were extra deep and pronounced, and she came to work in a greasy bun and no makeup, which basically meant she was invisible.

"Do you think your pattern here isn't obvious?" she asked, pointing to her face. "Honestly? Do you?"

The doorman's eyes darted left and right. "Huh? Miss, what are you talking about?"

Avery shook her head. He was an idiot. And so was she, for letting this get to her. So *what* if she was invisible to a doorman, as well as to most men over these last few days, who used to make small talk with her and hold the door open for her and generally act like she existed? Who cared if they thought she wasn't worth a second look now? Well, she cared. She could always rely on the quick hit of male attention to make her feel better about herself, but now she didn't even have that. She'd have to suffer through the pain of rejection with nothing to temper it. She knew her appearance was her biggest asset to men but, Christ, she was still a person. She shouldn't need to be dolled up to deserve a simple hello.

Back at the office, Avery decided to start the bridesmaids email chain to distract herself from waiting for Pete's reply.

From: Avery Russo
To: Emma Smith, Kim Garrett, Sandra Santana, Justine Hartford,
 Blair Montgomery
Cc: Morgan Feeley
Subject: Hi, bridesmaids :)

Hey ladies!!!!

Avery figured if she used enough exclamation points nobody would know she was on the verge of a mental breakdown.

174 ALEXIA LAFATA

My name is Avery and I'm Morgan's best friend and maid of honor. I realized I didn't know everyone in the bridal party, so I wanted to send a group email to introduce myself as well as get to know all of you! I'm so excited for this year and I hope you all are, too.

I also wanted to provide some information about our first order of business. Attached to this email are some photos of bridesmaids dresses. Morgan wants us to love the dress so she's asking us to choose, and we're all going to vote for our favorites. If you could send over your vote ASAP, along with your dress size, that would be awesome.

Best,
Avery

Blair replied, just to Avery, a few seconds later.

Thanks for finally sending this! Was wondering if I was going to have to do it. 😑

Avery rolled her eyes. She and Morgan had *just* finalized some dress options. She typed a reply.

I got it thanks!!!

"Are you writing a story for us?" Kevin called out from his cubicle.

Avery glared at him over the dividers. "No." Because she was a masochist, she peeked at her phone again to see if Pete had responded. He hadn't.

Kevin glanced up from behind his laptop, his reading glasses perched on his nose. "Sorry, I heard some enthusiastic typing and got excited."

Avery turned her phone face down again. A second later, she thought she heard it vibrate and turned it face up. But it was blank, except for a notification from her Seamless app asking her to rate her recent order from The Mansion. She sighed and flipped her phone face down again, but before her brain could tell her to stop, her fingers reached for it again to turn it back up. She groaned and turned it back down. Then up.

SHE USED TO BE NICE 175

Masochist, she thought. *I simply must be a masochist.*

Kevin rolled over to Avery's desk. "By the way, I have a second round of interviews at *Entertainment Weekly* today," he whispered. "For a principal product manager role."

"That's awesome!" Avery replied, also in a whisper. "I mean, I'll hate you if you leave, but that's very exciting."

"I'm just over this place." Kevin glanced over his shoulder. "Did you hear what happened with Patricia? A journalist at Bustle found one of her tweets from 2014 with the word 'faggot' in it."

Avery made a face. "Wow, that's shitty."

"I know. She kept it very hush-hush here. I only know because my friend at *GO Magazine* told me. You should Google her Notes apology. It's so pathetic. *I take full responsibility for what I said and I am committed to amplifying the voices of the blah blah blah.*"

"That is so lame."

Kevin nodded and rolled back to his desk, then Avery turned back to her laptop to dig into some work. *Metropolitan* broke a huge story today about a woman who accused famed TV producer Dave Moore of sexual assault, and Avery was tasked with writing all the social copy about it. Moore was behind all kinds of beloved classic comedy dramas, so this allegation was huge. Avery held her breath as she skimmed over *Metropolitan's* account of what happened, careful not to read too many disturbing details—a difficult task, considering she needed to get the language exactly right in her copy. Then she shared the story on *Metropolitan's* social media channels. It only took seconds for a torrent of replies to appear in their mentions. *These false rape accusations give a bad name to REAL rape victims,* replied one user. Another wrote, *Noo! Me & You is my comfort show!! I refuse to let there be a stain on its legacy.* An anonymous user replied with *bullshit. she's mad that he didn't give her a part in a show. typical Hollywood drama.* Yet another just wrote *stupid sluts*

Avery wrote the same social copy on Instagram, unwilling to do more than the bare minimum for this story. She hoped it would disappear soon so she wouldn't have to keep covering it, because if not, she might be right behind Kevin in quitting.

176 ALEXIA LAFATA

Her phone buzzed. She snatched it face up, and her heart stopped when she read Pete's name. She almost dropped her phone in the process of swiping it open.

Yea, that's cool. Where did you have in mind?

Avery squealed and responded immediately. *amazing!! how about Jimmy's Corner? tonight at 6?*

Jimmy's Corner was an unassuming but classic dive bar near the center of Times Square, which—Avery knew—was objectively the worst place in Manhattan, with its blinding seizure-inducing billboards stretching twenty stories high and hostile tourists taking photos on their iPads. But that area of Forty-Second Street was the easiest to get to no matter where you were in the city, and Avery didn't want to complicate things with Pete any more than she already had.

Three dots appeared on the screen. Avery's cheeks hurt from smiling. Pete was typing! He was using his fingers on the screen while their text message window was open! It was almost like they were touching.

Sure. See you then.

Avery spent the rest of the day avoiding work, specifically doing nothing more with the Dave Moore story, in favor of staring at the clock and watching the minutes drag. At 5:30 PM on the dot she bolted from her desk and hustled to the bar to ensure she arrived early, then ordered the strongest beer on the menu and grabbed two empty stools toward the back. The great thing about Jimmy's Corner, besides the unique boxing memorabilia decorating the walls, was that despite being right in the middle of the city's tourist trap, tourists rarely came here, meaning it was rarely crowded and there was always a place to sit.

Pete appeared at the front door at 6:10 with what looked like a fresh haircut, his shiny brown locks tamed while still retaining their signature thickness and volume. Avery's fingers pulsed with the need to touch them.

"Hey," Pete said when he approached her. His voice was cautious.

SHE USED TO BE NICE 177

"Hi." Avery gestured to the empty seat next to her, inviting Pete to sit. He obliged and waved down the bartender to order a beer.

"Put it on my tab," Avery insisted.

Pete didn't protest. He put in his order and then looked at her expectantly.

She wrung her hands out in her lap. Already her palms were sweating.

"Thanks for meeting me," she began. "I'm . . . very grateful for a chance to explain myself. Even though I probably don't deserve it." Again, Pete didn't protest. Avery wiped her slimy hands on her jeans. She hadn't prepared what she was going to say, which in hindsight was maybe a bad idea. "I'm sorry about this weekend. I shouldn't have kicked you out of my apartment without an explanation. But I'm still not ready for a relationship or anything . . ."

Pete's expression was blank. Waiting.

"Right now," she said.

He raised an eyebrow. "What do you mean?"

"I'm saying, I'm not ready for a relationship . . . right now." Avery took a long sip of her crisp beer to cool off. "But maybe . . . in the future. Like you said."

Pete tipped his head to the side, confused. "So you're changing your mind."

"Well . . ." Avery cleared her throat. "After you left my place the other morning, I realized that I . . . do like you." She hesitated as more panicked heat pricked the back of her neck. "Well, no. I didn't *realize*. I've known this whole time. I've just . . . been in denial?" She was so bad at this. "I wanna hang out more, is what I'm saying."

Pete leaned back in his seat and eyed her curiously. "Like how?"

Avery fidgeted, readjusted her sticky thighs. "I don't know. Like, dinner?"

"Dinner? I can get dinner with my mom." Pete sipped his beer, staring at her over the rim of the glass. "But I believe the word you're looking for starts with the same letter."

Avery squeezed her eyes shut and opened them again. "I wanna go on a date. With you."

Pete cupped his hand over his ear. "What did you say?"

Now he was just being annoying. But she deserved this. "I wanna go on a *date*," she said. "With you."

Pete laughed. "Now that's a sentence I never thought I'd hear from you." He took another gulp of his beer and patted his lips with a cocktail napkin. Was he making her wait for his answer on purpose? "But yes, sure, I'd love to," he said at last. "Even though you made me take the ungodly early ferry home while hungover without at least offering to get a bagel with me."

Avery's mouth quirked. "I'm sorry about that. I've been all over the place. It's no excuse, but work's been really busy, and between that and doing maid of honor stuff with Morgan for the wedding . . ." She swallowed in response to her own lie. The first of many she'd surely tell him. "I haven't been fair to you."

"It's okay." Pete gave her an affectionate nudge. "I get it. I'm just gonna rub it in a little more. I can't let you off the hook that easily."

They locked eyes for a few beats. Avery tore away her gaze, unsure of what to say next and growing more insecure with every passing moment of quiet. This would not be the first time she'd need to convince herself that she wasn't too much of an asshole for him. They sat in the heavy silence, with Avery wishing she could say more about why she'd been so aloof with him until now. He was clearly hurt and trying to hide it by keeping it light with humor, like they were each avoiding being vulnerable in their own ways.

"I guess not," she said softly.

He tossed her a small smile, indicating that maybe everything truly was fine. She stared straight ahead behind the bar, smacking her lips together to hide her own smile shoving its way through. She hoped that he would always be this forgiving and that she'd remain this open to him. Maybe soon he'd be able to trust her fully, and she him.

SHE USED TO BE NICE 179

"Just so you know, this doesn't count as the date," she said.

Pete laughed. "Don't worry, I'd never take a date to the hell-hole that is Times Square. Are you free Friday though?"

Avery hesitated for a moment, to make a feeble attempt at taking the power back. But it was pointless. Her defenses were down the second she'd texted Pete to meet up. And she could tell by the amused smile on his face that he loved it.

"Friday sounds great," she said.

And she'd never admit it out loud, but she loved it, too.

• • •

That Friday, before her first date with Pete, Avery spent an hour flipping through her closet to find something to wear. The more outfits she tried on, the more her body overheated, forcing her to peel everything off her sweaty skin like Velcro. She hated every single thing she owned. What was she *thinking* with this aggressively red wrap shirt, and in a size extra small no less? Even fucking Morgan wouldn't fit into this.

She felt the beginnings of a temper tantrum boil inside of her, so she settled on the first outfit she tried on, a black semi-sheer blouse and tight jeans. Then she spritzed perfume on the insides of her arms and the back of her neck, the parts of her body Pete would be the closest to when they hugged hello. It was a trick she'd learned from Blair. Which irked her to think about now.

She made her way downtown to Carroll Place, the Italian restaurant where Pete had made a dinner reservation. Butterflies fluttered in her stomach as her subway car flew underground, and she kicked herself for being such a cliché. But she hadn't been on what she would consider a real, meaningful date since Ryan, and his idea of a date was usually just burritos at the Chipotle down the street from campus. She didn't blame him—they'd been on a college budget—but still. This date with Pete felt different, was the first time drinks with a guy in her postgrad adult life could lead to more than just sex.

On her walk from the subway, Avery stopped in front of the passenger seat window of a parallel parked truck to study her reflection, smooth out her shirt, and fluff up her hair, pressing her mouth in a hard, nervous line. The night she ruined everything with Ryan was not going to continue ruining the rest of her life. Starting tonight, she was going to try to believe that she was worthy of good things in the present, no matter what happened in her past. She would give this thing with Pete a shot, and maybe eventually he could be her date to Morgan and Charlie's wedding, and not just as her armor against Ryan and her friends but also as her boyfriend. Maybe. Eventually.

Pete was waiting for her outside the restaurant with his back pressed against the wooden exterior. Avery's eyes lit up at the sight of him in a checkered button-down and pair of fitted black jeans. He smiled back at her.

"You look nice," he said. "Hot date?"

Avery rolled her eyes, but inside her heart swelled as she breathed in the mint and sandalwood floating off his shirt. He looked so handsome and smelled even better.

"Funny," she said.

Carroll Place was dark and cavernous, with deep red brick walls and twinkling chandeliers dripping from the high ceilings. Couples were snuggled together in two-tops and paired off at the communal table to the right, and upstairs on the second floor, at least what was visible from the lobby, it looked like more of the same. Avery was determined to not be overwhelmed by the implications of a place as romantic as this, by her questions about whether she deserved to be here with Pete at all, having this nice of an evening. While this was only a first date, it was still a date, and some indulgence and romance were allowed and even expected. She needed to just go with it. Pretend like she belonged here, with him.

A waiter led them toward a more private back room, to a small, intimate table dotted with a flickering white candle and situated right below a crystal chandelier. Soft instrumental jazz played from the speakers overheard. After they sat down, Pete ordered a Manhattan with an orange slice and a large square ice cube, and Avery

SHE USED TO BE NICE 181

ordered a glass of red wine. Avery couldn't believe they were doing this, that they were just a man and a woman sitting across from each other on a first date. It was so simple, yet so monumental, and now there was no turning back. Romance mode had been activated. The first layer of protection over her hardened heart had been sloughed away. Luckily the waiter arrived quickly with their drinks and Avery could take two huge gulps of wine.

"You seem nervous," Pete observed.

Avery put down her glass. She wasn't just nervous. She was terrified. She felt exposed and raw and they hadn't even started a conversation yet. Surely they were not going to dig into her traumas on the first date. She needed to relax.

"This is just new for me," she said.

"What is? Dinner?" Pete leaned closer to her and coolly picked up his drink, swirling the ice around in the glass. His calm self-possession only emphasized Avery's jitters.

She gave him a side-eye. "Yes, Pete. Eating is a foreign concept to me."

"Well, you've done it every night for twenty-three years. I'm confident you'll figure it out tonight." Pete smirked as the waiter came by to take their orders. He ordered mozzarella sticks for the table and the cheese ravioli for himself, and Avery ordered the large portion of spaghetti with meatballs. At least she could eat her comfort food to soothe her nerves.

"Great call on the mozzarella sticks," Avery said when the waiter left. "I'm starving."

"You know, you pronounce mozzarella like a real Italian-American from Jersey," Pete said. "*Muzz-a-dell.* That's spot-on."

Avery blushed. "I know. Everyone at Woodford made fun of me, but I can't pronounce it in any other way. Like . . . mozz-ar-ella." She overpronounced every syllable and shivered. "It feels weird."

"Actual Italians don't even say it like we do, but I don't care. Like, what even is capi-cola? It's *gabagool!*"

"Or how about cala-mari?"

"No," Pete said, cringing. "Anything other than *galamad* is painful."

Avery grinned mischievously. "Or mani-cotti?"

Pete covered his ears with his hands. "I can't! It's sacrilege!"

Avery laughed. "Just another reason I'm going to hell then."

"Right there with you. I don't believe in God anymore. It kills my mother and her *Lord's name in vain* bullshit. I grew up Catholic and everything, but as I got older I was like, why are all the priests pedophiles?"

Avery nodded in agreement. "And then they shame women for having sex with legal, consenting adults. I really bought into the Catholic purity thing growing up. My mom constantly reminded me that the only person she'd ever slept with was my dad, and not until their wedding night."

Pete scrunched his face. "I bet that's a mental image you could've done without."

"Definitely," Avery said with a chuckle. "She made it sound kind of romantic though. Like he was her one and only. I always thought that part of it was sweet. But the religious angle never sat well with me. It made me feel like I needed to apologize to God when I slept with my high school boyfriend. I was so scared of tainting myself with sex."

Avery tensed. How could she have revealed so much about herself already? But Pete was so open and easy to talk to. It was tough to keep her mouth shut.

"How times have changed," he joked as he took a piece of bread.

Avery gasped light-heartedly. "Slut shamer!"

"I'm kidding! I also had sex with you in that bathroom. I, too, am a slut."

Pete placed his white cloth napkin onto his lap. Avery did the same. She forgot that that was proper dinner etiquette.

"Have you noticed that the church is always almost exclusively filled with old people?" he went on. "My dad has a theory that it's because they're gonna die soon and need to reserve their spot in heaven."

SHE USED TO BE NICE

"Better there than the fiery pits." Avery paused dipping a piece of bread in olive oil. "Hold on. Aren't you not supposed to talk about religion on a first date?"

Pete shrugged. "Whatever. There are no rules."

"Is that so? Because if I remember correctly, you're the one who said we did this 'backward,' and that you knew what my naked body looked like before you knew my last name. You *love* rules."

Pete's lips curved into a smile. "I'll make an exception for you."

Avery wrinkled her nose. "Cheesy."

"You love it though."

"I implied nothing of the sort."

The waiter came by and set their steaming plate of mozzarella sticks down on the table.

"Now *that's* cheesy," Pete said, nodding at their appetizer.

"Okay, before we keep doing this, you should know that I despise puns," Avery said, the seriousness of her voice mostly, but not entirely, in jest. "My boss at *Metropolitan* loves them, but I will actively not write them in my social copy, even if one is right there."

Pete laughed. "Noted. I am in full support of finding little ways to make work tolerable."

"It's the only way to live."

"It is." Pete offered Avery the plate of mozzarella sticks, and she selected one before he grabbed one for himself. "Speaking of, I've started idly browsing some audio production job openings. Just seeing what's out there. But I don't think I'd ever actually quit my job."

"Why wouldn't you?"

"I'd have to cut my salary expectations in half, maybe even less. As soul-sucking as finance can be, I don't think I can do that yet."

Avery understood. She didn't like her job *and* didn't make a ton of money. At least Pete had one of those covered. "I get it.

Money isn't everything, but it would be naive for anyone to say it didn't make life easier."

"Exactly." Pete sipped his cocktail. "Maybe once I put away more savings, I can start to think about a career in music, which would be the dream. But for now, I'd be an idiot to quit finance."

Pete noticed Avery's water glass was low and casually refilled it with the jug on the table. Avery smiled at the gesture.

"Well, for what it's worth, I'd like you no matter how much money you made," she said.

Pete widened his eyes in mock-surprise. "Wait, you like me?"

Avery laughed. "Shut up."

At the end of the night, Pete paid for dinner and held the door open for Avery when they left the restaurant, two more gentle-manly gestures Avery couldn't help but clock and revel in. Outside, yellow lamps lining the street flickered above their heads, and a tipsy, handsy couple slid into a cab that drove down the block and disappeared. The couple reminded Avery that they'd approached *that* part of the first date, and she couldn't deny that she was looking forward to this. She enjoyed their dinner conversation, enjoyed all the little ways Pete seemed to want to take care of her already, but this was the moment she thought about the most: her hands wrapped around his neck, her fingers running through his silky hair, her lips surrendering to his with a sigh. If she bored him with talk of her upbringing or was at all awkward tonight, this was her chance to make up for it. Because despite how amazing Pete was, at the end of the day he was still a man, and men always secretly wanted this more than they let on, even when they were trying to be gentlemen. Or even, like Noah, when they weren't.

Pete pulled away from her embrace. "Let me get you a cab home."

Avery bristled, stung by the rejection. "Seriously? Just come over. Celeste is gone tonight."

Pete shook his head softly. "Not tonight."

SHE USED TO BE NICE

185

She huffed. How dare he embarrass her like this. "I'll get my own cab, thanks." She turned on her heel to walk away, until Pete spoke again.

"Hey, wait! It's not that I don't want to. Obviously I do. But, really? Sex on the first date? Have some class." Pete bounced his eyebrows on his forehead, signaling he was kidding.

Avery crossed her arms. "That's not funny. Are we never gonna have sex again now?"

Pete sighed. "Of course we will, Avery. But we started off kind of intense with that." He stared into Avery's eyes and laced his fingers through hers. "Why don't we just slow down a bit?"

Avery shivered at his tenderness. "It's hard to do that when you're touching me, you know."

Pete lifted his hands up. "I'll never touch you again."

"No!" Avery grabbed his hands and put them on her shoulders. "Don't stop!"

Pete laughed and slipped his palms around her waist, making her feel small and safe. He bent down to kiss her once again, this time without letting the kiss slide into anything passionate. Instead, he kept his lips loosely on hers, forcing her to slow down and focus on the closing space between them. She felt light-headed when he pulled away.

"It's very hard to resist you, trust me," Pete said. He put a gentle hand on her cheek. "But I want to savor getting to know you, now that I can."

Avery didn't know what to say. Her sexual experiences with other guys were always so animalistic and carnal, just a body using hers as a means to a satisfactory end. She rarely cared about what happened when they got drinks or during the actual sex afterward. It was the conquest element that she loved the most, the opportunity to see herself as someone who could take the wheel after Noah stripped her of that agency. But she couldn't remember the last time she'd been treated like this, like she was something delicate and precious. Like she was worthy of being taken care of, of being seen.

186   ALEXIA LAFATA

"Okay," she said, completely flustered. "Sure. Yeah. That sounds . . . nice."

"Now, can you please let me get you a cab? My mother will be so thrilled to know I was chivalrous."

Avery giggled in a fizzy kind of way. She was surprised that sound could still come out of her mouth. "Sure," she said. She knew she could hail her own cab—and she would have, since she didn't like taking the subway this late at night anyway, with all the crazies ready to use her for masturbation material—but she liked that Pete wanted to do this for her. She liked that she was allowing him to do this for her.

An empty cab pulled up next to them. Pete handed the driver some cash, then opened the door to the back seat for Avery. Before she slid inside, Pete put his hands on her waist and kissed her again, a little deeper this time, enough to leave her wanting more. Her lips tingled with the feel of his as she climbed into the back seat. And as the driver sped up the FDR, she looked out the window, beaming at the skyline sparkling across the East River.

• • •

"Why can't Pete keep his toothbrush at your apartment?" Morgan asked, taking a sip of her margarita.

A few weeks had passed since Avery's first date with Pete. Morgan and Avery were meeting for happy hour at Ofrenda, a delicious Mexican joint in the West Village, where little Mexican flags mixed with string lights hung across the ceiling and behind the bar. Avery felt unsure about Pete today. He'd slept over after they went out for Indian food last night, and this morning, she did a double take when she saw his toothbrush sitting in her cabinet, in the empty space next to her tampons. As if he thought he had a *spot* in her apartment now.

"I don't know," Avery said. "It's a lot of assumptions. It means you're confident enough to know that you'll be back."

Morgan blinked at her. "But he can assume that. You're dating."

SHE USED TO BE NICE 187

"We went on three *dates*. That doesn't mean we're *dating*." Avery ran her finger around the salty edge of her margarita glass as she mulled over the word. She definitely liked being around Pete, and there was something attractive about a guy who was so secure in his feelings for you that he thought nothing of leaving one of his belongings behind because he knew he'd get it next time. But Avery wished Morgan would use a more low-pressure word to describe what was going on. Something like talking or hanging out. "It just makes me uncomfortable. And is it that unreasonable for me to want to take things slow with someone?"

"No, it's not unreasonable, Avery." Morgan's voice was gentle. "But you can't let the mistake you made affect you forever. At some point, you have to forgive yourself."

A lump swelled in Avery's throat. If only Avery could tell Morgan the truth about that so-called mistake, about the shame that sat like an elephant on Avery's chest. Then Morgan wouldn't think moving on was so easy.

"I'm trying, Morgan. The fact that I'm going on dates with him is huge for me."

"I know it is!" Morgan put her hand on top of Avery's reassuringly. "I just want you to give yourself permission to open up, you know? Let him see you for the incredible person you are. You are so much more than that night senior year."

Avery took another bite of her taco. Morgan wouldn't understand. She didn't know how that night impacted everything Avery thought about herself, infiltrating her body like an incurable virus. When she looked in the mirror, she didn't see an incredible person. She saw someone who allowed horror to descend upon her through her reckless actions. She saw all the pieces of herself that Noah had taken from her, all the fragments of who she once was.

"Especially because I'm pretty sure Ryan is coming to the wedding," Morgan went on. "It's not a definite yes yet, but he told Charlie he's been saving up for the flight."

Avery groaned. "For fuck's sake," she muttered to herself. She slid her gaze to Morgan, who was trying not to frown. "I'm not blaming you. I know you warned me. I'm just—" Avery dug her fingers into her hair. "It's obviously going to be hard for me to see him."

"I know. I completely get it. But you have Pete now, right? And you like him, don't you?"

Avery gave a reluctant nod. "I like him a lot, Morgan."

"Good! Then you should try to allow him to make you happy again. Give him that chance. And give *yourself* that chance. Then bring him to the wedding and show everyone you've moved on. It will make them want to move on, too."

Avery knew Morgan was right. She would love to get to a place where she could bring Pete to the wedding, to not only prove to everyone that she was trying to be a different person now, but to also prove that to herself. And maybe Pete just left a toothbrush at her apartment because he didn't want to feel like a vagabond after trekking all the way from Staten Island. Or maybe he truly just liked her and wanted to keep seeing her. Either way, it wasn't like it was a proposal.

Avery swiped idly through Instagram while Morgan flagged the waitress for their check. She paused on a post from The Cut about the Dave Moore case. Another woman had come forward with accusations against him. This time it was actress Robyn Weasley, who claimed she hadn't gotten the lead role in the show *10 Things I Love About You* because she refused to perform oral sex on him. He ultimately forced himself on her anyway, and she was so rattled by the experience that she went fifteen years without stepping foot in an audition room. Avery quickly scrolled past the image of his saggy, wrinkled face, which looked like an actual ball sack. Her stomach stayed wedged in her throat as she tried to cleanse her phone screen with other posts.

"Awwww," Morgan cooed while she also scrolled on her phone. She showed Avery her screen, and Avery's heart raced as she realized she was looking at a photo booth strip of pictures of Noah and Blair, captioned *Best times with my love.*

Avery made a gagging sound. Despicable men were truly everywhere, like city rats. "Nobody wants to see that."

SHE USED TO BE NICE

"I think it's cute!" Morgan used her fingers to zoom in on the post while Avery preoccupied herself with something in the opposite direction to spare even her peripheral vision of Noah's face. She shoved the last of the chips on the table in her mouth. "I'm happy for Blair. I don't think she minds the long-distance either. She hasn't had the best luck with dating. Her mom's affair really messed with her."

Avery swallowed her chips. Some of them weren't chewed enough and scratched her throat on the way down. "Is her mom still with that guy?"

"Yeah. And now she wants to marry him and have his babies. Which is just sick, honestly. He's like a baby to *her*."

Morgan zoomed in on the post again. Avery's eyes snagged on it before she could look away, her brain taking a snapshot against her will. She saw the satisfied smile on Noah's face and the twinkle in Blair's eyes as she laughed and laughed; they were like a black and white sample image on a frame at a home goods store. No matter how hard Avery rubbed her eyes to dissolve the images, they wouldn't disappear. They only came stronger into view, making the fact of it clear as day: Noah was getting everything he wanted, and Avery was still suffering in silence.

But the wedding was only six months away now. She just had to hold it in a little bit longer.

16

LUSH GREENERY COVERED THE ceiling of Gallow Green, giving the illusion of being outside the city under a canopy of trees in a forest. Clusters of pink and white flowers bloomed from each corner and dangled toward the floor. The air smelled sweet, like pine needles, masking the scent of soot that normally permeated the air this side of Manhattan.

"Oh my *God*," Morgan said when she arrived, her long eyelashes fluttering in awe as she admired the space. "This place is stunning."

Avery beamed, smoothing down her off-the-shoulder sage green dress she'd gotten on sale at Anthropologie. Planning Morgan's bridal shower lunch with Gabriela had been a lot of fun. Gabriela was footing the bill and therefore led on most of the planning, but she gave Avery tasks that made her feel like she had a big role, too. First, Avery put together a guest list that didn't include Noah, which was incredibly satisfying and reminded her how much less stressful this event would be compared to the engagement party. Then she spent hours researching evites that matched the restaurant's ambiance and floral arrangements for all the tables. Gabriela also enlisted Avery to find a cool restaurant to cater from that Morgan's friends would love, with Gabriela bringing trays of arroz con gandules, tostones, and pernil for family.

Now Avery stood near the front entrance directing guests to the hors d'oeuvres and the poster board with "Morgan's Bridal

SHE USED TO BE NICE

Shower" written in swirly pink script on which they could sign. Guests mingled, signed the poster board, and helped themselves to gold-rimmed flutes of champagne stacked in a tower. Avery allowed herself only one glass to keep her head clear. She vowed, somewhat desperately, to stay optimistic that today would go smoothly, wiping the engagement party from her memory.

"Eat some, Avery," Gabriela urged, nodding at her homemade spread of food. "Before it gets cold. You must be ravenous."

Avery realized she was indeed starving after spending all morning setting up and gratefully made herself a plate. Just as she started eating and went to compliment Gabriela on how tender the pernil was, she heard a voice.

"The avocado toast looks soggy."

Blair's whisper was too loud, like it was meant to be overheard. Avery turned around. Blair and Emma were standing behind her in line at the main buffet, inspecting the selection of avocado toast, roasted chicken with vegetables, and Caesar salad.

"Welcome, guys!" Avery said brightly, refusing to let anyone to piss her off. "Help yourselves to whatever."

"Hey, girl!" Blair gestured toward the buffet. "This spread looks *delish*. Where'd you cater the food from?"

"The Silver Spoons Dining Room. It's that New American place on the Upper West Side." Avery kept her voice within a normal human pitch range, even though Blair did not.

"I've heard of them. Didn't the city close them down for unsanitary conditions? I read somewhere that they gave, like, thirty people norovirus when a cook didn't wash his hands after handling raw fish."

All the reviews Avery had read for this restaurant online were positive. Blair had to be lying. But she would not allow Blair to make her feel inadequate anymore, and especially not today.

"Well, luckily there's no fish from them, so we'll be okay," Avery said. "And they were plenty open today, so—"

"Any food can be contaminated with norovirus, though." Blair waved her hand. "I'm sure it'll be fine!"

192   ALEXIA LAFATA

Avery peered at the long picnic table next to the buffet, where
Morgan was happily chewing on a piece of her exceptionally
sturdy, virus-free avocado toast. Avery flashed Blair a joyless smile
as she loaded her plate with food and hustled away to sit next to
Morgan, who was in the middle of talking to her Grandma Peggy.
Avery had met Morgan's grandmother Margaret, affectionately
called Peggy, a couple of times, once in college and again during a
visit to Morgan's house in Rhode Island, but Avery wasn't sure if
she remembered who she was. Anyone, though, would be better
conversation than Blair.

"Oh, Grandma Peggy!" Morgan said when she spotted Avery.
"You remember Avery, right? You haven't seen her since before
your knee surgery."

Avery took Grandma Peggy's wrinkled hand. "So nice to see
you again. We're glad the doctor cleared you for travel."

Grandma Peggy smiled, revealing an impressive set of bright
white dentures. Her pearl earrings gleamed under the overhead
lighting. "Oh *darling*, nothing that bonehead doctor said was going
to stop me today. I was watching my granddaughter get married
whether he liked it or not."

Grandma Peggy lifted her half-empty glass of champagne in
salute and snapped her fingers to the beat of the music playing from
the speakers, the sleeves of her houndstooth lady jacket falling to
expose her bony wrists. Avery leaned in close to Morgan's ear.

"She knows this is just the shower, right?"

"I . . . think? My dad did tell her," Morgan whispered. "By
the way, you're doing a great job today. Everything looks gorgeous, and you picked a great restaurant. How are you doing right
now, being around Blair and Emma?"

No doubt Morgan was thinking about the engagement party,
fearing a repeat. But Avery refused to let that happen. "I'm doing
great," Avery said. "Blair had some shit to say about the buffet but
whatever, I'm ignoring it."

"Good, good." Morgan gave an encouraging smile. "I know
this has been tough on you, but I'm really proud of you." She

SHE USED TO BE NICE 193

paused, fixed her gaze right onto Avery and leaned forward a little. "But you'd tell me if there was something else going on, right?"

Avery's heart nearly screeched to a stop. "What do you mean?"

Morgan bit into a piece of her roasted chicken, taking her time chewing and swallowing it, like she was thinking. "Well, I know you're still upset about the breakup. And that you feel guilty about what you did. But after our conversation at Ofrenda, I just . . . want to make sure nothing else happened."

Avery glanced over her shoulder, for some reason. As though Noah had materialized and prompted Morgan's questions. "What else would have happened?"

Morgan put up her hands. "I don't know, Avery. I'm just putting it out there. Because sometimes you seem *really* upset. Like it's particularly difficult for you to move on. Or something."

"Yeah, because my whole life changed. I lost everything. And everyone. You were there."

Morgan held Avery's stare for a few curious beats. Avery didn't mean to sound so defensive. She just wasn't sure why Morgan was doing this right now, or what gave Morgan the impression that Avery was hiding something. Avery thought she'd been doing a decent job hiding her feelings about Noah lately, actually. Did her face give something away at Ofrenda when Morgan showed her those Instagram pictures of Noah and Blair?

"You're right," Morgan finally said with a sigh. "I'm sorry. I don't know what I'm thinking. I'm just checking in, that's all."

Avery softened. "Don't worry about me. Let's focus on you today."

And then—thankfully—they did.

· · ·

As the party wound down and guests began to leave, Avery helped Morgan load her gifts into large shopping bags to make them easier to travel home with. She'd just started dismounting the poster board when Blair stormed out from the bathroom, making Avery jump in surprise. She'd thought Blair had left.

"I have *incredible* news," Blair said to Morgan. "I just got off the phone with Noah. He said we can use his new mountain house!"

Morgan's jaw dropped. A disbelieving smile slowly made its way across her face. "Are you joking?"

"Nope! We're going to Colorado, baby!"

Morgan jumped up and down and grabbed Blair in a tight hug. Blair usually did her best to stay composed but this news must have been big, because even she started yelping with reckless abandon along with Morgan.

Avery narrowed her eyes. "What are you guys talking about?"

Morgan grabbed Avery's shoulders. "Noah's letting us use his *stunning* new mountain house in Colorado for a joint bachelor and bachelorette party!" Morgan inhaled deeply through her nose and exhaled dramatically out her mouth. "I can smell the fresh, unpolluted oxygen already."

A layer of sweat coated Avery's entire body. She had to spend a whole *weekend* with Noah? In his *house*?

"Wait, we're not doing separate parties?" she asked. "We're doing them together?"

"Yes!" Morgan squealed. "Sorry, I thought I'd told you. I like the idea of combining. It'll be fun!"

Blair swiped through photos on her phone, showing Morgan and Avery a massive stone mansion set high on a mountain and overlooking a twinkling lake. Thick stone beams stood in front of the house, and underneath the beams was a long, winding entryway that led to mahogany stained glass double doors. It was the exact kind of relaxing, scenic getaway in the middle of nature that Morgan would love. Gallow Green was a dumpster in comparison.

"Isn't it gorgeous?" Blair swooned. "Noah bought it after Meow Monthly hit two million monthly subscribers. The company really took off after they added dog and hamster care packages. Gosh, if I'd known Randall guys were capable of this, I wouldn't have dropped out of my Business of Econ class freshman year . . ."

SHE USED TO BE NICE 195

"Hold on, Morgan." Avery's chest was tightening. Fast. She barely had enough air to choke out the words. "Isn't . . . isn't the bachelorette party supposed to be a girls-only thing? Your last chance to . . . to celebrate being single with your girlfriends?"

"I *guess*," Morgan said, but it was clear she did not agree. "But I can't pass up on this. Look at this house!" She waved toward Blair's phone. "It's paradise."

Avery swallowed nervously. "But . . . but I already started brainstorming some stuff. I . . . I even found some bachelorette shirts. I found an adorable set with a white shirt that says 'I said yes!' for you and black ones that say 'We said party!' for us. They're . . . they're super cute." Avery felt small and stupid, like she was grasping for arguments she knew would not be persuasive. But she was desperate.

"Why don't you bring those shirts to Colorado? We'll wear them there!" Morgan insisted. "Look, I know you're not into the outdoors, but this house is everything I've ever wanted in a weekend getaway." Morgan was trying to speak calmly but failing; her energy was too high, her joy too unrestrained. She pointed at the photos on Blair's phone again. "Those mountains! Those *wildflowers*! Please? Be excited, for me?"

Avery scanned Morgan's face, wide-open and panting. A whole weekend. In Noah's house. Where Avery wouldn't be able to escape him no matter how hard she tried: His style would be reflected in the interior design choices; his favorite food and drinks would be stocked in the fridge; the scent of his laundry detergent would be embedded in the sheets she'd sleep on and the towels she'd dry her naked body with after a shower. He would be everywhere, reflecting and refracting back at her around every corner like a scary hall of mirrors.

"Of course I'm excited," she said, her smile so brittle it nearly crumbled.

There was nothing else to say.

17

WHICH DO YOU LIKE better w the dress? Morgan's text was accompanied by a picture of a gold necklace with a wide band next to a pair of long diamond earrings.

Avery thought it over, then wrote, *earrings. i think with a plunging neckline you need to go statement earring*

These kinds of conversations, in which Morgan would text Avery pictures of jewelry or hairstyles or silverware design and request her thoughts, were happening with increasing frequency since the bridal shower a couple of weeks ago. Today when Morgan texted, Avery had been following a burst of productivity that inspired her to clean out her fridge. She had just chucked a six-month-old loaf of bread she'd defrosted and forgotten about and an expired jar of mayonnaise that, when she opened it, was alarmingly chunky, into the garbage when her phone buzzed with Morgan's reply.

Thanks! I'll do that

Three dots appeared on the screen again. Avery wondered if Morgan was finally going to tell her that she'd decided on a centerpiece. Morgan was torn between a clear hexagonal bowl or tall glass cylinder adorned with either white ribbon or gold, and wasn't sure which combination would overshadow the flowers and which would complement them. Avery liked the hexagonal bowl and Morgan did, too, depending on which influencer's wedding she stalked online that day.

Btw hows Pete? Can we double date yet?

SHE USED TO BE NICE   197

Avery hadn't talked about Pete to Morgan since they discussed the toothbrush incident at Ofrenda, though Morgan was itching to reconnect with him and officially make him part of their friend group, which she probably hoped would encourage Avery to invite him as her plus-one to the wedding. But Pete was busy with work lately, always sending Avery Snapchats from his late nights in the office, sometimes even at 2 AM. It reminded Avery of what he'd told her about his music career dreams a few months ago at his parents' house. It seemed like the corporate world was not only sinking its teeth into him, but also taking a huge bite.

She tossed a smoothie bowl pocked with fuzzy green mold into the trash. *maybe. he's been really busy with work. i haven't even seen him much lately*

It surprised Avery how much she cared about Pete already. They'd only hung out a handful of times so far, and she was still getting used to the idea that he would actually stick around, but so far his presence in her life had inspired mostly positive feelings. Of course, the self-doubt still crept in sometimes; she always wondered if the next layer she peeled back about herself would be the one to scare him away. But so far he'd stayed. To be fair, though, he didn't know her *that* well yet, so his impression of her wasn't an impression of *her* and more an impression of the parts that she was willing to show him at this point, which was both a relief and a source of some stress. How long could they keep up these playful and mostly superficial conversations via text about movies and TV shows and funny memes? At some point he'd want more.

Her phone buzzed. *Well when he's free, we need to hang,* Morgan said. *And I know you're weird about the word "dating" so we won't call it double dating. We can call it a group hang! Just a casual group hang among some pals*

Avery knew people used the word "dating" in all kinds of different ways. But to her it felt so serious, like she was trying to find someone to settle down with. Or that whoever she was dating *was* the person she was trying to settle down with, that "dating" was synonymous with "relationship." That was why she preferred "talking" or "hanging out." It was the bare bones of the truth but the truth nonetheless, a way to honor what she and Pete were doing without the pressure that came with labels. Because the closer they got to a label, the more of herself she would have to give him. A label made things definitive, absolute, complete, when she'd only so far given him fragments. She didn't want to rush the process of letting him see more of her than she was ready to show.

But regardless of what she called it, it made her happy. *Pete* made her happy. Lately she found herself feeling disappointed when she didn't wake up to one of his late-night Snapchats. She also realized that if she wanted to bring him to the wedding, she'd need to get comfortable with him knowing more of her and integrating into the friend group. She knew Charlie and Morgan saw the best in her and would never have gossiped to Pete about what happened with Ryan whenever they hung out in Boston. A double date with friends Avery trusted would allow her to dip her toes into mixing Pete in with everyone else. She had less than six months to get comfortable with that, if she wanted to bring him as her plus-one in August.

ok let's do it, she texted. *what about karaoke? Planet Rose?* Avery smiled to herself as she remembered preteen Pete singing and playing guitar on his Instagram video. She'd love to watch him sing like that in person, all uninhibited and carefree.

Yessss!!!! Morgan replied with a string of heart-eye emojis.

Avery closed her fridge and opened a new text to Pete. Their last conversation was a debate over what happened to Tony in the finale of *The Sopranos.* (Pete said he was clearly killed; Avery believed it wasn't as obvious as people thought, even if it was true. They concluded that they'd do a series rewatch soon to confirm the clues together.)

She sent him a text. *wanna do karaoke with Charlie and Morgan at Planet Rose? when are you free?*

Her phone buzzed ten minutes later. *I'll actually finally be free Thurs. Sorry it's been insane at work but Thursdays are usually my slower day.*

that's ok! no shame in getting that bread

You know it. I miss you though.

SHE USED TO BE NICE 199

Avery held her phone to her heart, which had melted into a puddle. Then she darted her eyes left and right, embarrassed, like someone had caught her.

i might miss you a little bit too, she texted back. *MIGHT. key word Haha. Avery. You're impossible.*

. . .

On the night of karaoke, Avery was in such a good mood that she was convinced the guy at the pizza shop she stopped at beforehand slipped her drugs. She was about to take a bite of her dollar slice when she was startled by a dog barking close to her feet, making her yelp and drop her pizza. Disgruntled, she flung open the front door to Planet Rose, where Pete was already sitting at the bar and scrolling through his phone. He looked up, his face dotted with rainbow light from the disco balls hanging from the ceiling.

"Hey, you!" he called out.

Avery dug her hand into a bowl of peanuts on the counter and cracked some open without responding. Pete frowned.

"Uh oh, everything okay?" he asked.

"No," Avery muttered. "Some dog just barked at me and made me drop my pizza. He's lucky it wasn't a fifteen-dollar pad thai."

"Awww," Pete said with a tiny laugh. "You're not a fan of dogs, are you?"

Avery shoved a peanut into her mouth. "You think?"

"I remember how you reacted to Milo. He's scary, though."

"Whatever, I'm here. Hi." She kissed Pete hello. He kissed her back and pressed his body flush against her. The closeness made her woozy.

"Want a beer?" he asked. "I've got a tab open."

Avery nodded, and Pete ordered her a drink, leaning closer into her. All her nerve endings zeroed in on the spot where the skin on his arm brushed hers. She felt light-headed and anxious in a good way, like her feelings for him had already grown since the last time she saw him, like she was a preteen girl harboring her first crush, both scared and exhilarated to bump into him after class.

She really hoped that today would go well, that she could keep all her bad parts and past hidden from him for as long as possible.

A bell above the front door jingled, signaling Morgan and Charlie's arrival. Morgan lifted her eyebrows in Avery's direction and then darted her eyes to Pete. She scanned him up and down with a satisfied smile on her face. Avery shook her head. Morgan was never one for subtlety.

"Good to see you again, Pete!" Morgan said, pulling Pete in for a hug.

Charlie went next, shaking Pete's hand and clasping him on the back. "What's going on, man? I haven't seen you since college."

"I know, it already feels like forever ago," Pete said. "Small world, huh?"

Avery's heart swelled. She couldn't believe she was hanging out with her best friends and the guy she might, if she didn't reveal anything about herself that would ruin it, one day call her boyfriend. She never thought she'd be here again, with anyone.

Pete nodded at the bar. "You guys want a drink? I got the first round."

"Thanks! I'd love a beer," Charlie said. "Morgan?"

Morgan hung her purse on the back of the chair. "Vodka soda, please."

"You're brave," Pete said, laughing. "I think I had enough of those in college for the rest of my life."

"It's not by choice, trust me. I'm just trying to keep the calories low. Gotta fit into the wedding dress."

"I hear ya. The metabolism's starting to slow for all of us." Pete patted his stomach in sympathy, which was hilarious because Avery knew for a fact that he had abs. But if there was one thing Pete knew how to do, it was make jokes at his own expense. And Morgan laughed, which probably was his goal. "But congrats again!" he added. "Very exciting. When's the wedding?"

"August twenty-second. So soon!" Morgan beamed. "At the Brooklyn Botanic Garden."

SHE USED TO BE NICE 201

"They do weddings there? That's awesome. I bet it's beautiful."

"It is. It's amazing."

"And *very* expensive," Charlie added with a self-deprecating chuckle. "My best man hooked us up with a discount, though. He's a start-up founder and his company is pretty successful, so he's got some serious connections. He's probably gonna be on *Shark Tank*, actually."

"Wow, that's super cool." Pete sounded too impressed. Avery indulged in an eye roll. "I love Mr. Wonderful. He's such an ass but he's so entertaining."

"Totally," Charlie agreed. "Noah's been talking to the producers. Nothing's final yet but it's gonna happen."

Avery crossed her arms tightly over her chest. Of course Noah would be on *Shark Tank*, would continue to be successful and trick even more people into thinking he was not scum. She looked at Morgan and motioned to the blue binder of karaoke song choices splayed out on the bar. Morgan followed her over, out of earshot of the boys.

"Isn't that cool about Noah and *Shark Tank*?" Morgan said with a smile when they were alone.

Avery shifted her eyes to Morgan, then back to the binder. She flipped a page. "The coolest."

Morgan didn't notice Avery's indifference. She even kept smiling. "And it's so fun that Pete and Charlie know each other. It really is such a small world. Do you know Pete's astrological sign, by chance?"

"No, why?"

"Can you find out? He always seemed like an Aquarius to me, the couple of times I met him."

Avery laughed. "I truly don't care what his sign is, Morgan."

"Fine, fine. My overall point is, I like him." Morgan's brown eyes caught the light under the glow of the disco ball, her voice dreamy and full of hopeless romanticism. "I really hope you'll bring him to the wedding."

Avery looked over at Pete, and a warm pink blush spread across her cheeks when he met her eye. The more they hung out, the harder it was going to be for Avery to see herself *without* him at the wedding. She couldn't deny how special it would feel to have him on her arm, someone who saw the good in her in the face of so many people who didn't. Having Pete by her side could make the wedding not only tolerable, but enjoyable.

Morgan and Avery finalized their song selections, and Pete and Charlie joined them on the zebra print couch in the main karaoke room so that they could begin. The lyrics to Avery's song choice, "Delicate" by Taylor Swift, came up first on the projector. She took the mic, stood up, and began to sing. Or more like scream. She wasn't an amazing singer, exactly. She was talented enough to be in her high school musicals, but there was a reason she was mostly cast in roles that required more speaking than singing. But she forgot how much fun performing was, so she grabbed Pete's hands and dramatically serenaded him with the unbridled confidence of her seventeen-year-old self as he encouraged her and sang along.

While belting out a lyric, she felt the tickle of a breeze on her shoulders. She looked up. A white fan mounted on the ceiling had begun to spin, the blades whirring and picking up speed.

Her chest tightened. Her song continued to play, but she couldn't hear anything except the sound of the whirring growing louder above her. She swallowed and tried to focus on singing, but she had to be messing up, because she couldn't hear anything but the—

Whirr . . .

She'd forgotten all about that ceiling fan, the incessant low buzz it made while Noah pinned her down that night senior year and gave her bruises the shape of fingers wrapping around her wrists. It was the only other sound she'd been able to hear aside from his grunts and her own drunken voice trying to tell him no.

Whirr . . .

She remembered now, too, how freezing Ronald's bedroom was. Avery had no idea why it was that cold. It had been October

SHE USED TO BE NICE 203

in New England, yes, but the windows were closed, so no draft had been coming in, yet the fan was cranked up so high. Maybe Noah had turned it up on purpose to drown out her cries.

Whirr . . .

She took a shaky deep breath, trying to calm down. *You're in the East Village,* she reminded herself. *You're in Manhattan, in New York City, far from Woodford College, far from that bedroom with Noah—*

"You were so good!"

She'd finished?

Whose voice was that? Where was she?

"Avery? Are you okay?"

She blinked a few times, brought herself back to the present. She stared at Pete. She was somehow sitting on the couch next to him. "Hey, yeah, sorry," she said. "I'm just—"

Whirr . . .

Goosebumps erupted on her arms. She was suddenly frigid. "It's been a while since I performed like that. Guess I got overwhelmed."

"Well, you killed it," Pete said, his arm around her. "I'd for sure come to your concert."

Noah wasn't here. She wasn't in danger. She wasn't—

"Thanks," she muttered. "Hold on, I'll be right back."

Avery chugged the rest of her beer on her walk to the bar to get another one. The whirring sound didn't leave her head for the rest of the night, even as Pete serenaded her next with his karaoke song of choice. Even as they headed back to Avery's apartment together at one in the morning and snuggled under the covers in her bed. Even as she brushed her lips against his cheek and moved her naked body on top of him, trying to move on. Trying to erase that night senior year with more nights like these.

• • •

The following week, Blair came down from Boston to stay with Noah in Brooklyn for a few days, and Morgan suggested everyone come over for a pregame. Naturally, she encouraged Avery to invite Pete. But Avery was hesitant to invite him on another night out, embarrassed about how she'd acted toward the end of karaoke. She'd drunk much more than he had, almost puking in the cab during the ride back to her place and then knocking over the crowded shoe rack in her foyer. Somehow, though, Pete didn't seem to care. They had great sex the next morning, then took a walk to get bagels like nothing had happened.

And for the days that followed, it seemed, even more confusingly, that Pete's feelings for Avery grew. He'd started sending her good morning texts, wanting to FaceTime more regularly, and had taken to calling her "babe" on a semi-regular basis. Avery found this very suspicious. The insecure part of her thought he was only being sweet out of obligation, like he was taking pity on her or that she was some project he wanted to fix. The smaller, slightly less insecure part of her wondered if he was just encouraged by the double date with Charlie and Morgan. Like he knew that was her way of letting him in and allowing him to get to know her a bit more. She did her best to focus on the latter part and go along with his kindness, hoping his motives were pure and borne out of real feelings for her. Especially because she wasn't going to bring up her panic attack on her own.

Avery decided she'd acquiesce to Morgan's request to hang out, even if it meant she'd have to be around Noah for an extra unplanned night, but she wasn't comfortable bringing Pete around the larger group yet. It was a big enough deal that she took him on the double date and an even bigger deal that he'd witnessed her having a panic attack of such magnitude. She feared the other potentially worse triggers that awaited her if she were in the same room as Pete, Noah, and even Blair, as would be the case at Morgan's pregame. Who knew what random thing would set her off next and then what kinds of questions Pete would start to have about what was going on with her and her friends? He might not have noticed *this* panic attack, but she knew it wouldn't be the last one. Her panic attacks were like landmines she needed to carefully avoid, the explosions secrets she was not yet ready to share.

SHE USED TO BE NICE

"This feels like college!" Morgan said as she cranked up the music in her living room and began to dance. "I know, I have no rhythm. Don't tell my mom."

Avery laughed. Morgan was such an awkward dancer; Gabriela always made fun of her, saying Morgan couldn't possibly be her Puerto Rican daughter. Morgan used to do a handstand and twerk against the wall in their dorm room, and—God help her—her limbs were just out of control. The girl was all pointy elbows and scrawny knees.

Avery's laughter immediately stopped when Noah came into the living room and gave Charlie one of those stupid dude-hugs, with Blair following right behind.

"You know Blair, if you moved here, we could hang like this all the time," Charlie said.

"I know." Blair pouted stupidly. "I've been thinking about it. Just to be closer to Noah."

She kissed Noah's cheek. Avery flinched. Noah and Blair were officially together. Her Instagram was filled with repulsive couple photos accompanied by cringeworthy pun captions: a picture of her and Noah eating pizza with the caption *You stole a pizza my heart* (ugh); a picture of them on a dock in Maine, captioned *My Maine squeeze* (ewww); a picture of them holding kittens at the Humane Society, captioned *He's my purr-son* (gag). Eventually Avery couldn't sign onto Instagram without getting assaulted by the posts, so she had to mute Blair entirely. Real life, sadly, didn't have a touch screen.

Just five more months until the wedding, she thought. *And then you'll never have to see these people again.*

"It's hard with our busy schedules to find weekends to visit," Noah said. "I was gonna go to a conference in San Francisco this weekend for Meow Monthly, but I decided to stay, or else I wouldn't see her for so long."

"Speaking of, any news on *Shark Tank*?" Morgan asked.

"Not yet," Noah said. "But you'll all know as soon as it's confirmed."

Charlie gave him an enthusiastic high five. "So sick, dude."

Avery chugged her screwdriver in an effort to wipe the smear of disgust from her face. Then Charlie grabbed a handful of shot glasses and set them down on the coffee table in the living room, shouting at everyone to take one. Perfect timing.

Everyone threw their drinks back, reacting with varying levels of gagging. Morgan disappeared into the kitchen after she was done to grab a chaser and refill the snack bowls. Blair kept sputtering the loudest.

"Charlie, my gosh, was that raspberry Rubinoff?" she choked out.

"Yeah, it is . . ." Charlie sounded intrigued. "Why?"

Blair kept coughing before stopping abruptly to wipe her mouth. "I made a vow to myself that I'd never drink it again."

"Why not?" Noah asked.

Blair sunk into the couch and crossed her ankles. "No reason."

"Awww, come on! There's gotta be a story there," Charlie egged her on.

"Tell us, tell us, tell us!" Noah chanted.

"Okay!" Blair cleared her throat. "I . . . okay. Fine. I drank too much one night at school and hooked up with that guy with the mohawk."

Noah burst out laughing. "Wait, you hooked up with that kid? The one who walked around listening to heavy metal on full blast with no headphones?"

"That guy was in my history class! He was weird as shit!" Charlie smacked his leg, howling with laughter. "That's hilarious."

"Trust me, I regret it," Blair said, sounding mortified.

Noah looped his arm around Blair's shoulders affectionately. "It's not a big deal, babe."

"Yeah, in *your* opinion," Blair replied. "But *I* am embarrassed."

"You're being dramatic. It's fine."

Then Noah took a beat. Looked right at Avery.

And as she gulped down the rest of her drink, he added, "We've all had stupid drunken hookups."

SHE USED TO BE NICE   207

The acidity of Avery's screwdriver did nothing to disintegrate the tightness in her chest.

He knew. He fucking knew.

Is that all they are, Noah? she wished she could scream back, but the words were lodged deep in her throat and she couldn't dig them out. *Just stupid drunken hookups? What if one person was significantly more drunk than the other, couldn't stand up straight or speak in complete sentences? What would you have to say about those? About what you did to me?*

She buried herself in Instagram, her only real distraction from this current hell. But when she opened the app, the first post on her newsfeed was a zoomed-in picture of Dave Moore's crusty face and a caption summarizing the accounts of the two women who'd accused him of sexual assault. She quickly scrolled past it and clicked off her phone. Was there no escape?

"Avery, I've been meaning to ask, is Pete free the weekend of the bachelor party?" Charlie asked. "My coworker can't make it anymore so we have an extra room, if you wanna bring him."

Avery slid her gaze to Morgan, who'd just re-entered the living room carrying a bowl of pretzels. Morgan put the bowl down and clapped her hands excitedly. Had she put Charlie up to this?

"Oooh, yes! Invite him!" she squealed. "We need to even out the guys and the girls."

"Yeah, otherwise I'll look like I have no friends," Charlie said with a laugh.

"Who's Pete?" Noah asked.

None of your fucking business. "This guy I'm seeing," Avery said. "No big deal."

"His name's Pete DeFranco," Charlie explained. "We were buddies in college but lost touch after graduation, so Avery definitely knows him better now. We worked at G.E. Records together in Boston. I brought him around Woodford a few times, but I don't think you would've been there, Noah. Were you at the Dino-Whores party?"

Noah pursed his lips in thought. "Nope, can't say I was."

Charlie gave him a playful shove. "Randall kids were too cool for that, I get it."

"It's possible that I met him there," Blair offered. "But I have literally no idea. Everyone was in those ridiculous dinosaur costumes. I don't remember."

Avery looked at Morgan, who gazed hopefully back. It was as if Morgan thought the confirmation that Blair and Noah had never met Pete was all Avery needed to hear to bring him around the friend group. It certainly didn't hurt, but Pete meeting people from Woodford now could still risk him having conversations that Avery wasn't comfortable with him having yet.

Then she sighed. She supposed this integration would have to happen eventually if she wanted any shot at being normal again.

"Is it weird if I invite him to the bachelor party but not the wedding?" she asked.

"Who said you're not inviting him to the wedding?" Morgan teased.

"Okay, let me rephrase. Is it weird if I invite him to the bachelor party when I'm *not sure yet* if I'm inviting him to the wedding?"

"I think they're different," Charlie said with a bemused shrug. "The bachelor party is just a party, at the end of the day. The more, the merrier."

Morgan nodded. "Totally agree. The wedding is way more formal. Definitely a higher bar to entry. Anyone would understand that."

Avery needed to seriously think about all of this, if she wanted to keep seeing Pete. Which she did. And there would come a point where isolating him from her friends would seem strange, the ironic, self-fulfilling prophecy of not wanting him to suspect anything by behaving in ways that were suspicious. *That* might spark more questions from him than anything else.

"All right," she said. "Maybe I'll see if he's free."

"Yay!" Morgan cheered. "You should help plan the weekend, too. You were so good at doing the bridal shower. Why don't you and Noah find stuff for us to do in Colorado?"

SHE USED TO BE NICE 209

"Like drinking," Charlie added, holding up his beer.

"That sounds good to me," Noah said earnestly, like this was a serious request from his dumb investors that he'd prioritize immediately. Avery would've treated it the same way if she'd been asked to work on it with anyone else. But all she felt was panic. "Avery?"

She reflexively turned toward the sound of her name, then looked away when she realized it was Noah who'd said it.

"Here." Morgan took out her phone. "Let me text Noah your number—"

"No!"

The word flew out of Avery's mouth before she could stop it. She lunged forward and tried to knock Morgan's phone out of her hand, prompting Morgan to shriek in surprise. Avery's heart beat violently in her chest, inching up her throat. Everyone stared at her, alarmed and confused.

"Sorry," Avery muttered. *Chill out, chill out, chill out.* "I . . . uh, lost my balance for a second." Avery wiped the dust off her pants. Blair stared at her with one sharp eyebrow raised. Morgan's head was tilted to the side in worry. "It's fine, yeah. Sorry. You can . . . you can give him my number."

The crease in Morgan's forehead softened, and she slowly went back to typing. Seconds later, a *whoosh* sound came from her phone. "Sent!"

Charlie suggested they call an Uber before the lines at the bars got too long, and everyone murmured their agreement and gathered their belongings. Avery busied herself by helping Morgan clean up. Panic swelled in her chest, her hands trembling as she tied the drawstrings of a garbage bag into a tight knot. Should she change her phone number so Noah couldn't reach her? No, that would invite way too many questions. Who changed their phone number out of nowhere, for seemingly no reason?

But it was only no reason to everyone else. To Avery, Noah was the reason for everything. She just needed to keep pretending until the wedding that he wasn't.

18

COMEDY CELLAR SMELLED LIKE beer, old wood, and musty carpeting. A man holding a clipboard led Avery and Pete down a hallway covered in inky newspaper clippings into the main room, where the comedians would do their sets. Their second-row seats were so close to the stage, they'd be able to see sweat bubbling on the performers' foreheads.

"I thought this place would be much bigger," Avery said as she scooted over to make room for a couple seated beside her. It was her first time here at the iconic venue and she was excited, taking it all in. "My apartment is bigger, and that's not saying much."

"It's not," Pete said with a laugh. "Your place is small."

"Listen, at least I don't live with my parents."

Pete pretended to stab himself in the chest with a knife. "Ouch! You went there."

Avery looked around the venue, at the big mirror stretching along the back wall and the famous colorful "Comedy Cellar" sign lit up on the stage. Her gaze snagged on a framed photo of Louis C.K. hung up next to photos of other comedians who did stand-up here in the past. She frowned. She'd once been a huge fan of that guy.

She leaned in closer to Pete, grateful that he was one of the good ones. "Well, I'm happy we're here together."

SHE USED TO BE NICE 211

"Me too." Pete slung his arm across the back of Avery's chair, his delicious sandalwood cologne making Avery feel heady and exhilarated. "What'd you do last weekend?"

Avery didn't want to think about last weekend. The only thing she did after Morgan gave Noah her phone number was get progressively more drunk and resist the urge to text Pete strings of unintelligible words. At the bar, she realized she wasn't having a good time because she wished he was there, so she left alone before midnight, bought a slice of pizza that she ate in the cab ride home, and put herself to bed. She hadn't felt such an allegiance toward a man since Ryan. That she didn't want to stay out all night searching for stimulation, satisfied by the knowledge that Pete was on the other side of her *good night* text and she'd see him soon enough, felt something like progress toward a more stable emotional state.

"Not much, just hung out with some friends," she said. "What about you?"

"It was my cousin's birthday, so we had a little party at my aunt's house." Pete cleared his throat. "My mom actually asked about you."

Avery's ears perked. "Yeah? What'd you say?"

Pete nudged her, smiled bashfully. "Wouldn't you like to know."

Avery leaned forward, her heart warming at the memory of Gina, the familiarity of her. How awful Avery had been to cut their meeting so short that night on Staten Island. "I would, actually."

"Oh, nothing. She just asked where that nice girl was that she met a few months ago." He spoke in a relaxed and airy sort of way, like what he was saying wasn't a big deal, but Avery was relieved to hear that Gina still thought she was nice.

"And what did you say?"

"Well, first I told her you were more than just nice." Pete nuzzled into Avery's neck, making her ticklish. "I told her you were smart, and beautiful, and funny, and *fun* . . ."

Avery was momentarily disoriented by Pete's positive descriptors of her. Was he talking about her, or someone else? She almost felt like she was tricking him, the way he could only see so much

212 ALEXIA LAFATA

good in her. Or maybe it was possible that she wasn't so bad, if a guy as great as Pete thought she was great too.

"Pete, stop!" She giggled and shoved him away lightly. "We're in public!"

He blinked hard a few times while the rest of his face remained expressionless. "Avery, we had sex in a bar bathroom. The jig is up."

"Fair. I'm trying to be more civilized now, though. No more sex in public bathrooms, okay?"

Pete laughed. "That was my first time anyway, so that's fine with me. But if you change your mind, let me know. Would happily do it again."

A waitress came by to take their drink orders. Then the lights dimmed, the chatter quieted down, and the host, a scruffy man with a beer belly, came onto the stage and introduced himself as Steve. He told some jokes to loosen up the crowd before zeroing in on Avery and Pete, preparing to heckle them. He asked where they were from, and when they said New Jersey and Staten Island, he roared a dramatic guffaw.

"I'm so sorry for the both of you," Steve bellowed. "How did you guys meet? You both cast on the same season of *Jersey Shore*?"

"We met at a bar, actually," Pete called out.

"Whoa, how old-fashioned!" Steve gestured wildly to the crowd. "Isn't it crazy how meeting at a bar is now considered a meet-cute? You guys dating now or what?"

Pete glanced at Avery, like he was going to let her answer. She paused for a beat before replying, "Yes, we're dating."

"Well, *that* took a minute!" Steve looked knowingly at the cackling audience, as if the joke wrote itself. "Is that your final answer?"

Avery rested her hand on Pete's knee and told Steve yes, yes it was. And maybe it was silly to say the word "dating" out loud for the first time at a comedy show, but for the first time she didn't find herself recoiling at the thought. In fact, it finally felt right.

The show ended two hours later to a rambunctious round of applause. The venue cleared out into MacDougal Street, which bustled with crowded eateries, loud NYU students, and groups of stoners playing drums for cash. Avery looped her arm through

SHE USED TO BE NICE 213

Pete's. It was a perfect weekend night in early March, and winter was finally beginning to thaw into spring, and the air smelled like gravel and cigarettes and possibility. Tonight was the first warm night where Avery didn't need a jacket. Her good mood was buoyed when she and Pete stopped for dinner at a pizzeria and ordered a plate of mozzarella sticks, which had become their go-to appetizer whenever they went out to eat. Now, every time Avery saw a plate of mozzarella sticks, she thought of the man she was dating. Dating! She was so proud of herself for being able to say it.

"That host definitely had a crush on you," Pete said, biting into a mozzarella stick.

Avery licked marinara sauce off her finger. "You think so?"

"For sure. He wished he was on a date with you instead of me."

Avery bounced her eyebrows up and down. A date! They were dating! She wanted to scream it from a rooftop like a cringey rom-com character. "You jealous?"

Pete shrugged adorably. How one shrugs adorably, Avery was not sure, but Pete did it.

Avery thought about Morgan and Charlie's suggestion that she bring Pete to the bachelor party. Bringing him to Colorado next month could be a trial run for bringing him to the wedding in August. The latter was her ultimate goal anyway, and the bachelor party was more casual, smaller scale, and lower pressure, with some of the same people who'd be at the wedding. That weekend could be a test to see if Avery could successfully manage balancing her past and her present. If it went well—if Pete remained ignorant to what happened senior year—she'd feel more comfortable inviting him to the wedding, which was when she'd *really* have to be on her best behavior, thwarting panic attack triggers and keeping her past under wraps.

Plus, she'd finally named what she and Pete were doing for what it was. And instead of feeling anxious about admitting they were together, she felt settled and strong, like a tectonic plate cemented into place beside him. She wanted to celebrate that somehow.

"So, I have a question," she began. She leaned forward, the red upholstered cushion of the booth crunching under her thighs. "Are you free the weekend of April twenty-fifth? Morgan and Charlie are hosting a joint bachelor party in Colorado. Do you want to come?"

"Really?" Pete's face brightened. "I'm invited?"

"Charlie also asked about it, for what it's worth. I'm not just being one of those girls who can't go anywhere without the guy she's dating."

A smile danced on Pete's lips. "I wouldn't hate it if you were being like that, you know."

Avery blushed. "Well, I guess right now I am kind of being like that, since I'm the one inviting you. And since I really want you to come."

Pete leaned over the speckled Formica table to kiss her. "I'd love to. That's awesome. Thanks for the invite."

Avery's phone buzzed in her pocket as she took a bite of another mozzarella stick. She snuck a quick peek at the home screen and saw that it was a number she didn't recognize. She let it continue ringing and go to voicemail. But then it buzzed again.

"Sorry." Mid-chew, she pointed to her phone. "One second." She answered. "Hello?"

"Hey, is this Avery?"

Her eyes widened.

That voice. It would wake her from a coma.

She hung up and started coughing uncontrollably, spraying bits of cheese and sauce and breadcrumbs everywhere.

"Whoa, whoa!" Pete smacked her back, his eyes bulging in alarm. "Are you okay? Are you choking?"

Avery kept coughing and spraying food like a broken fire hydrant, trying to contain everything behind her hand. "No, I'm fine. I'm—sorry. I've just . . . forgotten how to swallow, apparently."

"Who was that?"

Avery shoveled more mozzarella sticks into her mouth, guzzling them down like she hadn't eaten in weeks. She wished she could chuck her phone across the room, but she knew she'd hurt someone from the force of the impact, so she shoved it inside her purse instead. She felt dizzy. Noah was on the other line. Noah's

SHE USED TO BE NICE 215

mouth was inches from the speaker on his phone. Noah's breath was in Avery's ear. Just like it was when he—

"Nobody. Let's eat," she said curtly.

Pete narrowed his eyes, both skeptical and concerned. "Is everything okay?"

"Yes."

"Do you want to call them back?"

"No, it's fine."

"Are you sure?"

"I'm sure."

Avery plastered a smile on her face like a shoddy paint job. But she could feel it chipping, and was grateful when Pete brought the date back to normal by talking about an issue he was frustrated with at work. Avery didn't need to focus too much on the details; she could just nod along and validate his feelings about wanting to quit, which was usually what she did anyway when he ranted about his job stressors. She was especially happy to do it tonight, to focus the attention away from her. Her reactions to Noah were spiraling out of control lately, in a much-too visible and obvious way. Unless she wanted everything she'd kept hidden to unravel before the wedding, she needed to get a grip. She was nearly in the homestretch. She couldn't fuck up now.

After dinner, Pete told her he had an early meeting the next morning and needed to get a full night's sleep in his own bed. He apologized and seemed disappointed that they wouldn't be spending the night together, but Avery was convinced that he wanted to get away from her because she'd made everything uncomfortable with the phone call incident. She sighed, annoyed that her brain provided the worst possible interpretation of their evening. Of course a man who wanted a night on his own couldn't possibly still like her. The only explanation was that he hated her now. Logically she knew this was probably a ridiculous insecure thought, but emotionally she couldn't help but wonder if it was the most accurate assessment she'd ever made about anyone.

She begrudgingly hailed a cab alone. As she slid inside, her phone buzzed again with a call from the same number. Nervous

216   ALEXIA LAFATA

sweat erupted on her palms; her hands were so slippery she could barely keep her grip on her phone steady. She should've known she wouldn't be able to avoid this phone call. Noah was obviously going to listen to Morgan and reach out to Avery to plan the bachelor party. He'd convinced everyone he was a nice guy, a responsible guy, a *good* guy. What a joke.

She pressed the green phone symbol slowly, like she was setting off a timer to detonate a bomb. "Hello?"

"Avery?"

She swallowed. "Yes?"

"Oh, good. I hope I'm not calling too late. It's Noah, by the way."

He could not have sounded more normal, like a regular person checking to make sure now was a good time to chat. And did he honestly think that Avery didn't know it was him, that his voice didn't haunt her in the deepest corners of her nightmares? Was he overcompensating or stupid? Or did he not care?

She stared out the window of the cab, trying to focus on the East River whizzing by as they sped uptown on the FDR to her apartment.

"You're not," she said, her voice blank. "What's up?"

"Cool. I wanted to chat with you about the bachelor party, if you have a minute? Since you said you were helping."

The river was moving so fast. The cab had to be going sixty miles per hour right now. "Okay," Avery said.

"Great. So the house is in Snowmass Village, this town outside Aspen. I could make a reservation at this Mexican place Friday night."

Avery thought about how cold the water was. "Sure, that works."

"It's good, trust me. I hosted my company for a retreat at the house once, and we started our weekend there. And then we can go downtown. Most of the bars are pretty chill."

There was no way the water was warmer than forty degrees.

"Then, Saturday morning, we'll go on the hike. It won't be too bad. Just a walk around the lake, maybe a couple inclines."

Maybe even thirty degrees. "Cool," Avery said.

SHE USED TO BE NICE

217

"And I was thinking it might be fun to separate during the day so both parties can do their own thing. There's shopping and nail salons downtown. The tarot card reader could be fun, too. I can text you some information, and you can book some stuff for the bridesmaids."

Or twenty degrees? Ten?

"Avery?"

Where in the world was the ocean that cold? "Huh?" Avery asked.

"Does that work?"

"Oh. Yeah."

"Great. Well, I think that's everything on my end," Noah said. "Just text me if you have any other questions or ideas."

Antarctica, maybe.

"All right, well . . . okay. Have a good night, Avery."

When Noah hung up, Avery came back down to earth, tried to forget about the sound of his voice so close to her ear, the heat of his beer breath from that night. She exited the cab in a frenzy and jammed her key into the front door of her apartment, then sprinted up the stairs to smoke a bowl and lie down on top of her comforter. The sound of the pipe crackling as she inhaled calmed her down, brought a welcome heaviness to her limbs and helped her become one with her bed. She was part of the mattress now. She was coziness embodied.

Her phone buzzed. Emma had sent an email in the bridesmaids chain with her dress size and her vote for her favorite gown. It looked like the official winner was the flutter-sleeve midi dress in the color "ballet." Avery loved that dress, especially the way the flowy sleeves glided over the upper arms, giving the illusion that they were toned. She'd need that for pictures if she'd be standing next to Morgan's skinny arm.

Morgan, she reminded herself as the last of her panic floated away in a cloud of weed smoke and she no longer knew where she ended and where her pillow and blankets began. She was putting up with Noah for Morgan. For her best friend's wedding. Which was almost here and then almost over. Almost, almost, almost.

She grinned lazily at her laptop and placed the order for the dresses. Then she fell asleep, dreaming about ruffles and chiffon.

. . .

A week later, ten brown boxes were piled in the lobby of Avery's building, each one delivered from Bella Blue, the bridesmaids dress company. Avery scratched her head, wondering why there were ten boxes when there were only six bridesmaids. She carried as many boxes as she could up the stairs and into her apartment, then opened one and splayed the dress on top of her bed. This was the right dress. She looked at the tag and saw that it was a size ten, which was her size.

She took out another dress and looked at the size. It was also a ten. Who else was a size ten? Avery thought she was the only one. She opened the bridesmaids email and read through everyone's sizes, confirming that she was, indeed, the only size ten.

She hurried back downstairs and grabbed a couple more boxes, then brought them back to her bedroom and tore them open, winded from her second up-and-down climb. They were the right dresses, again, but they were two more size tens. Avery's heart seized. How many size tens had she ordered?

She sprinted two steps at a time from her bedroom to the lobby and back again until all ten boxes were inside her apartment. Her pulse racing from the stairs and her mounting anxiety, she tore each box open and checked each size. Panicked heat pricked her chest when she realized that all of them—*all of them*—were size tens.

She checked the receipt in her email and nearly passed out when she saw the charge. Ten thousand dollars. To Morgan's credit card.

"Fuck!" she screamed. How high *was* she when she placed this order? She must have been so out of it. She hardly remembered placing the order at all, though she did remember Noah calling beforehand. What did they talk about? There was the sound of a river where Noah's voice should've been. She remembered something about the bachelor party. Had they discussed it?

Avery dialed Bella Blue's customer service number, trembling so violently that she barely processed when someone picked up.

SHE USED TO BE NICE

219

"Hello and good evening, ma'am," said a woman with a slow, syrupy California voice. "My name's Cheryl, how can I be of—"

"Hey," Avery interrupted. "I recently made a very big purchase and I need help getting it refunded as soon as possible. Like, now." She spoke extremely quickly, like if she did not get these boxes out of her apartment in the next five minutes they would explode.

"Sure thing, ma'am, we can help you with that." Cheryl, who had all the fucking time in the world, typed something on the other end. "Can I get your name for the order?"

Avery blanked on her name. Then, "Avery. Russo. Avery Russo."

"Sure," Cheryl said. "One moment."

Cheryl said nothing for an excruciating thirty seconds.

"All right, Ms. Russo. I've got it. On our systems, it's showing that the packages were successfully delivered to—"

"No, they weren't." Avery rubbed her temples. Her patience was wearing razor thin and her Jersey was threatening to emerge. "I mean, they were, but it was the wrong order. I ordered ten size tens and I only needed one, and now I have ten boxes and no idea how to refund them because I tore them all apart."

Another long pause from Cheryl.

"Okay, yes, sure ma'am, we can help you with that."

Avery's phone beeped with an incoming call from Morgan. Her heart fell to her stomach. She ignored it.

"Hmmm, let's see." Yet another pause from Cheryl. It should be illegal to employ anyone who operated this slowly in customer service. "It looks like your credit card company has blocked any activity going to your card."

"*Blocked?!*"

"Yes, ma'am. You'll have to call them to sort that out first and then we'll be happy to arrange a refund."

Avery's phone beeped again. Morgan. *Fuck.*

"Okay, thank you." She hung up with Cheryl and took a shuddering deep breath before answering Morgan's call. "Hey Morgan." She grit her teeth in a smile to trick herself into keeping the alarm out of her voice. "What's up?"

220   ALEXIA LAFATA

"Why the hell did Bella Blue charge us ten thousand dollars?" Morgan asked. Right to it. "I just looked at my bank statement, and I'm about to flip on my credit card company. This has to be a mistake."

Avery squeezed her eyes shut, bracing herself. "It's my fault."

"What?"

"I did the orders wrong."

"Wait, how? I thought we got crazy overcharged or something."

Avery reread the emailed receipt to make sure she wasn't hallucinating. She pinched her arm, touched her cheeks, rubbed her hands over her thighs—yes, this was reality, and the number on the receipt was not something she could make disappear with an antipsychotic. "I accidentally ordered ten dresses for myself instead of one size ten. Which means I probably did the same for everyone else."

Morgan didn't respond right away. *Fuck. Fuck fuck fuck fuck fuck fuck fuck.*

"Are you saying my cousin Sandra has *fourteen* dresses on her stoop right now?" Morgan demanded.

"Yes. Shit, yes. I'm so sorry."

Morgan exhaled loudly. Out Avery's window, cars honked at a cab driver who failed to immediately respond to a green light, with one driver screaming, "Move, asshole!" Avery slammed the window shut. There was enough tension in her apartment already.

"Jesus Christ, Avery. So now what? Did you call the dress company?"

"I just did." Avery braced herself again, lowering her voice to barely above a whisper. "Your credit card's frozen."

"Frozen?!" Morgan howled. "I just used it to order the flowers! Dammit, Avery!"

Avery rubbed her chest, willing her pulse to slow. This was just a mistake. People made mistakes, didn't they? Morgan knew that better than anyone. She was there during the fallout after Avery's mistake senior year. After what she *thought* was Avery's mistake senior year.

Because what happened that night was far from a mistake.

SHE USED TO BE NICE

And Avery didn't know how much longer she could pretend that it was.

It would, after all, make no sense to Morgan that Avery messed up the bridesmaids dress orders because she needed to soothe herself after talking to Noah. How much longer could Avery allow Morgan—could Avery allow *everyone*—to think she was a mess because that was simply who she was? Was she truly capable of continuing to pretend until the wedding that she wasn't hiding something? Yet how could she trust that everyone wouldn't think she was covering up for the fact that she'd cheated? If only everyone knew she'd been doing the opposite: that she'd rather people see her as a cheater instead of a weak, helpless victim. That she'd rather her actions that night be interpreted as something she had control over, instead of something she didn't.

But she'd had no control. She couldn't consent. *This was all Noah's fault.*

"I'm so sorry, Morgan," Avery pleaded, pacing back and forth by the foot of her bed. "Just call the credit card company and tell them it's not fraud. They have to understand, don't they?"

"Yeah, but now everyone probably has to ship the dresses back to prove it was a mistake before I can even get the refund, which I don't know if I'll be able to get because my card is frozen!" Morgan sighed. Loudly and pointedly. "You know what? It's fine. I doubt we're the only people in the world who have done this. I'll call the credit card company and figure it out."

"No, let me do it. Please. I was the one who did this."

"Well, they'll probably need my personal information, so it's easier for me to do it." Morgan's voice was firm. "I got it."

Then she hung up without saying goodbye.

19

AVERY PULLED HER THROW blanket closer to her neck. The sky on Saturday afternoon was dark, a thunderstorm looming overhead while an episode of *Vanderpump Rules* played on the television in her living room. Pete was snuggled up beside her on the couch. She hoped hanging out with him would help her feel better about screwing up the Bella Blue order. It had been a long time since she'd had a go-to person to call when she needed some company, though she kept her reason for "needing company" vague. All Pete knew was that the order was delayed, not the exact reason why.

"I'm sure you'll work it out," Pete had said when she'd told him what happened on the phone that morning. "You're busting your ass for this wedding. This is only a minor setback. Don't worry."

All Avery had wanted to do was berate herself. But Pete was confident in her ability to fix this. She wished she could believe in herself the same way he did.

"Thanks for saying that," she said.

"Of course! I'll come by in a couple hours. We'll do something to get your mind off of it."

Now Avery rested her head on Pete's shoulder. She knew she usually had Morgan to encourage her in moments like these, but besides the fact that Morgan wasn't Avery's biggest fan at the moment, Morgan had always had Charlie. Avery wasn't Morgan's number one priority the way Morgan was Avery's. Morgan would

SHE USED TO BE NICE 223

deny that if Avery ever said it to her face, but the fact of the matter was, things change when your best friend gets a boyfriend, let alone engaged. You can't have two number-one priorities. It's just math. Suddenly he becomes her default plus-one to parties and family events, becomes the first person she calls when she needs to vent. It's not that you as her best friend actively get demoted; it's more that he just takes your spot.

But Avery had her own person now. Someone she kept updated about the minutiae of her day, like her failed attempts at cooking chicken last weekend—she ended up burning it out of fear of undercooking it—and the squirrel eating a slice of pepperoni pizza that she saw on her walk to Duane Reade. Someone who even comforted her about the bigger stuff, like what was happening today. And it was better than she thought would be possible for her ever again.

"I'm so glad you're here," she said.

Pete squeezed her shoulder. "Me too." He fixed his attention on the television. "Damn, Raquel is *such* a good liar."

Avery laughed. "You're like those guys who pretend they hate 'girly' shows and end up becoming obsessed."

Pete didn't seem the least bit fazed. "No shame over here. I'm comfortable enough in my masculinity to admit it. This show is great."

"It's hot that you think that."

In the kitchen, the microwave dinged. Avery padded over barefoot and pulled out a freshly popped bag of popcorn. Yellow steam rose from the bag, filling the apartment with the scent of butter and salt. She poured the contents into a plastic bowl and sat back down on the couch next to Pete. He slapped her ass as she lowered herself into the seat cushion.

"You know what else is hot?" he asked. "You, today."

"Only today?" Avery teased. Her hair was in a loose bun on top of her head with strands framing her face, and she wore no bra and a thin pink tank top through which her nipples were visible.

Pete played with the strap of her shirt, let it fall and dangle against her skin. "You know what I mean." He kissed her bare shoulder.

"Stop!" Avery whispered, hoping he'd actually keep going—forever. "We need to watch the show!"

Pete paused the TV and dove his face into Avery's chest. "We'll watch later."

She arched her back into him and groaned as he slipped off her tank top. Warmth rushed between her legs. Her desire for Pete bloomed not from a frantic need for validation that she'd gotten used to with guys, but from a genuine longing for Pete and Pete alone. She welcomed the change, this feeling that she was allowing her happiness to depend on him so much. It was more vulnerable than she'd been in a long time, with anyone. But Pete treated her like a precious jewel, and continued to do so even as he found out more and more about who she really was. Where she saw a rock, he saw a diamond. It felt like a miracle.

"Should we go in my room?" she breathed.

Pete trailed kisses up her neck. "No. I need you now."

He ripped off his jeans while she slid off her leggings and pressed his naked body between her thighs. He moved her underwear to the side and slipped inside her easily, then pumped for a few delicious seconds before tapping her hip.

"Flip onto your stomach," he whispered.

Avery froze. She closed her eyes.

Noah's face burned behind her eyelids.

She threw the blanket over their bodies and pointed to her roommate's closed bedroom door. "Celeste is right there," she murmured. "She'll get so pissed if she walks out. Just keep it simple with missionary. So we can stay covered."

"I'll be quick, trust me, especially from behind. I'm gonna blow in ten seconds."

Pete threw the blanket back onto the floor and tapped Avery's side again. Her chest tightened. But she trusted him, didn't she? This was what it meant to be vulnerable, wasn't it? To do something that you were afraid of and hope for the best. To hope at all.

She turned over and held her breath. Pete leaned forward, pressing down on her back, and started to pump inside of her.

SHE USED TO BE NICE   225

She froze again. She couldn't do it, was catapulted right back to senior year, in that dark bedroom, under the whirr of that ceiling fan . . .

"Stop," she mumbled.

But Pete kept going, pressing even harder on her back, like he didn't hear her.

She winced and tried again. "Pete, stop."

"I'm so close," Pete moaned, his grip strong on Avery's skin. He still didn't hear her.

Or was he ignoring her like Noah had?

Nausea churned in her stomach. She couldn't speak any louder. She felt paralyzed, exactly like she'd felt that night after putting up a fight. "Pete, please stop for a—"

Pete yanked out of her with one swift motion and finished on her back, covering her in hot viscous liquid that trickled over her ribs and dripped down the side of her body. She stared at it. Bile crept up her esophagus, built pressure in her chest and her throat. Then she sprinted to the bathroom and vomited into the toilet.

Pete hurried after her. He knelt on the white tile floor next to her shaking body. "What the hell?" His eyes darted all over. "Avery! Are you okay?"

Avery lay her damp forehead against the porcelain, breathing in rapid bursts. Pete put his hand on her shoulder and tried to rub her back, but she shoved him away as hard as she could. He toppled backward onto the tile, landing with a *thud*.

"I told you to stop!" Avery shouted, hoarse from retching.

Pete searched her face, frantic and confused. "What? What are you talking about?"

"I told you to stop! And you didn't!" Avery tried to slow her breathing, but it wasn't letting up. She was still hyperventilating. She still felt Noah pressing down on her back, heard the ceiling fan whirring above her . . .

"Avery, I seriously do not remember you saying that. I swear. I *swear*."

226   ALEXIA LAFATA

"Well, I did!"

All the color drained from Pete's face, turning him a ghastly gray. "I swear I would have stopped if I heard you. I'm so sorry."

Avery's mouth tasted like acid, like bad vanilla yogurt. She lifted herself off the floor and stepped over Pete's legs, careful not to touch him. She stood in front of the sink, turned on the faucet, and cupped her hands under the water, then slurped some into her mouth and rinsed. Pete stood up next to her and watched her slowly and methodically clean herself off. Then he put his hand on her back and she leapt backward, recoiling from his touch.

"I want you to go." Avery pointed to the door, though what she really wanted was for him to hold her and never let go. To tell her they were going to overcome this, that everything was going to be all right.

Pete blinked at her. "Are you serious?"

"I'm dead serious. Go." *Stay,* she thought.

Pete tried to touch Avery's back again, but she flinched and wrapped her arms around her naked body, feeling too exposed. She dug her nails into her skin, leaving deeply etched half-moon marks. Who was she kidding? Nothing was going to be all right. She was so fucked up, beyond repair.

"Can we please talk about it?" Pete asked desperately. "What happened?"

Avery dug her nails even harder into her skin, as if she could claw the shame from her flesh. "I don't want to talk about it. I want you to go."

"I'm so confused. Please talk to me." His voice was gentle, but Avery could barely look at him.

"Pete, I swear to God. Get out of my apartment."

"But can't we—"

"GET OUT!"

Pete's eyes became glassy. He said nothing else. Only wordlessly gathered his things and left.

• • •

SHE USED TO BE NICE

Over the next few days, Avery's phone practically never stopped buzzing with calls and texts from Pete. It buzzed while she got drinks with Morgan at a new restaurant in Chinatown and while she was high on her couch watching TV. It even buzzed at work while she was once again writing social copy about *Metropolitan's* coverage of the Dave Moore case, because yet another actress had accused him of sexual assault, and this time it happened only a year ago, and it took everything in Avery not to chuck her laptop as well as herself out the eighteenth floor window of her office building. The buzzing became so unbearably constant, so mind-numbingly irritating, that she resorted to leaving her phone at home in the mornings before work and putting it in another room when she slept. Because *now* what explanation was she going to give Pete? He knew she liked sex. It was completely out of character for her to interrupt it. Had Pete never fucked her in her forbidden position before? She supposed not.

And besides, no excuse would justify screaming in Pete's face and kicking him out of her apartment with no regard for his feelings. Who *did* that to someone they cared about? Avery wasn't cut out for real intimacy. She didn't know how to be honest about what was going on with her. All she knew was how to yell at a man who only ever adored her and how to cut off all contact with him. How to act like they'd never known each other at all.

She thought about all of this on her way home from work several days later. She'd just rounded the corner onto her street, fantasizing about the sleeve of Oreos she was going to shove down her gullet, when she stopped in her tracks.

"Are you serious?" she asked.

Pete glanced up at her from his spot sitting on the stoop of her apartment building, his forearms resting on his knees. He laced his fingers together. "I'm very serious." His voice was kind but resolved, like this confrontation was happening whether she wanted it to or not.

Avery shook her head in disbelief. "How long have you been sitting here?"

"As long as it takes."

Avery shoved her way past him to jimmy her key into her front door. He shouldn't be here. He shouldn't do this to himself.

Pete stood up. "You need to talk to me," he insisted.

"I don't *need* to do anything."

"Well, you should."

Avery stormed up the stairs while Pete trailed behind. She was unable to speak to him but also unable to tell him to stop following her. She was ignoring him for his own sake, so that he'd go find someone who wasn't as complicated, because that would undoubtedly make him happier. But he kept following her, up the five treacherous flights of stairs to her apartment.

She briefly met his eye as she opened her door. Christ. If he wanted to risk being the target of another one of her outbursts, fine. He knew what she was about, and this was his decision as an adult man to move forward with her anyway.

She put her work tote down on the floor in her apartment and headed to the kitchen, where she took out a bottle of wine and two glasses. She poured some wine into each glass, the *glug glug glug* amplified in their silence. Then she slid a glass across the counter toward Pete. It was a small consolation, but she didn't know where else to start.

Pete took a sip while staring at her over the rim. Avery stared right back. There was no way Avery was speaking first. He wanted this, so he was going to speak.

"What happened the other day?" he asked.

Avery heaved a frustrated sigh. She tried to keep him away, and now she'd have to lie to him. He asked for this. "It was nothing. I was in pain, and I asked you to stop, and you didn't hear me. That's it."

"But you puked after. And screamed at me to leave."

Avery lifted her hands in the air in a dramatic shrug. "It was a lot of pain."

Pete made a concerned face. "That much?"

"I *guess*." Avery sat down at the kitchen table and looked straight ahead, sipping her wine. She could feel Pete staring at her, waiting for more. "It's—it's normal for sex to hurt from behind, okay? You get deep in there."

Pete sat down beside her, his eyes soft. "Well, are you still in pain? Were you bleeding?"

"No, I'm fine," she said quickly. "Everything's fine."

"Are you sure? If the pain was that bad, maybe there's something else goi—"

"No." Avery put her hand up to stop him. "I feel a lot better now. This has happened before." Avery's back pricked with sweat.

Pete chuckled nervously. "Well I obviously don't want to hear about that."

She whipped her head to glare at him. Absolutely nothing about this was funny. "What? Are you referring to me sleeping with other guys? You know you're not the only guy I've fucked, right?"

"Jesus, Avery." Pete massaged his temples. "I know that. I was teasing."

Avery twisted the stem of her wine glass between her fingers. She was such an asshole. And yet, he still wanted her. He still wanted this asshole. She didn't understand it, not even a little, but it made her happy all the same.

"Look, I'm sorry," Pete said. "I should've been paying more attention."

Avery stared out the window to avoid making eye contact. She felt tears brimming and wiped them away before they fell down her cheeks. Her body was betraying her so much lately, revealing all of her secrets.

"It's fine," she said, her voice clipped. "Can we not talk about it anymore? I'm sorry for not answering your texts. Thanks for coming over."

Pete searched her face. He scooted closer and wrapped an arm around her, keeping his worried gaze locked on hers. "Am I still invited to Colorado?"

Avery sighed into his embrace, then rested her head on his shoulder so she wouldn't have to look at him. "Yes, you're still invited to Colorado."

Pete gave her a gentle squeeze. She could tell there was more he wanted to talk about, more he wanted to ask about what happened. But she was putting a stop to this conversation. And that was that.

• • •

Avery sat on a bench across from a brightly lit three-way mirror at Kleinfeld for Morgan's dress fitting and stared at her phone. She and Pete hadn't spoken much since their conversation in her kitchen last weekend. Rationally, she knew he sometimes got slammed at work and couldn't text a lot during the week, but her insecure side figured the tables officially turned, that now *he* was done with *her*. She even had evidence: Yesterday, he sent her a Snapchat of a bowl of spaghetti and meatballs that he made "from scratch," according to the caption. Avery responded with, *looks so good. you gotta make that for me!* He wrote back: *Ha I will.* And then nothing else. It was driving her crazy. That period? Brutal. That "ha"? So much less easygoing than "haha" or "lol."

Morgan emerged from behind the changing curtain in her beautiful white gown with a big, openmouthed smile. She looked perfect.

But all Avery could muster was a flat "You look great."

Morgan grabbed a handful of the fabric on her skirt and flipped it over a few times to examine the shimmer. Then she smoothed down the bodice and sucked in her flat stomach, making her round, perky boobs pop out of the top in a demure-but-sexy kind of way. Avery wasn't in the mood to do this. She knew Morgan wasn't genuinely rubbing her beauty and joy in Avery's face, but that was what it felt like, and she wanted a second to indulge in some self-pity. Was that so much to ask, after everything she'd already put herself through for this wedding?

"I can't gain a *pound*," Morgan said urgently. "You need to pry *every slice of pizza* out of my hands."

She glanced over her shoulder at Avery, whose nose was buried in her phone, refreshing Pete's text message window and losing hope as no new white bubbles entered the screen.

SHE USED TO BE NICE   231

"Hey, did you hear me?" Morgan called out, a little louder. "I said you need to eat pizza for me."

Avery looked up. "Oh. Sorry. Don't worry, I will."

Morgan went back to admiring herself in the mirror. "I just want to feel beautiful on that day, you know? It sounds so lame to say that out loud . . ."

A few beats of silence passed. Morgan looked at Avery through the mirror, and it was only when Avery caught her eye that she realized she hadn't replied.

"You will be beautiful," Avery said in a voice she hoped was convincing and present enough. But she felt so terribly far away. "I promise. You always are. Even if you gain multiple pounds."

Morgan's mouth pressed into a line. She took a beat before saying, "Were you able to mail back the bridesmaids dresses, by the way?"

"Yeah, mine are all set. I know Blair's pissed that she had to carry all those boxes back to UPS, but she only had four so she can relax." Avery didn't have the energy to filter herself. Nothing seemed as big of a deal as whether her worst fear that she was too broken for Pete was coming true.

Morgan raised a brow. "I mean, sure. But I agree that it was annoying and could've been avoided."

Avery softened and met Morgan's eye. She put her phone down. She wasn't being fair. The fact that she'd messed up the bridesmaids dresses order was a huge deal, and she knew it.

"I know," she said. "You're right. I really am so sorry."

Morgan's face remained neutral. "Whatever."

Some minutes later—Avery had no idea how many—Morgan materialized fully dressed in her cropped jeans and white T-shirt. Avery hadn't even realized she'd started changing. She could really use a cigarette. She dug through her purse to find one as she followed Morgan out of Kleinfeld, but she must've left her pack at home because she came up empty. Her spirits brightened when she spotted a Halal cart across the street. Caffeine would suffice in place of nicotine.

"Thank God," Avery said after she and Morgan each bought a cup. She lifted her drink to her nose to let the nutty, earthy vapors revitalize her.

"Cart coffee is so underrated," Morgan said. "Even Blair, who you know is bougie about her coffee, thought it was great when I introduced it to her last week."

Avery paused taking a sip. "She was here *again*?"

"Yeah, visiting Noah. Those two are so in love. I wouldn't be surprised if they get engaged next."

A heavy, drowning sadness washed over Avery. Noah and Blair were in love, and Avery and Pete were . . . well, who even knew?

"Hey, are you okay?" Morgan asked. "Today was supposed to be fun but you've been out of it all morning. Kinda killing the vibe."

Avery stared down at the sidewalk, observing the mosaic of cracks and fossilized pieces of chewing gum etched into the concrete. The chipped burgundy polish on her fingernails caught her eye. A disgusting manicure: something else to add to her list of things to hate about herself. She glanced at Morgan's nails, painted a neat pale pink. Essie Ballet Slippers.

She stopped walking. "Can I have a hug?"

Morgan tilted her head in confusion but stopped, too. "You want a hug?"

Avery nodded. If things continued the way they were now, with Morgan being pissed and Pete being distant and Noah on the fast track toward his own happily ever after, these last few months until the wedding were going to wear her down to nothing.

"Of course you can get a hug," Morgan said. She held her arms out. Her citrus perfume wafted toward Avery in a way that made her want to cry, so she did. She did her best to hide her tears from Morgan, not wanting to ruin the day more than she already had. "Is everything okay?"

Avery sniffled with her cheek pressed against Morgan's chest. "Yeah. I'm fine."

But she wasn't. And she was getting really, really tired of faking it.

20

IT TURNED OUT PETE'S "ha" was not the omen Avery thought it was. On her way home from Morgan's dress fitting, he texted Avery asking to have a picnic in Central Park the following weekend. Avery felt light-headed with relief when she saw his name pop up on her screen and flew her fingers across the keyboard to accept his invitation. As she watched the word "Delivered" appear underneath her blue iMessage bubble, she thought about how just a few months ago, she'd have thought this suggestion was nauseating. Picnics in the park always felt so cringeworthy, like a performance of romance. Any traditional romantic gestures had always made Avery cringe. Buying a dozen roses or a box of chocolates required no original thought, which made it feel meaningless. And the mere knowledge that it was a romantic gesture put pressure on you to be grateful. You're a specific kind of bitch if you don't swoon over the teddy bear your boyfriend gets you for Valentine's Day. But now, Avery didn't even care about the cringe factor. In fact, she was thrilled to have a picnic with Pete, and not in spite of the romance but because of it.

"Wait, you're doing *what?*" Morgan asked the next day on FaceTime. She was in the middle of giving herself a pedicure, her foot propped up in front of her phone on her coffee table, bright pink toes wiggling on screen. "Can you please repeat that?"

Avery was in the middle of stuffing her dirty clothes into a bag to bring to the laundromat. The situation was dire. She was running out of underwear.

"I can't go to brunch this weekend because I'm having a picnic in Central Park with Pete," she said.

Morgan set down her nail polish brush dramatically. "I don't even know who you are right now."

Avery laughed. "I don't either."

"Like, you're having a picnic. In the park. With a guy who likes you. Am I dreaming? Is this really happening?"

The picnic was on a Saturday, on a beautiful spring day in April. The sun shone bright and strong, covering Central Park in a thick blanket of warmth. Pete and Avery walked hand in hand along the pathway through the lawn that overlooked Central Park West until they found an open spot beside a tree and away from the crowds and baseball fields. Pete laid down a red-and-white gingham blanket, then from his backpack he pulled out some mild white cheddar cheese, a box of buttery crackers, a bottle of pink rosé, and a wireless boom box. Cringeworthy, cliché, and perfect.

Avery nodded toward the boom box. "I've been trying to find a good one of those. Where'd you get yours?"

"My ex from college actually got it for me." Pete winced sympathetically. "Sorry, is it weird that I just told you that?"

Avery stiffened. It was only a matter of time before exes came up, and of course Pete would be so casual and unrestrained about sharing information about his. "No, it's not weird. We've all got exes."

"What was yours like?"

Avery chewed on her lip. "Let's not go there."

"Oh, come on. Here's my story, although it's kinda boring: She and I dated for a year but were just too different—we had different visions for our life and all that. It was a mutual breakup. Very cordial."

"No drama. Must've been nice."

"It was." Pete looked curiously at Avery, as a prompt. "Okay, your turn."

SHE USED TO BE NICE   235

Avery swallowed a hearty sip of rosé, then tried giving Pete's open approach a shot. "His name was Ryan. We dated for almost all of college." She stopped abruptly, couldn't bring herself to keep going; it was like she'd put her foot on the gas only to hit a stop sign.

"Why'd it end?"

Avery spent a few seconds picking at the yellow label on the cheese. And then, in her mind's eye, she saw it again: the ceiling fan. She felt dizzy as she watched it go, round and round inside her head.

Whirr . . .

A sudden chill ran through her, goosebumps turning her skin into Braille, despite how warm it was outside. She filled her cup with more rosé and swallowed a massive gulp, managing not to let the memory spiral into a full-blown panic attack.

"We just grew apart," she said.

Pete nodded, taking it in. Avery hoped he wouldn't ask any more questions. She hated lying to him. It was hard enough lying to her friends, but lying to Pete, to this incredible man who thought so highly of her, made her feel like her most reprehensible self.

"That simple, huh?" he said.

"That simple." Avery shrugged. "Shit happens."

Pete considered this. "Sounds like a good topic for you to write about."

"What is?"

"Life." Pete smirked at her. "Shit happening."

"Oh, yes. How riveting." Avery held her hands out, moving them from left to right in front of her like a marquee banner. "*Why Life Is Filled with Shit Happening* by Avery Russo. I can see the Pulitzer now."

Pete laughed. "Hey, I never said I was a writer. That's all you." His face softened, his blue eyes glinting in the sun. "I bet your writing is incredible."

Avery couldn't talk about the night that led to her breakup with Ryan, but maybe she could tell Pete about her writing. There was more than one way to let someone in. Her process of opening up to Pete involved this constant internal bartering, figuring out which piece of personal information would be significant enough to meet the current moment with him. Her secret about Noah felt like her most expensive good. Once that was gone she'd be depleted of everything.

"Here, I'll show you something I wrote in college." She took out her phone and tapped open the essay about reality television that she'd written for *The Golden*, then handed it over to Pete. Perhaps if she showed him her work, he'd feel satisfied enough and never ask about Ryan again.

Avery pinned Pete down with her eyes, her body tense and still as she watched him read her essay. Each time he reacted with a laugh or a nod or a "huh!" sound, Avery fought back the urge to dive headfirst into the reservoir in the middle of the park.

"This is amazing," Pete said. "Funny, informative, and makes me feel way less guilty about how much I love reality TV." He gave her back her phone. "You're an amazing writer." He cupped her chin with his hand, making her look deeply into his eyes. To really see him, for the way he was seeing her. "Don't forget about me when you write a bestseller one day."

Avery smiled. She'd done it. She'd let him in. It was only a little, and it wasn't everything, and she wasn't sure if it would make up for all the other times she'd pushed him away. But she was glad she could let her guard down some more. She was glad that Pete was patient, that he didn't give up on her when she acted cagey after Comedy Cellar or when she kicked him out of her apartment after sex in a blind rage. Maybe now, whenever Pete thought of her, *this* would be the moment he'd remember, above all those others.

Avery leaned backward on her hands, letting the rays of the sun seep into her face and bare shoulders. It was the most beautiful day of spring so far. On the walking path, people were jogging, riding bikes, and meandering aimlessly, while others were playing catch on the lawn or reading books on nearby benches. There was

SHE USED TO BE NICE 237

a long line in front of a blue and yellow Sabrett hot dog stand; Avery made a mental note to get one later. She glanced at Pete, who was also enjoying himself, grinning and peering around at their fellow New Yorkers thawing from winter. Avery was looking forward to the bachelor party in Colorado in a couple of weeks, to hanging out with Pete for several days in a row and seeing how he meshed with her friends. But right now, she wanted to take it one step further. To show him just how special he was to her. Because it turned out she didn't care how the bachelor party weekend went. She knew, no matter what, that she wanted Pete by her side for all of it. Good or bad.

"So, I know Morgan and Charlie's wedding isn't for another four months," she began. "But I was wondering. Do you want to be my plus-one?"

Pete leaned over their charcuterie board to kiss her. He pulled away slowly, gazing at her with an expression that looked something like love. And she gazed right back.

"I thought you'd never ask," he said.

• • •

Scout has been having diarrhea all over the apartment

It was far too early in the morning on a Monday for Morgan to be texting Avery about diarrhea, but here they were.

oh no, Avery texted back.

I need to cancel drinks tn. Charlie's gonna be home late from work so I need to deal with this

Morgan sent Avery a photo of Scout looking up at the camera with sad puppy eyes, his little body wrapped in a blanket like a burrito. Avery responded to the photo with a heart and told Morgan that she hoped he felt better. That dog was in great hands. Morgan was so maternal. Unlike Avery, who this morning realized she hadn't watered her monstera plant for three weeks, and it had begun wilting to its death.

Avery's phone buzzed again. *Call me after work tho? I wanna hear about the picnic!*

238   ALEXIA LAFATA

Avery smiled and wrote back *sure thing* 😊

She put down her phone and brought her attention back to her desk. Four women in total had now accused Dave Moore of sexual assault, and according to *Metropolitan* the latest development was that the Los Angeles police department was building a case to take him to court. Moore, as expected, denied every single allegation, his lawyers whack-a-moling each one as they popped up in what felt like rapid succession. Avery wondered what would even happen if Moore was brought to court. At least one victim would probably need a rape kit, for one, to have strong DNA evidence against him. But maybe at first these victims hadn't wanted to acknowledge that Moore had raped them, so why would they have gotten something called a *rape kit?* They should change the name of that to something else. Something that didn't require victims to admit what was done to them. Also, she'd read horror stories about how violating it was to collect samples for the kit. Who'd want to do that immediately after having already been violated?

Avery's heart slammed against her ribcage. She refused to contemplate this any further. This Dave Moore story was only further proof that #MeToo hadn't made any of the progress everyone thought it did. So many women spoke out during that movement, and for what? For this shit to keep happening and coming to light? For more readers, still, to say in the comments of *Metropolitan*'s coverage that the journalists writing about this case should kill themselves? The associate social media editor could handle this one later. Avery was over it.

"Morning, Avery," Larry said, leaning against Avery's desk. "Can I get some help making a video montage?"

Avery was relieved by the interruption. She helped Larry cut together some clips he had taken during a vintage car pop-up museum on the Upper West Side. As she finished showing him how to post the video to his social media accounts, her computer dinged with a message from Kevin.

Larry has 10k Instagram followers but I can't get an email back from a recruiter at BuzzFeed? Make it make sense

SHE USED TO BE NICE 239

Avery grabbed the box of Insomnia Cookies she'd bought on her way to work this morning and walked over to Kevin's desk. She'd remembered Kevin was hearing back from BuzzFeed today, his second choice after he didn't get the *Entertainment Weekly* job, and wanted to get him something to ease his nerves. She was glad at least one of them was pursuing their career dreams. Maybe one day she would find the motivation to join him, to try writing again in a real way. Then she'd never have to work on the Dave Moore story ever again.

Kevin gasped when he saw the white box. "You didn't."

"I did." Avery put the box down. "We'll use them to celebrate if you get the job. If not, we'll stress eat."

"What if Patricia asks what they're for?"

Avery pursed her lips in thought. "Your birthday?"

"It's next month anyway, so, close enough. Can you believe I'll be twenty-seven? Officially in my late twenties."

Avery pretended to be disgusted. "Wow. Should I call the nursing home? Reserve you a spot?"

"Don't waste your time. I'll be dead soon. Just like our racist uncles." Kevin helped himself to a chocolate chip cookie. "I can't wait to be out of my twenties. My sister is thirty-two. She says you care so much less about what people think in your thirties."

"That sounds nice. Probably because you're more secure in who you are by then. Or so I hear."

Kevin choked out a laugh. "Can you imagine what it would be like to not hate yourself?"

"I literally can't." Avery tried to keep her voice light, but the weight of the truth of her response nearly made her fall through her chair.

She thought about their conversation some more later that night, at home after work. Your twenties, she mused, were supposed to be filled with discovery, a time when you explored who you were and what you wanted out of your life. Yet all Avery was doing was running further from herself, further from the truth about what Noah did to her. She tried to push it away by skirting around conversations with Pete and being an attentive friend and maid of honor to Morgan, but those moments of success almost always came with a side effect of destruction. She could only run so far from the minefield of her past before another explosion affected her relationships and forced her to clean things up yet again. And although she hadn't been a mess for that long, already she'd gotten used to it, the way human beings can get used to any deplorable condition if they're steeped in it long enough. She was comfortable being this person, and the thought of the work it would take to confront the truth sounded exhausting, like an uphill battle she was too out of shape to climb.

But how much longer could she live like this, so scared of being honest about that night? She didn't know. Up until this point she'd lied to herself and everyone else. And in just a few short months the wedding would be over, and Noah and all her old friends would be out of her life for good, and then she'd feel less pressure around maintaining the lie. It was the finish line she had to cross, even if she had to army crawl her way there. She was looking forward to that immensely, to the exhale of relief of no longer having to think about any of this, because lately she felt like a wire pulled so taut that soon it would snap. Freedom was so close, she could taste it.

As she vowed to just keep moving forward, one foot in front of the other until it was all done, her phone vibrated with a FaceTime from Morgan.

"Tell me *everything*," she said when Avery answered.

Avery propped Morgan's face up on her bathroom sink, then continued brushing her post-shower wet hair in front of the mirror. "The picnic was great. The weather was gorgeous, and I showed him some of my writing. He loved it."

"Of course he did, Avery! You're a great writer."

Avery smiled. But she knew she was burying the lede. "And I invited him to the wedding."

Morgan gasped, clapped her hands excitedly. "You did? Oh my God! That's huge!"

SHE USED TO BE NICE

241

"I know! I was gonna wait until after the Colorado trip, to see how that went, but I'm feeling so good about him. It felt right to invite him now."

"I'm so happy for you. This is gonna be amazing!" Then Morgan's mood changed, darkening as she took a breath. "I guess this is as good a time as any to tell you that Ryan's coming. To the wedding."

A flash of heat pricked Avery's chest. She put down her hair brush.

"I know," Morgan sighed. Avery's face must've said it all. "I'm so sorry."

Avery leaned over the sink, pressing her palms into the edge. "Pete and I sort of had the ex talk. I mentioned I had a boyfriend in college but specifically *didn't* tell him anything about why it ended, or—" Avery massaged her temples. "And now he's *coming*? Are you *sure?*"

Morgan tucked a strand of hair behind her ears, her discomfort tangible through the phone screen. "I'm positive," she said in a gentle voice. "We got his RSVP in the mail yesterday."

Avery didn't know what to say. But also, there was nothing *to* say. Morgan had warned her. Still, Avery couldn't look at her.

"Fine." Avery picked up her hair brush again. "Whatever."

Morgan shot a glance off-screen, then stood up and started walking down the hallway of her apartment, keeping the phone steady on her face. "It's not like Ryan's gonna say anything. Why would he?"

"You don't know that. He might get too drunk and make a dick comment. You know how he can get." Avery fought a thick knot of hair at the base of her skull. "Or what if *I* act weird? What if *my* behavior around Ryan gives something away?" She yanked hard until she heard a ripping sound. "Things were going *so well* between me and Pete. This is going to ruin everything."

Morgan sighed as she settled into what looked like her and Charlie's bed. "Look, one thing at a time. Just focus on the bachelor party first. It seems like you've gotten better at being around everyone, so I'm hopeful you and Pete will have a good time. Have you been able to talk to Noah about the plans?"

Avery's stomach dropped at the reminder of that phone call with Noah, from which she couldn't recall a single detail. He'd told her to research some activities, but she forgot what she was supposed to be researching. She didn't even remember where in Colorado they were going. Snowsomething? Rainsomething? There was no way she'd call him back to confirm, though.

"Oh, yeah. Noah—" Avery paused. That was the first time she'd uttered his name out loud since college. "Noah called me. We talked about it."

His name tasted like poison on her tongue. The last time she'd said it was as a cry, a whimper muffled by an enveloping darkness. And now, in her nightmares, the sound of her voice begging him to stop jolted her awake all the time in a cold sweat, her body twisted in her dampened bed sheets. It was a sound she would never forget. A night of decisions she would never forget. And soon she'd have to see Ryan again, her scorned ex-boyfriend, the end result of that night coming palpably to life. With Pete right there to witness it all.

21

PETE STOOD UNDER THE awning of Monkey Bar wearing black slacks, a white dress shirt, and shiny dress shoes that gave him an extra inch of height. He'd made a dinner reservation here earlier in the week and had told Avery to wear something, quote, "nice." The tight black midi dress with spaghetti straps that she'd had since college was about as nice as she could muster on her current maid-of-honoring budget. She hoped it was sufficient.

"You look gorgeous," Pete said with a smile.

Avery smoothed down her straightened hair. "Thank you. You look great, too."

Pete blushed and hoisted his messenger bag over his shoulders. "Thanks. I met with a client today. Had to dress up a little extra."

"So even *they* hate your dorky vests?" Avery teased.

Pete laughed. "Hey, don't talk shit about my dorky vest. I know you love it. I saw that sparkle in your eye in the hospital."

"That sparkle is called intoxication."

Pete laughed again, then gestured toward the restaurant. "After you."

Avery pushed open the glass front door and led the way inside. As they stood in the foyer waiting for the maître d' to show them their table, Avery swallowed. Off to her right, vintage brass lamps illuminated a long bar with a dark wooden trim. To the left, in the dining room, burgundy leather booths were pushed up against a back wall covered in old-timey art, and round tables were draped in white cloth and dotted with tiny candles. The restaurant dripped with luxury, like a scene out of *Mad Men*. Avery wouldn't be surprised if Don Draper himself popped out from behind one of the red velvet partitions separating the rooms.

She sucked in a breath. She had hoped her date with Pete tonight could be their own private send-off before they left for Colorado next week, but for the last couple of days she'd been feeling uneasy about the news that Ryan was coming to the wedding. The thought of Pete and Ryan being in the same room was almost more than she could bear. And the romantic elegance of this restaurant wasn't helping to relieve any pressure.

Pete ordered some appetizers and a bottle of red wine for the table. A few minutes later, a waiter wearing a vest and black tie poured some of the wine Pete had selected into a glass for him to taste. He made a dramatic show of swirling the wine around, sniffing it, drinking it, and letting it sit on his tongue. His silliness helped relieve some of Avery's anxiety.

"Perfect," he said.

The waiter poured each of them a glass. Avery tried to relax. But she couldn't stop envisioning the nightmare of Ryan being at the wedding—Pete's one-way ticket to finding out what everyone thought Avery had done and disappearing from her life forever. Her past and present, colliding in a nuclear blast.

"Can you honestly tell the difference between those wines?" she asked, doing her best to stay present. "This place could serve me Franzia and tell me it's a hundred-dollar bottle and I'd have no clue."

"No, I can't tell shit. But it's fun to pretend I can. Look at this place." Pete gestured around emphatically. "You can't come here and not at least act like you know the difference between a cabernet sauvignon and a pinot noir."

"A what and a what?"

Pete pointed at her. "Exactly."

The waiter returned with a silver tray of oysters surrounded by lemons, sauces, and two tiny forks, all arranged on a bed of ice.

SHE USED TO BE NICE 245

Avery stared at the tray. She'd never eaten oysters before and had no clue what to do. She carefully picked up one of the gray and white shells.

"It looks like a booger," she observed.

Pete laughed as he sprinkled some of the more translucent sauce onto a shell and dug into it with a tiny fork. Then he tipped his head back to slurp the fish. He put the empty shell back on his plate.

"Tastes better than one, trust me," he said.

Avery mimicked Pete's motions, swallowing the salty, briny shellfish just like he did. "That was good." She smiled at herself. She felt like such a grownup, eating an oyster at a bougie restaurant with the man she was dating.

Don't think about the wedding.

"So, how was work today?" she asked as she took another oyster.

Pete shrugged. "It was all right. I've been advising on a merger and it's taking forever. One company is getting cold feet at the finish line, and my MD has to do a lot of handholding."

"Ooof. That sounds terrible."

"Yeah. And this meeting we were having about it today was running late, which it always does—these old guys in suits can talk your ear off. So I told them I had to go meet my girlfriend for dinner and we'd finish tomorrow."

Avery nearly choked on her oyster as it slid down her throat. "Girlfriend," she repeated slowly, like it was a foreign word she needed translated. He'd never called her that before. "Is that what you've been calling me?"

Pete looked taken aback. "I guess, yeah. For a little while." He paused, tossed her a questioning glance. "Is that weird to you?"

Avery repeated the word inside her head to try it on. *Girlfriend,* she thought. *Pete's girlfriend. I'm Avery Russo, and I'm Pete's girlfriend.* It was lovely, that word. And it made sense for where they were at. But it was also a sign that Pete trusted her, was committed to her, that they'd reached the final frontier of vulnerability. All she was doing in return was lying to him.

"Well, how long have we been doing this thing?" she asked.

Pete blinked hard. "This *thing*?" He sounded irritated, rightfully. "Thing" was flippant. "I don't know, several months? We *are* exclusive, aren't we?"

Avery nervously wrung her hands out in her lap. "I mean, we haven't discussed it, but . . . yeah, I haven't been with anyone since we reconnected." She tried to see herself through his eyes, as someone he'd want to call his girlfriend. But the kind of girlfriend Pete deserved wouldn't have a history of infidelity. She wouldn't rope him into toxic situations, the way Avery would if she brought him to the wedding and Ryan were there. She would be sweet and gentle, supportive and emotionally available, not a cold-hearted bitch keeping this massive secret from him.

The waiter came by with their steaks and set them down on the table, filling the air with the scent of butter and garlic. Avery felt the urge to rip off her dress, throw on a leather mini skirt, and do something reckless, something to show Pete she wasn't the girlfriend type, since apparently her irrational, emotional behavior the whole time they were dating hadn't made that clear.

Pete exhaled loudly, angrily, and took a sip of his wine. "What do you want, Avery? Tell me what you want me to do here."

Avery ripped off a piece of bread and popped it into her mouth. She couldn't stand pretending to be someone she wasn't and watching Pete fall for her bullshit. It wasn't fair. He had no idea what he was getting himself into. He shouldn't do this to himself. She needed to protect him. Put him back at a distance.

"I don't think our relationship is what you think it is," she said as gently as she could.

Pete watched her chew, his dinner remaining untouched in front of him. "As in, you're *not* my girlfriend?" he demanded.

Avery didn't know how to make him understand without telling him everything. And she just couldn't. Not now, not yet, not ever. "I'm sorry. I'm just not ready for that label."

SHE USED TO BE NICE 247

Pete pressed his lips into a line. "I don't get it. Am I ever going to be able to call you my girlfriend?"

Avery gave a small shrug. "I don't know." Another lie. Because if she were her normal self from before senior year, she would love the label, would welcome it. But now it just made her nauseous with guilt and fear. She could see it all unfold: Pete accompanying her to the wedding and shaking Ryan's hand, introducing himself as her boyfriend. Pete and Ryan talking while Avery was off doing some maid of honor obligation. Ryan getting too drunk and making some comment. *Good luck with that one,* he'd say, tossing his chin in Avery's direction. *You'll probably want to keep her on a leash.*

"You don't *know?*" Pete unrolled his silverware more loudly than he needed to. "You're seriously doing this?"

Avery slowly set down her napkin on the table. The wedding day was the last stretch, the final showtime, and coming up so soon. Any goodwill Avery had built by being a great maid of honor throughout the year would mean nothing if she fucked up at the wedding because she was so stressed about keeping Pete from learning about her past. She was even having doubts about the bachelor party now, too. She wasn't anywhere near strong enough to balance both her fears of being around Noah and her desire to impress Pete. No doubt she would ruin something, even in that casual of a setting.

No, she couldn't do this. She couldn't do any of this.

"I also don't think you should come to the bachelor party," Avery said.

Pete blew all the air out of his mouth.

"Or the wedding."

"What the *fuck,* Avery?!" Pete pinched his face in confusion. "Are you breaking up with me?"

Panic simmered in Avery's stomach. "No! I just think we should take a step back. We . . . we're getting too serious. I need to slow back down."

Pete cut forcefully into his steak, his knife screeching against his plate. "This is the normal, natural progression of a relationship.

We date for a few months. You become my girlfriend. I come with you to weddings. How is this so *difficult* for you?"

"It doesn't have to be like that. Everyone does relationships differently."

"No they don't, Avery. This is how it goes. And if you disagree with that, then . . ." He shook his head. "Then we need to be done here."

The panic in Avery's gut roared to a violent, overflowing boil. "Wait a minute. So it's your way or no way? That's not fair."

"We've been doing it your way this whole time! Do you realize that? You've controlled this whole thing! I'm your fucking marionette! It's fucked up!"

Avery felt her pulse inside her ears. "But I was clear with my intentions from the *start*, Pete. I even told you I didn't want a relationship!" She was grasping now, digging her heels in, knowing she was making it worse but unable to stop, a freight train barreling down the tracks. "And you know what's fucked up? Forcing women to do things they don't want to do. *That's* fucked up."

The waiter flitted by and asked with a megawatt smile how everything was. Avery stared at the table. But Pete was right. Again. She was in control of their whole relationship, which she once preferred but now, with Pete, it didn't feel right. He was at her mercy, devouring the smallest bits of herself she doled out, like a starved raccoon digging through trash for food scraps. Why would he want to be with someone who did that to him, someone who thought bits and pieces of herself were enough and half the time remained aloof?

Why would he want *her?*

"I don't want to wait for you to let me in anymore," Pete said. He was calmer now, the arrival of the waiter having diffused some of the tension. "I'm tired of fighting for you."

Avery's breathing became shallow. She was about to lose him. Her vision went dark. "Pete . . . please . . ."

Pete sprung up from his chair and stormed away from the table. Customers and wait staff parted for him as he bolted through

SHE USED TO BE NICE 249

the restaurant toward the front door. Avery sprinted to catch up to him, grabbed hold of his shoulder once they were outside under the awning. But he shrugged her off.

"It's over, Avery. I'm done."

And then he was gone.

• • •

A couple days later, Avery's phone buzzed with a text. Not from Pete.

I'm taking Scout to Carl Schurz Park. Come hang?

Avery rubbed her eyes. She was lying on her couch with a throw blanket draped over her body. The television was off, and the wind whistled forcefully outside the closed window. Scout's gastrointestinal issues had improved, the fact of which Morgan celebrated by sending Avery videos of him playing tug of war with his toys. Avery was as happy for him as she could possibly be within the bounds of her state of misery.

i'm busy, she replied to Morgan.

Just for a sec? I'm so close to your apartment!

Avery peered around her living room. Empty bottles of booze were strewn on the coffee table, and wet, crumpled tissues were piled up in little mountains on the floor. The air was stale and rancid from the mess and lack of ventilation, the kind of pungent thickness that hangs when you've been home sick. She knew Pete was better off finding happiness with someone else, but she wished that someone else could be her. She wished she could just be *normal*. Nothing she was doing made the power Noah had over her go away. The more she pushed that night down, the harder it sprang back up in her face later, like one of those awful jack-in-the-box toys.

Her phone buzzed with another text from Morgan. *Please? I've barely seen you lately because of Scout*

Carl Schurz Park was half a block from Avery's apartment, but the thought of leaving the safety of her depression cave made her want to die. Then she sighed. She figured she hated herself, not

Morgan; in fact the only thing she had left at this point *was* being a good friend to Morgan. She threw on a Yankees cap and floated toward the park, where she found Morgan wrestling a chew toy with Scout's mouth.

The park was lively today, with parents pushing oversized strollers and joggers in colorful spandex running up and down the pavement. New spring flowers bloomed in the gardens along the walkway. The benches overlooking the East River were occupied with people admiring the still blue water cut by a barge and the bridge standing tall in the distance. Avery got a closer look at the barge. It was actually the Honey Boat, a large vessel filled with millions of gallons of the city's wastewater, aka shit.

She pointed at Scout twirling around and rubbing himself into the grass. "He looks like he's feeling better."

"He is, thankfully," Morgan said. She sounded tired. She adjusted her oversized sunglasses; Avery noticed her skin underneath lacked its normal retinol-treated shine. "I had to get a new credit card after that whole thing with the Bella Blue order, but the company accidentally mailed my new card to my parents' address in Rhode Island instead of mine. So I'm still waiting for it. I had to use my dad's card for Scout's medicine. He wasn't pleased with the cost."

Avery's chest ached. This dog could have died of dehydration and it would have been all her fault. She couldn't take any more fucking up. Please someone make the fucking up stop.

Scout peered at her with his floppy tongue sticking out of his mouth. Avery flashed him a tiny smile to hide her anguish while Morgan fluffed his fur.

"Well, I'm glad he's okay," Avery said.

"Me too. Wiping his ass every hour was getting tiring."

Avery scrunched her nose. "That's disgusting, Morgan."

"Hey, it happens. Especially if you want to be a mother one day. But maybe Pete can take diaper duty."

Avery tripped on a rock, losing her footing. "We broke up, so that won't be happening."

SHE USED TO BE NICE

Morgan slid her sunglasses onto her forehead like a headband to look Avery in the eye. Her face fell. "Really? Are you okay? What happened?"

Avery peeked at her phone to see if Pete had texted her, but her notifications were agonizingly empty. She wasn't surprised. Why would he text her? She'd uninvited him from the wedding and from the rest of her life, and he had dignity. At this point, with everything she'd put him through, he would probably never speak to her again, only affirming that she was exactly as damaged as she thought she was. That she was as unlovable as she believed.

"Nothing," she said. "It just didn't work out. And I don't want to talk about it."

Morgan eyed Avery sadly, but soon the sound of Scout barking at their feet grabbed hold of her attention instead. Avery startled, jumped a small step away from him. It was so embarrassing that she'd never not interpret any sudden animal movements as threatening. But Scout had doubled his size since the engagement party and was officially big enough that Avery didn't seem like that much of a baby for fearing the wrath of his jaws sinking into her flesh.

Morgan noticed Avery's stone-cold expression and let out a laugh. "He's harmless, Avery. Just pet him. Maybe it'll help you feel better. Dogs tend to do that."

Avery hesitated, pretended to busy herself by looking at her phone. "I don't want to."

"Just a little one?"

Avery sighed and stuck her arm out straight toward Scout's back, keeping the rest of her body at a distance. Morgan gently led Avery's fingers toward his fur. After a couple of strokes, Scout turned to face Avery and barked, making her recoil.

"He's excited!" Morgan exclaimed. "He loves you. Look at his tail wagging like crazy."

Avery shoved her hands in her sweatshirt pocket. "I'm good on the petting."

Morgan shrugged, and suddenly her face broke into a massive grin. "Hey!" she called out. "What are you guys doing here?"

252   ALEXIA LAFATA

Avery followed Morgan's line of sight.

No. Not now. Please, not now.

Noah stood several yards away across the path wearing a blue Humane Society vest with his arm wrapped around Blair in the same blue vest. They were surrounded by dogs wearing similar orange vests, the words "ADOPT ME" written in bold black letters on each one. Noah fed a brown short-haired dog some kibble while Blair massaged his shoulder, and Avery darted a scowl from Blair's hand to Noah's grin as he admired her. How was it fair that Noah was in this stable, loving relationship while Avery was just brutally dumped? *Again?*

"What's up?" Morgan said enthusiastically to Blair. "I had no idea you were visiting. How long are you here for?"

Blair affectionately wiped a speck of dirt off Noah's vest. "Just until tomorrow. I'm here to start looking at apartments!"

Morgan gasped. Avery, too, made a tiny choking sound.

"Are you serious?" Morgan asked, her excitement building as quickly as Avery's stomach was roiling.

"Yes!" Blair said. "We're moving in together!"

Morgan clapped her hands. "Yay! Finally!"

Noah kissed Blair's temple. "It's true. We can't wait," he said. "She'll probably start volunteering with me, too. I'm here every Saturday."

Avery glared at Noah from underneath her baseball cap as he fed more kibble to other dogs. He didn't deserve this. He shouldn't be allowed to be happy. It should be that the more evil you were, the less potential your life had for joy.

"I remember!" Morgan said, nodding. "I forgot it was at this park, though."

"This park is *so* nice," Blair added. "I could see myself running here. I would've gone this morning if it wasn't my time of the month."

"Ah, so that's why you've been snappy with me today," Noah murmured. "You're on your period. It all makes sense now."

SHE USED TO BE NICE 253

Blair gave him a lighthearted smack. "Oh, hush."

Morgan had bent down a few feet away to pet a snappy Yorkie, who was now trotting way too close for comfort to Avery's feet. Next to the Yorkie was a hefty black and white husky also prancing around dangerously close. Noah crouched down to give the husky a toy to wrestle with, and the dog yelped and jumped to Noah's giggles and delight. Avery looked at Blair to see if Blair was stewing on her own about Noah's period comment, but Blair was all smiles watching Noah happily play with the dogs. Avery felt like she was suspended over herself, watching with incredulity as the scene below her unfolded.

"Why don't you pet Rex, Avery?" Morgan asked as she joined Noah in petting the husky. "He's not barking. I know that's what freaks you out."

"Go on," Noah said. "Don't be shy. He won't hurt you."

Avery shot a suspicious glare at Rex while Morgan did her best to encourage Avery with nods. Avery looked like such an icy bitch next to Noah, with his dedication to animals and his volunteer work and his devoted relationship. Sometimes he was so good he could even trick Avery. And then she'd remember. She'd remember her unraveling into a shell of the person she once was, behaving in ways that made her almost lose Morgan and, now, lose Pete. She'd remember it all, because she was still living it. Because Noah was thriving while she was barely holding on.

"Do it! Do it! Do it!" Morgan chanted.

Backed into a corner, Avery grazed Rex's fur with her fingers. She'd barely touched him when he whirled around and chomped a mouthful of her flesh with his teeth.

"Jesus!" she cried. Little bright specks dotted her vision. Her hand throbbed in agony.

"Oh no, are you all right?" Morgan asked.

Noah put a toy back in Rex's mouth, and in response Rex growled and huffed and barked. "He's just being playful," Noah said. "It's a playful bite. Does it to me all the time."

Avery wrapped her fingers around her hand. The wound beat hard under her skin, like it had its own pulse. "No, he bit me because you riled him up."

A dot of blood pooled on her finger. Noah winced. "Oh, shit, you're bleeding," he murmured. "Sorry. I'll get a first aid kit."

A moment later he approached Avery with a roll of gauze and a bandage, then gestured to look at her hand. But instead of showing him, she stared him down, a crackling fury catching fire inside of her.

"Don't touch me," she hissed, because she knew that if he did, it would all come back. The helplessness as she stared into his eyes and tried to get away. The pressure on her wrists as he pinned them onto her back and made her bruise. The whirr of the ceiling fan as it tickled her bare skin. The moment he went from a nice guy in a button-down and pair of chinos to a cold-blooded rapist. Bearing his teeth, leaving his mark on her flesh.

22

NOAH'S FIVE-BEDROOM, WOOD-BEAMED MOUNTAIN house was located on a gated five-acre property in Snowmass Village, a town fifteen minutes outside Aspen. The house had an indoor pool and diving board, an extravagant home theater complete with a popcorn machine, and three separate decks, each with a perfect view of the snowcapped Elk Mountain range. Inside every room were several floor-to-ceiling windows from which you could see even more of the mountains, somehow. Avery couldn't believe how many windows there were, with the sun pouring into each one and casting beams of rainbow light onto the shiny hardwood floor. The sheer number of windows seemed to taunt her, reminding her how untouchable Noah was.

"This place is unreal," Morgan said, her eyes misty with awe. She'd spent the first ten minutes of their arrival sitting on the cream couches on the front porch under the stone archway, staring off into the distance. Now she stood in the living room with the rest of the group as they admired the elaborate chandeliers hanging from the sky-high ceiling and the massive fireplace crackling across a couch draped in thick chenille blankets.

Avery kept her expression neutral. She didn't want to give Noah any more satisfaction than he was already getting.

256   ALEXIA LAFATA

"You're making me look so bad, Noah," Charlie said with a laugh as he rolled his luggage up against the wall. "Now I've gotta get one of these for Morgan."

"What's with all the security cameras?" Parker asked, nodding toward a camera mounted in the corner of the foyer.

"Can't be too careful," Noah said. "This place was a multimillion-dollar investment. I've only had it for a couple of months. And I live too far away to keep an eye on it in person."

"There's one in literally every room," Viraj called out from the kitchen. "You trying to spy on us?"

Noah gave a half-hearted, tight-lipped laugh, the kind that indicated he was not amused. Avery felt sick. Did this mean there were cameras everywhere, even in the bedrooms? She suspected Noah did lots of nonconsensual spying on women, if so.

"Hilarious," he said, deadpan. "They're mainly down here, and then upstairs in the hallway only. You guys are welcome to the footage anytime."

"Hey, where's Blair?" Emma asked, looking around.

"Her plane was delayed." Noah rubbed his hands together excitedly, his mood switching like a light. "Okay, gang! We've got a dinner reservation at Venga Venga! Let's head out!"

Avery scoffed. Gang? What did he think he was, a fucking camp counselor?

After a twenty-minute Uber ride, they arrived at the restaurant, where Noah didn't even need to tell the hostess his name for her to know who he was and that he'd made a reservation. It reminded Avery that she'd made no reservations this weekend, for anywhere, and had never called Noah back about any of the plans. She could barely grapple with the reality of spending an entire weekend in his house, let alone contribute to planning said weekend. Another part of her believed that if she didn't call him back, she could convince herself this weekend wasn't happening. But watching Noah give a breezy, confident hello to the restaurant owners like he was the town mayor smacked the reality of it all

SHE USED TO BE NICE

across Avery's face: She was here and this was happening. She was about to spend the weekend at her rapist's house.

"That car ride was gorgeous," Morgan swooned as they sat down at their table. "I've never seen so many mountains in my life."

"Wait until you see the views on the hike tomorrow," Noah said with a smile. "You'll lose your mind."

Morgan loaded guacamole on a chip. "I looked it up! It looks so beautiful."

Avery turned to Morgan. "Did it say the hike was difficult?" Avery watched Noah give a waiter a friendly pat on the back and enthusiastically shake his hand. She could not be more disgusted by the whole display. "I'm severely out of shape."

"The website said moderate," Morgan replied.

"No, don't worry, it'll be easy," Noah added as the waiter left.

Avery scowled at him. She hadn't asked for his input, but of course he was giving it anyway. Of course he would only care about himself and be oblivious to what Avery wanted.

"Great," she said flatly.

"Yeah, it's the least strenuous hike that also offers the best views." Noah put his arm around Blair, who'd taken a cab from the airport and met them at the restaurant. "Blair can vouch for me. She helped me choose the best one."

Blair replied by shifting her eyes in his direction and saying nothing, then leaning away from him and sipping her margarita.

Avery raised an eyebrow. That was odd.

Noah unwrapped his arm from around Blair's shoulders and took a sip of his beer. Blair still didn't look at him. Avery removed a taquito from a platter and bit it in half, observing Noah and Blair from across the table.

"I'm pumped to work out outside in the fresh air," Charlie said. "I hate the gym. I need to breathe actual oxygen, not some old dude's sweaty socks."

"You're welcome to use the gym at the house, too, if you want," Noah said. "No old dudes."

Charlie laughed in shock. "You have a private gym? Damn, that *Shark Tank* money's doing you good."

Pride oozed from Noah like unidentified liquid from hot city garbage. "I don't want to share too much yet, but. . . ." He dipped a chip in salsa and smiled. "Yeah. It's pretty good."

"I still can't believe you got Mark Cuban to invest!" Morgan squealed.

"Believe it. You'll see how my pitch went down when the episode airs this week."

Everyone around the table murmured their excitement, but Avery was focused on Blair and the fact that she wasn't reacting, which was incredibly out of character. Normally she would've been the first one to brag about Noah's appearance on *Shark Tank*. But all she did was stare down at her plate and push her food around in silence.

Avery leaned over to whisper in Morgan's ear. "Is Blair okay?"

"I think she and Noah are fighting," Morgan whispered back. Avery blinked. "Oh."

"Well, cheers to you, man," Charlie bellowed. He lifted his beer in Noah's direction, and everyone else followed suit. "Congratulations on making a deal with a shark."

"Hear, hear!" Viraj shouted.

Avery shot her eyes to the corner of the table, where Noah had started murmuring something in Blair's ear. Blair's eyes bulged as her lips moved rapidly in response, her brows furrowed like she was pissed. Avery couldn't stop staring at the two of them, overwhelmed by her need to know what was going on.

She tapped Morgan on the shoulder. "Do you know what they're fighting about?"

Morgan shrugged. "I'm not sure. She didn't tell me. You know Blair, so prim about her business."

Avery and Blair made eye contact for a beat before Blair went back to pushing around her food.

Back at the house later that night, Avery heard Blair washing up in the bathroom upstairs. Noah was in the bathroom, too,

SHE USED TO BE NICE 259

watching Blair dab eye cream under her eyes with her ring fingers. The door was cracked open. Avery pressed her body against the wall around the corner, listening hard.

"Can we talk?" Noah whispered.

"I'm not in the mood to talk," Blair replied.

"Don't ruin the weekend over this."

"Go away."

He sighed and left, leaving the door cracked open. Avery watched him disappear into a bedroom before poking her head into the bathroom. She winced at how much it smelled like Noah in here. His grooming products, organized in the corner of the sink, released his scent like a carbon monoxide leak poisoning Avery's lungs.

"Hey, Blair," she said.

Blair glanced at Avery, then flicked her gaze back to the mirror. "Hey." She rubbed lotion on her elbows, filling the room with the smell of coconut.

"You okay?" Avery spoke carefully, as kindly as she could. "Sorry, I just, um . . . the door was open."

Blair twisted the cap on her lotion and put it back in her toiletry bag. "Yeah. I'm fine."

She brushed past Avery and out the door.

• • •

Everyone woke up at the most ungodly hour the next morning for the hike. Avery pulled her matted hair into a low messy bun and threw on a pair of leggings and an oversized T-shirt. Charlie reacted to her trudging down the stairs all disheveled and exhausted with a good-natured laugh.

"*Someone's* happy to be alive," he said.

Avery gave him a pained smile. She'd stayed awake all last night tossing and turning, trying to figure out what was going on between Blair and Noah. She didn't even know why she cared. Couples fought all the time, so it was probably nothing, and it wasn't like she and Blair were friends anymore. But she couldn't forget about it. She had to know what was going on. She'd understand whatever Blair was going through. Avery knew more than anyone how awful Noah was. It was certainly possible that Blair was in the wrong in their argument, because she was awful in her own right, but Avery hoped that wasn't the case. She hoped it was Noah who'd started it, giving her confirmation that he was the bad guy she'd finally admitted to herself that he was. Using the word.

"I'm not a morning person," she replied. "Or an outdoors person."

Morgan appeared beside Charlie in a matching white leggings and crop top set. Her shiny ponytail sticking out of her white baseball cap swung as she bent down to lace up her hiking boots.

"Oh, stop," she said. "It'll be fun!"

Noah jogged down the stairs in shorts and a muscle tank, with Blair sulking behind him. Noah put his hand out to her, but she refused him.

Avery narrowed her eyes.

"The trailhead is a quick walk from the house," Noah announced to the group, who'd all gathered in the foyer. "We should be there in no time. And wait until you see the mountains. The sun casts these shadows right under the peaks, and they shine through the tree canopy to create these incredible shapes when we're on the trail."

Noah sounded so stupid, talking about the mountains and trails nearby like he carved them from the fucking Earth himself.

Charlie clapped his hands together once, loudly. "Let's do this!"

The walk to the trailhead was not quick like Noah had suggested. It was at least a mile. They'd barely started the hike when Avery's scalp tingled with itchy sweat. Morgan, sensing Avery's struggle, fed her words of encouragement until they reached the trailhead. Once there, they pressed onward, starting to make their way up an incline under a canopy of trees. The shade from the trees made the climb a little easier, but after they rounded a corner and approached a more vertical incline, the drop to their left

SHE USED TO BE NICE

growing steeper as they ascended, the sun's rays beat directly down on the tops of their heads. Avery's chest burned in agony.

"I need to stop," she breathed, panting hard.

Morgan stopped next to her and rubbed her back. "Just push through. A few more steps. You can do it."

"My hamstrings are killing me." Avery dug into her bag for her water bottle and chugged it. Over her shoulder, a few yards behind, Blair was walking alone. Avery pretended to stretch so she could get a better view of Blair, but she must've lingered in her stretch for a beat too long, because Morgan scoffed.

"This isn't that difficult, Avery. You're delaying the whole group."

Avery blinked at Morgan. "What?"

"We're walking up the exact same incline that you walk uptown on York Avenue."

Avery glanced at Blair again, then looked back at Morgan, whose face was twisted in impatience. "It's not at all like that," Avery said.

"Yes," Morgan snapped. "It is."

Morgan stormed ahead, her feet crunching hard against the rocks and twigs on the forest floor. A few seconds later, Blair caught up to Avery and floated past her on the trail.

"Blair! Hey!" Avery called out, jogging lightly to match Blair's pace. Finally, a moment alone.

Blair raised an eyebrow. "Hey?"

"How are you? I'm breaking a sweat right now. Literally dying."

Blair picked up her pace, and Avery did her best to match it as knives stabbed her chest with every intake of breath. Blair gave her a confused glare while Avery flashed her friendliest, most reassuring smile, hoping to remind Blair of the rapport they'd once had in college. Avery didn't want to do the whole fake nice thing they'd been doing since this wedding season began. She wanted to have a genuine interaction, one that was reminiscent of their relationship's better days, so that maybe Blair would open up.

"I'm doing fine," Blair said warily. "This really isn't hard."

Avery fanned her face. "You and Morgan need to get my ass to the gym." She laughed and flashed another wide smile that bordered on psychotic. "Next time you come to the city, we'll all go."

Blair tossed her a strange look before jogging away until she caught up with the rest of the group at the first viewpoint. Avery lagged behind, still winded, but eventually made her way to the flat spot of the trail that looked out onto a panoramic mountain range. Each mountain was a different shade of purplish blue, and they faded into each other like a gradient as they stretched farther into the background, with the last peak blending into the color of the sky. Avery would've thought it was gorgeous if she weren't so distracted by thoughts of Blair and Noah.

"This summit is the lowest one we're gonna see today!" Noah's voice sliced through the crisp, quiet air. "There are even more beautiful views up ahead. Let's keep going!"

Everyone trekked onward, and Avery took wide-legged strides to try keeping up with their pace. Her lungs were on fire.

"I hate this," she mumbled to herself.

Morgan shot her a frustrated glance and stormed a few feet ahead, but Avery was in too much physical discomfort to react. She guzzled more water and wiped her mouth with the back of her hand. After a few more seconds, she stopped again.

"I'm sorry," she squeaked. "Hold on."

Morgan groaned as she turned around to face Avery, her muscular thighs clenching. "Come on, Avery. At this rate we're never gonna make it to the summit."

Avery rested her hands on her knees. In front of her, a pile of leaves whirled a mini tornado low to the ground. "I'm trying, Morgan. I'm not in great shape."

"I don't understand. You're twenty-three years old. It's a walk with the tiniest incline."

Avery glared at her. "Why are you being such a bitch right now?"

Morgan crossed her arms. "I'm not being a bitch."

SHE USED TO BE NICE

"You're being a bitch."

Avery tried to strut away to stick her point, but after two strides she realized she was going to vomit if she didn't slow down. By the time the queasiness passed and she looked up, Morgan had disappeared.

• • •

After the hike, the bridesmaids separated from the groomsmen and made their way to a spa, the first of many stops on their girls-only afternoon in Aspen. As they walked through town nestled in the mountains, passing red-brick buildings with black awnings and outdoor dining spaces surrounded by bright green hedges, Avery watched Blair pick at a hangnail while the other bridesmaids talked about how beautiful the hike was. Avery tried strategizing a way to get Blair to talk, but they wouldn't have any more alone time today. And even if they did, there was no way they could magically reconcile their differences enough for Blair to feel comfortable venting to her about Noah.

"We're here!" Morgan called out.

Up ahead was a building with natural brown stone siding, lilac windows, and a winding pathway leading to a front door with a sign that said "Relax." The bridesmaids sat inside the foyer of the spa as they waited for a receptionist to call their names. Blair continued biting her nails while the rest of the bridesmaids gabbed about the hike. Avery remained silent and observant, until she felt a nudge on her arm.

"You worked up a sweat out there," Morgan said.

"I tried," Avery replied distractedly. Blair suddenly gasped quietly in pain and put her finger to her mouth, sucking what was probably blood from her nail. "I was nervous when we were crossing that wet muddy area, though." Avery stared at Blair's finger. "Me and Blair almost slipped over there. Didn't we, Blair?"

Blair looked up, startled. "Oh. Yeah. Rough spot."

"Gravity's the worst," Morgan said, oblivious to Blair's anguish. "You should've worn hiking boots." Morgan nodded toward Avery's black Nike sneakers, which were caked with dirt. "Would've been easier to navigate that terrain."

Avery shrugged. This was so unimportant. Didn't Morgan care that one of her best friends was hurting? "I don't have hiking boots."

"You should've gotten a pair. They have cheap ones." Morgan tilted her ankle to show off her brown boots tied up with red laces. "I got these online at a discount sporting goods store."

"Well, I'm not gonna spend money on something I won't need," Avery said. "I'll probably never hike again after this weekend." She watched Blair continue pressing her lips to her finger, wondered if she needed a bandage.

"Oh, I know," Morgan snapped. "You've made your hatred of the outdoors *crystal* clear."

Avery darted her eyes back to Morgan. "What? No, I didn't mean like—"

"Morgan Feeley, party of seven?" the receptionist called out.

Morgan bolted up from the couch. The rest of the group followed as the receptionist led everyone down a dark hallway lit by twinkling candles. Soft instrumental music played from speakers mounted on the ceiling, and eucalyptus oil misted into the air from diffusers perched on ledges outside each massage room. Avery swallowed, torn between being an attentive maid of honor and getting to the bottom of what was happening with Blair and Noah. She spent the whole hour in her massage room jittery and tense, trying and failing to summon the eucalyptus's calming powers.

When she finished, early because she cut the session short when the masseuse touched her back, she sat in the foyer and waited for the rest of the bridesmaids. One by one, they trickled out with relaxed, sleepy smiles on their faces. Blair came out last. Her right sleeve was scrunched up, revealing a ring of green and yellow bruises around her wrist.

23

AVERY'S NERVOUS SYSTEM JOLTED into high-alert. She remembered wearing a sweatshirt to cover her own bruises for weeks after that night senior year, even on days that were unseasonably warm that fall.

Could this mean what she thought it meant?

The thought plagued her the whole walk to the psychic center, where the bridesmaids were greeted by a kind Black receptionist. The woman was stunning, with smooth, glowing skin and dark brown hair wrapped in a gold turban, but Avery could barely spend a second admiring her before the dizzying image of Blair's bruises flashed inside her mind again. Perhaps this was why Avery was so curious about what was going on between Noah and Blair: because subconsciously she wondered if Noah had taken advantage of someone else. Injuries shaped like that, like long narrow lesions curling around bone, could only be explained by someone's meaty fingers wrapped tightly around your wrists, holding you down against your will. Just like Noah had done to Avery.

Avery's heart hammered in her chest as she massaged her wrists and scrutinized Blair, who seemed unaware that Avery had noticed anything.

Finally, Blair caught Avery's eye. "What's your problem?" Blair barked after everyone sunk into a chair in the waiting room.

266   ALEXIA LAFATA

A mushroom-shaped table lamp glowed burnt-orange in the corner. "Why are you looking at me like that?"

"Yeah, you're being weird," Morgan added. "You were quiet on the walk over here, too."

Blood rushed in Avery's ears. "No. Sorry. I was just taking in the surroundings. Aspen is very pretty."

"So *now* you appreciate nature," Morgan muttered to herself, so softly that Avery would've missed it if her senses weren't so heightened.

Avery slid her eyes from Morgan to Blair, trying to relay a telepathic message: *Is it true, Blair? Did he do this to you, too? You can tell me. We used to be best friends.*

The tarot card reader finally arrived in a royal blue caftan and layers of brown beaded necklaces that rattled like maracas when she moved. She introduced herself as Katanjai, their "spiritual guide" for the day. Avery heard Blair's phone buzz in her pocket, and Blair scanned the screen before shoving it back into her bag.

Avery once again tried to communicate telepathically. *Was that him?* But Blair didn't look at her.

Katanjai led the group to a room in the back of the center, waving around a hand adorned with turquoise rings on each finger. Blair shuffled behind and sat down in the last empty vinyl chair set up in front of a large circular table. Avery alternated between staring out the window flanked by bamboo curtains behind Katanjai and staring at Blair's wrists, wondering if she should say something or mind her business. Avery never would have talked to anyone if they'd mentioned her wrists senior year. She would have lied and kept her pain inside, just like she'd done over the last year.

But it wasn't too late for Blair. It didn't have to be.

Maybe, if Avery couldn't save herself, she could save Blair.

"Shall we do the bride first?" Katanjai asked.

Morgan gave an enthusiastic nod. Katanjai took out a deck of tarot cards and shuffled them around with a series of elaborate hand movements. Blair tugged her sleeves over her wrists, gripped them with her hands. Avery couldn't stop staring.

SHE USED TO BE NICE

267

Katanjai made a *hmmm* sound, steepling her fingers together and studying the card she'd flipped over for Morgan. "This is a great card. You're destined for eternal love and prosperity."

"Really?" Morgan asked hopefully.

Katanjai nodded. "Your life with your new husband will be long, filled with happiness and money."

Blair went from tugging at her sleeves to gazing at the crystal ball in the corner of the room. Avery wondered what she was thinking, what she wanted to know. That everything would be okay? That she'd be doomed to suffer forever from what Noah did to her?

"Can I go next?" Blair asked.

Katanjai smiled. "Sure, darling. Come, come."

Blair scooted over to the center of the table. Katanjai flipped the next card and blinked a few times in shock. Avery watched intensely, like she was getting her fortune read, too.

"Oh. Ooooh," Katanjai said.

Blair's eyes darted around the room. "What? What?"

What? Avery wanted to scream.

Katanjai cradled Blair's fingers in her hands. "This is an interesting card . . ." She moved her finger along the cobblestone path printed on the card. "See this road? As it winds, it disappears into the horizon and plunges into darkness. And there are mountains in the distance, in front of that dark backdrop." Katanjai squeezed Blair's hand. "There are challenges for you up ahead, my dear. Daunting challenges that will—"

"No!" Avery slammed her palms on the table and stood up quickly, her chair screeching against the floor as she chucked it back with her hips. "Don't listen to her, Blair! That card is lying!" It was lying. It had to be lying. How many more challenges was she—were *they*—supposed to face?

"Avery!" Morgan cried. "What are you *doing*?"

Avery couldn't stop. She didn't want to suffer anymore. And she didn't want Blair, someone who was once one of her best friends, to suffer either. She didn't want any woman to suffer ever again. Her purpose was suddenly crystal clear. Noah was done for.

268 ALEXIA LAFATA

Avery gripped Blair's shoulders, her fingers cramping as they dug into Blair's skin. "You aren't damned to whatever darkness is in that card, do you hear me?" She could see the whites of Blair's shell-shocked eyes. "You can overcome this."

We can overcome this.

Blair wiggled her way out of Avery's grip and crossed her legs, muttered something about Avery being a weirdo. Morgan darted a furious gaze between Blair and Avery, but Avery ignored her. This was bigger than Morgan and the wedding, bigger than Blair betraying Avery and turning all their friends against her. And Avery needed to do something about it.

• • •

The last stop on the bridesmaids' tour of Aspen was a beer garden, where Avery achieved the perfect level of buzzed—confident but not manic, loose but not stumbling. She needed all the liquid courage she could get. This was their final stop before they went back to the house, and Avery had officially decided that she was going to confront Noah about what he was doing to Blair.

"We're leaving now," Morgan said when she approached Avery, who was happily letting a middle-aged man in a cowboy hat twirl her around.

Avery's mood dampened. She thought she had at least another hour. "Why do you wanna leave? Aren't you having fun?"

Avery was hoping to buy some time before this confrontation. Because even though this was the right thing to do, even though she wished someone had confronted Noah for her in college like she was about to confront him for Blair, she was terrified. But she couldn't live with herself knowing he was torturing other women the way he tortured her. This confrontation was for the greater good. For all the women who were still afraid to speak up. For the woman she herself had been for way too long.

"I am having fun," Morgan said with a shrug. "I'm just getting tired. And hungry. So, I'm ready to go."

SHE USED TO BE NICE 269

Avery flicked her eyes to Blair. Blair would support her. Blair didn't want to see Noah yet either. "Blair, back me up. You don't wanna go back yet, right?"

Blair tilted her head, confused, and said nothing. Avery tried to be sympathetic, to put herself in Blair's shoes. Blair had to be scared of Noah just like Avery was. For so long, Avery, too, had struggled with knowing how to act around him, whether being friendly was easier than being quiet was easier than screaming for help. But now she knew what to do. Now, fury bubbled inside her like lava ready to erupt.

Morgan huffed. "Avery, enough. We're leaving. I'm calling the Uber." Then she muttered under her breath, "Though technically that's supposed to be your job . . ."

When the bridesmaids arrived at the house, the groomsmen had already begun cooking dinner, with Charlie chopping vegetables and Noah manning the grill outside on the porch. Plates of potato salad and corn on the cob were spread out on the table, with wildflowers dotting the spaces in between. Noah thought he was so welcoming, so pure with his intentions to give everyone a fun weekend. But Avery saw right through him, into the sludge of his insides. She grabbed a beer from the fridge and took an aggressive swig, resisting the urge to slam his face into his grill.

"Everything looks and smells amazing," Morgan said as she admired the setup on the dining room table. "Do you guys want any help?"

"No way!" Noah called from the porch. "Nobody help. Everyone grab a drink and have a seat. The only reason I'm letting Charlie chop the vegetables was because he threatened me with a steak knife if I said no." Noah threw a steak on the grill; the meat sizzled and an enormous flame lit up in front of his face. He sprung backward and laughed. "Hell yeah, now we're cooking!" He popped his head into the living room. "Blair, help me bring the steaks in?"

Blair didn't respond, went to grab herself a beer instead. Then she floated back into the dining room, where everyone else was gathered around the table and had begun serving themselves from the plates of food.

270 ALEXIA LAFATA

"Blair! Come help!" Noah called again.

Avery clenched her beer bottle so tightly it nearly burst apart and sent glass flying out like a grenade. "She doesn't want to! Leave her alone!"

Blair shot Avery a look. "Goodness, Avery, how much have you had to drink?"

Avery put her hand on Blair's shoulder. "You don't have to do anything he says," she muttered, disregarding Blair's comment. She craned her neck to shout at Noah again. "Leave her alone!"

Morgan yanked Avery's beer out of her hand and slammed it on the table. "What is wrong with you today? You're being a psycho."

Noah stepped inside the house. "What's going on?" He glanced at Blair, prompting Avery to jab a shaky finger at him.

"Fuck off, Noah! Nobody wants you here!"

"Why are you being so rude to him?" Morgan shouted. "I don't understand you. You snarled at him when he tried to help you in the dog park, and you never once called him back to talk about this weekend. I know you don't want to be here but you could at least *pretend*."

Avery had no idea where that last comment came from. She looked sadly at Morgan. "What are you talking about? Of course I want to be here."

Through her peripheral vision, Avery watched, her stomach in her throat, as Noah whispered something in Blair's ear, until Morgan stole Avery's attention again by grabbing her arm with her perfectly manicured fingers and forcing Avery to look at her. Her engagement ring glowed against the backdrop of the early evening sun seeping lazily in through all the windows. Tears burned in Avery's eyes, threatened to fall down her cheeks. She knew she was ruining even more of the bachelor party than she already had, but she couldn't go back now. Not when she already mustered up the courage to confront Noah, after she'd spent so long in silence.

"No, you don't care at *all* about this weekend!" Morgan cried. "Noah said he called you to help plan our activities, and you were

SHE USED TO BE NICE

so spacy on the phone. I told him you'd get back to him and you didn't! He had to plan everything by *himself*."

Avery's eyes darted back and forth among Noah and Blair and Morgan, unsure who to give her attention to first. Her stomach lurched again when Noah kissed Blair's cheek.

"Plus my dog almost died and it would've been *your* fault if I couldn't get his medicine in time," Morgan continued. She was trembling with rage now. "And you didn't order the shirts!"

Blair's face was devoid of color, her pale lips barely moving as she responded to whatever Noah was saying.

Morgan grabbed Avery's arm again. "Avery! Are you even listening to me?

"No!" Avery said, then quickly backtracked. "I mean, yes! I mean . . . what shirts? What are you talking about?" Avery imagined Noah's cologne lingering in Blair's nose, his hand pressing firmly on her back . . .

"The shirts! The bachelorette shirts you said you were gonna bring. We talked about it at the shower!"

Blair leaned away from Noah again, and Avery clenched her fists. She wanted to wring Noah's neck until his face turned purple. She wanted to douse every room in gasoline and light this mansion on fire. She wanted—

"You're not listening to me!" Morgan yelled again.

"No, no, I am listening. I swear . . . It's just . . ." Avery rubbed her eyes to reorient herself. When she opened them, Blair was scooting away from Noah on the couch, yet for some reason he was creeping toward her, closer and closer and—"Noah raped Blair! I know he did because he did it to me too."

Avery glared at Noah, whose mouth hung open in shock. Their eyes locked.

She did not—would not—break his gaze.

Blair stood up and put her hands on her hips. "*Excuse* me?"

Avery took a shaky deep breath. She felt the pressure on her back, heard the ceiling fan spin above her. *Whirr . . .*

272   ALEXIA LAFATA

"You keep avoiding him," she said. "And you have those bruises. I thought—"

"That absolutely *never* happened," Noah insisted.

Blair shook her head. "Noah's just making us move to San Francisco so he could be more in the start-up world and I . . . I'd already made all these plans to move to New York City and—" She cut herself off and glared at Avery. "Why am I telling you this? It's none of your business. And for you to accuse Noah of . . ." She shook her head again. "My goodness, Avery. He would never do that."

Avery swallowed. Maybe Blair was just scared to admit what happened. Avery couldn't fault her for that. She understood completely.

She pointed to Blair's arm, the evidence. "But . . . but you have bruises. On your wrist. Like the ones I had. You've been covering them with your sleeve."

"Because we used restraints!" Noah shouted.

Everyone whirled to face Noah.

Fuck, Avery thought.

"Noah!" Blair muttered through clenched teeth. "We weren't gonna tell anyone that."

"Yeah, well, that was before someone accused me of being a *rapist,*" Noah spat. "We use restraints in bed during sex sometimes. And I accidentally tied them too tight and that's why Blair's wrists are bruised."

Noah's penchant for dominating women in bed came in all forms, it seemed. Consensual *and* nonconsensual.

He looked at Avery again. "So, there you go," he went on, seething. "I didn't rape her. And I didn't rape *you* either."

There was the word again, shot like a bullet.

The shame tightened its grip around Avery's neck, choking her into silence, like it had done every single day since that night senior year. But for the first time, with everyone's eyes on her, she felt herself wriggle out from under its grasp. She didn't want to gasp for air anymore. She wanted to breathe.

"Yes," she said, quiet and almost eerily calm now. "You did."

24

SILENCE EXPANDED IN THE room. A strong gust of wind blew the scent of charcoal from the grill into the house.

Avery couldn't believe she'd said it out loud. Confirmed it was real.

"What do you mean?" Morgan asked. It was the first time she spoke since Avery made the accusation.

"What the *fuck* are you talking about?" Noah snapped. "I nev—"

Morgan held her hand up to shush him. "Avery. What do you mean?"

Avery closed her eyes. If only she could shove the truth back into the little box inside her head, where it had existed as a seed of a thought, a fragment of her imagination, an encounter that she'd told herself was an accident, a mistake, not a big deal. Where she'd wanted it to stay forever. But now it was out.

"I said exactly what I meant," she said.

Noah made a loud scoffing sound. "Are you fucking *kidding* m—"

Morgan held her hand up to Noah again. "When?"

"Senior year," Avery said, her pulse climbing. "That party at Viraj's apartment fall semester. Remember when everyone thought I hooked up with Ronald?"

"Yes," Blair said. Her voice was firm. She was sitting next to Noah with her hand on his thigh.

"Well, I didn't hook up with him." Avery's heart was nearly beating out of her chest, the vibrations visible through her shirt. She swallowed. "Viraj just saw us in Ronald's bedroom and assumed it was Ronald. What really happened was that I was taken advantage of. And it wasn't Ronald who did it." Avery shifted her gaze right to Noah, boring straight into his eyes. "It was Noah."

"What the hell?" Viraj cut in.

Blair turned to Noah. "Wait, you actually had sex with her?"

"He didn't have *sex* with me, Blair. He r—" Avery felt faint. The word was so violent and aggressive, something she only thought happened in back alleys, at gunpoint, by a stranger. But it was the truth. "He raped me."

Everyone was speechless. A few people looked at Noah, waiting for him to respond.

"I have no idea what you're talking about," he said. His lack of concern was spine-chilling. "You were drunk. We both were."

Hot anger shot through Avery's veins. This motherfucker. "That's not true at *all*. You were fine. I could barely stand up straight."

Noah rolled his eyes. "Oh, come on, Avery. We were all drinking that night. If drunk sex is sexual assault, then everyone at this table has been sexually assaulted."

"That is one-hundred percent true," Viraj added. "I've been nearly blackout for most of my sexual experiences, and I've never cried rape."

"I'm not *crying* anything!" Avery shouted. She could hear the desperate shrill in her voice. "That's what it was!"

"But Noah was drunk, too," Viraj said. "Does that mean you also took advantage of him?"

"No, I know for a fact I was out of it—way more out of it than him. I had to work so hard to even form a sentence." Avery glared at Noah, willing him to look at her and acknowledge what he'd done. "I tried to get him off me and tried to say no and he didn't listen." She glanced hopefully at Morgan for backup, but Morgan just sat in her seat, staring at her plate.

SHE USED TO BE NICE 275

"That did *not* happen, Avery," Noah said. "That's ridiculous. We were in college and we hooked up. That's it."

Avery felt like she was breathing through a straw.

"Plus, if you were that drunk," Parker said, taking a corn on the cob from a tray, "how could you be so sure of all these details?"

"Good point," Viraj added, helping himself to potato salad.

"The fact that we're implying Noah did that to anyone is horrifying," Blair said with a shiver.

"I would *never* forget that night." Avery had started this whole conversation so strong, but now her confidence wavered. She'd been wrong about Blair's bruises. Could she be wrong about this too? She wouldn't forget, wouldn't she? She didn't just let people believe she cheated because that was what happened, right?

"But you could have," Blair said. "You have to acknowledge that possibility. If you were as drunk as you say you were, you don't know *exactly* what happened."

Avery always remembered that night in flashes: Noah's green eyes, the strength of his grip on her wrists, the pressure on her back, the whirr of the ceiling fan. But between those flashes was nothing. It was like being submerged under water and coming up for air, over and over again.

Noah's face and ears were red with fury. "This is absurd. I didn't rape anyone."

"You probably just regret hooking up with him because Ryan dumped you right after," Blair said simply, like the case was closed and there was no use arguing anymore. "Don't blame Noah because you don't want to admit you cheated."

"That's not at *all* what's happening here," Avery said. But she was losing steam.

"Well, if it was really sexual assault, why would you wait this long to say something?" Viraj asked. "Better yet, why didn't you report it?"

"Another good point," Parker said, his voice muffled from potato salad.

"Because this would be a crime just like . . . I don't know, like burglary is a crime," Viraj said. "If someone robbed my house, I'd report it that *day*. It's the same idea. But you didn't do that."

Avery glanced at Morgan again. Her best friend still hadn't moved, still hadn't spoken. She just stared helplessly at her dinner plate, stealing occasional glances at Charlie, whose face was ashen.

Finally, Charlie spoke. "Is this true, Noah?"

"Of course it's not true!" Blair cried.

"No, dude," Noah said emphatically. "Seriously? Come on. We were drunk and we hooked up. Nothing more."

Avery lightly shook Morgan's shoulder. "Morgan, you don't think I'm lying, do you? Do you?"

"No," Morgan said with less conviction than Avery hoped. "Of course not."

Blair raised a confused brow. "Are you saying you think Noah did this?"

"Please tell me you believe me, Morgan," Avery begged. "Please."

Morgan massaged the back of her neck uneasily. "Avery, I—"

"See?" Blair jabbed a finger in Morgan's direction. "Even Morgan isn't buying it."

"I never said that, Blair," Morgan said firmly.

"But he didn't do it!" Blair was indignant. "He's such a good guy. You know he is."

Avery sunk slowly back into her seat. She felt like she was in a courtroom on trial for murder, which was ironic, considering she was the one who'd spent the last year feeling dead inside. All around her, everyone was defending Noah, the chorus of voices in her jury blending together until they were indistinguishable from each other, until all she heard was that ceiling fan.

"Noah would never do something like that."

Whirr . . .

"We've all been there. She was drunk."

Whirr . . .

"She just doesn't want to be blamed for cheating."

Whirr . . .

"It's a cry for attention!"

SHE USED TO BE NICE

Whirr . . .

"She—"

"Okay, you know what?" Morgan shouted, so loudly it bounced off the walls and echoed throughout the house. The conversations stopped. "We're done talking about this."

"Hey, don't blame us," Blair said with her hands up. "Avery started it. We're just defending Noah."

Morgan pointed at Blair. "This conversation is *over.*"

Everyone hesitated before serving themselves from the trays of food once again. Nobody spoke. The only sounds were chairs scooting back and forth across the hardwood floor and silverware clinking and scraping against dishes. Avery didn't get herself any food, could hardly bring herself to move. All she did was watch Morgan cut up a piece of eggplant and shove it in her mouth, and think to herself, *How could you?*

She fled from the dinner table and stormed up the stairs, shaking with sobs as she dove into her bed and buried her wet face into the pillow. She'd never felt more alone in her entire life. This loneliness was even more acute than when everyone ditched her senior year. At least back then she told herself she deserved it, because she'd let everyone believe that she cheated, that she'd just made a mistake, to the point where even she could believe it, too. It was so much easier to accept being treated horribly when you thought you deserved to be treated that way.

But now her head was all mixed up and she didn't know what was real anymore. What if Noah *didn't* take advantage of her? What if she *did* cheat? She did let that narrative take off without correcting anyone. Why would she do that if there wasn't a nugget of truth to it?

She squeezed her pillow tighter and kept sobbing until a bone-deep exhaustion pulled her under. Soon she fell asleep, and awoke hours later numb and needing to pee. She rubbed the crusts of sleep from her red-rimmed eyes and tiptoed into the hallway, toward the bathroom, passing Morgan and Charlie's room. Their door was closed.

278   ALEXIA LAFATA

"What if he's lying?"

Avery stopped after hearing Morgan's impassioned voice muffled through the wood. Avery leaned her ear against the door, straining to hear.

"Why would he lie?" That was Charlie now. "Noah's a really nice guy."

Avery pressed her ear harder against the door, heard the *tss-tss* of cologne spritzing.

"But why would Avery lie? What would she gain from lying?"

"I don't know, Morgan. I don't know anything right now."

"Exactly. You don't know anything. You especially don't know anything about Avery." There was a pause. "You don't get it. She's been a mess this year, in a way I've never seen. It's not like her to be like this. She was always so put together, so responsible." Another pause. "He did it, Charlie. I know he did."

"How do you know?" Charlie whispered.

"Female intuition."

Relief poured into Avery's body. *Morgan believes me.*

"What are you suggesting we do?" Charlie asked with a sigh.

Morgan mumbled something incoherent. Charlie's voice became quieter, too. Avery pressed her ear so hard against the door that she nearly fell through it. She heard a drawer opening and slamming shut, then shuffles of footsteps growing louder and coming closer to the door. She scrambled to stand up and brush herself off, and the moment she was upright the door swung open. Morgan was dressed in black flare leggings and a white tank top, her freshly showered hair combed and dangling wet at her sides. The hollows underneath her eyes were stained purple.

"Hey," she said.

"Hey," Avery said back.

Laughter erupted from downstairs. Charlie murmured, "Let me go check on that," and put his hand on Avery's shoulder as he passed her.

Morgan and Avery stared at each other in silence. A few heavy, loaded beats passed before Morgan spoke. "Can we talk?"

SHE USED TO BE NICE 279

Avery said nothing, just followed Morgan to the front yard, where they sat side by side on the cream couches under the stone archway. The early evening air was crisp and refreshing, the perfect setting to watch the sun disappear behind the mountains and fill the sky with streaky reds and oranges. It could've been a beautiful night, a beautiful weekend, if not for this. If not for Avery.

"I don't know what to say," Morgan said quietly.

Avery picked at a loose thread on the couch. "Yeah, well, you didn't have much to say inside either, so . . ." Her voice trailed off. She wasn't mad at Morgan, exactly, for not defending her at dinner. She was just sad. And not quite sure where they went from here.

"I think I was just shocked."

Avery blinked. "Shocked."

"Yeah. Shocked that Noah could do something like that." Morgan leaned back on the couch and chewed pensively on her lip. Then she met Avery's eye. "I don't want you to think I don't believe you. I do believe you. I just . . . I just can't believe you didn't tell me."

"I didn't tell anyone. I didn't even tell myself." Avery stared into the sunset. The trees stretched high into the sky and rustled with the sounds of birds and insects settling in for the night. "I mean, I thought it was my fault. I know we're not supposed to think that. But I really did get too drunk and wear a slutty outfit to that party. And I was definitely giggly. It would've been easy for him to think I wanted to hook up. And then I failed to stop him once it started."

Morgan reached for Avery's hand. Avery knew what so many people still thought about rape victims: that it was their fault, that they put themselves in a compromising, vulnerable position, that they could've prevented it if they hadn't acted in *this* way or *that* way. It's the equivalent of someone leaving their wallet hanging out of their pocket and getting pickpocketed. It's hard not to think that person should've safeguarded their stuff better. Avery knew women weren't wallets, but society was just as quick to label them as objects, so really there was no difference.

"But you didn't want to hook up," Morgan said. "And him thinking you did is not on you. At all."

Avery sighed, feeling all at once validated by her best friend and devastated that this really happened.

"I know," she whispered.

Morgan buried her face in her hands and dragged her fingers across her eyes. "I'm so sorry. I wish I could've been there for you. I feel like I made it worse."

"You didn't make it worse. How could you have known? Noah's done so much for your wedding. He helped you guys with the venue and got you your dream dog. And look at this house! Nobody, not even you, could've known he was a bad guy underneath everything. He fooled everyone."

Morgan put her arm around Avery. "I love you. I hope you know that."

Avery leaned into Morgan's embrace. The sounds of laughter drifted from inside the house, through the open window. Avery peered inside. Noah and Blair sat on the couch in front of the fireplace with their feet perched on the ottoman, relaxed and happy like everything was fine. Avery shuddered as she watched him take a generous sip of his beer and plant a kiss on Blair's cheek.

Morgan exhaled an irritated breath. "And I'm uninviting him from the wedding."

Avery untangled herself from Morgan's grip, squared her shoulders to look at her. "Morgan. You can't."

"Why? I can't keep him around knowing what he did to you."

"You're the only person who cares what happened. Kicking him out would be more drama than it's worth. This is why I didn't want to say anything in the first place. I didn't want it affecting the wedding." Avery searched Morgan's face. "Please don't do it."

Morgan sighed. "Avery—"

"Please," Avery begged again. "Don't."

They sat in silence for a long time after that, until the sky was almost black and the porch lamps dinged on, flooding the couch with light.

25

AVERY DESPERATELY WANTED TO go to bed, but Morgan, Charlie, and the rest of the wedding party were gathering on the porch in the back of the house. And although Morgan told Avery that she was welcome to go upstairs and call it a night, Avery didn't want to leave Morgan hanging. Because as awful as tonight was, this was still her best friend's bachelorette party, and Avery needed to do at least one good thing this weekend to make up for ruining everything else.

She opened the screen door to the wraparound back porch. The stars twinkled in the night sky, like sparkles spilled over a piece of black felt. Morgan and Charlie weren't there, but Avery had heard their voices so she was sure they were somewhere. Noah was nowhere in sight either, but he, too, couldn't have gone far. The prospect of him popping up made Avery tense with anticipation. Everyone would surely cheer when they saw him, showing him their support. Because he was the hero. To them, he deserved all the benefit of the doubt in the world. He was the founder of a start-up, a wealthy philanthropist, a dog lover. God, Avery *hated* dogs. How could anyone sympathize with someone who hated dogs? Avery was nobody's idea of a victim. She binge drank, had lots of sex, could be kind of cold-hearted at times. Of course everyone doubted her story, like any court of public opinion would. A real court would be just as bad, if not worse.

282 ALEXIA LAFATA

She wondered about the Dave Moore case, about the lawyers who were collecting evidence to bring him to trial. What would happen if she took Noah to trial? Even if she'd had one of those rape kits, real DNA evidence that connected Noah to the crime—which she didn't—she'd have to relive that night over and over again in excruciating detail, in front of lawyers, police officers, members of a jury. It was bad enough to have flashbacks when she wasn't talking about it. In a trial, she'd have to recall every single thing, out loud, using her voice. What she could recall would trigger unspeakable panic, and what she couldn't would be used against her. A jury wouldn't even consider the fact that it was completely reasonable for someone's memory to be fuzzy in the circumstances of that night: She'd been drunk and she was human, and humans, in general, have imperfect memories. And, as she'd learned while down a Wikipedia rabbit hole one night, the brain shuts off its ability to code memories during traumatic situations. It was a defense mechanism, a way to protect itself, so she would never have remembered everything anyway.

But none of that would matter. Deliberations would ensue, and Avery wouldn't hold her breath for a positive outcome. She once read in a *Metropolitan* story that out of every 1,000 rapes, 975 rapists serve no jail time. And that's only referencing reported rapes. The majority go unreported, so the real number was much higher. The decision after deliberations, then, would be clear: Noah would receive no punishment, and it would be concluded that it was a messy drunken hookup between two horny college kids, as these things were. The jury would lament about how unfair it would be for Noah to suffer for the rest of his life because of one night, indifferent to the fact that Avery was already damned to that exact thing.

Avery looked around the spacious back porch. Emma and Parker were in the hot tub several yards away. Beside the hot tub, Viraj and Blair sat in two Adirondack chairs next to a boom box perched on top of a small table. Morgan still wasn't out here. Neither was Charlie. Avery could have sworn she'd heard both of their voices, or else she would have stayed in bed upstairs.

SHE USED TO BE NICE

Without making eye contact with anyone, she sat down on the love seat in the far corner away from all the activity, then brought her knees up to her chest and hugged her legs. She stared out onto the lake, at the rippled surface sparkling beneath the moonlight and the faint shadowy outline of the mighty mountains beyond. She tried to admire the scenery, but she knew Noah would come barging through the back door any minute and ruin her calm.

Morgan's voice carried through the air again. Avery stood up, listened closer. It sounded like it was coming from the other side of the porch, the part that extended along the side of the house. She heard Charlie, too.

And then suddenly Noah rounded the corner, brushing past Avery. She startled. He yanked open the screen door that led inside the house and slammed it shut behind him. Blair jumped up from her seat to hurry after him.

Avery stuck her head around the corner from where Noah emerged. Morgan and Charlie were standing on the deck and facing each other, Charlie leaning against the railing and Morgan against the house. Both of them were looking down at the ground. The flood lights attached to the house illuminated the tops of their heads in bright white light, casting deep shadows on the valleys of their faces.

"What the hell was that?" Avery asked.

They jerked their heads up, meeting her eye.

"It's done," Charlie said. "He's out."

Avery's heart thudded. "What are you talking about?"

"He's no longer the best man," Morgan added. "And he's no longer invited to the wedding at all."

Avery stared at Morgan. She'd specifically told Morgan *not* to do this. She was fucking fine! She wasn't curled up in a ball in her apartment afraid of being touched or something, like a typical rape victim. And she'd gone this long gritting her teeth in Noah's presence. She'd planned to power through the rest of it until August, knowing in just a few months he would become only a memory once again.

284 ALEXIA LAFATA

"But I told you I didn't want that!" she pleaded. "Why did you do that?"

Morgan sighed and crossed her arms. "Avery, it's our wedding. If we don't want him there, he's not going to be there."

This wasn't supposed to happen. Avery hadn't even intended to say anything about what Noah did to her. She was just going deal with him this weekend, like she'd been doing this whole time. This was hell. If everyone didn't hate her already, they would *really* hate her now.

"You didn't need to do this," Avery said with a groan. She rubbed her hands up and down her face in distress. But a flicker of joy, too, ignited inside of her. She would never have *asked* Morgan and Charlie to kick Noah out of the wedding. But obviously, in her ideal world, the sooner she could never see him again, the better.

"Yes we did. We needed to do it because we believe you," Charlie said. "I don't doubt your story for a second. I even—agh, fuck." Charlie ran his hands through his hair.

"Just tell her," Morgan urged. "Tell her what you told me."

"Tell me what?" Avery asked.

"Goddammit," Charlie mumbled. He squared his shoulders to face Avery. Then he sucked in a breath. "I can't stop thinking about what I saw after that party senior year." He ran through that sentence so quickly that Avery had to replay what he'd said inside her mind to fully comprehend it. Charlie *saw* something?

"You were so drunk that night," he went on. "I figured maybe you were stressed with schoolwork, blowing off steam. But we were all drunk, so, whatever. Then the next morning, on my way home from the gym, I saw you run out of the apartment crying."

Charlie slid down the railing to sit on the patio floor and rubbed his temples with his thumbs. Morgan sat beside him. Avery remained quiet and standing, waiting for more.

"I knew you weren't with Ryan, because I ran into him in the dining hall when I stopped for breakfast," he continued. "And I had no idea what you'd be doing sleeping over Viraj's place. So I

SHE USED TO BE NICE

asked Parker what he thought. I was like, do you think something bad happened? Like clearly alluding to the possibility of sexual assault. Because you looked really upset when you ran off. Your makeup was running, your hair was all messed up. And Parker told me I was contributing to the *pussification of America* by suggesting that." Charlie pulled the skin on the sides of his head taut. "But I saw you crying. I saw you with my own two eyes. And then I let it go, like a useless piece of shit, when Viraj and Blair and everyone else started saying you cheated. I figured you were just upset after you realized you slept with Ronald."

Avery kneeled down so that she was eye level with him. "Charlie, please. This is not your fault."

"I don't know. I feel like I should've questioned everyone more."

Morgan smoothed down a loose curl at Charlie's temple. "I doubt you're the only person who saw Avery crying. I wish *I* saw. I have no clue where I was that morning."

"I bolted into our shower," Avery said. "All the tears washed away. Nobody saw. Except Charlie, I guess."

Charlie frowned. "I should've asked you if you were okay, instead of just going along with what everyone else said. I'm an idiot."

"You're not an idiot, babe," Morgan said.

"She's right," Avery agreed. "You're not. And if you asked me if I was okay, I would've lied. I had planned on continuing to lie tonight, for what it's worth. I was gonna lie forever."

Charlie stared out at the lake, his eyes glassy. An owl made a loud hooting sound that echoed in the direction of the mountains. "I can't believe Noah was involved. I did *not* see him that night. That I know for sure."

Avery had always considered Charlie a good friend, but they'd never shared a moment like this, something that unlocked a new level of their friendship. It was a surprising but welcome side effect of all of this that she could feel closer to her best friends than she did before.

"Nobody else saw him either," she murmured. "Well, except Viraj. But he didn't know it was Noah, so I guess I don't count it."

"Viraj's a dick. I never liked that guy much anyway." Charlie sighed. "And I can't even look at Noah anymore." He searched Avery's face, his gaze soft. "I'm so sorry, Avery. For everything."

Avery gave Charlie a small forgiving smile. Then she shook her head, mostly to herself. "I can't believe you guys are kicking him out of the wedding. Are you sure?"

"Avery." Morgan leaned in close. "I've never been more sure of anything in my life."

"What about the venue? Are things weird with his connections now?"

"We already paid using the discount. He can't exactly take that back now."

"But who's gonna be the best man?"

"I'll figure it out," Charlie said. "Someone else will step in. We have time."

Avery couldn't believe it was that easy. That Morgan and Charlie were just doing this, no questions asked.

"Everyone's gonna hate me," Avery muttered. "Even more than they already do."

Morgan pulled Avery in for a hug while Charlie rubbed Avery's back. Avery's eyes burned with tears.

"You've got us no matter what," Morgan whispered.

Avery wiped her eyes. She felt so held. So supported. So loved.

• • •

Avery went back inside the house after her conversation with Morgan and Charlie, wanting a moment alone to process everything. She ran her fingers through her matted hair, which was still soaked in sweat from the hike and salt water from crying. She was desperate for a shower, but using Noah's towels or shampoo would only make her feel dirtier. Resigned to her filth, she put her hair in a bun, then went to the kitchen to grab another beer from the fridge and sat on a stool in front of the island. She was eager to get out of

SHE USED TO BE NICE

287

Noah's house as fast as she could, but while she was here she might as well drink his alcohol.

Noah suddenly appeared in the kitchen carrying a water bottle. Avery jumped. He twisted open the lid, lowered the empty bottle into the sink, and turned on the faucet. He had one of those massive forty-ounce Stanley cups that would take forever to fill up, so he wouldn't be budging from that spot for twenty seconds. Avery distracted herself by chugging her beer.

Halfway through his refill, he said, "We need to talk."

He dug his hand into an opened bag of Ruffles beside the sink, then put a chip in his mouth and licked his fingers clean. Avery's body jolted with a memory—those fingers on her skin, the way she rubbed her flesh raw in the shower the morning after he'd touched her and watched her blood swirl down the drain.

"There's nothing to talk about," she said.

Noah turned off the sink. Twisted the cap on his Stanley. "Actually, there is."

He tried to make eye contact with her, but she wouldn't look at him. Her pulse throbbed.

"This whole thing is ridiculous. You know that, right?" he said.

Avery slid her gaze to meet his. He took a few steps toward her, but she pressed her back against the stool, urging him not to come closer.

"You know, the thing about how I *raped* you." He said the word like it was theoretical. "Come on. You can't just go around saying shit like that."

He took a long sip of his water. Avery imagined him choking to death, drowning.

"But you did," she said plainly. "That's what happened."

Noah rolled his eyes. "Spare me," he hissed. "You were all over me that night. And then we hooked up. It's not the big deal you're making it out to be."

Avery drew in a long breath and moved her attention to her beer bottle, picking at the label and rolling up the wet paper into tiny balls. She willed the strength from her conversation with Morgan on the porch an hour ago, from the way Charlie and Morgan had believed her so easily, to carry her through this confrontation. She needed to remember everything she knew to be true about that night.

"Noah, I was just being nice," she said. "Just because someone is being nice to you doesn't mean they're agreeing to fuck you." She flicked one of the wet paper balls away. "Also, you knew I was dating Ryan. Why in the world would I be all over you?"

Noah slapped his hands against his sides. "What do I know? I thought maybe you guys were in a fight or had broken up or something. I wasn't keeping track of every development in your fucking relationship. And you and I were hanging out all night."

"We were *all* hanging out." Avery looked him right in the eye. "In a *group*."

"You and I weren't with the group the whole night. You followed me upstairs. *You*"—and here Noah pointed at her—"wanted to be alone."

"No, you're misreading that entire interaction. It was an oven in that basement and you said you were going to get some air, and I agreed that was a good idea. That's all that was."

Noah let out an exasperated sigh. "What about when you were getting handsy with me in Ronald's bedroom? You were *very happy* to be alone with me in there."

Avery drank the remaining few sips of her beer and chucked it into the recycling bin, where it clanked loudly against other empty glass bottles. "*Handsy?*" Her nostrils flared. She rose from her stool. "You mean when I was trying to pry you off me? And then when you held my wrists behind my back against my will? Is *that* what you're referring to?"

"Against your will? Are you serious?" Noah's agitation was mounting, spittle forming in the corners of his lips. "Girls *like* rough sex. Just look at Blair. She's into it. And that's what we were doing, too."

SHE USED TO BE NICE 289

"That wasn't what we were doing, Noah. *I* was not 'into it.' I was trying to get away. And you would've known that if you'd checked in with me even *once*."

Noah said nothing for a few seconds, just shook his head repeatedly as he moved to the other side of the island. Avery remained standing, panting hard.

"Jesus Christ, you're a tease," Noah muttered to himself. He met her eye again. "So now it's my responsibility to *ask* if the girl is doing okay? Why didn't *you* say something?"

Avery had tried to say something that night. Her limbs and tongue were heavy with booze, but she did her best to communicate that she did not want to have sex with him when they were in the bedroom. And it wasn't enough.

"I did say something," she said. Her voice was unyielding. "I said no. Or at least I tried very hard. You ignored me."

Noah scoffed. "I didn't *ignore* you. *You* didn't communicate clearly enough."

Even if Avery's attempt to get Noah off of her was unclear and sloppy, shouldn't the mere *attempt* have been enough for him to stop? Why would he proceed to have sex with someone who wasn't fully enthusiastically engaged in the moment? She supposed when a man saw you as only a body and not as a human, the words that came out of your mouth didn't matter.

"You can't be this stupid," she pressed on. She stayed strong, felt something powerful coursing through her veins. "Have you never been super drunk before? You're not exactly functioning at maximum capacity. Anyone who looked at me would've known that I couldn't give consent."

"*Give consent,*" Noah repeated in a derisive, high-pitched voice. "You sound like one of those ugly blue-haired feminists who don't shave their pits."

"And you sound like a rapist. Because that's what you are."

They stared at each other for a few beats, Avery holding steady on his steely gaze. She searched his stone-cold expression for a flicker of fear. He knew there were people who believed Avery

290 ALEXIA LAFATA

now, people like Morgan and Charlie, which was a risk to his nice-guy, charismatic start-up founder image. He'd have to explain to everyone—his colleagues at the Humane Society who'd helped him adopt the puppy, the Meow Monthly investor who'd connected him with a discount for the Brooklyn Botanic Garden, his whole inner circle of friends and family—why he was no longer the best man in his friends' wedding.

But that wasn't Avery's problem.

He went over to the sink and swiped his Stanley off the counter before leaning in close to Avery's ear. His breath was hot and yeasty, frothing in his mouth. Avery remained still.

"You're right," he said, his voice low and hard, cutting in its quiet. "And I'd do it all over again so that bitches like you know your place."

When he left the kitchen, Avery curled her hands into fists on the table. What a despicable excuse of a man. Of a human being.

"Fuck you," she spat after him.

He didn't hear her. He'd already disappeared. But it was the start of him finally getting what he deserved.

26

OVER THE NEXT MONTH, *Metropolitan*'s search traffic decreased at a frighteningly rapid pace. Google rolled out algorithm updates several times a year to reduce the visibility of low-quality content across the web, and this update was hitting *Metropolitan* hard. The site was losing rankings across dozens of search engine results pages.

"We rely on Google for over half of our pageviews," Patricia said to Avery and Kevin, who unfortunately hadn't gotten the job at BuzzFeed, in a meeting in her office. She alternated between pacing from one end of the room to the other and leaning as far backward in her large leather chair as she could go. "I thought Avery's social media research was gonna help, but it doesn't seem to be doing much."

She stared pointedly at Avery.

"I don't know that the traffic we'll get from any platform will make up for this loss in the near term," Avery said. "We have the most potential to grow on Instagram currently, and I can shift my focus to building that out more, but even that isn't going to be an overnight thing."

"And we need more people specifically focused on Google," Kevin offered. "Avery can only do so much when she's also focusing on our other platforms. SEO is an entire discipline that—"

Patrica heaved an impatient sigh. "SEO analysts aren't in the budget this quarter. Kevin, why don't you take the lead on what's

292   ALEXIA LAFATA

going on with Google? And Avery, you focus on our other platforms. There, we have a plan."

Patricia put on her reading glasses and looked at her computer, as a dismissal. Kevin and Avery walked back to their desks in defeated silence.

Avery spent the next few days posting on *Metropolitan's* Instagram as often as she could without irritating their followers. She knew their audience loved candid photos of celebrities doing normal things, like Hailey Bieber licking an ice cream cone or Adam Driver scraping gum off the bottom of his shoe, so she posted a couple of those to rack up likes and comments. By the end of the week, she'd amassed five thousand new followers and a thousand clicks to *Metropolitan* articles from Instagram Stories.

Metropolitan had also run a timeline of every major event in the Dave Moore case, starting from the first allegation and ending with the four women currently trying to bring him to trial. Predictably, the story was blowing up online. Some people were supportive of *Metropolitan's* coverage, including a prominent actor from *One Happy Valley* who tweeted the article and wrote, *I wish all the victims nothing but the best.* Other people, though, were insensitive trolls. One reader commented on the article that the victims were looking for publicity, as "evidenced" by the fact that one of them had just begun to star on a new TV show. A Republican pundit posted paparazzi photos of one of the victims drunk at a bar, her eyelids fluttering, and wrote, *Presented without comment.*

Avery posted a few more Instagram stories on the *Metropolitan* account before switching to her personal one for a break. Scrolling through her feed, she froze when she came across a picture of Blair and Noah facing each other and smiling, an engagement ring sparkling on Blair's outstretched hand, and a caption that read, *I have found the one whom my soul loves. So blessed to say I'm marrying my best friend!*

Avery scrolled through the deluge of comments under the post, her stomach twisting tighter with each flick of her thumb.

Congrats!

You guys are so cute!

SHE USED TO BE NICE 293

OMG YAY!
♥ 🫂🧑‍🤝‍🧑🐣

Avery leaned back in her desk chair and took slow, even breaths, in through her nose and out through her mouth. There had once been a time when she thought Blair's betrayal couldn't get any worse. What could be worse than one of your best friends insulting you behind your back and turning all your other friends against you when you needed her support the most? Well, this. This was worse.

Avery took a screenshot of the Instagram post and sent it to Morgan. Morgan called her immediately.

"I know," Morgan said, sounding just as flabbergasted as Avery.

"Like, is she serious?" Avery asked.

"Unfortunately, she is. We kicked her out of the wedding, too."

Avery's jaw dropped.

"It's sociopathic to me that Noah admitted to you that he did it yet continues to lie and deny it to everyone else, including— clearly—Blair," Morgan said. "It's like he purposely wanted to make sure *you* knew he knew what he was doing that night so that, in addition to the assault, now he also gets to make you out to be crazy. Meanwhile Blair refused to acknowledge even the *possibility* that you were telling the truth. Even Viraj and Parker were like, 'Who knows?' when Charlie and I talked to them. I'm not saying their response is ideal, but it's better than outright dismissing Noah's involvement."

First Noah, and now Blair. Morgan and Charlie's unflinching support was more than Avery could've dreamed of. She had severely underestimated her best friends' love for her. That she was worthy of any support at all was still something she was getting used to. And the fact that Noah admitted what he did to her gave her a strange kind of satisfaction. It was gratifying, she supposed, to get his confirmation of what she knew to be true—not that she needed it to know it was true. But the thing she'd gotten confirmed was the fact that she was raped. This wasn't exactly a victory she wanted to celebrate.

"And then Blair has to go ahead and *marry* him?" Morgan made a guttural sound of disgust. "Sorry, but fuck her."

Although Avery was thrilled that Noah and Blair weren't coming to the wedding, that wouldn't magically fix every issue he had caused. He was still the reason Avery kept men at a distance, the reason she felt so unlovable. The reason that Pete had dumped her.

Avery's heart sank to the floor of her cubicle. What she wouldn't give to see Pete right now, to melt into his tender embrace and laugh at his dumb jokes and feel his confident, reassuring presence. At this point their relationship felt like a dream, the details slipping away the harder she tried to remember them. Did Pete miss her like she missed him? Did he even think about her? She wondered what he was doing. She closed her eyes and fantasized about the weight of his arm draping across her side and his face snuggled up in her hair. She'd rarely let him spoon her when he slept over, and he'd always joke about how lonely it was on the other side of the bed. But whenever she did let him pull her in, the warmth of his chest on her back felt like sunshine.

She suddenly remembered that she still hadn't followed him back on Instagram. She'd resisted doing it the whole time they were together. "I see enough of you in person. Do we need access to each other's entire digital footprints, too?" she'd said one Saturday morning while they were lying in her bed, splitting a plate of pancakes from the diner. In his very charming way, Pete had replied, "I want access to every part of you."

She wanted that, too. She wanted him to know everything. Everything she'd been too scared to tell him about her past.

She typed his username into her search bar. She knew following him back would give him a notification. Maybe it would get his attention, like a flame shot into the sky by a ship abandoned at sea. She tapped Follow.

• • •

Avery hadn't known what she expected to happen after she followed Pete back on Instagram. But what did happen was nothing.

SHE USED TO BE NICE 295

She let a full week go by before she called him, her heart racing as she dialed his number. If she wanted to talk to him, she'd have to summon some bravery, whatever morsel she'd found in Colorado, and reach out to him directly. She listened as her phone rang into his voicemail. Then she hung up and tried again, and still nothing.

She checked the time. It was Thursday at five. Pete could be in a meeting. More likely, he was ignoring her. But she remembered Thursdays were generally his slower, more normal day, when he got off work closer to 5:30. They'd gone on their date to Monkey Bar on a Thursday, did karaoke with Morgan and Charlie at Planet Rose on a Thursday. There was a chance she could catch him on his way home.

She rode the subway up to midtown to Pete's office, which was inside a skyscraper on Park Avenue. The shades of pink in the early evening sunset reflected against the glass side of his tall, towering building. Avery felt very small from where she stood on the sidewalk, craning her neck up to watch the building disappear into the clouds and then trailing her eyes back down to the imposing revolving front door. A few yards away from the entrance was a massive circular bench made of cement. Avery made her way toward the bench, climbing up the long steps that stretched nearly half the block, and sat down. She crossed her legs and waited as the warm early summer breeze caressed her bare arms. Lots of men in dorky fleece vests emerged from that front door. She watched them intently, hoping that soon one of those men would be hers.

Finally, at 6:30, he appeared. Hair slightly overgrown, sleeves of his blue button down rolled, vest tight against his core. Her breath caught in her throat.

"Pete!"

Pete whirled his head around and froze as his gaze settled on Avery. She strode toward him but was careful to keep her distance when she stopped walking, not wanting to scare him away by getting too close.

"I was hoping I'd catch you," she said.

Pete tossed a glance behind her shoulder. "Have you been waiting here . . . ?"

Avery nodded.

"How long?" he asked.

"I would've waited as long as it took for you to come out."

Pete didn't budge. He just sighed. "What do you want, Avery?"

Avery's eyes burned with tears. Already. She missed him so much, but his tone was disapproving. He was also probably creeped out, even though he'd once ambushed her outside of somewhere he knew she'd be, too. It was arguably creepier of him to wait at her apartment building that one time. At least this was a public space.

"I just want to talk to you," she said.

"About what? There's nothing left to say." He didn't sound unkind. Just neutral. Heart-wrenchingly apathetic.

Avery didn't know how much time she had with whatever amount of attention Pete was generously offering. He could walk away any minute and she'd be speaking into the abyss. It was now or never. And if he didn't believe her about what happened senior year, at least Morgan and Charlie still did. Her foundation of support was stronger now, able to stand on its own.

"I wasn't honest with you about something when we were dating, and I think it made me act like a bitch," she said.

Pete shook his head. "I don't understand."

Avery looked back at the cement bench. "Can we sit?"

"I'm fine right here." Pete crossed his arms, readjusted his stance so that his messenger bag sat higher on his shoulder. "What could you possibly need to tell me? You've done this kind of shit before."

"I know. But this time it's different."

"I really can't keep doing this, Avery."

Avery swallowed down the lump in her throat. "You remember Morgan and Charlie, right? Their wedding?"

"Yes. Obviously." His words were sharp, impatient.

Just come out with it, she thought. *You're taking too long.*

SHE USED TO BE NICE 297

"Well, their best man is this guy named Noah, who I also, um, know from school." She was sputtering a bit. "He, um . . ."

She hesitated for a long time. Pete waited.

"He raped me."

Avery averted her gaze, shifting her eyes to stare at the ground. An ant crawled toward the toe of her loafer. She squished it into the concrete.

Then she looked at Pete. His eyes were wide.

"Holy shit," he gasped.

He put his messenger bag on the ground beside him.

Now she had his attention.

"Yeah . . ." she said.

"Did Morgan and Charlie know that?" Pete asked.

"Well, no. Not until recently. Senior year I got drunk at a party and Noah brought me to this guy Ronald's room. He held me down, and . . ." Avery paused, feeling light-headed. "But nobody saw Noah—they only saw me with who they thought was Ronald. And I was dating my ex at the time, so everyone thought I, um . . . cheated." She paused again. "I hardly remembered anything the next morning, and I woke up feeling really . . . violated."

She reached over her shoulder and massaged her back, the spot where Noah pressed down the hardest. Pete just looked at her, his lips slightly parted and his eyebrows furrowed, waiting for more.

"Anyway," she continued. Beads of nervous sweat dotted her forehead. "I felt so dumb for putting myself in a compromised position, you know, getting too drunk and giggling with Noah too much. Like I made him think I was flirting and wanted to sleep with him. And when everyone thought I'd cheated on Ryan, I just went along with that story, because it was easier to admit to being a cheater than it was to admit that someone did this to me. I was terrified to admit that it happened. But now everyone knows the truth. I kind of lost it in Colorado and confronted him in front of everyone."

Silence lingered between them. Pete's face was impassive but seemingly in flux, like he was at the crossroads of several different emotions and figuring out which one to lead with.

Finally, he frowned. "I'm so sorry that happened to you."

Happiness bloomed inside Avery's chest. He believed her. Make that three people now. "Thanks," she said.

"I'm just—" Pete ran a hand through his hair as the details of what happened calcified in his mind. "I'm shocked. You always hear about this stuff, but you never think it'll happen to someone you know."

"Yeah, well . . ." Avery shrugged. "Here I am, I guess."

Pete stayed quiet for a few beats. He appeared at a loss for what to say next. "Well, what are Morgan and Charlie gonna do? If he's the best man."

"They kicked him out of the wedding. But the rest of the bridal party doesn't think Noah did anything wrong. They all still think I just got drunk and cheated and that I'm trying to pass the blame. They're reacting exactly how I thought they would if I ever came clean."

Pete inhaled a shaky, angry breath. "That's beyond messed up. They think he's innocent?"

Avery nodded. "Even though in Colorado he admitted to me that he did it. But of course he's still lying to everyone else."

Pete's eyes grew slightly more open. "What a bunch of *douchebags*. All of them."

Avery made a face like *yup*. "I mean, that's what normally happens with these things anyway. Doesn't matter what the truth is. Have you been following the Dave Moore news? Just watch. I bet he'll lie low for a few years, then come back and win an Emmy."

Pete had to know Avery was right. He lived in the same backward world that she did. "I want Noah dead. I want to skin him alive."

Avery laughed. "Good luck with that." The breeze started picking up, tickling Avery's cheek and whipping her hair across her face. She tucked a long strand behind her ear. "But, yeah. Now you know everything."

Pete gave a small smile. "Well, thank you for trusting me with this."

SHE USED TO BE NICE

Avery wrapped her arms around herself. The sun was almost fully set behind the skyscrapers, cooling down the air and darkening the sky. Pete's face was tinged with the orange-blue of dusk. He and Avery were still the same distance apart as they were at the beginning of the conversation. She took a tiny step closer.

"I think the problem with us was that I didn't think I deserved your affection," she began. "I had this huge secret I was hiding not just from you, but from everyone in my life. I thought what Noah did to me was my fault for so long, and I was afraid people who thought I cheated on my ex wouldn't believe me if I told the truth. I felt awful that I let something like this happen to me. I was so disgusted with myself. I felt so broken. It was just . . . constant self-loathing." Avery sighed. "And it trickled into our relationship. It made me feel like I wasn't good enough for you."

"I'm really sorry to hear that." Pete sounded stiffer than Avery would've liked. She could feel him slipping away and his well of compassion running dry.

"I'm not naive enough to think we could get back to where we were, with us dating or you wanting to come to the wedding." Avery bit her lip to stop herself from trembling. "But I was wondering if you wanted to . . . grab a drink. Or something." She held his gaze, tried to stay brave. "I'm sorry if that's too forward. I just . . . I just miss you. I can't stop thinking about you, and I'm scared I ruined it. Well, I mean, I know I ruined it now. But I'm scared I ruined it forever."

Avery's words hung heavy, suffocating, as Pete gave no immediate response. She tried not to beat herself up for the horrible way she'd treated him this year, for the horrible way she behaved in general, with everything. But she couldn't help how she dealt with her pain. You can't control the survival tactics your body deploys when it feels under attack, the way chameleons can't control their skin changing to blend into their surroundings in the face of a threat. It's biology. But she hated that she'd hurt Pete with her behavior, hated that he was in the crossfire of her attempts to survive.

"Look, I appreciate you coming by," Pete said, in a tone that suggested he was leading up to his answer. "Even if it was slightly stalkery." He tossed her a grin.

Avery grinned back, hope making her heart flutter. "Hey, remember when you waited for me outside my apartment after our fight? Grand ambushing gestures shouldn't be new to you."

"I know. You're right."

Avery held herself tighter, her teeth chattering from the wind. "So . . . that drink?" She was fully cold now, and the sky was almost black. But she would wait here all night for Pete's reply.

"Can I think about it?" he finally said.

Tears pricked Avery's eyes, built on her lash line and threatened to fall. It was too late. It was over.

"Okay." She felt like a deflated balloon. "I understand. Just text me, I guess."

"I will." Pete cleared his throat and picked up his messenger bag. A flicker of something crossed his face. Sadness? Regret? She wasn't sure. "Get home safe. And have a good night."

She closed her eyes as he turned around to leave. "You too."

27

WITH THE ARRIVAL OF August came the oppressive, suffocating heat, the kind that made most New Yorkers flee the city and return in September when the weather was at its best again. It meant Morgan had started wearing her wedding shoes around her apartment to break them in, had intensified her workouts so her arms and shoulders would be extra toned in her dress, and had assembled the gift bags she would bestow upon each of the bridesmaids the morning they arrived at the Brooklyn Botanic Garden. The wedding was in just three weeks now, and Avery's excitement for Morgan and Charlie only slightly outweighed her stress over seeing Ryan and her old friends again. At least she wouldn't have to see Noah, or Blair for that matter. It was undoubtedly a bright side, certainly the kind of positive thinking her new therapist, Dr. Banshol, would approve of.

It had taken forever for Avery to find this woman. Once Avery decided, reluctantly, that she probably needed some professional help to get through all of this, the search for a therapist who didn't suck was grueling. Everyone was booked with clients already, and so few people called her back after she left them messages. Finding someone she connected with was a whole other challenge. She'd needed a therapist to help her through the process of finding a therapist. But Dr. Banshol had an office a few blocks from her apartment and a gentle but firm disposition that Avery needed.

They'd only had a few sessions so far. They didn't get into many details of the sexual assault during the first session, but Dr. Banshol started poking at it in the second session, trying to help Avery push past her reflexive feelings of guilt and self-blame. It wasn't like Avery thought she was going to heal overnight, but being confronted with Dr. Banshol's questions and hearing herself waffle back and forth between blaming herself and blaming Noah only solidified that her road ahead would not be short.

Avery attended a couple of group therapy sessions, too, also reluctantly, per the advice of Dr. Banshol. Listening to fellow victims—and survivors, as some called themselves, though Avery probably wouldn't use that word for herself; it felt more suited for people who'd been through life-or-death tragedies like wars or cancer—sharing their stories put a hard stone of anger in Avery's stomach, the same anger she'd felt when she thought Noah was abusing Blair. Who knew rapists came in so many different forms? There was the woman who had panic attacks whenever she was in small spaces, a side effect of getting sexually assaulted in a bathroom on a yacht. There was the teenager whose stepfather took advantage of her at least once a week for years, and the guy who was drunk at a party and came to with a girl on top of him filming the whole encounter. Every story, one after the other, was somehow worse than the last. Avery mostly listened during these sessions, not yet ready to speak the details about her story aloud to strangers. But the fact that she was there meant people inherently knew that she was a victim, too. It was enough exposure for now.

One night, after group therapy, Avery met her parents at J. G. Melon, a burger restaurant on the Upper East Side. Avery had been tempted to cancel, but she'd made these plans before she started group and she hadn't seen her parents in a while. The last time she'd seen them was when she spent the whole weekend listening to her mom drone on about the men who could have taken advantage of her while she was drunk after Doc Holliday's. Which was a conversation she was not interested in continuing today. But she tried to see it from her parents' perspective. They were protective,

SHE USED TO BE NICE

and part of her could see herself saying the same thing to her own daughter one day, despite knowing the kind of offensive cultural messaging it perpetuated. It would only be out of love. Out of not wanting her daughter to end up like her.

When her parents' cab pulled up in front of J. G. Melon, her mom climbed out and hustled over to squeeze Avery in a hug. "We've missed you, honey," she said.

Avery had been surprised by her mom's suggestion that they come into the city. Her parents hated Manhattan, were suburban-ites through and through. Whenever they visited, Mom lamented about all the dog shit on the sidewalks, and Dad told her he couldn't understand how people lived in such tight quarters. All they did was complain: about the dirty subway, the high rent, how "dan-gerously close to Harlem" Avery lived. They were happiest in their little conservative bubble in New Jersey. Avery would never forget the fight they'd had when she insisted white privilege was real, and Mom said that "insulted" all the "hard work her father put into their family."

"I missed you too," Avery said.

"How did you get here?" Mom asked, already in a panic. "Subway? I hate the idea of you going down there by yourself. The crime rate in your area has got to be astronomical."

Here we go. "It's fine, Mom. I feel very safe."

"Can't you move somewhere with a doorman?" Dad asked. "We'd feel so much better if you had that extra layer of protection."

"If you want to pay the rent that kind of apartment would cost, absolutely."

Inside the restaurant, they were seated at a table right near the bar, below a row of televisions mounted on the ceiling. The table was covered in a green-and-white checkered tablecloth, with salt and pepper shakers and a ketchup bottle gathered in the center. Avery had specifically chosen J. G. Melon not only because it boasted one of the juiciest burgers in the city, but because it was the safest choice for her picky parents, who mostly stuck to the same two Ital-ian restaurants within a five-mile radius of their house.

"What's new, honey?" Dad said after the waiter took their food and drink orders. "You guys getting ready for the wedding?"

Avery nodded. In addition to therapy, she'd also been busy with last-minute wedding tasks, like scheduling mani-pedi appointments for the bridesmaids and drafting her maid of honor speech. "Yep. It's just a few weeks away now."

"I forgot to ask you how Colorado was. Morgan's pictures online looked beautiful."

Avery fiddled nervously with the tablecloth. "Oh, yeah. It was fine."

"Whose house was that?" Mom asked. "It was stunning."

"Noah's. He's a friend of Charlie's." Now that Avery had told some people about her sexual assault, she wondered if she should tell her parents, too. Didn't they deserve an explanation for why their daughter had changed so much over the last year? With their conservative tendencies, though, could Avery trust them to believe her? Morgan, Charlie, and Pete already did. Maybe there was more support available to her waiting with open arms, if she'd just let herself be held.

"Well, he must be *very* successful to afford something like that," Mom concluded.

A journalist on one of the television screens in the restaurant suddenly began discussing the Moore victims' accounts of what happened during the assaults, focusing on how Moore tied a blue bandana around the base of his shaft to keep himself erect. Avery blew bubbles in her Diet Coke to block the information from entering her brain.

"Goodness," Mom scoffed, nodding at the television. "All these women want is attention."

"And money," Dad said.

Avery took her lips off her straw. "What did you just say?"

"They want to sue Moore for his millions," Dad said casually, like this was a widely known fact. "Money talks. These girls are full of it."

"*And* they get to go on the news," Mom added in the same factual tone. "I bet one of them is an aspiring actor auditioning for her next emotional TV role."

SHE USED TO BE NICE

Avery couldn't believe what she was hearing. Her parents weren't just conservative. They were fucking conspiracy theorists.

"That's a little ridiculous, don't you think?" she said. "These women are getting so much shit right now. I see it at work all the time. If *Metropolitan's* social media replies are filled with death threats just because we're *covering* the story, I can only imagine what the women themselves are dealing with."

Dad shrugged. "I doubt those women will care about a bad tweet when they're raking in the dough."

"Dave Moore won't go anywhere," Mom said with a wave of her hand. "His shows are too good. The networks need him for content."

Avery felt the rising tides of fury unearth themselves from deep inside her. What kind of nonsensical reaction were her parents having right now? What kind of nonsensical reaction would they have to *her?*

She thought about the people in group therapy, about the women coming forward to share their abuse at the hands of Dave Moore. She thought about Noah and his appearance on *Shark Tank* and their confrontation in Colorado. About his admission. So many perpetrators, getting investments in their start-ups and prestigious Emmy awards and forgiveness from ignorant people like her friends and parents and idiots on social media. Still. Even after #MeToo, even after the illusion of cultural progress had been made.

A forest fire of rage lit up inside Avery's stomach. Something else needed to change. More of these predators needed to be taken down.

Including hers.

• • •

Avery stayed up researching all night, every night, for almost two weeks. Hunched over her laptop in the darkness of her bedroom, the bright blue light making her bloodshot eyes pulse in their sockets, she wrote down everything—everything she wanted the world to know. It poured out of her like a gushing waterfall emptying into the mouth of a river.

306   ALEXIA LAFATA

A few days before the wedding, it was ready.

From her seat at work, Avery watched the writers and editors gather for their pitch meeting in the conference room. She grabbed her laptop and hustled over to join them, then sat down in an empty seat a few chairs away from Patricia, who was typing something on her laptop with her reading glasses perched on her nose. Kevin walked by and gave Avery a thumbs up through the glass window. She couldn't have done what she was about to do without his help.

The meeting began at Patricia's introduction. Everyone fired off new ideas and stories they were working on. One writer pitched an in-depth look into the lies Republicans told about abortion, including their belief that abortion involved ripping a baby from a mother's womb moments before birth. Larry was getting to the bottom of a situation in which a bus driver refused to drive until a wheelchair passenger was strapped in, but the straps were so tight that they'd made other patrons bleed; he wanted to hold the MTA accountable for the lack of compassion and poor transportation design.

Patricia turned to Avery next.

"What about you?" Patricia asked. "You have any pitches for us?"

Avery sat up straight and cleared her throat. "Yes," she said. "Yes I do."

· · ·

Noah McCormick, Founder of Meow Monthly, Accused of Sexual Assault

By Avery Russo

When you picture a "rapist," the image of Noah McCormick, the charismatic start-up founder of Meow Monthly, a popular subscription service providing toys and necessities for pets, probably doesn't come to mind. A man who has dedicated his life to nurturing and caring for animals is incongruous with a person who can commit such a heinous act of violence.

SHE USED TO BE NICE

307

But that's the thing about rape, or at least my rape. It doesn't always happen in the context that you'd expect. Mine didn't happen in a deserted back alley by a stranger in a hoodie holding a knife to my throat. It happened at a crowded party during my senior year of college, when nobody noticed that Noah McCormick led me upstairs to a stranger's bedroom and took advantage of me when I was too drunk to clearly, convincingly say no. And believe me, I tried.

After Noah McCormick appeared on an episode of *Shark Tank* and accepted an offer from Mark Cuban, Meow Monthly generated an extra $15 million in sales and is projected to earn double that by the end of the year, according to *Forbes*. While Noah racks in millions for his beloved company, I've been suffering from horrific flashbacks, hypersexuality, and mental instability because of what he did to me. I was dating my boyfriend at the time that Noah sexually assaulted me, and after it happened, my ex broke up with me because he thought I'd cheated on him. And I didn't say anything to change his mind. The fact that I didn't cheat—that it was, in fact, rape—remained a thought inside my mind that I refused to speak aloud, lest it become real. Until now, I've kept this all a secret from my friends and family. I twisted the narrative in my head, framing the night like an irresponsible drunken hookup to protect myself from the truth. Being a cheater, to me, was less painful than being raped. But now, I'm ready to say it: I was raped.

And I'm not alone.

In the last year, four women have come forward to accuse Dave Moore, famed creator and producer of iconic dramedies such as *Me & You, One Happy Valley,* and *10 Things I Love About You,* of sexual assault. The allegations have spurred the #NoMoore movement, a hashtag that's become a rallying cry to put a stop to the harrowing epidemic of sexual assault that still persists even after #MeToo. The movement has spread quickly throughout social media, with women like me feeling empowered to chime in to share their own stories and experiences—proving this issue is just as prevalent as it's ever been. Today, one out of every six women has been a victim of attempted or completed rape in her lifetime, with college-aged women being an even more likely target—and yet only twenty-five out of 1,000 rapists will ever go to prison.

It's time, finally, to say #NoMoore to powerful men getting away with these despicable acts. And maybe think twice if you were planning on subscribing to Meow Monthly for your pet needs.

• • •

Avery's essay had gone live around ten the previous morning, racking up dozens of comments and social media shares. Now, in the conference room at *Metropolitan's* office, she and Kevin watched their analytics tools closely, mesmerized by the pageviews to the story skyrocketing with no signs of slowing down. Patricia was thrilled, both praising Avery for her bravery and encouraging her to think of follow-up ideas to generate more traffic.

The traffic to the essay started climbing even higher after Noah posted a response on his personal Instagram account: *The allegations made against me by my former classmate Avery Russo are completely unfounded. Avery and I had a consensual sexual encounter during our senior year of college. We were BOTH drinking at the time of the encounter, as is normal for college students engaging in sexual activity. I vehemently deny that I sexually assaulted her, in any way, shape, or form.*

"What a piece of shit," Kevin said as he read Noah's message.

Knowing that Noah might react this way—especially if he wanted to sue for defamation later—Avery had done all the research she could to cover her bases before she published the essay. It could easily be argued that Noah's status as a start-up founder meant he was a public figure, so for one the burden of proof on

SHE USED TO BE NICE

309

him to sue for defamation was high. But more importantly, he would only have grounds if her accusation was false. And he knew just as well as she did that it wasn't.

"I'm so glad we tricked him into giving us the password to his security cameras," she said.

"Me too," Kevin said with a smile. "Writing a convincing spear phishing email from Panasonic about 'suspicious movement' was my easiest coding job ever."

The audio proof that Avery had of her and Noah's conversation in his kitchen in Colorado probably wouldn't be admissible in court, since it was retrieved illegally. But she had it. She had his clear admission that he'd raped her. Nobody besides Kevin knew that she had this audio, and as of now she planned on keeping it that way. But if Noah sued her, she could anonymously release it to the media or elsewhere in the court of public opinion as a blow to Noah's credibility.

Noah had also technically given everyone at the bachelor party permission to see whatever security footage they wanted. A good lawyer could argue that Avery merely took him up on that offer.

"Are you sure that account is gone now, though?" she asked uneasily. She still couldn't believe they'd pulled this off.

Kevin nodded vigorously, definitively. "Absolutely. Noah will never know where the email came from. I had one of my engineers do it on his grandmother's old-ass Dell."

"I knew Noah would jump on the message. That house is his baby." Avery met Kevin's gaze, put a grateful hand on his arm. "Thank you so much for helping me with this."

"Girl, are you kidding? This was my *pleasure*. I will gladly help you take down any straight white man. Let alone a rapist."

When Avery had told Kevin her story, his eyes welled with tears. He'd confessed that he'd been sexually assaulted, too, by the guy he was dating in high school. He was fifteen and had technically lost his virginity to him, but Kevin didn't count it. Hacking into Noah's email gave Kevin a taste of the revenge he didn't get as a teenager.

Avery knew she wasn't the only person in the world who'd been sexually assaulted, but it was always so easy to forget that,

310   ALEXIA LAFATA

even as more women and men came forward amidst the #NoMoore movement. Every time she heard a new story, she remembered all over again how rarely justice was served. She hoped her essay could move that needle forward, bringing her one step closer to healing. Dr. Banshol had helped her realize that keeping her sexual assault a secret festering inside of her had exacerbated her self-loathing, as though the act of keeping it silent reinforced that it was shameful. And it had felt incredible to write it all down. She found it was so much easier to write about it than it was to speak about it in group. She felt like she'd turned herself inside out and cleansed herself of the toxins. It was how she always used to feel after a good writing session: purged and clearer-headed.

But she didn't share her essay on any of her social media accounts like she once shared her *Golden* columns. Directing people to it herself would invite another layer of exposure she didn't need. People could find it themselves if they really wanted to. She'd only texted it to Morgan and Charlie, both of whom reacted with hearts and words of support. And of course Noah reacted to it on his Instagram, where anyone from Woodford College who followed him would see it. Other major media outlets were covering it, too, Avery's name splashed across headlines and homepages in ways that made her feel somewhat brave but mostly terrified. She avoided her DMs and turned all her social media private, knowing based on her experience covering the Dave Moore case what she was in for. She desperately hoped this was just the obsessive twenty-four-hour news cycle at its peak and that soon most of the public would move on. At least some of the reactions so far were positive, though, like Mark Cuban announcing his support of her and that he was taking a step back from his involvement in Meow Monthly. A couple of her female classmates from Woodford even texted her that Noah had tried similar shit with them at parties, getting them alone when they were drunk and then initiating "rough sex."

Avery didn't know what Noah would do now, if anything. But she'd made a choice and she had to keep going. She had a wedding to attend.

28

A VERY PEEKED OUT THE window of the dressing room, at the exquisite setup for Morgan and Charlie's outdoor ceremony. Cherry blossom trees and weeping willows surrounded the ceremony space, which was filled with rows of white chairs lined up perpendicular to a long aisle that led to an altar covered in pale pink roses. Unfortunately, rain was predicted within the hour, right around the time of the start of the ceremony. Avery hoped it would hold out a bit longer, though the sky was gray and overcast in a way that signaled an impending storm. All morning, Morgan was stressed about the possibility of getting married in the alternate indoor ceremony space, a sterile-looking conference room with smelly carpeting and unflattering fluorescent lighting.

"Everything's going to be fine," Avery said calmly as she held a mug of Yogi stress relief tea to Morgan's lips. Morgan didn't want to move too much while getting her hair and makeup done, so Avery spent the last hour alternating between feeding her tea and a mimosa, both to relax her. "Happy thoughts."

"Happy thoughts," Morgan murmured. She inhaled deeply and released an *ohm* sound, the exhale rustling her fake eyelashes. "Happy. Thoughts." She met Avery's eye. "And I wish the same for you."

Avery gave her a small smile and carefully popped a piece of watermelon from the fruit salad into her mouth so as not to disturb her completed makeup. If Morgan was pissed about the timing of

Avery's *Metropolitan* essay, she didn't show it. If anything, she seemed proud. She also must have shown her parents the essay, because Gabriela and Joe each texted Avery their support after it went live. Avery's mom, too, surprised Avery by calling her crying yesterday.

"I don't want to distract you from the big day tomorrow," she'd said between sniffles on the phone. "But I just want you to know that Dad and I are here."

"I appreciate that," Avery had replied. She was skeptical of what "here" meant, considering her parents' views about sexual assault victims, but she was willing to hear them out after the wedding.

Strong gusts of wind pummeled the window, rattling the glass. Avery bit her lip and looked outside to see if the chairs were still standing. She was also, if she were being honest, looking for Ryan. She'd heard from Morgan that he was on his way, and already some guests were hanging out near the ceremony setup, waiting for the procession to begin. But she had no idea what she was going to say to him. She hadn't exactly anticipated her story being out there the way it was now.

Morgan groaned as she watched the clouds rolling in outside. "I swear, if it rains . . ."

"Rain means a good marriage," Emma called out from the corner, where she was getting her hair curled. The smell of burning hairspray tickled Avery's nostrils. "Don't they say that? Isn't that a thing?"

"No, people only say that to make brides feel better when everything's going to shit."

The makeup artist swirled the final touches of eyeshadow into Morgan's crease while a hairdresser pinned a strand of hair into the loose bun at the nape of her neck. The only thing missing was Morgan's wedding dress, which hung in a white garment bag behind the dressing room door. But even now, wearing only her white silk robe, Morgan looked stunning.

"Well, at least you look gorgeous, and that's all that matters," Emma said. She dabbed a budding tear away. "Oh, no, my makeup . . ."

SHE USED TO BE NICE 313

Morgan pointed at her. "Save your tears. If you're not all crying as I walk down the aisle, I'm gonna go back up and walk down again until you are."

Emma shifted her eyes to Avery before burying her face in her phone. She hadn't said anything else to Avery since the bachelor party in Colorado, merely tolerating her presence on various last-minute text threads and email chains with the other bridesmaids. Nor had she said anything about Avery's essay or Noah's response. Today was probably not the day to talk about all of that anyway, but Avery couldn't help but feel the presence of a massive elephant in the room regardless.

When Morgan's makeup was finished, Avery helped her step into her wedding dress, then smoothed down a crystal twisted out of place. With the last button secured, Morgan stared at herself in the mirror and fanned the tears from her face.

"I'm a bride," she choked out.

Morgan turned around to face the bridesmaids admiring her with awestruck gasps while a photographer snapped pictures of everyone's reactions. Now that Morgan was ready, the ceremony could finally begin.

The bridesmaids headed outside. The sky was still gray and bloated with rain, but everyone remained optimistic that the bright white crack between the clouds would soon turn to blue. They hid behind a barn around the corner from the ceremony space, shielding Morgan from the guests' and Charlie's view. By now, most guests had filed in and were seated on the chairs facing the altar, filling the air with soft murmurs of conversation.

"You ready?" Avery asked Morgan, flicking a blade of grass off her spaghetti strap.

Morgan took a long, deep breath, then exhaled into a smile that lit up her whole face. "I've been ready since I met him."

Avery put her arm around Morgan's waist, gave her a squeeze. Then Avery settled into her spot toward the back of the line of bridesmaids and held her flowers low at her hips as instructed by the wedding coordinator.

Suddenly Emma turned around to face her. "I hope you're happy."

Avery's heart thudded. "What?"

Emma rolled her eyes. "As if we didn't read your essay destroying Noah's character."

Emma faced forward again and said nothing else. Avery remained silent, unsure of what to say back, if anything, in this cramped, intimate space. Why did Emma only confront her when Morgan was out of earshot, the processional was starting to unfold in front of them, and they couldn't cause a scene?

"Let's not right now," Avery whispered as quietly as she could.

Emma tossed a gaze over her shoulder. "So selfish," she muttered.

Avery was tempted to spit back a response. To defend herself or beg for understanding or call Emma a bitch. Then she remembered what Dr. Banshol had told her last week, something about building her self-esteem and not deriving her value from other people's criticisms. She decided against reacting; instead she fluffed up the flowers in her bouquet while repeating Dr. Banshol's advice to herself like a mantra. *Another person's opinion of you is not a fact,* Avery heard her therapist's voice inside her head. *What makes someone else more qualified to know you than you?*

While finalizing her stance, Avery found Ryan's eye across the lawn. Her breath hitched at the sight of him. He was one of the last guests to arrive; he held an envelope in one hand and kept his other hand tucked into the pocket of his slim-fit navy suit. He held her gaze for a beat before breaking away, but Avery couldn't read his expression, if there was one of note. Maybe he didn't realize that he was looking right at her.

A ray of sun suddenly warmed her shoulder, and she looked up. The clouds were finally beginning to pass, opening to reveal the clearest cerulean sky. Then, a few seconds later, the organs began to play.

• • •

SHE USED TO BE NICE
315

After the ceremony, the guests were ushered to the cocktail hour held outside the reception hall on the patio, where lilies and other aquatic plants made their serene way floating across small pools. While the guests stood in line for the bar and congregated around tall cocktail tables, the wedding party gathered by the pond to take group photos before the sun set. Morgan and Charlie lined up in the middle, with Parker next to Charlie as the replacement best man and Avery next to Morgan as maid of honor.

"Wait!" Avery shouted at the photographer. She tilted her head back to study Morgan's teeth, then dug a fingernail into her gum line. "You had a piece of food in there."

"Wow, thank you," Morgan said.

Avery didn't need to talk to anyone as they took pictures, which was great, though her essay about Noah still pulsed like an electrical charge in the air, invisible but alive and quivering. Avery could only infer that the "we" Emma mentioned earlier was the rest of the bridal party. They were probably sharpening their pitchforks in some separate group chat, ready to skewer Avery.

"Hey," Morgan said to Avery as everyone else dispersed after the photos were done. "Just checking in."

Avery laughed. "You're not supposed to worry about other people on your wedding day."

"Well, this is my best friend we're talking about. It's different."

Morgan spoke to Avery like she was the only person on the lawn, despite the droves of guests who were certainly waiting to be greeted. Avery let it be the permission granted to share some of what was happening.

"According to Emma, it sounds like everyone's read the essay."

Morgan didn't look shocked. Her expression was more neutral than anything else, with a hint of sympathy. "How do you feel about that? Are you surprised?"

Avery shrugged. "I guess not. Especially after Noah's public denial."

316   ALEXIA LAFATA

"Such an asshole." Morgan peered across the lawn at Ryan holding a plate of food by the seafood buffet. "Have you talked to Ryan about it yet?"

Avery chewed nervously on her lip. "I don't know how. Or if I should."

"I'll leave that decision up to you. And I'll support you no matter what."

Morgan pulled Avery in for a hug. Avery's eyes welled with grateful tears, because she knew Morgan was telling the truth. If it weren't for Morgan and Charlie's support in Colorado, Avery might never have found the strength to support herself. A crest of gratitude swelled in her chest.

"I know," Avery said. "You've always supported me. All versions of me. I can't thank you enough for it."

Morgan smiled and took Avery's hand. "Come on." She nodded toward the reception venue. "Let's go inside together."

The reception was held in a massive glass-walled dome near the cocktail hour patio. White lamps attached to white metal rods hung from a ceiling that curved downward to enclose the guests in what looked like hundreds of white-paneled windows. The trees and flowers blooming outside in the gardens, visible through the glass from the inside, were backlit by a sunset approaching its finale below the horizon. Avery put her evening clutch down at her seat at the head table, which was covered in sprinkles of pink rose petals and small cream candles. Already the table was plated with the first salad course, a spring mix tossed with walnuts and apple slices drizzled in a balsamic vinaigrette. Avery had helped Morgan select the menu, a mix of dinner and dessert options catered from Gramercy Tavern and The Freakin' Rican, in addition to helping design the tablescape. It was gratifying to see her positive influence woven into the evening, despite all the negativity from the bridal party.

Avery gripped the back of her chair, her eye on the door from where guests were trickling in. She watched to see when Ryan would join them. As she waited, she picked idly at her salad to give her something to do, but then a couple minutes later, just as she

SHE USED TO BE NICE

was about to give up, he appeared, laughing with Viraj and holding a beer.

Ryan and Viraj walked over to Viraj's seat at the head table, across from where Avery stood. Viraj put down his drink and fiddled with something on his phone, avoiding eye contact with Avery. But Ryan looked up.

"Hey," he said, nodding in Avery's direction.

Avery met his eye. She sucked in a breath. Did Viraj tell him something just now? "Hey."

"How are you?"

Avery pursed her lips. Should she be honest? That *was* her new thing lately.

"I'm fine," she said. "No, sorry—it's weird. A little. Seeing you."

Ryan exhaled a brief chuckle. Viraj disappeared, had taken off to talk to Charlie near the dance floor as the band started warming up. Ryan and Avery were alone, as alone as you could be in a banquet hall filling up with a hundred and fifty people.

"I feel the same," Ryan said.

They looked around, each of them waiting for the other to break the ice. It might be too early in the night for a real conversation. Ryan was likely only on his first beer. Avery, meanwhile, had been forced to acknowledge in therapy that her drinking was unhealthy, so she was doing her best to stay sober tonight, meaning this was about as loose and open as she'd get.

"It's good to see you, too, though," she said, out of the knee-jerk politeness that plagues you when you're not sure what else to say. "I'm sure Charlie's happy to have you here."

Ryan gave a small smile, probably out of similar politeness. "Yeah, I'm glad I could make it."

An emcee took to the mic, telling everyone to find their seats because they were about to start serving the first course.

Ryan jerked his head across the dance floor in what Avery figured was the direction of his table. "Well, I guess I should go."

Avery wasn't sure what Ryan knew about her allegation against Noah, if he'd seen her essay or Noah's response online. The only

318   ALEXIA LAFATA

thing she knew was that he'd planned to come here and have fun
with his friends. And at some point tonight, when the guys were
several drinks deep, he would join them in thrusting his suit jacket
upon the back of his chair, rolling up the sleeves of his sweaty,
translucent white button-down shirt, and dancing like a moron on
the dance floor. That would be his focus tonight. Not Avery.

Avery behaved accordingly, with no expectations. She ate her
grilled pork shoulder entrée and made conversation with Morgan's
cousin at the head table. She moved her body on the dance floor,
twirling Morgan around and scream-singing their favorite songs
together, even dancing with Titi Julia when the band stopped to
allow Gabriela to play some salsa on Spotify. She took silly pictures
with Charlie adorned in the sunglasses and hats that the band
tossed out into the crowd. She had a heart-to-heart with Joe about
how grown-up Morgan was. She watched Morgan and Charlie cut
the cake and wipe frosting on each other's noses. She gave a speech,
ignoring whispers from the bridal party to focus on speaking
directly to the bride and groom.

"To Morgan and Charlie, the greatest friends I've ever had." She
raised her drink, a ginger ale disguised in a champagne flute, toward
Morgan and Charlie at their sweetheart table. "Here's to a lifetime
of happiness and love. No two people are more deserving."

Thirty minutes later, after Avery finished her piece of cake,
she headed to the bar for another ginger ale. The dance floor was
at its peak, and the groomsmen's shirts were one button away from
coming off entirely as the band geared up to play "Mr. Brightside."
Ryan got in line behind Avery. His tie was loosened around his
neck and his eyes were bloodshot.

"What's up, Avery?" His voice was louder than it was a few
hours ago at the beginning of the night. He was definitely drunk
now.

Avery flicked her head over her shoulder. "Hey, Ryan."

The speakers shook so hard Avery thought they might topple
over. Bright white spotlights moved about the dance floor as people started yelling alongside The Killers.

SHE USED TO BE NICE

319

"So, I heard," Ryan began. "About Noah."

Avery turned to face him. "You did?"

"Charlie told me everything." He ran his hand through his sweaty hair before meeting her eye. "Why didn't you say anything to me last year? I knew you better than anyone. I would've believed you."

Avery wasn't sure how to react. Did she believe that he would've believed her? It was easy for Ryan to say that now, after he saw that other people like Morgan and Charlie were on her side. But in the immediate aftermath of that night, emotions were high, especially Ryan's, and nobody suspected for a second that Avery wasn't completely at fault. If Ryan had had any suspicion that she didn't cheat, he could have asked her point-blank if something else had happened. His claim that he knew her better than anyone meant very little if he didn't leverage it when it mattered most.

"That's nice of you to say," she said.

She ordered her ginger ale and Ryan ordered another beer. The loud music and exuberant crowd filled what could've been an awkward silence while they waited for their drinks. But Avery didn't want to elaborate. She was fine with letting Ryan think he would have had the correct reaction. Maybe he would have. It was a better reaction than she imagined him having, regardless of whether it was true.

"I'm not just saying it to be nice, Avery," he said. He sounded more distraught because he'd been drinking, but she could tell he was being genuine all the same. "I mean it. I'm serious."

She gave him a small and somewhat strained smile. There was no reason to make Ryan think he was a bad guy for not immediately assuming she didn't cheat senior year. He had just been hurt and reacted to the situation according to his pain. Avery knew all about that.

"I know, Ryan. I believe you."

The bartender returned with their drinks. Ryan took his and held the bottle up in salute, seeming satisfied. "Well, I'll see ya on the dance floor," he said.

Avery smiled, more earnestly this time. "See ya there."

With her drink in her hand, Avery walked outside for a break from the crowd. She sat down on a wooden bench and took off her nude heels, massaged her aching feet. In the distance, dozens of fireflies dotted the space above the grass, and the cicadas' cries rattled and reverberated in the silent night air. A rustling sound came from behind a bush, the kind made by a small animal or a child who'd gotten lost. Avery leaned over to the side.

"Hello?" she called out.

It wasn't immediately clear through the darkness that it was Pete who'd rounded the corner. Avery had to blink a few times to adjust to the low light. She had to wait for him to come closer. She had to convince herself that he wasn't a mirage.

"Pete?" She stood up. "What are you doing here?"

Pete put his hands in his pockets. He was in a suit. The suit she imagined he would have worn if he'd come as her plus-one tonight. And he looked perfect.

"Well, I knew you'd be here," he said with a grin. "And I . . . well, I had to see you. I saw your story covered in the *Wall Street Journal* this morning."

Avery smiled. "Of course you read it there. Classic finance bro."

Pete chuckled softly before slowly making his way toward her. Soon they were so close Avery could taste his minty breath. She felt the vibration of every cell inside her body.

"I'm not proud of how I reacted when you came to my office," he said. "I was overwhelmed and still hurt, I guess, from everything. And I'm sorry."

Avery shook her head reassuringly. "You have nothing to be sorry about."

"Yes I do." Pete leaned in closer. "Because what I should've said was that I think you're amazing. And beautiful. And strong. And, now, so brave for telling your story." His blue eyes sparkled under the moonlight as his gaze stayed soft on hers. "I'm in awe of you. I couldn't go another day without telling you that."

SHE USED TO BE NICE 321

Avery's heart beat hard under her dress. She was elated to see him. Elated and in disbelief that he was here, at the wedding, like he should've been this whole time. "Well, you're pretty awesome yourself."

"Nah, I'm just a wedding crasher. Even though I was technically invited."

He looked sheepishly at her. Avery longed to put her arms around him. To kiss him.

"You absolutely were invited," she said. "I never should've uninvited you. I was just afraid of what you'd find out about me before I was ready to share it."

Pete nodded. "I understand that now."

He flicked his gaze to the ground, let the moment of silence sit between them. When he looked back up, he met Avery's eye and smiled, his straight white teeth as beautiful as ever. Avery smiled back, just as shyly, as hopefully.

"But how about we start over?" he asked. "Are you free for dinner next weekend?"

Avery thought of all the times she'd lied to Pete. All the times she pretended she was okay, that she wasn't barricading the storm of her past from destroying the promising beginnings of him in her present. There was power in pretending, Avery knew. It made her feel strong and untouchable. But pretending wasn't what made her powerful. Because even if she didn't realize it, she was powerful all along, every part of her: her good and bad sides, her past and her present. She just needed to believe it. To let him—to let everyone—see all of her.

"Well, you're here, aren't you?" she asked. "Why don't we eat something now?"

Pete glanced over Avery's shoulder toward the venue. "You sure Morgan and Charlie won't mind?"

She took Pete's hand, laced her fingers through his. "Not at all."

And then she led him inside.

ACKNOWLEDGMENTS

I'VE WANTED TO WRITE novels for as long as I can remember. While some little girls dreamed of becoming ballerinas or princesses, I dreamed of becoming an author. So, thank you, first and foremost, dear reader, for giving this unknown author's debut novel a chance to take up space on your bookshelf. I am so honored.

Thank you to the two incredible women who changed my life forever: Taj McCoy, my agent at Laura Dail Literary Agency, and Jess Verdi, my editor at Alcove Press. Taj, you took on this book when I thought I'd already set it aside for good, and it's because of your belief in me that I didn't quit trying entirely. I'm so grateful that you welcomed me with an open heart. Jess, you saw everything this book was and everything I hoped it would become, and your ingenious creative vision turned it into a work of art that I'm so proud of. It's one of the biggest thrills of my life that we got to work together. Both of you made my wildest dreams come true.

Thank you, Veronica Park, for getting me my start and for teaching me everything you know about the publishing industry and the craft of storytelling. I carry your lessons with me wherever I go.

Thank you to some of my earliest readers, closest creative confidants, and fellow authors Zara Barrie, Candice Jalili, Hannah Orenstein, and Joe Trezza. I'm so lucky to be friends with so many

ACKNOWLEDGMENTS

talented writers who inspire me, challenge me, and give me moral support. Thank you as well to every author I've chatted with online, met in person, or befriended in some way or another throughout the years I spent trying to get published. Nobody understands this industry quite like we do, and I'm just really happy to be here with all of you.

I'm so grateful for the love and support of my friends who encouraged me as a writer every step of the way. Val, thank you for reading more early (and often bad) versions of this book than anyone else. Meaghan, thank you for sprinting to my apartment with flowers when I finally sold this book, and for helping me craft an authentic half Puerto Rican/half Irish background for Morgan. Missa, thank you for listening with empathy and compassion as I lamented about who I'd be if I failed at becoming an author. There are too many other friends to name, but just know I appreciate you all more than you know.

Thank you, also, to my frousins. Elizabeth and Gabriella, thank you for loving my cringey middle school fan-fiction and never letting me forget about it (not that I'd ever want to). Lauren, thank you for showing me how cool reading is. Taylor, thank you for being the first family member to read my book!

To my colleagues at Vox Media, thank you for making my day job so fun and fulfilling and for being so excited about my side hustle as a novelist. To everyone I was lucky enough to cross paths with during my time at Elite Daily, thank you for teaching me that I had what it took to make a career out of writing. Special thanks to Emily McCombs and Faye Brennan, two women media legends, whose mentorship I will forever cherish. To my fellow members of Asinine Sketch & Improv Comedy at Boston College, thank you for molding my sense of humor and helping me exercise my creative writing chops. To my editors at *The Heights*, also at Boston College, my dream to write professionally was forever solidified when I saw my name in print for the first time.

To Marjorie, Mac, Julie, Kate, Josh, and John, I'm so lucky to know you all. Thank you for the warmth, the laughter, and the

ACKNOWLEDGMENTS 325

cocktails (and an extra thank you to Julie for the legal consulting!). It meant so much to know that you were all cheering me on as I worked to become a published author.

To Scott, my "evolved" man, thank you for seeing me at my best, my worst, and everything in between, and still loving me for who I am. You inspire me every day and give my life meaning. Forever is nowhere near long enough, but it's all we've got. I love you so much.

Thank you to my parents. From helping me "publish" a picture book I wrote and illustrated at seven years old to telling everyone you know about my debut novel at thirty-one, I have never doubted your belief in me as a writer. Thank you for nurturing my ambitions, for instilling in me the utmost strength and confidence, and for always being proud of me. I know I can do anything because you will both be there to catch me if I fall.

Finally, thank you to the survivors. I started writing this book during the height of the #MeToo movement, when women's stories of sexual trauma were gaining rapid widespread attention. Over the last several years since #MeToo, it's easy to feel like nothing has changed. Men are still able to be successful despite being known sexual predators, while so many women still suffer in silence and are not believed. Thank you for your courage to keep going.

DISCUSSION QUESTIONS FOR
SHE USED TO BE NICE

1. Did you have any preconceived notions about sexual assault before reading *She Used to Be Nice*, be it about victims, perpetrators, or the act itself? How have your ideas changed, if at all?

2. Like Avery, many victims of sexual assault experience hypersexuality as a response to their trauma. Discuss the role sex plays in Avery's life and coping process after her rape.

3. Do you agree with the way Avery handles learning that she will be in the wedding party with Noah? Should she have told Morgan right away or was she correct to keep it a secret for the sake of the wedding? If you were in Avery's position, what would you have done?

4. During the confrontation at the bachelor party in Colorado, Avery's friends pepper her with questions about why she didn't report what happened senior year. Why might a victim of sexual assault not want to tell anyone what happened to them?

5. There are everyday moments of sexism chronicled throughout the book, like Avery getting catcalled by construction

DISCUSSION QUESTIONS FOR *SHE USED TO BE NICE*

workers, Morgan lamenting about people thinking she looks tired without makeup (which men aren't subjected to), and Charlie's coworkers objectifying a female colleague in a crass way. How do these moments contribute to our society's view of women at large? Why is it important to illustrate this in a book about sexual assault?

6. At the engagement party, the friend group discusses an incident in which a police officer at Woodford promises he won't get a sophomore who stole food from the dining hall in trouble if she blows him. Noah downplays this incident, suggesting the girl should've told the police officer to get lost, and laughs off the fact that the police officer wasn't intimidating because he was "a hundred and fifty pounds soaking wet." What does this interaction say about our society's understanding of power? Discuss the flaws in this understanding.

7. Despite not knowing what Avery is going through, Morgan tries her best to be a good friend. What would you do if you sensed that your best friend was struggling with her mental health the way Avery is? Is Morgan a good enough friend, or should she have done more?

8. What might someone like Avery who is recovering from sexual trauma need in a romantic partner? Do you think Pete embodies those qualities?

9. Throughout the book, Avery is pushed harder and harder to come out with her secret, but she only does so when she suspects that Noah is abusing Blair. If that moment didn't happen, do you think she would've eventually told someone or continued to keep it a secret?

10. Which character's reaction to Avery's truth in Colorado felt the most realistic to you? Which reaction aligns the closest with how you think you would've reacted?

11. Charlie tearfully shares that he wishes he'd questioned what he'd heard when the rumors about Avery's infidelity spread during their senior year. Have you ever believed a

DISCUSSION QUESTIONS FOR *SHE USED TO BE NICE* 329

nasty rumor about a classmate without interrogating whether it was true? What would you do differently now, if anything?

12. Avery's sexual assault happened at a party on campus during her senior year of college. What can colleges do to create safer environments for their students and decrease the risk of sexual violence?

13. Discuss all the ways Avery is an "imperfect" victim. Did these qualities cloud your judgment of her story? At any point, did you not believe her?

14. Avery often laments that the #MeToo movement didn't do anything to help her feel better about coming forward with her story. As a society, do you think we are better or worse off than we were before #MeToo?

15. What do you think will happen next, now that Avery's essay about her rape is live online? How will she navigate her relationship with her parents and their differing political beliefs? Will Noah sue her or come after her in some other way? What will happen between her and Pete?